AT THE CROSSROADS

Georgia sank back on the sofa to align her thoughts. She knew she was falling in love with Nick Culletti, but feared the consequences of a relationship with a younger man, especially an actor on his way to the top of the celebrity heap. Maybe she'd just be in the way. Maybe she was a mother image, for God's sake!

And, of course, there was Jake Pierce. Apparently he had disappeared from her life as mysteriously as he had entered it, and for that she was grateful; but one could never be certain about a man like Jake. He was dangerous, possibly schizoid. Everything about him was excessive, especially his sexual prowess. Georgia feared him most of all because of the hypnotic spell he appeared to cast over her. When Jake was in the room, she seemed to have no will of her own, and this was terrifying. She'd never felt that kind of emotion before. On the one hand, she despised the feeling, while on the other, it exerted a peculiar fascination. That ambivalence was the disturbing element.

Georgia hadn't worked since the "Angels in White" stint, and had finally dismissed the idea of securing a "straight" job. Management had secured the right tenant percentage to turn the apartment building cooperative, and she had only a few months to come up with the cash or get out. But somehow things would work out—they always had in the past. Meanwhile, she looked forward to seeing Nick on Sunday night . . .

(Cover photograph posed by professional model)

Also by Pat Gaston:

LOVE TO BE LOVED

THE LOVE ARENA

Pat Gaston

To my dear friend Suzy Keane,
who is better known as "Doodles."

Book Margins, Inc.

A BMI Edition

Published by special arrangement with Dorchester Publishing

Printed in the United States of America.

PART I

LUST

Lust mingled with fear
is the Devil's own cocktail.
—P.G.

PROLOGUE

INTERNATIONAL INTERIOR designer Billy Bright scanned the headlines of the afternoon *Post*, then promptly prepared himself a stiff drink, his palms wet . . .

In another part of the city, casting director, Margo Sweet, and makeup wizard, Teddy Morrell, sipped exceedingly dry martinis at the Plaza Palm Court, both wrapped in mutual, guilty satisfaction . . .

At three o'clock, actor Nick Culletti folded the paper under his arm and strolled calmly back to the set to resume filming a jeans commerical, experiencing a peculiar lack of surprise or pity . . .

On the terrace of his Riverside Drive penthouse Lucky DeSantos read and reread the headlines, wondering if the news had reached Georgia Bonner Sandborne and syndicate boss Louis Gerfinski who were at the moment blithely sailing the blue waters of the Caribbean . . .

All were in some way touched by the bold, black print.

Glamour girl found slain in posh east side pad. Kiki Blake Sandborne, widow of former Arkansas Governor, multimillionaire Victor Sandborne, was discovered strangled to death in her town house on East Forty-eighth Street late yesterday by a maid returning from a three day vacation. The thirty-five year old jet set beauty was found lying on red satin sheets. Gems valued at three-hundred thousand dollars were missing, and authorities feel the motive was robbery. An alarm system failed to go off, indicating the victim knew her assailant or assailants.

CHAPTER ONE

As NIGHT settled over the city, fog drifted in from the river wrapping glittering Manhattan in a veil of gauzy gray. Traffic, more frustrating than usual, was punctuated by the impatient sounds of a thousand horns beeping their irritation. Four-letter words rang from the mouth of an angry taxi driver suddenly stalled. Rain began slowly, then came down in a steady stream—pedestrians raced to beat the lights—traffic cops, arms waving, whistles squealing, remained dry under cumbersome orange slickers. There was a perceptible urgency, as if the masses of people feared irrevocable damage from the sudden downpour. Hansom carriages, their horses tired and wet, lined the corner near Central Park South. Bergdorf's, Tiffany's, and the stately Plaza Hotel loomed magnificent and secure. A Silver Cloud Rolls glided to a halt at the hotel's entrance, causing the uniformed doorman to jump to attention. Nearby a shoeless bag lady huddled in a doorway, alone and ignored. She lit a cigarette, observing the passing parade with a wistful smile.

A few blocks west on Fifty-Seventh Street, the Marty Saks television talk show was airing live. The dressing room door of the Green Room, a haven for guests about to appear, was slightly ajar. Production assistant Robbie Hale hesitated a second, then popped his head inside and addressed a beautiful blonde woman who sat at the makeup table.

"Hi, Miss Bonner. I'm Robbie Hale. You probably don't remember me, but we met last week in Marty's office. You have about five minutes. The segment on transsexuals is almost over."

She turned and faced him. "Thanks. I'll be ready. At least I hope so." Her voice was husky and trembled slightly. Robbie suspected she was nervous, but that wasn't unusual. Everyone got a case of the jitters before appearing on the hot seat with Marty Saks, especially live. The fabled talk-show host was known in some circles as "Marty the Terrible," and it was said that his interviews made the Spanish Inquisition seem like a Sunday School picnic.

"You look super, Miss Bonner, really great. I remember you from the soaps."

He remembered her from the soaps, all

right—as the leading lady on "Mother's Children" almost ten years ago. She'd been good, too, but her real claim to fame had come from her personal life. Marriage to former Arkansas Governor Victor Sandborne had catapulted her into overnight headlines —ACTRESS MARRIES MILLIONAIRE—to love happily ever after. Not quite. Not quite the expected faily tale ending. After three years there was trouble in paradise. Society columns were filled with veiled items linking Victor Sandborne with another woman, a lady of mystery. Who was she? How could she destroy the perfect marriage? What strange powers did she possess? Then more headlines—divorce, pictures in the *Post* of a handsome, graying Victor and the voluptuous *other woman* in Las Vegas— another wedding, and then, not quite a year later, Victor Sandborne was dead. Some said he deserved it—served him right.

But what had become of the injured party, Georgia, the deserted wife? She'd simply faded away like the setting sun into temporary oblivion. There were rumors of a nervous breakdown, alcoholism. Others whispered she'd become a nun! And now, here she was about to appear on the Marty Saks T.V. Show. She was nervous, all right, thought Robbie. She had every right to be.

He lit a cigarette. "Look, Miss Bonner," (he liked the fact she was using her own name) "don't let Marty throw you. He's harmless.

11

Just imagine him and the entire bunch out there with all their clothes off. That should do it. I'll be back in a couple of minutes to take you to the arena."

Georgia nodded and continued to concentrate on her reflection in the large well-lighted mirror. She had become her own best critic, an expert at camouflage, a genius at maintaining the striking illusion that some still referred to as "Gorgeous Georgia Bonner."

Already she'd spent twenty minutes shading a slightly crooked nose into one of perfection, and blocking out tiny lines that had only recently appeared under her dark, luminous eyes. She was five foot seven, amazingly slim, with high, full breasts and long legs that went on forever. A perfect body for jeans and slacks. Her shoulder length wheat-colored hair was naturally blond, but few believed she didn't resort to the bleach bottle. It was simply a quirk of nature, like her complexion which was the color of creamy milk.

Georgia *was* nervous. Her hand trembled slightly as she applied lip gloss with a tiny pointed brush. She'd always hated her mouth, thinking it was too full and pouty, but men loved it and she'd done a dozen cosmetic ads in her earlier modeling career. One page in *Cosmopolitan* had been devoted entirely to a close-up of her scarlet lips touting a new brand of lipstick. Now she stood up and

12

appraised herself. Not bad for thirty-six, not bad at all, she thought wryly. In all fairness, anyone seeing Georgia Bonner on a good day would not guess her to be a day over twenty-five—well, maybe thirty. Her looks had held up well through the years.

She wore a gown of black lace over nude satin, cut modestly high at the neck with long tapered sleeves, sleeves that hid scars on her slim wrists, long healed razor scars inflicted in one drunken moment of despair after Victor's death. But she wouldn't think about that now, not tonight. Tonight she needed all her resources. Tonight was important—she mustn't blow it.

Diamond earrings glittered at her ears, and a jeweled heart hung from a platinum chain around her neck. A silver flask containing a mixture of vodka and orange juice nestled inside her handbag; just for security reasons, she'd told herself coming over in the taxi, just for a little "Dutch courage." Lord, how she needed it! The room was empty now, but in case someone came in, she stepped inside one of the stalls, removed the flask from her purse, took a healthy slug, then another and another. The effect was immediately rewarding. A delicious, warm sensation spread through her, producing a calm, floating feeling in which the demons nipping at her heels were put to rest, at least for the moment. She emerged from the little cubicle, gave herself a last glance in the mirror, then turned at the sound of Robbie Hale's gravelly voice.

"Hi, Miss Bonner. Me again. All ready? Marty's in fine fettle. But you can handle it, Miss Bonner. My money's on you. Just follow me. It's a little dark down these stairs, so keep close."

Georgia drew in her breath and followed the man out the door. Why in hell hadn't she taken another little nip? She was definitely going to need it.

Inside the studio, Georgia felt perspiration running down her sides from under her arms. The lights were hot. Marty Saks, his clear blue eyes assessing every detail of her face and gown, smiled as she was introduced and seated. "Georgia Bonner . . . nice to see you looking so svelte after such a long, long time. I'm not going to pry about where you've been hiding. Suffice to say, we've missed your lovely face." Marty was being nice—softening her up. He respected her for coming on the show.

"Georgia, I realize you've put the past behind you, but our viewers would dearly love to know how a woman like you managed during that difficult period. I mean the divorce from Victor, all the publicity, his re-marriage, then his death . . . so untimely." Marty's voice softened, becoming intimate, almost beguiling, begging her to open up. "There are thousands of other women out there all over the country who I'm certain have had similar problems."

A sudden fury surged through Georgia, then subsided, leaving her almost calm. After all, what did she expect?

"Look, Marty, my life with Victor is over. He's dead. He was my husband, but he's dead. Even though we were no longer married, I tried to be his friend." She didn't add, *He made a terrible mistake, but it was too late.* "I've been picking up the pieces of my life the last three years. I was in a sanitarium for a year"—an audible sound of sympathy from the audience as she delivered this bombshell—"and now I'm back and I need to work. I'm starting slow. I'm in an off-Broadway play at the moment, 'Goodbye Tomorrow.' We're in rehearsal." She paused. "We're in rehearsal but we need more financing. Always money." Marty's cologne was getting to her. It was awful. She prayed she wouldn't sneeze.

Marty paused a full moment, allowing her revelations to sink in. He was still annoyed that his original plan had been foiled—to present both Mrs. Sandbornes on the show together, not letting either know the other was to appear. Georgia Bonner Sandborne, wronged wife; Kiki Blake Sandborne, the other woman, face to face. What sparks! What drama! But of course, decadent, devious, and so-o-o desirable Kiki had declined the offer. Marty tapped his pencil on the desk, feeling sweat on his upper lip at the thought. "Off-Broadway . . . I see . . . I see . . . Sounds good, Georgia. Well, good luck with it. You deserve it. You've paid your dues. But now, to get back to Victor. How did you two meet, by the way? Was it when he was Governor, or later here in New York?"

Georgia adjusted the little mike clipped to the neck of her dress and took a deep breath. How had they met? It was etched in her mind like a photograph . . .

She'd been the star of "Mother's Children" for two years and was just beginning to feel secure, a small miracle considering her background—her pitiful childhood, the early deprivations, her only home a cabin in the pines. Her only parent was Grandmother Taia, her only friends the animals in the woods. At sixteen, working as a waitress after Taia's death—no money, never knowing who she really was, never knowing her parents—propositions, passes everywhere she turned. Then modeling in Dallas, a disastrous love affair with a married oil tycoon, and finally the long trip to New York. Three commercials, an ill fated sit-com, and then, because of her long friendship with Margo Sweet, "Mother's Children."

Victor Sandborne had entered her life on cue, as if he'd been written into the script as the perfect love interest. Tall, handsome, fifty-eight-year old Victor—security, love, happiness, all rolled into one. On their first date at 21, Victor conducted business over the phone like a reigning potentate while she, the beautiful young queen, reigned at his side. All eyes were on the striking couple—Victor's picture had been on the cover of *Fortune* that very day. He exuded the smell of power and success and she had a part in it all, touching the roughness of his tweed jacket, inhaling the scent of his cologne, tingling when he accidentally touched her fingers . . .

She faced Marty squarely. "How did we meet? I'm afraid that would take hours, but it was after his first wife, Caldonia Heinz, was killed in a plane crash. We met here in New York when he took over Sandborne and Company. We were married a year later."

Marty nodded. "Yes, of course. Now I recall. Those little Sandborne stores are all over the place—computers, televisions, all kinds of electronic gimmicks. Have a few shares of that stock myself. My brilliant financial advisor had to do something right after insisting I buy condos in Iran!" Everyone laughed. "Incidentally, Georgia, you're from Arkansas yourself, aren't you? I mean, seems I read some place you were a farmer's daughter, or something like that."

"Yes, I'm from Arkansas. Kernsville."

"A little louder, Georgia. You're too soft, speak up."

"I said yes, I'm from Arkansas—a small town called Kernsville. It's near Little Rock." She had a sudden impulse to do a chorus of

"Little Girl from Little Rock," but refrained. God, what was happening? Too much booze . . . careful . . . careful . . .

Marty smiled. "Kernsville. Never heard of it." He winked into the camera. "Now don't send me any letters from Kernsville, folks. We know you're out there." He turned to Georgia. "Enough about geography and your roots. How's your love life, Georgia? Any men? You're still a very beautiful lady."

Georgia was momentarily thrown off balance. "My love life?" She attempted to smile, but again images from the past flooded her mind. Victor, standing in the bedroom of their Sutton Place penthouse, an odd look on his face, announcing calmly, as if he were at a board meeting, that he wanted a divorce. Just like that—cold—not the Victor she'd known before the abortion, though the operation had been at his insistence. "I'm too old for children, Georgia, you should have taken precautions."

But that wasn't the real reason. She couldn't bear to face the real reason. He had dismissed her sexually the moment she'd become pregnant, as if by impregnating her he had at the same time rendered her undesirable. And all because of Grandmother Taia. She never should have told him, but she trusted him, trusted his love for her. She sat there accepting his terms, too stunned to fight back, too hurt to lift a finger, drained, shriveled inside and worst of all, the guilt; as

18

if she were somehow to blame. But that was before she'd known about Kiki Blake. The old cliche, "the wife is always the last to know."

Back to reality. "My love life, did you say? My love life's just dandy, Marty. How's yours?"

Marty didn't smile. "We're discussing *your* love life, Georgia, not mine."

"I said it was fine," repeated Georgia suddenly filled with a spurt of energy. "Frankly though, I'd rather talk about what I came on the show to discuss—'Goodbye Tomorrow.' I play a schizoid nymphomaniac who seduces three men in Act One." That should get the little ferret's attention! But the director chose that moment to wave them off for a commercial break. Damn!

It was a little hotel on the west side of the city, Forty-Fourth and Broadway, to be exact, a stone's throw from Times Square, where approaching darkness spat out a parade of tarnished, third-rate decadence, both repugnant and alluring.

Inside one small room Jake Pierce glanced around at the shabby, depressing decor and cursed the lack of opulence in his present lifestyle. A black and white television sat precariously on a milk crate, and he moved the dial impatiently, annoyed at everything he saw. The commercials featuring glamorous women were his pet peeve. Shirtless and clad in skin-tight faded blue jeans that hugged his muscular bottom like another skin, the deeply bronzed, full-blooded Mohawk Indian flipped the tuning dial again, then stopped short and stared at the screen.

It was that dumb talk show. "Tell All." A beautiful blonde was chattering away to the host, Marty Saks, who really had her going. Jake liked Marty because he delighted in baiting his guests, making them appear foolish without their realizing he'd set them up. The show was the most popular in that time slot, and there were rumors that it would go national. His interest piqued, Jake sat down on the floor near the screen. Shit, what a gorgeous dish! If he had her here right now with all her clothes off, he'd know what to do, all right. He smiled at his sudden erection, then, fascinated, continued to watch while the delectable nitwit rambled on and on about some rich, famous ex-husband who'd kicked off. She seemed nervous, but he hadn't an ounce of sympathy. Life at the top was a cinch the way these babies got it. Marry a millionnaire, that's all it took. Take some poor sucker over the hurdles, maybe even knock him off.

Annoyed, Jake ground out his cigarette and went to the kitchen for a cold beer.

Women! Nothing was ever enough for them. All they wanted was everything—sex, position, money, a career—what the hell didn't they want? thought Jake, ignoring the

fact that his prime source of income was derived from the female sex. They didn't make
women like his grandmother, Blue Pearl,
anymore. That's why the fuckin' country was
in such a mess.

He sat back down and watched the rest of
the show. Christ! This lady was talking her
fool head off. The dumb broad almost gave
out her address and telephone number. Now
what was she rambling on about? He turned
up the sound. He liked her voice. Low and
husky, not tinny like some dames. R. R.
Malloy's was her favorite little bistro—the
way she pronounced *bistro*, so elegant . . .
After the show. She said something about
drinks after the show, then tossed her long
hair, revealing glittering earrings dangling
from those dainty white ears. Diamonds
fairly dazzled him from the screen. Now she
was full face. He spotted something dangling
from her neck. Sparkle, sparkle!

Jake smiled to himself and allowed his
mind to wing through dark musty corridors.
Sudden energy shot through him—excitement, anticipation—just the way he used to
feel astride the broad back of a Brahma bull
a split second before they opened the chute.
He hadn't made a good score in a long time,
not a really good one. Penny ante stuff—but
this was cream, whipped cream. Real class. A
challenge, like the bulls!

He flipped off the set and went to get
another beer. R. R. Malloy's . . . East Side . . .

21

he felt himself harden inside his jeans and decided to jerk off and think about the blonde. That chick was just asking for it.

The director signaled once more . . . three minutes to go. Marty seemed determined to discuss everything under the sun other than the play, including Georgia's favorite saloon; and before she knew it, the time was up. The show was over. Georgia breathed a sigh of relief and vowed never to do a talk show again unless she had a gun to her head. Dutifully, she shook hands with Marty, silently putting one of her grandmother's hexes on him, and slipped outside the studio.

The cool, damp air felt good to her flushed face, and she glanced frantically around for her closest friend, Margo Sweet, who had attended the show with her husband, John. The rain had stopped for the moment, but the sky remained black and starless.

Suddenly Georgia spotted Margo striding toward her, a smile on her wide face. As usual, the well-known casting director was wearing a pair of exquisitely tailored slacks which had become her trademark and the envy of all. Margo was forever pictured in some candid pose in *Women's Wear Daily* looking chic and successful, attired in one of her marvelous pantsuits. Actually, they were all handmade by an eighty-year old Chinese tailor on Mott Street, but few were privy to this fascinating bit of fashion information.

Margo held out her arms. "Georgia, you were good, really good. I mean you handled yourself superbly. John and I sat in the rear so our faces wouldn't be a distraction, but the audience loved you. I could tell." The two women embraced with real affection.

"Thanks," said Georgia, beginning to feel a slight letdown from the alcohol she'd consumed earlier, "but I'm glad it's over. And, of course, you're just being kind as always. Marty barely gave me a chance to talk about the play, but I guess facing the public again is a big step for me. Hi, John, I'm glad you're here."

She turned and faced Margo's tall, slim husband who, though in his fifties, gave the remarkable appearance of a man in his thirties. When he spoke, his voice was low, well modulated, the trained voice of an actor or announcer. In actuality, John Sweet was a lawyer. "Let's not stand out here gabbing. I have a strong feeling you need a drink," he joked.

R. R. Malloy's was jumping with its usual frantic activity. The famous restaurant and bar, now a landmark on Third Avenue, generated an energy that was tangible. Hamburgers and beer were a specialty of the house, but everything from soup to nuts was served with a smile.

Celebrities crowded in, attracted by the casual atmosphere. Even former First Lady, Jackie Onassis, made an occasional visit.

Tiny, the seven-foot bouncer/maitre'd, waved Georgia, Margo and John to a small table covered with a red and white checkered tablecloth. A handsome young waiter took their drink order. The juke box blasted loudly, and Georgia immediately relaxed and felt better.

Well into the third round of drinks, John gave Georgia one of his lawyer-to-client looks. "I don't want you to misunderstand what I'm about to say, dear girl, but just remember I'm looking out for you the way I would Margo here." He paused and lit a cigarette. "I happen to know those expensive earrings you're wearing belong to Betty, so don't you think it would be a good idea if we stopped by her apartment before it gets any later and dropped them off? I mean, we live close by, so actually it might even be more convenient to simply drop you off first. Then Margo and I will wind our way home and deposit the jewels with Betty before she sacks out. You know, not take chances."

Georgia wanted to laugh. How like a lawyer . . . no loose ends. But, of course, he was entirely right. She sipped the last of her stinger. "John, you are such a diplomat. What you really think is that I'm getting drunk and might just lose the little gems, and you may be right. Here." She unfastened the glittering objects from her ears and handed them to John. "Now they're in your capable hands, but I think I'll stay awhile. You know, unwind a little more." She patted his arm. "You two go on. I'll hop a cab home, or maybe even walk if the rain stops." Her voice sounded surprisingly sober for one who'd consumed a great deal of alcohol in the past few hours. She knew she was drinking too much, but it was the only thing that seemed to relax her, give her some release.

"I mean it, darling, take the crown jewels and go get some sleep. I'll be fine." She paused. "If I must be brutally frank, I'm not in the mood to be alone in my apartment just yet. The little taste of Marty, the stimulation of the show and all—you understand." ·

In reality, she'd spotted an interesting dark man sitting in the corner who'd been giving her the eye for an hour. Somehow it seemed a harmless diversion, the little flirtation. Actually, she wanted to forget the show, forget money problems, and maybe even have some fun.

"Well, okay," replied Margo, who from long experience knew it was hopeless to argue with Georgia. "If you're sure. I've got a hell of a day tomorrow." She adjusted the lapel of her perfectly tailored jacket. "That damn hosiery commercial—if it's not jeans, it's something just as aggravating. The girl for this one has to be really super, gorgeous, great legs . . . and unfortunately, she's got to act! Some order."

She glanced at Georgia. "You'd be divine, darling, but she also has to be in her twenties.

Apparently the ad agency thinks women past thirty-five evaporate or simply don't wear hosiery. Same with jeans. They've gone about as far as they can go on buns, I think. But let's not get me started on that subject." Everyone laughed and John requested the check. After paying, they hugged Georgia goodnight and left the restaurant.

Georgia sat for a moment reflecting on her two good friends and wished she could be more like Margo. There was a woman who appeared to have a built-in security that glowed like a lighted candle. She was the epitome of the word "together" thought Georgia. Her personal life with John was flawless, her career wildly successful, and she appeared incapable of making the stupid, everyday mistakes that seemed to plague others. Yet she was kind and empathetic, always managing to be where she was most needed with a genuine concern. And if that weren't enough, she had a superb sense of humor. Georgia drained the last of her stinger and decided she was damn lucky to have Margo as a friend.

At that same moment, Jake Pierce ground out his last Lucky Strike and once more made eye contact with Georgia. This time she met his gaze squarely and smiled. He congratulated himself and felt a fresh surge of excitement—like riding a loco bronc for twenty seconds.

He ambled across the room and stopped at

her table. "Excuse me, beautiful lady, but I'd dearly love to buy you a drink now that your friends have run off and left you."

Jake waited for Georgia to reply. She looked better in person, better than she had on his black and white television screen. Her coloring was what made her a beauty. All that taffy-colored hair and those big brown eyes, and that skin—just like a gardenia.

Georgia eyed the swarthy-skinned man up and down. He was clad in tight-fitting western pants, a beige silk shirt, and short boots; but it was the unusual silver belt around his waist that held her interest. Her glance drifted to his crotch, then back to his strangely attractive face. She noted a jagged scar over his left eye. Thick, coarse, black hair worn long covered part of it. There was something common about him, but none the less interesting—like a cactus.

She answered, her voice low. "You've been staring at me all night. Do we know each other? You look familiar, are you an actor?"

Jake sat down and motioned for the waiter. "I'm Melvin Smith." Where the hell did that name spring from, he wondered. Well, it was as good as any. "I'm in town for the toy convention, and speaking of toys—you're some doll."

Georgia's face remained set. She didn't laugh.

Jake lit a cigarette and offered her one. "Not funny. Right? Well, what I was trying to

say was what a pretty lady you are."
Suddenly he got a rush. The diamond
earrings were missing from her ears. "What
are you drinking by the way?" That seemed
more her speed. The waiter hovered nearby.

"Well, I've been on stingers, but for now,
just a coffee and brandy." She paused. "Skip
the coffee, make it a Courvoisier."

"Fine. Hear that?" The waiter nodded.

"Got it. And for you?"

"Oh, scotch, straight, water on the side,"
answered Jake.

He turned his full attention to Georgia. She
was a lush, he could tell, or turning into one.
This would make his job easier.

"Tell me about yourself, gorgeous. We
don't have ladies that look like you in
Kansas."

"Is that where you're from? Kansas?" He
was beginning to become a bit blurred, but
he seemed alright, a man in the toy business.
He didn't look like a man in the toy business,
probably had a little girl at home. Suddenly
she wanted to cry. She felt the tears.

He glanced at her, confused. "What's
wrong? Something I said?"

"No. No, it's just that I hate the rain."

"Rain? Rain? What are you talking about?"
He thought the rain had stopped hours ago,
but when he glanced around the room, he
spotted couples arriving, dripping wet and
carrying umbrellas.

"Oh, I see it is raining. But, no problem.

I've got a car parked right outside. I'll be glad to see you home."

Georgia looked him in the face and replied evenly. "Thanks, Marvin, but I'm not ready to leave yet. You go on." Suddenly she decided she didn't like him. The entire incident was a mistake. She wanted him to disappear, leave. She fumbled around looking for a cigarette, avoiding Jake's glance. "I really want to be alone to think."

Jake understood. He was not intelligent or educated, but extremely cunning—like an animal. That's how he'd managed to stay out of jail all these years.

He grinned at Georgia and stood up. "Have it your own way, sweetheart. See you around." And then he was gone.

Four A.M. . . . last call. Last frantic call before the bars emptied out leaving everyone to their own private miseries.

Georgia finished her fourth brandy and was really quite drunk. Not so drunk that she couldn't walk or talk clearly. No one would ever think to see her and she was in a haze, a pleasant alcoholic haze. She congratulated herself on her demeanor and ordered the check, clear as a bell.

Marvin hadn't been so bad after all. Now she was sorry he'd left. She felt lonely. Everyone seemed to have a partner, someone they liked or loved. Everyone—except her. Again, she wanted to cry.

She finished the brandy, paid the tab, and made her way out accompanied by the strangers from the bar who were accustomed to the booze and late hours. Even the rain didn't seem to affect them. Georgia looked around frantically for a cab. Of course, there were none. The rain came down in sheets. What was it F. Scott Fitzgerald had said about four o'clock in the morning? The loneliest time on earth. She agreed. No umbrella. She could barely see her hands in front of her. It was a real downpour. Shit!

Laughing couples shielded by umbrellas deserted the shelter of the awning and scampered drunkenly down the streets, singing and sloshing through the water like children.

Suddenly Georgia was all alone, standing there under the street lamp in front of the dismal empty saloon. She peered down at her ruined black satin pumps. Where in hell had all the cabs gone?

And then, like some magician's trick, he materialized from out of nowhere, car and all. Jake pulled his old Buick close to the curb, opened the door, and called out. "Come on, Georgia. Get in before you drown."

She happily obeyed. Her hair dripping wet, she slid in the seat beside the man who suddenly loomed like a knight in shining armor.

"Thanks. Wow, what luck. Just in time. I'm wet to the bone—at least to my shoes." She kicked them off and fumbled in her little beaded bag for a cigarette. She lit it with a gold Dunhill lighter and stared at the silent man at the wheel.

He didn't look the same, somehow. His mouth was a grim line. His eyes were black like licorice, high prominent cheekbones, all that long black hair, dark skin. Christ! He was an Indian! Suddenly she wanted to laugh and ask him if he'd brought his bow and arrow. She restrained herself and sat back while he expertly guided the car through the teeming rain. The windshield wipers were of little help and Jake concentrated on his driving. At last they arrived, and Jake parked at an empty space near the canopied entrance of her apartment building.

She turned to him. "Look, I can just hop out right here. Thanks so much for rescuing me; it's terribly late, and I have a monster day tomorrow." She lied and hiccupped at the same time. "I'm certain you have to get home." Her thinking was hazy, unclear, she really should invite him up. But why? She was exhausted.

Jake took her hand and smiled. "Look, kid, I'm beat. That drive was something else. It's four-thirty in the morning, and I need a drink. There's nothing open. Surely you'll reward a poor cuss who rescued you from the storm—just one?" It was difficult for Jake to be condescending—he hated it! He wanted to pull her out of the car, march upstairs, and do exactly as he pleased, but he patted her arm reassuringly. "You look as if you could use a belt yourself."

"Well, okay. Come on—but just one. Follow me." She slipped out of the car and ran into the lobby; Jake close behind. He noted with interest that the uniformed doorman sat comfortably in front of the package room, fast asleep.

Upstairs, Georgia opened the apartment door, entered, and flipped a switch that immediately bathed the room in a soft rosy glow, highlighting plants in every conceivable spot.

Jake stared for a long moment and felt a wave of envy. This was just the kind of pad he'd like. Not too feminine, not too fancy, paintings, good furniture—and live, growing things.

"Nice . . . nice." He sat in a large pale green velvet chair in the corner. Georgia slipped out of her shoes, threw her black silk coat that was surprisingly dry across the sofa, and went to fix drinks. "Thanks. It could use a slight overhaul redecorating, I mean. What's your pleasure?"

"Scotch is fine," he called out.

She was feeling dizzy now and couldn't find the scotch. At last she located the bottle, poured two shots in glasses, added ice and water. She returned to the living room, handed Jake his drink, then went to the stereo. The music was soft and low—Sinatra.

Georgia sat in a small French provincial

chair nearby and sipped her drink, her head was beginning to spin badly. Suddenly she couldn't think of what to say. She looked at Jake; a peculiar expression was on his face, his eyes narrow, mouth grim, shoulders hunched like an animal ready to spring. Georgia felt a jolt of apprehension.

He hadn't touched his drink, just sat there studying her silently. Come to think of it, he didn't talk much.

At last he spoke. His voice had changed, now it was low, guttural, commanding. "Look beautiful, no point in wasting time." He got up and came striding swiftly across the room until he stood directly in front of her.

Georgia felt a little shiver up her spine.

"I don't want a big fuss, and above all, I don't wanna hurt you, so just do what I say."

Georgia started to rise from her chair, but he pushed her back down. "Sit still. I'll tell you when to get up. Now, I'm gonna count to three. By the time I finish, I want you to have those rocks you wore on the show and every other piece of jewelry in this joint, right out here in plain view. Got it? And don't get smart 'cause you're drunk, baby, whether you know it or not, and no match for ol' Jake here. Now get moving. One . . . two . . . now hustle." He produced a long gleaming switchblade from his pocket and slashed the air like a Samurai warrior.

Georgia thought she must be dreaming.

She was stunned, taken aback. At first it simply didn't sink in—the words—was it a joke? Some kind of new sexual turn-on? Oh my God! She stood up and moved to the center of the room, the glass still in her hand.

"Jewelry? Jewelry? What the hell are you talking about? What makes you think I have and jewelry? Are you insane? Who the hell are you anyway?"

Her voice sounded strong, positive. She had yet to feel the surge of fear and panic that was gathering strength inside her.

"I don't have any jewelry left, except for what I'm wearing." Thank God she'd given John Betty's earrings.

Jake grabbed her roughly by the arm and spun her around, his eyes blazing. "Shut up, cunt. Don't expect me to believe that any dame married to Victor Sandborne has no money or jewelry—that I ain't buying! Now hustle." He sliced the air with the knife just inches from her nose.

Now real fear began to rise inside her. Her stomach was a tight little ball, her throat dry, hands wet, and the horrible thought that everyone would hear she had been found murdered and drunk in her own apartment. God, that just couldn't happen.

Miraculously, Georgia Bonner was suddenly cold sober, her mind clear as a bell. Must be the adrenalin of fear at work. She stood up very straight and faced Jake Pierce. "Look, this is all I have." She slowly unfastened the clasp and handed him the diamond heart. Her voice was calm, solemn, almost fearless. She walked to the Chippendale desk and handed Jake a pile of unpaid bills. "I have these; lots of them."

He grabbed her by the shoulder and shook her like a rag doll. "Stop it, you're lying. What do you take me for? An idiot? You're a lying, cheating whore, and if you don't shut up, I'm gonna mess that gorgeous face up good and proper." He held her face in strong hands and squeezed her chin; his eyes glittered darkly. She felt weak in the knees, like she might faint, but she fought it off. When he released his grip on her she made a dash for the door, but he was right behind her. One long arm reached out and snapped her body around, pinning her arms behind her in a vise-like grip.

"Please stop. You're hurting me." Her face was contorted in agony. The man shook her like a puppet without strings. Her head snapped back and forth. Now his voice was low and shrill with rage. "Don't try that again, you fool, or you're really gonna be sorry. Just do as I say—don't scream. Nobody would hear you through these walls, and if they did, forget it, by the time they got here . . ." He flashed her an evil grin and then held the knife to her throat. She felt the coldness of it against her skin.

She was trembling visibly. "Please . . . please . . . don't . . . don't. I've got something

else for you, just let me go . . . just let me go."
Her voice was low, and appealing, just the
way she used to do it on the soaps when they
told her to make it seductive—sexy.

Jake released her. They stood looking at
one another—the hunted and the hunter.
"Well, go ahead! Get it, and no tricks this
time. Hurry."

Rain pelted the windows but faint streaks
of dawn were visible on the horizon. The
blinds were open and the flimsy drapes only
partly drawn. She stood for a second, looking
out, trying to regain her equilibrium. And
then she headed for the bedroom. It was a
long chance, but the only one she had. There
were no other choices. She'd already sold most
of her jewelry, and the few remaining pieces
were in her safe deposit box.

Inside the feminine bedroom she began to
disrobe quickly. First her wet dress, then
pantyhose and bra. She mustn't dwell on
what she was about to do. Save herself—that
was the main thing—nothing else mattered.

Now she was naked. Somehow, rather than
making her feel more vulnerable, she felt
more in control. Her body had been good to
her in the past, gotten her things she'd
wanted. It was a beautiful, firm body with
large breasts, nipples pink and erect, a tiny
waist, long slim legs, and smooth white skin
that most men found totally irresistible. She
arranged herself on the bed, legs slightly

apart, and called out, "Marvin . . . come in the bedroom. You can come in now."

Jake stood in the doorway and stared at the naked girl lying there so seductively. She reminded him of those calendars he used to hide as a kid, the ones with nude women in all sorts of provocative poses. For a second he was stunned, then felt himself hardening inside his pants. Somehow he couldn't help himself. It was the direct way she did it, right to the point. Well, hell . . . why not? He'd always wanted to fuck one of these ritzy society dames.

Jake didn't speak but he undressed rapidly, throwing his clothes in every direction. Suddenly the jewelry, his neat little plan, nothing seemed to matter except to get to this woman with everything he had.

Georgia lay there on the bed and watched the tall muscular man approach her. She felt nothing, not repulsion, not desire, not fear— nothing. She must still be drunk, numb. That was it.

He slid into the bed beside her and snarled, "Okay, baby, here I am."

His hands cupped one breast almost savagely while his mouth sucked hungrily at the nipple. He moved to the other breast, fondling her, tonguing her, as if he were starved. Low animal sounds came from his mouth, and then he was between her legs, eating her, licking her, running his long dark fingers up inside her, playing with her clitoris. His concentration was intense, like someone possessed. Georgia felt herself becoming aroused. God! This was the final insanity. He cupped her ass in his large hands and raised the lower part of her torso near his face.

"This is eatin' pussy, baby . . . real eatin' pussy."

And then he spread her apart, tonguing and lapping at her until, despite herself, Georgia reached a climax. He laughed with a coarse, ugly laugh, and shoved his big hard member deep inside her. He moved over her rapidly, like a rider in a rodeo. More . . . more . . . faster . . . faster, and then with a wild cry, he came and flopped across her belly, exhausted. Not once had he ever kissed her mouth.

Georgia lay there not daring to breathe— not daring to say a word—afraid the mood would once again revert back to one of hostility.

Long moments elapsed. He didn't budge. Didn't utter a sound. Christ . . . he was asleep . . . asleep! She couldn't believe it. She almost laughed out loud. God, the power of sex. But it seemed too easy. Was he really asleep or just pretending, like a cat with a mouse?

She moved ever so silently . . . testing . . . testing . . . easy now, she told herself. Easy . . . She edged herself slowly out from underneath him and lay for a moment aligning her thoughts. She heard his heavy, even breathing, a little snore. God, he was out cold! Maybe he'd been drunker than she'd thought, or on something? She decided to chance it. Her heart was thumping wildly in her breast.

Georgia slid silently out of bed and tip-toed barefoot into the hallway. Once there, she opened the closet door and, still naked, slipped into a raincoat, boots and an old Pucci scarf that dangled from the hook.

Something fell to the floor with a thump. She drew in her breath, panic flooding through her. Shit! She'd knocked over some books. God . . . she prayed he hadn't heard. Then, not wasting another second, she picked up her purse and fled out the door.

Once in the hallway she walked to the exit door and raced down two flights of stairs, just in case he might wake up and come looking for her. She was still numb inside as she rang for the elevator. The real terror had not yet flooded through her. But it would come. She knew it would come, delayed reaction. She was always great in a crisis. But afterwards . . . well, then she came apart at the seams.

The elevator came to a halt and she fled out into the streets. People were on their way to work. They stared at her. She must look a mess. She wondered about the man in her apartment. How had he known so much about her? Actually, that wasn't too hard to figure.

She hadn't exactly been a recluse.

The police. She'd run right over to the 19th Precinct. Suddenly she paused and thought about the obvious consequences of that move. Publicity . . . questions . . . endless questions about how she'd met him. They'd find out she'd picked him up in a bar. Lord! Then suppose they couldn't hold him? The man was probably deranged. He'd come back after her for sure. No, she couldn't chance it.

Already she was headed in the direction of Seventy-Second Street and Second. Teddy Morrell's apartment was just around the corner. He'd know what to do.

It was still raining and the dark skies were streaked with a peculiar pink and gray. It felt like the middle of the night. At last she arrived at Teddy's. There was no doorman. She searched frantically for his name, found it, and rang the buzzer. Luckily, he was on the first floor. He answered through the intercom, fuzzy, half asleep—annoyed. "Who is it, for Christ's sake?"

"It's me, Georgia. Let me in. Emergency."

The buzzer clicked the door open and in seconds she was in the dry safety of her friend's cozy apartment. Teddy stood there in shorts, his eyes red, mouth open in surprise. "What on earth's happened, Georgia? You look awful. Sit down, I'll get you a drink."

Georgia flopped down on the sofa and began to sob uncontrollably. Teddy sat beside her, patting her shoulder, urging her to drink the scotch and milk. "There . . . there . . . Georgia, it can't be that bad. Drink up, and tell Uncle Teddy all about it."

The sobs subsided and she blurted out bits and pieces of the story, pausing to take long swallows of the drink. Teddy lit a cigarette and handed it to her.

"Lord, girl, you're worse than me, picking up rough trade. But thank God you're okay. Margo and I told you to loosen up, have some fun, but not go cruising some nut-cake."

He got up and walked to a closet. "Here, put on one of my robes and relax. I've got a lousy promotion at Bloomie's all week, have to show up by ten. I'll have time for some coffee. And Georgia," he patted her hand. "you stay right here til I get back. You look like a drowned rat."

Georgia nodded. "Thanks, Teddy. I'm exhausted alright but the first thing I want is a bath. And then, I think I could sleep forever."

CHAPTER TWO

JAKE AWAKENED with a start. Wary, like an
animal in unfamiliar surroundings, he
sprang out of bed suddenly conscious of his
whereabouts and glanced quickly around the
bedroom. Spotty images flashed across his
brain. Even when drunk, Jake had total
recall. And he had been drunk last night.
Drunker than usual, certainly drunker than
he should have been. The booze, combined
with half a joint and two quaaludes, had done
him in.

He stood for a moment in the center of the
room and felt the unseen presence of Georgia
all around him. It was her perfume. He could
still smell it. The delicate odor of her sex was
on him, too. He felt an immediate erection.
Shit! What a debacle. No jewels! A great roll
in the hay, but no jewels. And then he remembered the pendant—he'd stashed it in
his pocket.

And the girl. Where was she? Gone for the cops? No! Not a dame like her. She'd be too embarrassed, Jake rationalized. After all, she'd invited him into her bed, hadn't she? Face it, she wanted him. All women did!

Jake smiled to himself as he dressed. His clothes were all over the place. He ambled into the kitchen, poured himself a stiff shot of scotch, lit a cigarette with the gold lighter he'd lifted off Lorna, and sauntered casually out the door of the apartment.

Avoiding the eyes of the doorman in the lobby, he stood for a moment in front of the building to collect his thoughts. Then he headed toward Third Avenue at an even pace, not feeling the cutting chill in the winter air.

Bloomingdale's, on the corner of Fifty-Ninth and Lexington, was a madhouse that day. Teddy stood at the Eve of Roma counter and attempted vainly to appear his usual cheery, smiling self. Under the circumstances, he found this a difficult assignment. His insides churned at the thought of Georgia's dilemma, and he was in no mood for the preening, twittering women who pressed three-deep against the counter waiting with remarkable patience for his makeup wizardry.

The moon-faced dowager now in the chair beamed a smile in his direction, then closed her eyes as he began what she foolishly expected to be a miraculous transformation.

Sometimes Teddy felt empathy for these women. Other times he was amazed and delighted with the results, but today he only wanted to finish, and get the hell back to the apartment—and Georgia. He hoped she'd slept a little. Despite the fact that he was homosexual, Teddy honestly loved Georgia. In his own way, he probably loved her more than anyone else on earth. Georgia Bonner was the feminine side of Teddy, and when something unpleasant happened to her, it was as if it had happened to him.

Once more he attempted to concentrate on the large, florid face of the woman in the chair. He tweezed stray hairs from her caterpillar eyebrows, powdered down her makeup after adding just the right touch of Roman Glow blush, then, satisfied, handed her the mirror.

"There you go, Mrs. Stein. Simply divine. This new florita base is perfect for your skin tone. Perfect!"

The woman inspected her face with obvious satisfaction. "Oh, Teddy, if only you'd come live with me, I'd look like this always!" she tittered happily as Teddy spotted his assistant, David, making his way slowly through the crowds. He had obviously slipped outside for a quick smoke. It was near Christmas, and the store was jammed.

Teddy bent down and whispered something in David's ear, then turned his attention back to Mrs. Stein. "Look, my dear,

David here will tend to your every need and take your order. I really must dash, have a doctor's appointment," he lied. "Can't be late for that, you know. Your bonus for today will be our new blush. Enjoy! Bye now, see you soon." He patted David's shoulder, murmured a hurried, "Thanks, kid," and turned to leave. He squeezed his way through thickening crowds, and felt he'd suffocate.

The store was aglow with tinseled decorations, golden angels and Santas looming about like a drunken nightmare. The scent of heavy perfume combined with the body heat of hundreds of shoppers, caused Teddy to feel faint. Shit, if he could only get out the Third Avenue door, he'd have it made.

At last he was in the cold, crisp air. A uniformed Santa Claus rang the bell from the Salvation Army, and the sight of the same little man who'd been selling roasted chestnuts near the corner of Third and Lexington was reassuring. He hailed a cruising cab, and within minutes he was inside his own apartment.

Georgia was sitting up in the middle of his king-size bed smoking a cigarette. "Hi, am I glad you're back! I slept for a while, but kept waking up in a cold sweat. I'm still nervous as a cat! Is it raining? What time is it?"

"No rain. And it's four-thirty." He sat down on the bed beside her. "I think you're making a big mistake by not going to the police—"

"No, Teddy! I have my reasons." She

blushed crimson at the thought of Jake's mouth all over her body, his bruising, animalistic lovemaking. "What the hell good would the police be? They'll simply get their jollies asking me how I met him, etcetera. And then I'd get a long lecture on the evils of drink and picking up strange men in bars. All of which I already know. So forget it." She lit another cigarette. "He's welcome to anything he can carry out. The diamond heart, that bugs me the most. I could wring his neck for that."

Teddy patted her shoulder. She looked so vulnerable in his blue silk bathrobe, sitting there trying to act so strong and brave. Teddy wanted to hug her. Instead, he headed for the mirrored bar to make them both a drink.

"Guess I never told you about the time a few years ago when I had a snoot full at Bogart's one night. Well, my girl, I met a really groovy number who appeared to be the essence of charm and good breeding. Quite naturally, I invited him back for a nightcap; and presto, Mr. Nice Guy turned into a wild man. Pulled a gun on me. He tied me up and cleaned out the apartment." Teddy handed Georgia a tall, stiff drink. "So there! You're not the only one whose foot has slipped a bit. But I can tell you this much—never again. I learned my lesson well that night. Now I only play in my own back yard! I'll call Billy in a few minutes, and he can go with us back to your place."

Georgia smiled and sipped her drink.

Teddy would take care of everything. She'd even ask him to do her face today. She was too exhausted to bother.

Six o'clock. Georgia, Teddy and Billy Bright, accompanied by Lee the doorman, gingerly opened the door to Georgia's apartment. They entered cautiously, as if expecting some monster to pop out from nowhere. The place was as silent as a tomb, a faint stench of scotch and stale tobacco still hung in the air.

Teddy turned to Georgia. "Nary a sign of the culprit. He's gone, that's for certain. Can you tell if anything's missing? Everything looks so neat."

"Looks like the dear boy helped himself to a drink," Georgia answered. "The scotch is demolished. Everything else seems to be in order. Except, of course, the pendant is gone. Damn! I was hoping he wouldn't take it."

Georgia wanted to cry. Somehow she'd hoped maybe—just maybe—the man would have had a streak of gentility and left the diamond heart behind. But then, Georgia Bonner had always been a dreamer!

Billy called out from the bedroom. "Everything's okay in here except the bed's a mess and a lamp turned over. Drawers seem to be in order, doesn't look like anything is missing. But what the hell is that smell?"

Teddy and Georgia entered the room followed by Lee, who had made a note to change the locks on the door. Georgia wrinkled up her nose. "Oh, Lord! That's Patchouli. He was wearing it. It is a musk fragrance, a base for other perfume, the hippies used to wear it. Anyway, it sure as hell stays in a room." She patted Billy on the arm. "Come on, guys. Let's close up and get out of here. I'll treat you to dinner at *Friday's.*" They all agreed, and quickly left the apartment.

Friday's, at Sixty-Third and First Avenue, specialized in hamburgers, big drinks reasonably priced, a juke box, and an atmosphere that attracted a crowd of people who preferred jeans to jackets and ties.

The three friends were ushered to a table against the wall, then ordered a round of drinks. The silence at their table was deafening. What could anyone say?

Teddy finished the last of his vodka martini, and patted Georgia's hand. "You're welcome to stay with me tonight, hon, just in case you still have the heebie-jeebies about sleeping in your own place." He glanced at the slim, blond man sitting to his right. "Billy only stays on weekends. His career, you know!"

Billy Bright lit a cigarette. "Don't be snide. I work like a dog all day long with a lot of demanding, spoiled wives, who can't make up their minds whether they want a decorator or a baby-sitter. By ten o'clock all I want to do is sleep—and *alone!*"

"Come on, boys, no fighting. At least not tonight, I'm not able to cope. I've had enough aggravation to last me a month. Teddy, you're a luv, but if I don't stay in my own bed tonight, I may never feel really comfortable there again. It's like getting back on a horse after you've been thrown. You understand, don't you?" Both men nodded.

"Oh Lord, in all the excitement I completely forgot about Margo. She was in one of her motherly moods last night. I should have called her. Incidentally, this little incident is between the three of us, okay? I'm not wild for anyone, *especially Margo*, to find out the gory details. You understand?" She flashed them both a dazzling smile, then glanced at the menu. "Ummm . . . baked trout. Strange, but I'm suddenly starving to death."

Later, back in her own apartment, Georgia lay across the enormous bed and dialed Margo's number. She had put on fresh linens, and stuffed the old ones down the incinerator. Somehow, that made everything seem all right—almost as if it had never even happened. Her night of horror.

"Hi, Margo, it's me. Just checking in. Sorry I didn't call earlier, but I had dinner with Teddy and Billy. How are you dear? Did you find the girl for the hosiery ad?" She was talking too fast. Clever Margo would know something was amiss.

"Georgia! What the hell? It's eleven o'clock. I was worried sick. Tried to call you last night, but you must have had the phone off the hook; busy . . . busy . . . for hours! But at least I knew you got home safely."

Georgia had a perverse desire to laugh at that but kept silent and sipped her scotch and milk while Margo prattled on.

"As to Miss Legs, well, we're down to three finalists; all good-looking, of course, but something is missing. One girl, Nancy Nellis, is damn good, has the quality we need, a bit too skinny in the leg department—but the face is to die! The writers are enraptured with their copy, and in all fairness, it's funny as hell." Margo paused. "I can tell by the silence that I'm boring you to death, or you're tired. And frankly, so am I. John's due in the D.A.'s office at the crack of dawn, so I'll say goodnight, Georgia, sleep tight. Talk to you tomorrow."

Margo hung up the phone, thinking it had been an extremely one-sided conversation. Georgia didn't sound right. Victor's death, and sudden remarriage just prior to his death, still affected her. And all that confusion about the money! John had handled the case and came up empty-handed. Georgia never had a copy of the will naming her as beneficiary, and of course none could be found. Sometimes she felt Georgia reveled in her sudden lack of security, wallowed in self-pity, dwelt on the past too much. And that

50

razor episode! That time Margo had really been concerned. She feared Georgia was becoming an emotional cripple, but she'd improved the past few months. Except for the drinking, of course. If only she could meet a decent man like John, settle down, and find out what contentment was all about. That stupid off-Broadway show was no help. Margo secretly felt the production would never get off the ground, and so far she'd been correct. What Georgia needed was a good commercial, something she could sink her teeth into. She'd have to get busy and set something up for her.

Margo stood in front of the bathroom mirror and brushed her teeth. She smiled at her reflection, and felt a pleasant tingling in her mouth. One thing she had was beautiful teeth. Amazingly enough, she was never jealous of Georgia, or other, younger beauties—at least not anymore, mainly because she had an inner serenity that no one could touch. She had long ago come to terms with herself. She adored her job—that, and her relationship with John. As far as Margo Sweet was concerned, she had it all. She dabbed perfume behind her ears, then went to the bedroom and slipped into the bed beside her husband. He turned and took her in his arms. "Just a hug, darling. I'm exhausted. If I fall asleep, you turn off Johnny!"

* * *

51

Across town, Jake Pierce turned off his own TV set and glanced around the ugly little hotel room with disdain. He didn't spend much time here, but it still bugged him to have to live this way—a hovel! He thought about Georgia's apartment. Now that was real class. And so was she, even though he hated to admit it. He'd gotten a real charge out of making it with her, too. It was a trip and a half. As a general rule, Jake got his kicks hurting women, not loving them!

Somehow the fact that he'd enjoyed the sex so much with Georgia irritated him. Like she'd put one over on him.

Now he sat on the one over-stuffed chair in the little room, swigged beer from a can, and remembered how it had been when he was a kid on the reservation in Canada. No shoes to wear to school, that had been the worse. And always knowing you were different—a redskin! He'd never understood what that meant. He had dark, almost golden brown skin. It was smooth and beautiful except for the scars left by the bull. But you got used to everything, mainly because you didn't know any better. The poverty, the isolation, the feeling inside that you didn't belong.

He laughed to himself recalling how he and the other young boys used to lie in wait for the girls in the woods, then grab them, hold them down, suck their little titties until they screamed in panic. That had been a hoot, a source of fun. He'd managed to get laid for the first time at age ten. From then on he'd been addicted. It was like a drug, a woman's body. He loved it. Playing with the other boys, massaging their cocks, became a secondary pleasure.

Jake smiled at the memories and poured more beer. Once when he was sixteen, just off the reservation, he'd picked up an eighteen-year old college student. One of those idealistic types who wore horn-rimmed glasses, drank too much and wrote poetry. He'd holed up with the girl for a long weekend, and during that period of time managed to come fourteen times. The girl was amazed and exhausted, but he was just getting his second wind.

And then he'd moved in with his grandmother who owned some property and a small motel by the lake. He had liked living there. The eighty-year old Blue Pearl was the only woman he'd ever really respected or felt any affection for. He'd never known his own mother. She'd run away when he was three, after his father died of acute alcoholism, an affliction suffered by many Indians attempting vainly to secure a fast hold in the white man's world.

Later he joined a rodeo in Texas that took him all over the southwest and turned out to be the real high point of his life. He suffered injuries, many from the Brahma bulls. He was gored on five different occasions, but he always went back for more, determined to master the wily, dangerous animals, who would one day prove to be his downfall.

And then it happened! He was gored in the thigh, his back wrenched. That was the end of his rodeo days. But he often journeyed back to Riodosa where the final accident had occurred—the one that kept him off the circuit for life.

Nostalgia, that's what kept bringing him back. Nostalgia for the bulls, and the smell of horse manure, and sawdust. Yes, and the sweet smell of success. Because Jake Pierce had been a half-assed star in his rodeo days, and shit . . . he missed the crowds cheering, urging him on. "Ride 'em, cowboy!" And the women that gathered in each town—they were easy pickins. He liked that. The women and the liquor.

But those days were over. His "Star Days," as Jake liked to think of them, and so he'd journeyed to Brooklyn and holed up with a group of Indians who did iron work. Climbers, they were called. There were entire little pockets of these people, still striving valiantly for a niche all their own. They were a part of the working people who built the skyscrapers and bridges, and who for some peculiar reason were not afraid of great heights. No one could ever figure it out—how Indians seemed automatically addicted to alcohol but by some quirk of nature, fearless and agile atop the highest building.

Jake was in seventh heaven. He loved the

work, the money was good, and up thirty floors he felt free, in control—like a bird without wings. Again he felt like a star, a performer for the crowds down below.

And then he'd made a giant mistake and married that little cunt who turned out to be a hooker. He almost killed her when he found out. Two months after their separation his back had started to act up, pain him, his thigh where the bull's horn had pierced clear through his flesh, throbbed at nights like a tom-tom in his Red Bone record album. And he'd almost fallen on a new construction job —reconstruction of a bridge. That was the end of that. No more iron work. No more feeling the camaraderie with the other men swapping stories over boiler-makers in the local bar, feeling that he belonged—somewhere, at least.

Money! You had to get it somehow. He'd never go on welfare. He was an Indian! Too proud to take charity. But not too proud to steal!

And the women. They provided a source of income. Sometimes they were only too willing to hand over cash for services rendered—like Lorna on Park Avenue with her strange fetish. He didn't have to force them. Jake wasn't handsome in the traditional sense, but what he did possess was a strong, untamed animal-quality which, though sleazy and corrupt, nevertheless appealed to a certain type of female. Oddly enough, Jake had scored highest with the privileged class. They always felt a certain guilt. He became an expert at working on that Achilles heel.

And, of course, there had been some men along the way—like Martin, the antique dealer in Toronto. He'd been only twenty then, and the few hundred he'd gotten out of that deal seemed at the time a small fortune. Peanuts!

Jake lit a cigarette and allowed his mind to drift back once more to thoughts of Georgia.

He remembered her standing there, so afraid at first, and then when he'd walked into the bedroom, she was lying there so appealingly, so desirable. He kept remembering her dark eyes, begging him not to hurt her.

He glanced at the diamond pendant and fingered it softly, carefully, almost as if he were touching her warm smooth skin. Maybe, just maybe, he'd better pay her another little visit.

CHAPTER THREE

On Friday, Georgia reported to rehearsal a half-hour late. The other members of the cast were sitting around the little renovated off-Broadway theatre drinking coffee out of paper containers.

"Hi, Georgia. You look awful. What the hell happened? A spat with a new lover?" Joan Katz, the play's second lead, laughed snidely.

Georgia shot the younger girl a piercing look. "Sorry to disappoint you, but no—no lovers' spat. Guess I'll have to resort to cosmetic surgery. Why don't you join me, Joan; you could use it, even at your age."

Georgia wasn't in the mood for the girl's humor this morning. Since the robbery, she hadn't slept a full night through. She was tired, depressed, and full of an unknown fear.

"Everyone here? Where's Forrest?"

"Here I am, darling." The tall blonde director fairly sailed across the room. He paused in front of Georgia. "May I say, Miss Bonner, that you were simply superb fencing with the dreadful little man Marty Saks on TV the other night. Too bad the little bastard didn't let you talk more about the play. But anyway, you got in a couple of plugs. Unfortunately, we haven't raised another cent. So today I think we'd better concentrate on Kelly's rewrites; see how it all reads.

Georgia nodded. "Right. And look, Forrest, forget Saks' show. I have. It's a waste of time. We'll get the money somewhere, I'm certain of it. It'll just take time. Meanwhile, let's go to work!"

The cast sat around in a circle and read Kelly's rewrites. Georgia hated them; they were awful—at least she thought so. Everyone else seemed pleased. She must be going off her rocker. It was all beginning to get to her. The numbness had worn off, and a terrible feeling of apprehension had set in. She thought she saw the man everywhere she looked, even in the lobby of her building. Of course she'd been mistaken. Once she thought she'd spotted him at the supermarket.

She went up on her lines, and everyone glared at her accusingly. Sometimes she wished she could chuck the whole thing and just relax and be taken care of by some man. Life seemed such a struggle.

After rehearsal she hopped a cab from the west side and told the driver to let her out at

Sixty-Third and First. She needed to stop in the liquor store and buy some wine. She looked forward to a cool drink, a TV dinner, or maybe order out for a pizza. Nothing too taxing.

Georgia had dressed carefully that day. She wore slacks, a turtleneck cashmere sweater, boots and a short lynx jacket. She got out of the cab and darted into the stationer's on the corner to buy a package of cigarettes and a newspaper. That was when she saw him. At first she thought she was mistaken again. She adjusted her dark glasses, and looked carefully, cautiously.

There he stood, outside the phone booth across the street from the stationery shop, his profile clearly visible to her. He was wearing skin tight levis, an open shirt, a leather jacket. A cigarette dangled arrogantly from his lips. He looked younger—better looking than she'd remembered. Well, she was surprised she even recognized him; she had been quite drunk that night. She looked again, holding the newspaper up near her face. It was the same man alright. Georgia stepped further inside the newsstand just as he turned around. She could see him full face now, but he couldn't see her. Her heart was pounding so hard she thought she'd faint. Her hands trembled as she paid the man behind the counter, and decided to avoid the liquor store. She could always order when she reached the apartment.

Georgia unlocked her door cautiously. The man had disappeared by the time she'd slipped out of the stationer's, but that in itself was nervewracking. Could she have imagined seeing him? Was she coming apart at the seams? Was he watching her? Following her for some reason? Did he think she'd gone to the police? Surely he wouldn't be crazy enough to come back—or would he?

Georgia went to the bedroom and changed into her favorite soft, fluffy granny gown. Somehow that gave her a feeling of security. She laughed to herself and dialed the number of the liquor store. Imagine! Feeling secure because of a cuddly nightgown. She *was* going nuts!

After placing her liquor order she stretched out on the sofa. Her back and neck ached. Nerves no doubt. Also, she hadn't been getting the proper exercise. What she really needed was a good workout and a swim at the *Club Vertical* up the street.

Suddenly the phone rang. It was probably Margo just checking in. She had managed to keep the "night of horror" a dark secret from her best friend—so far.

Georgia answered, her voice soft. "Hello. Hello, is anyone there?" Shit! No one was answering—probably a wrong number. Georgia hung up the phone as the doorman buzzed from downstairs. She jumped as if she'd been shot. It was only the wine delivery.

60

She went to the door, opened it a crack, paid the boy, and then struggled to open the nicely chilled bottle. She poured a large goblet to the brim, then added strawberries. She loved it that way, it looked so pretty. Made her feel luxurious—like a princess.

She settled back to enjoy her drink, turned on the pink lights, and the hi-fi. Sinatra's smooth voice filled the room. Georgia allowed the wine to take hold, lull her into a mellow mood. God! She really had to forget that crazy night. It was over. Finished. Why did she feel this nagging worry, as if it was only the beginning—the beginning of something really bad!

And then the phone rang again. This time there was music at the other end. Glasses clinking. But no voice. No other sound. Georgia hung up the instrument, filled with a growing anxiety. Face it. She thought it was the man. Well, if it was, how in hell had he gotten her number? She was unlisted. And then she remembered. The stupid number was written big and bold across the base of the phone for anyone to see.

Georgia felt ill. She picked up the instrument, turned it over, and flipped a switch that automatically eliminated all sound. Now anyone calling would think she wasn't home. It was inconvenient, but the best she could do. At least for the time being! She finished the wine, curled up to watch reruns of "Baretta" and was soon fast asleep.

* * *

Two days later Georgia left rehearsal in a mood of depression. The play was being abandoned. Not enough money had been raised to continue paying members of the cast even half scale, and the worst of it was, there didn't appear to be any hope. Little interest had been generated in the work of the ambitious new playwright, and so they had all decided to call it quits. It had started as such a promising venture. But then Georgia had desperately needed something to give herself focus, and again she had made a mistake. Failed herself and the cast.

Of course, that wasn't entirely true. She couldn't be held responsible for their financial dilemma, even if they all secretly thought she had the cash to back the damn production herself. Why the hell did everyone think she was loaded just because of her marriage to Victor? The more she tried to explain, the more no one believed her. She'd given up trying.

Joan Katz and a couple of other actors invited her to have a drink around the corner at *Dart's*. She agreed, and within an hour the little bar was filled with familiar faces. Georgia felt awful. She promised herself not to drink too much. It was too early.

Suddenly, Forrest, the director, accompanied by the playwright, Kelly, appeared in front of her at the bar. "Just came by to buy you a drink, Georgia. All that work, down the drain. I'm really sick. Shit, I turned down a bit in the chorus of *La Cage* just so I could direct." Forrest stared at her with a touch of hostility in his gaze. "When they told me you were the star, at first I didn't like it much. You know, married to Victor Sandborne, loaded, dilettante—" He laughed nastily. "But then I thought . . . well, she may be a bit of a has-been, but she still has all those ritzy friends, all those friends with nice big bucks. How wrong can you be? Right, Georgia?"

Kelly stood by as if in silent agreement. "So here we are. All out of a job, and no rich friends to come to our aid. What's the matter, Georgia dear, losing your touch?"

Her glass clattered to the floor and shattered into a thousand pieces. Georgia stood up from the stool defiantly, flung ten dollars on the bar, and walked out without saying a word. She barely made it to a taxi before the tears came. She told the driver to take her to *Green Feathers* on Sixty-Eighth Street, then sat back and let the tears flow. That bastard Forrest! She never had liked him.

"Here we are, lady."

Georgia glanced at the meter, opened her Gucci bag, and paid the fare. She tipped the driver a dollar just for not having bugged her about why she was crying.

Inside it was dim, cozy, and offered a refuge for those who needed to hide—even from themselves. Georgia liked to think of the place as her relief station. Somehow, when she walked through those doors, sat down at the bar, ordered a drink, put a quarter in the juke, she felt secure and safe. Snug as a bug in a rug. She laughed to herself and repeated the little rhyme out loud. "Snug as a bug in a rug."

"What was that again, Georgia? Never heard of that drink!" Johnny Pato, the bartender, smiled and poured her a scotch and water. "There you go, beautiful."

Georgie smiled and sipped her drink. The juke was playing an old Sonny and Cher tune. She ordered another drink, drank it rather fast, and then ordered another. She'd sip this one. Savor it. Bette Midler wailed about married men. Michael Jackson hissed *Beat It*.

Georgia ordered another round. The place was filling up. People stood at the bar, or filtered to the back to play darts or be seated for dinner. Georgia wasn't hungry, but a dim voice in her head told her to order something to eat, at least a bite, or she'd get very, very drunk. Shit! She wanted to get very drunk; maybe she was very drunk. She nibbled on a pretzel and smiled to herself; she felt good, really good.

"New York . . . New York," then "My Way" . . . Sinatra! God, how she loved Sinatra.

She ordered another round and let herself drift with the music. For the moment all she wanted was to feel absolutely nothing.

Not far from *Feathers*, on Sixty-Third and

First, in a little jazz bar called *Gregory's*, sat Jake Pierce. He ordered his third round of drinks, lit a cigarette, and thought about the woman he was stalking. Somehow she was different from the others. He could do things with this one, manipulate her, really enjoy himself. There was just something about her.

Jake sipped his drink and thought about the others. Take good old Lorna Karp—and come to think of it, that's just what he'd done! He smiled, enjoying the secret joke. Lorna was rich, sixtyish, still good looking enough to want a man, and willing to pay! Two hundred dollars to be exact . . . just like clockwork. And all he had to do was screw her at dawn in Central Park! Easier said than done; but never mind, he'd managed. And just when dear ole Lorna had thought he was her friend. God, how he'd wanted to laugh in her face. That was when he'd taken the extra set of her keys and had them copied. Next step, use them when she was out of the apartment, hand the loot to Jerry, the fence, and sit back and wait for the cash to roll in. Simple as pie. Jake laughed to himself.

So far there'd never been a hitch. So far the women never—but never—went to the cops. He ordered another drink and wondered who was screwing Lorna in Central Park these days.

Then he thought about Georgia. He remembered everything about her. The way she smelled. The way she walked. That nice finishing school way she talked. Just like the little girl when he was a kid on the reservation, the little blonde princess who came with the other children from the nearby school to stare at the Indians. Improve their social conscience. Stare at the animals in the zoo, was more like it. He remembered how the little blonde girl had smiled at him—offered him candy. Secretly, he'd been touched, but then when he'd tried to take the candy, talk to her, she'd turned and run away screaming.

Jake felt real anger now. Bile was rising in his throat. Suddenly he not only felt his cock inside Georgia, but his strong hands pressing tightly around her neck as well.

Jake finished the drink, paid the tab, flashed the hostess a suggestive grin, then ambled out the door into the cold night. It had started to snow. Just a few flakes. It wasn't sticking. He stood on the corner and appraised his surroundings. This was Georgia's neighborhood. He liked it. Somehow it combined all the things he associated with Georgia—and women like her. He liked the feel of it. There was something in the air here. You couldn't quite put your finger on it. Was it wealth? Power? A Rolls slid silently by. Adventure! That was it, thought Jake. You felt adventurous in this neighborhood, like anything could happen.

The light turned green. Jake crossed the street at Sixty-Third and First, then headed towards *Green Feathers*. He'd heard about the place. Tonight he'd go there!

At first it was difficult to adjust his eyes to the darkness. The swirling lights on the juke box added to the confusion. It was crowded and smoky. The place smelled of pretzels, perfume, and booze. He started toward the bar, then stopped short. At first he wasn't certain, but then he saw the way she tossed the mane of hair, laughed out loud. In a flash, he knew it was Georgia. And she was drunk. He knew that also. He congratulated himself. Christ! What timing!

For ten minutes he stood at the bar and watched her unobserved. Watched her flirt and drink, and toss her hair around. He wanted to grab her, pull her up from the bar, shake her, tell her she was making an ass of herself, a jerk. She was supposed to be a princess, not a drunken slut. Jake glanced at his watch. He paid the tab, and waited outside in the shadows.

Ten minutes later, out she came, staggering slightly. She must have been in that bar for hours. He heard her laugh to herself. She paused outside the door and lit a cigarette. He felt like reaching over and knocking it out of her hand. Didn't the little cunt know ladies didn't smoke on the street?! She ambled along, not quite walking a straight line, and Jake followed a few paces behind.

He studied her as she walked. She was

wearing designer jeans, a fur coat. Her boots were flat. They gave her a peculiar gait. Women walked differently in high heels. Her hair bounced and shone under the street lamp. Flakes of snow caught and melted on her back.

Jake could stand it no longer. With one long stride he was beside her. He took her arm and whispered, "Don't be scared. I won't hurt you. Don't yell, or I *will* hurt you. Just keep walking. Keep walking."

A scream froze inside Georgia's throat. It caught and hung there. "My God! Where did you spring from?" She was suddenly almost sober like the other time. "Why? Oh, God, please, what do you want?"

Jake stopped abruptly and pushed her inside an empty doorway. He voice was low. Almost a purr. "Look, sweetheart, I'm here to help. Help you get home because you're drunk again." He felt her stiffen. "This—" he pulled out the diamond pendant from his pocket and dangled it in front of her nose—"I believe, belongs to you, if I'm not mistaken."

Georgia nodded dumbly and remained silent until they reached her apartment. Jake kept a tight grip on her arm. In the lobby, the doorman smiled and tipped his hat. Jake whispered in her ear, "Don't say a fuckin' word, kiddo," and then they were in the tiny elevator face to face. He loosened his grip and they stared at each other. "What do you want?" Georgia's voice shook now. She was scared silly, like she's awakened from a nightmare to find it wasn't a dream at all, but stark reality! "Look, I don't have another piece of jewelry, just lost my job today—"

Jake squeezed her arm. "What the hell are you talking about?" Job? This ritzy broad never had a job in her life. "What job?"

The elevator stopped, and they were in front of her door. "The show. 'Goodbye Tomorrow.' It was Off-Broadway, and I was making a little money, not much, but a little —and it folded—we couldn't get backing. Angels—" What the hell was she telling this madman all this personal stuff for? She prattled on wildly, took out her key, and opened the door. Jake pushed her inside. She turned on the plant lights, the room was again bathed in the pale pink glow. Jake locked the door and sat down, staring at Georgia, who stood nervously in the center of the room.

"Please, don't hurt me. I'll give you all the money I have—it isn't much—"

Jake stared at her with glittering black eyes that suddenly told her everything. She relaxed. She was on familiar ground. It wasn't money he was after, she could tell by the bulge in his tight jeans—it was her!

"Well, would you like a drink? And what's your name?" She nervously laughed. "You neglected to tell me the last time."

"You just forgot, sweetheart." His voice was sarcastic. "I *said* my name was Melvin.

69

But it ain't. It's Jake. Jake Pierce. And yeah—
I'll have a drink, you got good scotch."

His eyes never left her for a second as she
went to the bar and poured them both a
drink. Her hand trembled slightly, but she
was amazingly calm under the circumstances. Somehow, the worst had happened.
He was here, finally. No more wondering if
he would or would not come back; if he was
or was not in the neighborhood or on the
phone. It was almost a relief. She handed him
the drink.

"Thanks." He sipped the drink carefully,
slowly, studying her every move. "Sit down.
Over there, so I can look at you." He pointed
to the brocaded sofa across from where he
sat. Georgia obeyed and sat demurely sipping
her drink. What happens now? she wondered
warily. She licked her lips nervously, crossed
and uncrossed her legs. What should she do?
Scream? No, that would be useless. No one
would hear and he might just kill her. Or
maim her! Better play it his way. Cool. Easy.
She sipped her drink slowly. His eyes bored
through her. Her nipples hardened, she felt
naked, and remembered their last encounter.

As if reading her mind, Jake put his drink
down and walked toward Georgia. He
seemed to be moving in slow motion. She was
paralyzed. Fascinated. His body was like that
of a predatory animal—long, lean and
muscular. She remembered the scars. The
long coarse black hair gave him a peculiar

feminine look for one who exuded such a vulgar masculinity. The black eyes narrowed as he came closer—they were evil snake eyes. His mouth was a thin cruel line. And then she noticed the gold earring worn on one ear only. He was so close she could smell him— the peculiar musk odor mingled with sweat and alcohol.

Georgia felt dizzy as he pulled her to her feet. He was so tall. He gathered her in his arms and kissed her long, and sweet, and penetrating. His tongue worked her lips and mouth the way it had her clitoris. Expertly. She offered no resistance, and allowed him to hold her. His chest pressed against her breasts. Now he took her tongue in his mouth and sucked it, demanding that she respond. His teeth held her lower lip. He bit her slightly. No blood. Just to let her know he had control. She moaned and he did what he'd been wanting to do all night—he slapped her across the face. Not hard, but a stinging slap that stunned her slightly. She stood there and he laughed, "Just so you know who's boss, baby."

She said nothing. Wanted to sob. Hit him back. Run. But she said nothing. Did nothing. Just stood there like a snake with its charmer. And then he unzipped his fly and produced his cock. It was hard and stood out like another arm.

"Get down on your knees, princess. Get down on your knees and suck it. Do it right now!" he ordered in a low voice that caused shivers to ride up and down Georgia's back. "Go ahead, princess. Down on your knees. Get to work."

Georgia, like a good actress taking direction from an honored director, sank to her knees and took the man's penis in her mouth. She sucked him fast and well, knowing that to hedge would only prolong things. He stood there smiling down at her, holding her blonde head with one hand. Over and over she let her tongue flick over the head, and then she determined to finish it. See what he'd do about that! Her fingers touched his balls. Lightly she massaged them, urging him on. Her mouth was filled with him now, and suddenly with a shuddering cry of ecstasy he let go. She felt the warm liquid in her mouth.

"You're pretty expert at that, baby. Now get me a drink and we'll talk."

Georgia fixed them two strong drinks and handed Jake his without a word.

He smiled at her. "You know, you're not a half bad dame, if you'd stop with those phony airs. Oh, here. Here's your necklace."

He tossed the diamond heart into her lap. Georgia spoke for the first time in minutes. "I guess I should say thanks." She paused. "And I do. Thanks for returning it."

She felt like she and Jake were old friends. Old enemies would be more like it. But the one thing she didn't feel was terror. Somehow that had evaporated when she'd had his cock in her mouth . . . then she'd been in control. They finished several more drinks, and Georgia was by this time quietly ossified. Jake seemed able to hold enormous amounts of booze without the slightest problem. He seemed in no hurry to leave, and Georgia wondered hazily if he ever would. Perhaps this was her punishment for all the wrong, wicked things she'd done in her life . . . to remain here forever, trapped with Jake Pierce.

And then he stood up and began to undress. Georgia watched as he slid out of his tight Levis, shorts, sweatshirt, socks and boots. There he stood: naked, nonchalant, unconcerned. More comfortable, in fact, than he'd been earlier. Totally in command. Georgia wanted to scream. Shout. But when he pulled her to her feet, she leaned against his hard chest weakly. He held her with one hand, and with the other unfastened the brassiere under her blouse and fondled her breasts. Softly.

"Get undressed, Georgia. Get all naked and go lie down in the bedroom. Hurry up, princess, take it off."

Georgia went to the bedroom as if in a dream. She seemed hypnotized, not able to function until Jake spoke. Gave the order. She undressed. When she was naked, she lay across the giant bed, her blonde hair cascading across the pillow. In he came, striding towards her like a warrior ready to take his captive maid.

And then his mouth was all over her, wetting her, sucking her mouth first, then her nipples. Her breasts were wet as he cupped first one then the other with his large hands, working the nipples with his lips and tongue until Georgia cried out in heated passion. She had never felt a sensation like this before. It was as if her body was something this man had been denied all his life, like a satisfying meal, and now, starved, he was given his wish.

He tasted every inch of her. She moaned as he took her clitoris between his lips and massaged and played with the delicate tissue. His tongue took over and he seemed obsessed with this new delicacy. Over and over he let his tongue work in a steady rhythm, then once more all of her filled his mouth. He pressed her forward so that nothing would be missed. She moaned. He raised his head, and smiled that evil smile. His lips were wet from her, and she experienced erotic waves of ecstasy that left her limp. Back again, his tongue slipped way inside this time. Over and over again, as if he were fucking her with his long tongue. Unable to stand it a moment longer, Georgia came with a shuddering spasm.

Jake, with one swift movement, had his cock inside her—moving, moving, urging the spasms to continue, as Georgia moaned, cried out, and felt the penetrating hardness. Over and over he rode her, stirring up one orgasm which melted into the next. Georgia tangled her hands in the Indian's hair and gave in to the violent sexuality that had invaded her entire being. He continued to ride her tirelessly. His cock touched new secret places and she found herself rocking with this despicable man who had robbed and humiliated her.

New colors formed a kaleidoscope in her brain. God! What was happening to her? She didn't care. Once more she gave in, and allowed the man to feel her every emotion. Over and over she came, and then he leaned forward, still astride her, and pulled her face to his. He kissed her mouth, inserting his tongue and holding her tightly, kissing her so deeply that she felt she was dying. And then he raised his head from her mouth and cried out like a wounded animal. A strange, wild scream as the final throes of passion hit him wave after wave.

The two lay quietly for a few moments, and then Jake went to the bar and poured them both drinks. Georgia didn't know what to say. She was dumbfounded. Utterly without words or thoughts. Spent.

"Here, princess."

"Thanks." She accepted the drink, downed it rapidly and almost immediately fell into a deep, alcohol-ridden sleep. When she awoke to the sharp ring of the phone the following morning, Jake Pierce was long gone.

Georgia lay there and listened to the phone
ring. Her head felt as if a thousand little
creatures were housed inside with tom-toms
all beating in maddening rhythm. She
decided not to answer. In was just too early,
and she felt too lousy to cope. Anyway, it
might just be him, and she really couldn't
bear to think about last night. Not now.

She reached over and switched off the
sound, then lit a cigarette. It tasted awful,
just like she felt. Well, what the hell did she
expect? A million drinks—and sex, sex, sex.
Suddenly a wave of nausea swept over her.
Nausea and remorse.

It was eleven o'clock. Not so early, after all.
She climbed out of bed naked and ambled
into the kitchen for a cold beer. She washed
down two Bufferin with the liquid, and sat in
the living room by the window sipping the
Coors.

What the hell was happening to her? Most
certainly she had to take hold of something
tangible before it was too late. Last night
should never have happened. Now what? The
first time was understandable, but *again?*

And she'd enjoyed it! That was the worst of
it, she actually enjoyed that animal pawing
her, making love to her, like the savage he
was. She'd been drunk, of course, drunk and
upset about the play, but that was no excuse.

If she hadn't been at *Green Feathers* alone,

the entire thing would never have happened. Or would it? She'd been unable to get the man out of her mind since the first time. What on earth was wrong with her now?

Certainly the time spent at Green Oaks had allowed her to recover from Victor, but this new episode smacked of disaster. She remembered the doctor's warnings. "Georgia, sometimes you're like a moth with a flame, always courting danger. One day you'll fly too near the fire and singe your wings. Watch it! It's self destructive and you don't need that."

Georgia pondered the recollection a brief moment, then decided to slide down under the comforting warmth and security of the satin quilt once again. She'd hide a while longer, then call Margo. That always made her feel better.

CHAPTER FOUR

It was three in the afternoon. Margo sat in her office smoking and feeling guilty. Cigarettes! Would she ever be able to give them up? She'd promised her doctor she would, and she had—about twenty times.

There was a hesitant tap at the door. It opened and there stood Lew Kaylor, head of Feine, Dalton and Goldstein's business affairs department. Lew delt with legal documents: contracts, the unions, etc. A quiet, efficient man in his fifties, he stood for a moment until Margo beckoned him inside.

"Well, what can I do for you, Lew?" The man appeared nervous, unlike himself. Margo smelled a hint of alcohol across the room. He sat down near her desk and spoke. "Look, Margo, I hope we can keep this little conversation just between ourselves." She nodded, and he continued.

"I'm embarrassed really, but . . . hell, might

as well get to it. It's like this. I have this friend—a young girl   very young." He paused. "She's an actress, needs a break. Well, actually . . . to be perfectly accurate . . . she's a model and wants desperately to land a commercial. I've got her pictures, resume, the works." He dragged nervously on his cigarette. "Well, what I had in mind, Margo, is simply this . . . the next time you need a Brooke Shields type," he smiled, "she's a dead ringer. If you could kind of edge her in front, so to speak. Not that she would need it, but it couldn't hurt. She's so gorgeous and so ambitious." His voice trailed off. "I'd be glad to make it worth your while."

He noted Margo's look of shock but continued. "What I mean is, she'd be willing to give you half of each year's residuals on any commercial you got for her. That's not illegal, Margo. You know how these things work."

Margo lit another cigarette and secretly cursed Lew for stimulating her bad habit. "Frankly, Lew, I'm a might surprised, to say the least. You, of all people, should be aware that while I wield a powerful sword in some areas, in others I'm on the back burner. That's just for starters. And while we both know all kinds of things go on in the industry, I've built a reputation on integrity. In other words, I've had these offers before; and even if I accepted, which I wouldn't, there's the account executive, art directors, and let's not

79

forget the writers—all of whom have a giant say in who does what. Tell your friend to go out and get some experience and stop trying to make it the easy way. There is no easy way anymore, Lew, I thought you knew that."

Lew Kaylor glanced down at his folded hands in embarrassment. "Hell, Margo, I know you're right. But, oh, God! I'm in a hell of a mess. I'm hooked on a Lolita. Me! Me . . . Lew Kaylor, who never strayed from the straight and narrow. I don't understand anything anymore. Girls, sirens at age twelve . . . it's devastating. All that smooth skin . . . all that youth . . . just throwing it at you at a time when you're starting to feel like Father Time."

Margo thought he was about to cry. Her voice softened. "Come on, Lew, it happens to every man sooner or later. You know men go through a change of life same as a woman. You'll get over it. Buy the kid a fur coat. That should keep her quiet."

"Thanks for the advice, Margo, but I'm just not myself. She's got me crazy, and she's only eighteen. Lord! I could be arrested!"

Margo suddenly had the desire to laugh. "Don't worry about it. She'll have a birthday soon, then you're on safe ground. And don't be concerned about your secret. I've got a million of 'em."

Lew thanked her and left the room; his dilemma still unsolved. Margo glanced at her watch and decided his problem seemed childish compared to her own pile of troubles.

Headache Number One: *Lariat* Jeans, a top account. So far, over fifty young men from various agencies had been screened for the new commercial, and only seven had qualified for a second video tape callback. Not one possessed the combination of masculinity and elegance the clients required. Those boys from Israel, owners of Lariat, were perfectionists, and demanded the best for their multi-million dollar product.

And then, of course, there was Georgia. They'd been through so much together. Sometimes Margo felt like an older sister, or even a mother to her dear friend, who had been a source of concern in the past few years. Now that she seemed motivated, now that she'd emerged from her protective shell, the sure cure was work . . . work . . . work.

The Milk of Mango account—that was it, thought Margo, checking her large gold-bound appointment book. They were always on the lookout for a particular type of beauty to tout their famous cream; a cream purported to bring eternal youth to its users. Margo had decided long ago that where beauty was concerned, women would swallow anything provided it was packaged and marketed correctly. Shit . . . maybe the damn stuff worked! Anyway, she'd add Georgia to the audition list for Tuesday.

Suddenly, the little desk phone light

flashed. A reminder that Lariat Jeans remained an unsolved problem. It was her next appointment. She sat back and awaited still another young hopeful with overly developed triceps and tight buns.

The young man was from The Conway Agency, and there was no doubt about his masculine sex appeal. He was sandy haired, square jawed, tall, with muscles that looked as if they'd been greased with oil and worked on at some gym for hours on end. And he had a certain presence. Margo was encouraged. She handed him the copy.

"Look this over for a few minutes, and then let's have it. There are only a couple of sentences. Just read it straight. I want to hear your voice quality."

The young man studied the script, his hands trembled slightly. He swallowed hard, faced her, and began to read.

One line was enough. Margo wanted to scream. His accent was so thick, you could cut it with a knife. Texas! A real drawl. Funny, she hadn't noticed it when they first met. Well, he'd said very little.

"Thank you so much, Mr. James. Your looks are right, but the accent . . . sorry. You should try to get rid of it, unless you plan to go into westerns."

He thanked her, smiled shyly and left.

Margo lit another cigarette, vowing to quit again tomorrow when the pressures lessened.

She picked up the phone to call Georgia.

Tuesday morning. Margo's outer office was filled with good looking women, all with something in common. They were over thirty. Georgia decided she was as bad as the rest, afraid of becoming old, unattractive and unloved. No wonder the entire aging female population bought the damn cream. She glanced around the room at the others and picked up their fears and anticipation; it was tangible, like animals in a jungle, all vying to be queen of the herd . . . top banana . . . the chosen one. Georgia hated competing. She would have made a lousy athlete.

At last it was her turn to read the copy, and oddly enough Margo's presence served to make her more nervous than she would have been had the casting director been a stranger. Georgia donned enormous apricot-tinted glasses and slowly read the lines. It was difficult to avoid laughing.

"Just a tiny bit of this marvelous substance rubbed nightly into my skin, and I awaken to a brighter, more beautiful, more self-assured me. Radiant, that's how I look and how I feel."

The male actor read his part. "Yes, darling, you look marvelous. Just as young as the day we first met."

"Thank you, sweetheart," Georgia responded. "I find that tiny lines do disappear just like magic. It's almost as if

83

Milk of Mango is magic, darling, just like our life together." (They embrace.)

Suddenly, all Georgia could think about was Jake Pierce. She wanted to shout out something like "Milk of Mango is superior stuff for orgies. Just spread a tiny bit over your entire body, then call every man you know." Georgia smiled to herself and finished the copy, grateful that those listening with such rapt attention were unable to read her mind.

Later that night Margo called and told her she'd given a good reading, but it appeared the powers that be preferred a Latin-type for that particular commercial. A slim, dark woman in her mid-thirties had been asked to come back with two others to be video taped. Georgia remembered thinking how much the woman had reminded her of a young Dolores Del Rio.

"You know, dear, you were damn good," continued Margo. "I was proud of you. Now that you're out of that stupid play, I can concentrate on setting up some really worthwhile auditions. Milk of Mango isn't the end of the line. Let's see, I have something coming up next week for a wine commercial. They need extras, too."

"Come on, Margo, you don't have to play the diplomat with me. Face it. I'm not a good commercial type. Anyway, you tried."

Georgia felt her throat constrict. She'd be damned if she'd let Margo know how hurt she was over a stupid thing like a TV commercial. "Thanks anyway . . . talk to you later. I've got a thousand things to do . . . bye-bye."

Georgia hung up the receiver and lay across the giant bed. Why did she feel so God-awful? Maybe she'd never work again. Maybe she was too old—or looked too old. Things seemed to be in such a mess. The Jake Pierce episode. Money.

.Well, it was all her own fault, believing Victor about the will, the trust fund—but nothing in writing. What a fool she had been! Not saving, thinking the alimony would last forever. How the hell could she have been so stupid considering what her earlier life had been like? Men—shit! Teddy 'was her only true male friend, and in a sense he wasn't even a man, if you wanted to get technical. She dialed his number. It rang and rang.

Teddy Morrell walked into the living room of his apartment just as the telephone stopped ringing. He picked it up; there was silence. That always infuriated him, to pick it up just as the party on the other end hung up. He took off his cashmere topcoat, flung it across the sofa, and sat down.

It had been a long day. The Bloomingdale's promotion was happily over, and it was just a few days until Christmas. He'd done nothing about it. Somehow he wished Christmas would just come and go without his having to buy a single gift, wrap a single package; and, of course, Billy was behaving strangely . . .

again. It always seemed to happen around the holidays. People tried too hard. 'Tis the season to be jolly.

Teddy poured himself a drink from the mirrored bar and sat in front of the little tree. The lights blinked on and off, lulling him into a peculiar mood of nostalgia. A time to remember. . . .

Teddy Morrell had not always been his name. He'd changed it from Morris Organsky because he simply didn't feel or look like a Morris Organsky. Nor did he feel comfortable in the middle-class, Jewish family in the Bronx. His father had died when he was six, and his mother had been almost relieved when he moved out of their two-family home leaving her with a younger sister, Shirley.

Manhattan seemed a continent away, but he took the subway ride when he was eighteen, rented a furnished room on the West Side, and attempted to become an actor. He was doomed to failure, though he could pass for an English nobleman in appearance with his patrician features and well modulated speaking voice. He was determined to do something in the arts, and for a time he was kept by a well-known portrait painter who did nude sketches of him in every conceivable position.

Still, Teddy regarded himself more male than female, and he was able to function with some women, if he so desired. The point was, he rarely desired. It was the male body that excited and satified him sexually, and the male personality. That was what it was all about. He loved the masculine gender. They were more direct. He felt more comfortable with men than women on every level.

The affair with the artist came to a dramatic conclusion when Teddy found himself pictured in five pages of *Spur*, an erotic magazine for men. Apparently the artist had also a penchant for taking pictures when Teddy was asleep or unaware he was being photographed.

Rather than infuriating him, Teddy accepted the money offered by the contrite, guilt-ridden artist, who by this time was hooked on cocaine, and hied himself off to Rome.

At the time, Rome was cheap and interesting, especially to those involved in the arts and particularly those who had not yet made a deal with life. Those who were still seeking.

Teddy checked into an inexpensive pensione, a boarding house with atmosphere and meals. The wine-soaked *la dolce vita* suited him just fine.

One night, at a little bar on the *Via Sardinia*, he met and got thoroughly drunk with a close friend of the fantastic woman who owned and operated the cosmetic empire known as Eve of Roma. Ross White was American and had a beard like Santa Claus. He was a writer and had become interested in Teddy primarily because he seemed an excellent character for his next novel. However, they became really good friends and eventually Ross introduced Teddy to the fabulous Eve.

Teddy, who had always had a flair for cosmetics, was delighted when several weeks later she offered him a job as an apprentice makeup artist in her Roman salon. Naturally, he accepted. He was down to his last hundred *lire*.

Teddy remained an apprentice for a short time only, and soon became the most sought after makeup wizard in Rome. Some of his ideas were bizarre, but they pleased the eccentric tastes of the variety of women he worked on daily. The cosmetic queen took great pride in the fact that her own discovery had become such a hit with the magnificent women of Italian society and cinema. There were various reasons for Teddy Morrell's success. One, he was a good artist, devising makeups for the individual rather than sticking to what was in vogue. But more than his talent, he understood women. He could advise them on what to do and what not to do with their current lover or husband with such accuracy because he also understood men. Teddy Morrell played both sides of the fence—and won!

And then one afternoon he received a call from Patsy Capri's agent/manager at The Excelsior Hotel.

"Look, Mr. Morrell, everyone around here

says you're the best makeup artist in the land, so if you can race right over in ten minutes and get the lady in shape for her premiere tonight, there's three hundred in it for you—as well as my undying gratitude. This broad—I mean lady—is driving me bananas. Let's put it this way, Mr. Morrell. Patsy is a famous star and a shade on the temperamental side. You understand?"

Teddy did not have to be bribed to meet Patsy Capri, drunk or sober. She'd been his favorite since puberty. Now she must be forty or so. He'd followed her tempestuous career: suicide attempts, broken marriages, headlines, not to mention her notorious bouts with the bottle and drugs. He looked forward to his task with relish.

Teddy arrived at the star's suite at precisely five o'clock and was greeted by the sight of Patsy stark naked, sitting in the middle of an enormous bed, with empty glass in hand.

"You can stop right there, my friend, unless you tell my fuckin' manager to return the bottle he hid."

Teddy paused, eyed Patsy from head to toe, then remarked, "God, what a gorgeous body. Too bad you're going to ruin it. How about champagne instead of the hard stuff? Doesn't hurt as much. I'll order." He walked to the phone and calmly ordered a bottle of French champagne from room service. He put down the receiver, then walked towards the bed.

Patsy, suddenly embarrassed, pulled a sheet over her ample breasts. "What did you say your name was, young man?"

"I didn't say, but it's Teddy Morrell, and I can't wait to get my hands on you."

Suddenly Patsy began to laugh. The champagne arrived, and Teddy poured them each a goblet. "To you, Miss Capri. To a real star . . . and to tonight. Now, put down the glass and let me get started. First go wash your face," Teddy ordered. "Your old mascara is smeared. Then come back and we'll begin."

Oddly enough she obeyed, and with the sheet dragging behind her, one of the world's most famous women went to the bathroom, washed her face as Teddy had directed, then returned to the bedroom, dropped the sheet, and stood stark naked smiling an elfin smile in his direction.

"What now, Mr. Moto? What now? How about giving me a little before we start the face."

Teddy stared right into her large, limpid, brown eyes that were slightly bleary from too much booze. "Sorry, Miss Capri, but I never mix business with pleasure. At least not until I've finished with business. So, sit down in front of the *poudre*, and let's get started with that face. When I'm finished with you, I can guarantee every man at the premiere will want to screw your ass off!"

Patsy Capri sat down still naked and

replied, "Well, Mr. Morrell, whether you know it or not, tonight you're my escort for this lousy Guinea premiere, so make your magic and then go change into a monkey suit." She had become remarkably sober. Teddy believed that like the child she was inside, she had enjoyed teasing her manager and the others who hovered about, fearing their investment would fall apart. Her shock tactics had not worked with him. He'd been accepted.

"Fine, Miss Capri. But relax now and let me do the base and your eyes." Teddy smiled. "You do your own mouth. That's a very personal thing. Then I'll dash home, change, and be back to fetch you in nothing flat." He noticed with curious satisfaction that the champagne glass had remained untouched.

It was a night to remember. The crowds swelled and chanted. How they loved her! How the Italians adored the tempestuous, bizarre, beautiful American actress, who so suffered for love—for her art—for her lost youth. The pathos in that sultry voice, the sadness in those limpid brown eyes truly picked at the heart strings.

Teddy had been so proud to be at her side. He remembered wondering who her last husband had been, her last lover. One daughter had committed suicide, or was it a son? Her past was so strewn with misfortune, it seemed synonymous with her very name.

Tonight she was breathtaking in a silver beaded gown, her face flushed from champagne and excitement. The premiere had been an overwhelming success. Again Patsy Capri had transformed herself into the public's image of a glamour queen, vulnerable, head lowered in humility, with worshipers at her feet. And he, Teddy Morrell, had been a part of it all. Heady stuff!

After the premiere party they sneaked away, hitting every hot spot in Rome, including *Harry's American Bar* where the entire place rose and greeted Patsy with a standing ovation.

Champagne at *Brick Top's* . . . dawn at the fountain of Trevi. Patsy removed her rhinestone sandals and dangled her bare feet in the water. Teddy had been drunk and filled with such glee. When he'd awakened at noon the following day with a naked Patsy sprawled at his side, his first impulse was to flee, but she rolled over and smiled. "You're really super, baby, and to think I thought you were a fag. Let's have a Bloody Mary for Christ's sake! My head is splitting."

Teddy stumbled around her enormous suite searching for vodka and the little portable ice chest she carted everywhere. The Italians weren't much on ice. And they'd sat together in the king sized bed sipping drinks . . . rehashing the evening . . . laughing . . . kissing . . . behaving like children. Teddy was enchanted. He felt protective towards her, he liked her, but mainly, for the first time in his entire life, Teddy Morrell felt like a real man.

Three weeks later, much to the astonishment of all, Patsy and Teddy were married in a quiet little Roman church, with only Eve and Ross White present. The Papparrazi went wild, rushing about snapping pictures as they emerged from the church enroute to Eve's villa for a champagne reception.

Patsy was due back on the coast to begin a T.V. series, and Teddy closed up shop in Rome, and joined his wife in Los Angeles. Thanks to her contacts, he soon became the top makeup artist in Hollywood, and even wrote a book on the subject of Cosmetics and Careers. However, life with a tempermental, fading super star was not easy. He became her baby-sitter when she embarked on one of her famous binges; watching how much she drank, counting the endless pills; and finally, even keeping track of the men. That was the worst—the men.

After she and Teddy managed to make love successfully several times, suddenly, like a child with a used toy, she lost interest. Disregarding his feelings, she went merrily on her capricious way inviting every available stud, from the Valley to Beverly Hills, into her bedroom.

Once he returned from a weekend in New York to find Patsy drunk, an ensign's rumpled white uniform in the bedroom, and cash and jewelry missing from the bedroom safe.

The uniform was the puzzle. He could make no sense of Patsy's explanation, except that she had met the officer at a bar on La Cienga and brought him home for a drink. The uniform was there, but where was the body? Bits and pieces of the scenario emerged, and after questioning the bartender for an hour, along with a C-note as incentive, Teddy discovered that the Ensign was a hustler who merely rented the uniform as a costume in order to entice his victims, giving his character more credence. Three of Teddy's best suits were also missing (they must have been the same size) and all his gold cuff links. The culprit was never found, but Teddy's adoration for Patsy was on the wane.

And so when she took that final overdose, he was saddened but exhausted—drained physically and mentally. He felt used up, as if he'd been the last ditch for the star. Her estate was left in utter chaos, and Teddy, as spouse, was legally bound to pay all debts and back taxes. He sold his shop in Beverly Hills in order to settle, but as luck or the fates would have it, Eve, now firmly established in The Big Apple, offered him employment there on a temporary basis, doing important clients and promotionals. One day he'd have his own salon again, but so far, that day had not arrived.

It was at about that time that he met Georgia who was also trapped in turmoil and needed a real friend, someone she could trust. Her marriage over, a career in limbo, emotionally drained, she had withdrawn into herself to lick her wounds—but he had helped.

Finding themselves kindred spirits, they developed a warm supportive rapport that was satisfying to both. Teddy adored Georgia, and vice-versa. There was little strain on their relationship. Georgia had her problems but was a paragon of virtue compared to Patsy Capri.

Billy entered the picture a year later, and though he felt somewhat foolish, Teddy imagined himself to be really in love for the first time. Things between the two men had developed nicely for a time, and then Billy Bright, a talented but somewhat spoiled interior designer, began to exhibit signs of restlessness; forgetting appointments, skipping dates, calling at the last minute to say something had come up. Teddy had become desperate and he had done something for which he was deeply ashamed. He'd hired a private detective to follow Billy.

That reminded Teddy. The ringing phone when he'd first arrived, perhaps it was the private investigator. Joe Chance was his name. What a name! Teddy went to the phone and dialed the detective's number.

"Hello, Mr. Chance? It's Teddy Morrell

here. Anything to report?" He felt such a fool.

At the other end of the line, the short, balding ex-cop chewed on a cigar and wished he was in another profession. "Not much, kid, except that friend of your stops in occasionally at the baths on Twenty-Third Street. And he's been seein' a lot of a dame . . . someone by the name of Kiki Sandborne."

Teddy interrupted. "Mr. Chance," (every time he spoke that name he wanted to smile.) "I'm certain you're aware Mr. Bright is a successful interior designer, and like me, spends half his life with women, so that's hardly a revelation. Is that all?"

The detective mashed out his cigar. The office had begun to smell and he was expecting the cute little hooker over for his once-a-weeker.

"Look, Mr. Morrell, I'm aware what your friend does for a living, but we have him under twenty-four hour surveillance. I took the late shift myself. Mr. Bright has been seen entering Miss Sandborne's townhouse at East Forty-Eighth Street at midnight for three nights running—Wednesday, Thursday and Friday, to be exact—and not reappearing until eight o'clock the next morning. Strange hours for decorating, ain't it?"

Teddy hung up the receiver. A cold chill down his back. Suddenly the name Kiki Sandborne registered like a slap in the face. Of course, that was the girl who'd married Georgia's ex-husband!

Teddy went to the bar and poured himself another drink—a stiff one.

He turned and glanced at the little tree with its twinkling lights, remembering suddenly that he and Georgia were invited to Margo's for a gathering on Christmas Day. He'd invest in some really nice gifts; after all, Christmas came but once a year . . . thank God!

CHAPTER FIVE

"Merry Christmas! Merry Christmas, everyone. Come in, come in. Welcome!"

Margo, attired in a green silken pantsuit—whipped up by Mr. Tai, of course—stood in the doorway of her large duplex townhouse greeting her guests. Her short cropped hair, streaked with gray, was beautifully coiffed; emerald earrings glittered at her ears; and a welcoming smile wreathed her face.

Georgia and Teddy arrived simultaneously and, after hugging Margo and placing their colorfully wrapped gifts on the hall table, went immediately to shed their coats.

John added more wood to an already hearty fire, giving the room a cocoon-like coziness. Lew Kaylor and his wife, sipping eggnogs and gazing reflectively into the flames, sat side by side in identical Queen Anne chairs upholstered in pale apricot satin. Bing's old standby, *White Christmas*, played softly in the background as beautifully dressed people, the women shimmering in sequined blouses, the men dapper in dinner jackets, wafted about the perfectly appointed room. Some paused, forming little clusters like perfectly tended flower arrangements, chatting and laughing, all seemingly free—at least temporarily—from the woes of the world.

Sex scandals, child abuse, trouble in the Middle East, political figures under severe scrutiny, and crime . . . crime . . . crime! Everything appeared to be happily blocked out this Christmas night.

The Sweets' duplex easily could have been a page from any issue of *Town and Country* or *House Beautiful,* so much time and care had gone into the decor. Billy Bright had done the decorating, and that especially pleased Teddy. The long table was a picture of yuletide beauty with Baccarat crystal; tall, glowing candles set in antique candelabra; and thin, delicate china edged in gold. Mistletoe hung at propitious spots, and twinkling lights from the giant fir tree provided an atmosphere of holiday delight.

Georgia always felt a warmth and security here, almost as if it were a fortress against the terrors of the outside world.

She glanced at herself in the large gilt-edged mirror. Tonight she was wearing red, her favorite color of late. It was a simple dress, but she always felt good wearing it, particularly at Christmas time. She wore matching satin sandals with tiny, rhinestone spiked heels and very little makeup. Her eyes were done beautifully with a new kohl pencil and a bronze shadow, but she wore only a tinted gloss on her full, sensuous mouth, and tonight, *Opium*, her favorite perfume of the moment. Tomorrow it would be something else. She definitely was erratic when it came to scents. Just last week she'd been in love with *Jungle Gardenia*.

Teddy came up from behind and patted her on one bare shoulder. "You look gorgeous, honey. Come on, let's go meet the guests." He took her hand, and they walked toward Margo who was busy introducing director Mike Marvoni, and his new, nineteen-year old wife to several new arrivals.

She turned to Georgia and Teddy. "Hi, you two glamour dolls! Where's Billy?" She glanced at a jeweled watch on her arm. "It's getting late. I called and invited him myself. After all, this is his baby. Everyone's been raving about his work, especially the bedrooms upstairs. He'd better not disappoint me."

"Guess he'll be here later. At least that's what he said when I spoke to him yesterday," said Teddy, sipping his eggnog and wishing he had a good stiff drink of scotch instead of this milkshake shit. Trust Billy to be disappointing on a holiday.

Margo was immediately sorry she'd asked,

noting Teddy's expression. "Come on, you two, mingle, for God's sake. Help me get the party going. Dinner will be served in an hour. If he's not here, he's not here; but I can tell you, I'll be hopping mad."

Billy arrived twenty minutes before dinner was announced, and Teddy breathed a sigh of relief. He wanted to chastise him but greeted him as if nothing was wrong. Billy offered no excuse for his tardiness, and Teddy asked for none.

The dinner was superb, and with all the wine and brandy, everyone was pleasantly high—not drunk, but exuberant and gay. Georgia proposed a toast, and Margo felt her little holiday soiree a giant success.

A little after midnight, Georgia, Teddy and Billy said their goodbyes and stepped out into the cold, wintery night. Georgia was wide awake and filled with nervous energy. "Let's stop off someplace and have a night-cap, okay? You said you had something to tell me, Teddy dear."

Teddy hesitated. He'd decided earlier in the evening not to mention his conversation with Joe Chance to Georgia. He'd sit on it awhile. "Let's skip it tonight, Georgia." He glanced in Billy's direction. "Frankly, I think Mr. Bright here and I have some things to discuss. I mean, he's made himself so scarce lately, we've got a bit of catching up to do."

"Of course, I understand," answered Georgia, disguising her disappointment.

Tonight, somehow, she'd felt especially vulnerable. Even with the glamour and revelry of Margo's party, she still dreaded going home alone on Christmas. The three figures stood talking near a street lamp as bits of snow swirled around them like so much white powder. It had almost stopped, but tiny flakes still floated about, sticking to the trees in Central Park and giving everything an ethereal, almost fairy-tale appearance—like a *Hallmark* card. Georgia's face was damp, her hair beginning to hang limp. She pulled her mink coat more tightly around her. "Let's walk awhile. I need the air. To hell with the muggers."

"Right you are," smiled Billy, taking her arm. Teddy took her other arm, and they stepped gingerly along the walkway watching carefully so they wouldn't slip and fall. Late carolers could be heard in the distance.

Suddenly Georgia stopped short. "What's that noise? Hear it? Something's crying. Sounds like a baby."

Teddy cocked his head. "I hear it too. Where's it coming from?"

The three glanced around the asphalt covered with snow but saw only their own footprints forming a little pathway. Abruptly, Georgia broke away from the two men and walked toward a long row of trash cans.

She bent her head, listening intently.

"There it is again. Hear it? It's coming from inside that trash can. I'm going to see." She took hold of the lid and removed it haltingly.

Teddy was quickly by her side. Billy looked on. "Lord, Georgia! It might be a bomb!"

She turned and faced him. "You must be insane. A bomb? Oh, Teddy, you've got some imagination."

"Can you see anything? It's so bloody dark. Maybe it's a wild thing. Don't put your hand in there, for God's sake!"

But it was too late. Georgia had already reached inside, feeling around amidst orange peels, bottles and otther loose garbage, only to touch a soft, little body. It moaned like a wounded child, and Georgia pulled out the tiny ball of silver and white fur snuggling it close to her breast. It appeared to be a baby toy poodle, the tiniest creature Georgia had ever seen. She stood for a moment holding the little animal up under the street lamp while Billy and Teddy looked on in amazement. "It's a little doggy! My little Christmas doggy, and I'm going to keep it forever."

They proceeded immediately to Teddy's apartment to examine the animal more closely under better lighting. Georgia was incredulous. Someone simply had abandoned the creature which couldn't be more than a few days old at best.

Teddy warmed some milk, and they all three stood around like nervous parents urging the puppy to eat, but it chose to ignore their entreaties and simply cried a sad, little lament for its lost mother.

"It doesn't know how to eat. It had a mama, and now it doesn't. I'm going to get a doll bottle tomorrow and feed it that way. Who could have done such a cruel thing? If we hadn't come along, the poor, little thing would have died by morning."

Teddy studied Georgia closely. "You're something else, my dear. Women abandon babies everyday, so how can you be shocked that some son-of-a-bitch would throw away a dog? Boy, are you living in a dream world! Maybe it's got rabies. Still, it's amazingly clean for having been in a trash can."

Georgia sat with the dog in her lap and smiled. "This little powder puff is mine now. The damn fools that threw it away obviously were unaware that French poodles are valuable. They could have sold her and made a buck. I'm going to name her Powder Puff."

Billy handed both Teddy and Georgia a drink. "How the hell do you know if it's a she or a he? It's so tiny. God, it looks like a rat. Are you sure it's not a mouse?"

Georgia was indignant. "Billy, I'm gonna smack you. It's a French poodle. Maybe mixed with something else, but who cares. The two of us are going to travel life's road together, so there!"

She held the puppy up to the light and stared into its little, black eyes.

Miraculously, it had stopped crying as if it knew it had been rescued.

A half hour later Georgia said good night, and with Powder Puff wrapped snugly in one of Teddy's velour towels, left the apartment accompanied by Billy who insisted on seeing her to a taxi.

The snow had ceased, and now there was an enormous moon peeking through the clouds. Billy hailed a cruising cab. The cab ride seemed to take forever, but the little dog remained amazingly quiet. Georgia wondered idly if it had been drugged.

Once inside her own elevator, Georgia pressed her floor button and smiled at two men in dinner clothes accompanied by a stunning, young model who Georgia recognized as the girl in the *Viscount* cologne commercial. They exchanged Christmas greetings and glanced inquiringly at her little bundle as the automatic door opened on the tenth floor.

Georgia got out, stood for a moment in front of her own door, and fumbled for a set of keys. It proved to be a bit awkward, what with her newly acquired, furry friend clutched to her breast. The tiny face of the puppy peeked out at her, and Georgia smiled and kissed its cold nose. She put the dog, along with her purse, on the carpeted floor and then turned the first key which opened the door immediately. Odd. She must have forgotten to lock the second lock. That was particularly dangerous these days, considering that there'd been a murder just two streets over last week; and the week before, her friend, Suzy, had been robbed while she napped.

Wary, Georgia entered her living room cautiously, and at first glance thought she was in the wrong apartment. Once before she'd gotten off the elevator by mistake on the ninth floor and tried to open 9F. Now she stood staring, attempting to orient herself.

The entire room was in total darkness except for the glow of candles casting eerie shadows against the wall. She clutched Powder Puff and wanted to scream but remained rooted to the spot unable to utter a sound. She couldn't believe her eyes. It was a bizarre tableau, like a painting or an X-rated film clip. There, in her large velvet chair, was Jake Pierce—completely naked except for a silver Indian chain around his neck. He was stretched out, almost in a reclining position, fast asleep, with a half-empty bottle of scotch between his legs. His body was dark, smooth and muscular. In the light of the candles it appeared to glisten as if it had been oiled. The muscles of his arms and legs were curved and beautiful. The long, coarse, black hair hung almost to his shoulders. In repose, he resembled a statue.

Georgia's first reaction was to turn and run. Realizing how foolish that would be, she approached the sleeping Jake. She wondered if he was drunk. She felt her face go hot as she stared at his nakedness, and then a languid feeling hit the pit of her stomach. Her nipples under the red jersey dress hardened and pressed through the material. She hadn't worn a brassiere.

At that moment, Jake's black eyes opened and stared straight into Georgia's face. "You're late, kid! I almost got drunk waitin' for you. Where the hell you been, all dressed up like that? Out with your fancy friends?" He acted as if he owned her, as if he had a right to be here and question her like this. "And what the hell you got all wrapped up there? A baby?"

"No, a puppy. I found a puppy." She lay Powder Puff on the sofa, then stood at Jake's feet continuing to stare at him in utter fascination. Her voice trembled. "What the hell are you doing in my apartment? How the hell did you get in, for God's sake? What right have you got to keep bugging me like this?" She was shouting now, angry and frightened, completely off balance.

Suddenly, with that feline quickness that was so deceptive, like a Siamese cat that springs through the air and is on you before you know it, Jake was on his feet. He pulled Georgia into his arms. "With a key, sweetheart . . . a key. I know people in the key business. You've heard of keys, haven't you? They open doors. Now, shut up!"

His mouth was on hers. He smelled of alcohol and Patchouli. She tried to resist, tried not to react, hating herself; but it was useless. He was kissing her now, working his tongue inside her mouth in that sensuous way, making her want to respond, kiss him back. Now he was licking her lip gloss with his tongue, sipping at her as if she were a delicious fountain. Georgia's coat slipped to the floor, and as he undressed her slowly in the candlelight, she forgot everything else— even Powder Puff, who had gone to sleep on the sofa unaware of his mistress' dilemma.

They both stood naked, facing each other in the candlelit room. Jake looked at her and smiled. "You're gorgeous, Georgia, beautiful like a white goddess. I'm going to taste every inch of you, hold you, make love to you till you beg me to stop." His voice was low, intimate, almost a growl.

She remained silent as he led her to the sofa and pushed her gently down against the satin pillows. Then he knelt between her legs and gently pressed her thighs apart. He smiled and touched the pubic hair with his long, dark fingers, the tips barely touching her clitoris, urging it to respond. "That's beautiful, Georgia. You're wet . . . hot . . . but be patient, I don't want to rush. Wanna take my time . . . enjoy."

Georgia still had not spoken as Jake bent his head and began to suck her. She moved her body against his mouth as he flicked his tongue over and over, faster and faster. He took both hands and opened her further apart, running his tongue up inside. Her eyes were closed, her body arched. She trembled as Jake held her fast and continued to suck and manipulate her clitoris gently, then applying more pressure. She moved against him, then came with a little cry, not recognizing the sound of her own voice.

Jake smiled and pushed her flat on the sofa. He straddled her body, moving over her, allowing her to feel his member penetrating deep inside. Georgia drew his dark head to her mouth and kissed him deeply. She entwined her fingers in the thick, coarse hair and allowed herself to feel the fire between them while he continued to move in a sensuous rhythm that soon brought them both to a slow, exhilarating climax.

Jake was the first to speak. "Aren't you sorry you didn't get here sooner, Miss Bonner? Something tells me that whoever you were with couldn't make you feel the way I just did. And the evening is still young."

With that, Jake Pierce picked her up and carried her into the bedroom.

Georgia awakened the following morning to find Jake in the kitchen feeding her new found friend. He sat on a stool holding the tiny dog in his lap, a small bowl of milk in the other hand. The dark muscular man was shirtless, wearing only his usual faded blue

Levis, but he held the animal with a gentleness Georgia would never have thought the Indian possessed.

"Well, hi! How do you like my new baby? She didn't make a peep last night. I almost forgot about her. I see you two are acquainted already."

Somehow Georgia felt easy with Jake . . . comfortable. She didn't bother to analyze why. He was here; they'd made violent love once more, and though she knew the whole thing meant trouble, she didn't have the energy to engage in any complicated moral issues. And he looked so handsome and serene, like a father with a new baby.

He smiled at Georgia. Jake rarely smiled. "I love animals. Where'd you get this little tiger? Didn't have him last night. The little devil is eatin' for ol' Jake. See, the milk's almost gone. When I was a kid on the reservation, I had a dog—not a pretty dog—but I loved the bastard. We used to go fishin' together." Jake paused and a ferocious look crossed his face. "Somebody drowned him, one of the other kids. I found out who it was and broke both his arms."

Momentarily taken back, Georgia was silent and put on a pot of coffee. She felt almost domestic. As the day progressed, Jake appeared to have little to do except laze around her apartment and help himself to food and drink. Georgia cut off the phones. She felt guilty about Jake. This was her red

110

wagon, and she planned to pull it up the hill with as much secrecy as possible.

At four o'clock, Jake led Georgia back into the bedroom and removed her robe. They made love once more, and this time he was gentler, not so savage, not so ferocious—almost loving. He seemed more like a friend. She didn't feel so helpless, like she was a victim completely under his evil magnetic spell. And then later, over drinks, they began to talk.

Jake lit a cigarette and studied Georgia closely. "You know, kid, I could almost get to care for you, but there's just something I can't put my finger on. Guess it's the finishing school upbringing, or being married to a tycoon ex-governor, all that dough. You know, better than us Indian trash."

Georgia sipped her white wine and replied, "Well, Jake, you're in for quite a jolt. You see, I'm not really what I seem. I mean, not what others sometimes imagine." She paused. "At sixteen, after taking care of my blind Grandmother for two years before she died, I fled. I mean, I just took off from this tiny little burg I was raised in that didn't even have a movie house and split. I've been on my own ever since. I was a waitress in Texarkana, a model in Dallas, and, frankly, as to Indian trash, you may be interested to hear, my own Grandmother Taia was mulatto. Supposedly, my Grandfather and Father were both white so that doesn't leave me with much black blood, but I'm still technically part black. So how does that grab you, Hiawatha?"

Jake's mouth opened in surprise. "Black! Your grandmother was black? You're full of shit. You're whiter than snow. What the hell are you tellin' me?"

Georgia had to smile at Jake's confusion. "Just what I said. My mother and father disappeared when I was a baby. Grandmother Taia said they were murdered, but no one was really certain what happened. I don't even know if she was telling the truth. All I know is that I loved her more than anyone on earth, and after she died, it was like the end of the world. So, you see, Jake, you're way off base."

Jake dragged on his Lucky Strike. "My God! Just like me. My grandmother, Blue Pearl, raised me. I was a kid on a reservation, you know, like in the movies, except much worse . . . real disaster. Everyone was ashamed of me, even the Indians—and I don't blame them. My old man died of booze, and I never got a peek at my mother. Some said she was a beauty and became a whore. Who knows? I wouldn't have blamed her. But enough about that, how did you get hooked up with a fancy dude like Victor Sandborne? Did he know you were passing, or did he care? Shit, I still can't believe it."

"Not so hard to believe," answered Georgia, "if you knew the facts. Look, Jake,

I'm in my thirties now. When I was twenty I came to New York and became a model first, then an actress. I made good money. Margo Sweet, the top casting director in this town, is my best friend, and that didn't hurt. I did soaps. I was even the star of 'Mother's Children,' and then I met Victor. It was like a dream. I fell in love with an image. You know, Victor Sandborne, ex-Governor, rich, respectable and sooo handsome. He seemed so solid, like no one I'd ever met before. Yet he was exciting, alive, and I felt secure in his love for me. And when we were married, I thought, boy, this is everything I've ever wanted out of life."

She lit a cigarette. "You see, I never was one of those ambitious women for a career. I mean, I just wanted to be loved, so it wasn't all that traumatic when Victor insisted I give up the soaps. You see, I thought my future was set in cement. Anyway, I lived an interesting life; country home, penthouse in New York . . . Everything moved along beautifully —at first. Then Victor seemed preoccupied, he stayed late in the city a lot, and I proceeded to get pregnant though in all fairness, I knew he wasn't all that wild to have kiddies. I thought with me it would be different—but it wasn't.

"One night, after a lot of wine, I told him the real unedited story of my life, Grandmother Taia included, and he hit the ceiling. I never knew a man could change so completely. I was miserable, and when he flatly insisted I have an abortion, at first I refused, but then I gave in." Tears came to Georgia's eyes. "That was the worst mistake of my life. I can never have children now, something went wrong. I never in a million years thought the truth about my smidgen of black blood would make a difference to a man like Victor in this day and age, but my God—it did! Underneath, Victor was a racist."

Georgia looked away from Jake's penetrating gaze. "I should have hated him. Right? Wrong, I still loved the bastard and I floundered around trying to save the marriage. Of course, things were never the same, but I refused to give up. We grew further and further apart, and finally one day he simply asked for a divorce."

Jake interrupted. "What a bastard. But you gave him the divorce, right? That's what *you* would do, not make waves. Then what happened?" He was genuinely interested.

"Yes, I gave it to him, but I wasn't happy, as you can well imagine. I got drunk a few times—had hysterics—threatened—did all those things women do and shouldn't do when the man they love tells them he wants out. Anyway, after the air cleared, we sat down and he arranged a financial deal that paid me a certain amount over a period of time." She paused. "After that period of time he said his lawyers would set up some kind of trust. Anyway, it had something to do with taxes. You know, all that business mumbo-jumbo. I was like a trusting, stupid child. Next scene, enter Kiki Blake. I was seeing Victor from time to time, and then I began to realize he had someone else, probably had for a long time. That explained a lot. I confronted him, and he admitted it, but he said she was really nothing to him—a plaything. He even called her his sex therapist, someone to amuse him. We continued to see one another, and he continued to see Kiki. Then one night at dinner, he told me she was giving him trouble, blackmailing him. No real threats, just letting him know she knew the score about all the checks and jewelry he'd given her and not reported to the IRS."

Georgia poured them each more wine and continued. "That same night he took his will from the hall safe and showed me its contents. I was stunned. Except for a few minor bequests, Victor had left everything to me. He told me my financial worries were over, that one day I'd be a rich heiress and could produce my own shows. Can you imagine how I felt? How grateful I was after it all had happened?

"Later, when he married Kiki Blake, I thought my world had collapsed. I just couldn't believe it. The betrayal . . . the lies . . . and he wouldn't even talk to me. It was maddening. His friends were as stunned as I, but he ignored all of us and became almost a recluse. It was the strangest thing—so unlike Victor. And then, almost a year later, he was dead. Heart, the doctors said, but I never knew Victor to have a moment's worry with his heart. In any case, the will naming me as beneficiary disappeared and apparently he'd drawn up a second leaving Kiki the works. McMillian and McMillian, his executors, behaved as if I was a maniac, having delusions. The Widow Sandborne got everything. I had a breakdown and went to a sanitarium for a rest, but that cost a pretty penny. Everything just gave way, my nerves . . . I'm fine now."

Georgia looked straight into Jake's eyes, wondering why she'd told him all these personal things. Somehow she felt better for having done it, like a burden had been lifted —a purge. "I've got only a few months left of my alimony payments, then *finito!* I'm right back where I started, a little older, a lot wiser."

Jake finished his drink in one gulp and took Georgia's hands. "That's some story. Sounds like one of those modern romances. I'd never have believed it if I read it somewhere." He paused and grinned. "Now what the hell am I gonna do? I was just about to hit you up for a loan."

Georgia almost spilled wine all over her new lounging coulottes. "A loan! Well, my friend, I'm afraid you've come to the wrong place. And Jake, while we're on the subject, I'm really in no position to become involved with a man at this time, especially one who's in the same spot as me. Forgive my frankness; but face it, we met in a hell of an unconventional way."

She paused, taking note of Jake's peculiar expression. "I know you returned the pendant and all, but you did try to rob me . . . and the sex, I can't deny I enjoyed it, but Jake, this has got to be the last time. I can't have you popping in and out of my life. Hell, you don't even bother to pick up a phone. You're like some kind of phantom. I'm certain you understand."

Georgia felt her face flush. She wondered why the little speech should have unnerved her so.

Jake remained in a sitting position but suddenly he grabbed her wrist in a vise-like hold. "Look, Yellow Hair, don't be givin' me orders. That's the one thing I can't abide. Whether you know it or not, you're gettin' as hooked on me as I am on you; otherwise, why didn't you throw me out last night? For once, you were sober."

Georgia recoverred herself and lit a cigarette. "Good question. Well, it was Christmas night, and frankly, I was curious how you got in and . . . and . . ."

"And," Jake supplied, "you were damn glad to see me. You knew I'd come back. You were just waiting for me, Yellow Hair, just waiting for me to make love to you until you were so exhausted nothing mattered but sleep, sleep that blocks out all problems, all worries. And that's why you didn't throw me out. You're hooked on me just like you're startin' to get hooked on the sauce, but take it from an expert, gettin' hooked on ol' Jake is a lot easier on the liver—and a lot more fun."

With that little speech he stood up, stretched, then pulled Georgia to her feet facing him. "I'm leaving now, Yellow Hair. I've got business, but I'll be back. You can count on it."

Georgia took his hand. "Jake, please, I like you . . . I really do . . . but this can't go on. I've got a life to live, such as it is, and I can't always be wondering when you're going to pop up again. I've got to get back to work. It's not easy. It isn't as if I was Liz Taylor making a comeback." She wrinkled up her nose. "Hell, I may have to go to Katherine Gibbs, you know, take a secretarial course."

That remark appeared to go over Jake's head. "At least telephone, okay? And give me back the keys; you said you had keys."

Jake smiled, picked up his leather jacket from the sofa, patted Powder Puff, then paused at the door. "I was only kiddin'. You left your door unlocked. I mean, you didn't lock both locks, and I have a way of pickin' a lock when it's not secure. Don't worry." He smile and was gone before Georgia could utter another word.

She somehow managed to put Jake out of her mind for the rest of the day and decided to telephone Margo to verfiy their matinee date for *La Cage*. George Hearn, an old friend of Margo's, had given her house seats, and they were both looking forward to the performance on Saturday.

CHAPTER SIX

SATURDAY AFTERNOON Nick Culletti stood behind the bar of the famed *Alamo Saloon* on West Forty-Sixth Street and allowed his mind to wander. He was sick to death of booze, drinkers, loud music, and boring conversations with people he'd probably never see again. However, it was a living of sorts, until that big break came along. Modeling, and the few acting jobs he'd so far managed to land, barely paid for his room, drama lessons, and other necessary expenses. Bartending seemed a necessary evil. At least the tips were good, and the place attracted a theatrical crowd—actors, agents, models, people on the fringe of show business.

The jukebox was blaring as Nick wiped down the bar with a Handiwipe, then poured himself a small glass of red wine. Flip Casey was coming on to relieve him for an hour, and the big, blonde Irishman was a welcome sight. It was a matinee day, and the joint would soon be filled.

"Hi, Casey! Am I glad to see you. I'm going in the back to have a few with Sam and Lucky. If anybody should try to get me—you know, if some big shot producer should call and page me for a starring role in his new production—well, you'll know where I'm at."

Casey smiled and slapped Nick on the back affectionately. "Right, Mr. Newman, right—I'll know where to find you."

They both attended Gladys Marlow's drama classes, and Casey and the other students regarded Nick as a real talent.

He had the looks alright—six feet tall, the grace of a bull fighter, and handsome in that dark, pretty but tough way that caused girls' hearts to flutter.

Nick sat down in a large booth opposite Sam who looked up and smiled at the sight of his friend. The grey-haired black man raised his glass of *Lone Star* in salute.

"How you doin', kid? Keepin' in shape?"

Sam had been Nick's trainer when he was eighteen. The boy had shown real promise as a light heavyweight in the old days—days before that night in Newark when Sallic Fox, fresh out of San Quentin and with murder in his eyes, had injured Nick's arm badly. The fight had been called, but Nick had never been the same. He quit the ring and embarked on an acting career.

Nick studied Sam for a minute. "You asked

if I was in shape? Well, I couldn't take on Sallie Fox, but I work out at Dukey's Gym an hour every day. Guess I'll pass." He raised his glass. "Here's to our great and shining future. We're still partners. Just hang in there, good buddy. Keep the faith."

Sam nodded and glanced at his watch. "What time is Lucky due?"

"Any minute now," answered Nick, anxious for his friend's arrival. "You know, every time I clap eyes on that guy, no matter how long it's been, I still get a flash of the two of us back when we were kids in the home."

Sam drained the beer from his glass and studied Nick in silence. Each time they met with Lucky it was the same thing. He brought back old memories. Sometimes, for Nick's sake, he wished the older boy had never gotten out. Years back when the two had been arrested, Lucky, no longer a juvenile, had been sent to prison; Nick to Boys Town. They had lost contact until that amazing coincidence last year when Sam and Nick had run into Lucky in a bar on the West side.

Lucky, all slick and connected, even rated a bodyguard. Sam had been filled with anxiety, but Nick had been ecstatic at being reunited with his long lost comrade.

"Hey, Sam, here comes Lucky now," Nick smiled, "with Juju, of course. Shit, that mother must weigh three-hundred pounds." Nick was referring to the whale-like body-guard who was Lucky's constant companion.

Sam turned and observed the enormous creature who strode with surprising grace through the bar as if checking for concealed enemies who might be expected to emerge at any moment from behind the bar or under a table. Nick secretly felt this was theatrics on Lucky's part, but it was not until the entire room was cased that tall, thin, beautifully-groomed Lucky emerged from a black Caddy and entered the room like a reigning potentate. He should be the actor, thought Nick with a certain pride, as Lucky, dressed entirely in beige cashmere—complete with Gucci shoes—made his way admidst admiring glances and veiled whispers toward Nick and the back booth. Juju sat down like a concerned parent at a table nearby.

"Lucky, sit down, man. You look like the cover of *Gentlemen's Quarterly*. Remind me to borrow that outfit the next time I have an audition. That's a room rocker, man!"

Nick knew how secretly proud Lucky was of his fashion flair. The gangster had been limited to grey cotton pants and shirts at the orphanage, then the drab clothes of prison.

Nick remembered the time he'd stolen a tablecloth and fashioned a pair of shorts and a shirt out of the red-checkered material. Nick had loved it, but the nuns had had a fit—and that delighted the boys.

Lucky casually thew his topcoat to Juju with one graceful gesture and sat down opposite Sam and Nick.

"Greetings, gentlemen. Glad you like the rags. Special from Dunhill's. This entire ensemble set me back a mere eight-hundred dollars." He opened a solid gold cigarette case and retrieved a cigarette which he tapped against the tabletop before lighting. "And you, my friends, look as if you've been sent on a treasure hunt in Alexander's basement."

Both Nick and Sam laughed and ordered Lucky's favorite drink—Dubonnet over ice.

"How's the acting business, Nick? When you gonna get smart and throw in with me? What the hell have you got to show as an actor? Three shows in that damn class and a commercial that's only seen in Jersey."

"Not just Jersey, Lucky. It's not syndicated. I mean, not national, but it's for a famous sporting goods house. Anyway, I have an audition next week for a Broadway show. A small part, but a good one. Ernie's sending me over for a reading."

Sam remained silent while Lucky lit his cigarette, at long last. "Okay, okay—don't get defensive. Just thought I'd ask." He turned and motioned to Juju who sat sipping a beer. "Juju, go to the car and get the loot for the boys." The hulking man stood up and without a word walked out of the saloon.

Lucky smiled mysteriously and smoked his cigarette while Nick and Sam exchanged quizzical looks. Moments later the bodyguard returned, carrying a shopping bag. "Here's the stuff, boss."

The thin, dark man reached inside the bag and produced two beautifully wrapped gifts. "Merry Christmas, boys. Merry Christmas!" He handed the packages to a startled Nick and Sam who accepted the offerings in stunned silence. A few days late, but Christmas just the same.

"Go ahead, open 'em. They wrapped 'em at the store. Remember that rotten orphanage? We didn't get shit. Go on, guys, open 'em."

Inside Nick's box lay a solid gold initialed cigarette case with matching lighter and five crisp hundred-dollar bills.

Sam's present was a Macy's gift certificate for three-hundred dollars and a gold key ring with the figure of a fighter attached.

They both looked at Lucky in disbelief. Nick was the first to regain his voice. "God, Lucky, what the hell? You hit the lottery? I don't know what to say. Thanks." He clasped the older man on the shoulder. "I always wanted a gold lighter. Hope I don't lose it."

"Yeah, man, what a hell of a good present," said Sam. "The least we can do is buy you a drink, for God's sake. Sorry it can't be something more."

Lucky had remained silent, enjoying the obvious pleasure and surprise of his two friends. He laughed quietly. "Think nothin' of it, guys. When Nick here makes it big on the silver screen, he can give me a free ticket to one of his movies—or maybe, I can manage him. Who the hell knows? I'm thinking of expanding my line of business to include the entertainment field. You know—records, TV, night clubs. Saw a little club out in Jersey for sale last week. Might just buy it. Well, boys, I got to travel. Things to do, eggs to lay." Nick always remembered him repeating that line when he was a kid in the orphanange. *Things to do, eggs to lay.*

The giant Juju, having been given some secret signal, was on his feet and assisting Lucky with his coat. Nick and Sam both rose and embraced the gangster. "Thanks again . . . thanks again, Lucky." And then he was gone.

Nick glanced at his watch. "Guess I'd better get back to the bar, Sam. See you later. That Lucky . . . he's something else! He's got it made. What a generous guy. Go on, have fun at Macy's; get yourself some new duds. You can use 'em."

Sam smiled and turned to leave. "He's got it made alright, but how long can it last? I've heard rumors about Mr. G. He's been running things a long time, and when he goes, Lucky's in trouble."

Nick ignored Sam's pessimism and headed for the bar where Casey was waiting to be relieved.

The cocktail crowd was beginning to drift in. Twilight in New York—the time for dreams, anticipation, a time to savor what the night might bring. Everyone headed for their favorite hangout.

Nick paid little attention to the two women seated at the far table against the wall. It was partially hidden by a palm tree, but then it became hard to ignore them. They were so obvious, both staring at him like they'd seen a ghost. The blonde was some looker. The other one was older; tanned, elegant, well-dressed, like she might be a horse breeder—one of those society types. Why the hell didn't they stop staring? Nick was accustomed to women making passes at him, especially when they'd had too much booze, but these two were something else. Now the older one was approaching the bar. What the hell did she want?

Margo faced Nick from the other side of the bar and smiled. "Forgive me for being rude, my man, but I'm a casting director and oddly enough you may be just what we've been looking for. I mean, I think you are. By the way, what agency are you with? You are an actor or a model, aren't you? Well, aren't you?" Her voice was a bit sharp.

At first Nick was too shocked to speak, and then he threw back his handsome dark head and laughed. "You've got to be kidding! I feel like Lana Turner in Schwabs drug store. I mean, you are serious?"

She smiled and handed him her card.

"Fiene-Dalton-Goldstein . . . Margo Sweet.

Not *the* Margo Sweet?" Nick was incredulous. "Hell, I've been trying to get in to see you for six months."

"Well, that's the way it goes," announced Margo. "Here I am in the flesh, and if you wouldn't mind, I'd appreciate it if you'd come out from behind the bar and give me a look at your buns. The job is a jeans commercial, Lariat Jeans. You've got the right look, right age. Just come out a second. It's important. We're about to lose one of our best accounts. My friend and I were at the theatre around the corner and we just popped in here for a drink. It's fate."

Several customers at the bar were obviously listening, and one of Nick's regulars, a director, announced loudly, "Go on, Nick, for Christ's sake. Let the lady see your butt!"

The others laughed, and Nick wiped his hands on a towel and came striding out from behind the bar, his face hot with embarrassment.

"Okay, okay . . . here I am. Look, I'm on duty. Can't we do this someplace else?"

Margo looked him up and down with a professional eye and remarked cooly, "Look, I won't be certain till I see you on video tape, but I know you're good. I can tell. I know what they want. Be in my office on Monday morning—nine sharp—and don't be late! By the way, what's your name?"

Nick smiled and tucked her card in his

128

pocket. "My name is Nick. Nick Culletti. I'm Italian."

Monday morning Nick was five minutes early. The receptionist took his name, called Margo, and he was ushered into her office without further ado.

"Good morning, Nick. Say hello to Bernard Rich and Manny Coh. These two gentlemen own Lariat Jeans."

The two men muttered amenities, then shook hands with Nick who imagined the owners of a multi-million dollar manufacturing business would be a bunch of old, grey-haired birds, not these slim, attractive men in their thirties or forties. How had they managed to do it, he wondered.

"Sorry I seem dumbstruck. It's just that I never thought you'd be so young."

The men laughed and the shorter one, Manny, chuckled. "We grow up fast in Israel. That's where we're from. I mean, we were born there, but now we live in New York. Now, Nick, would you mind climbing into a pair of our little beauties? Face it, jeans are all pretty much alike. It's how you promote what you've got that counts. The man who becomes the Lariat Jeans symbol has got to ooze virility. That's the man thing we want to say. *I am man . . . sexy . . . bold . . . successful . . . sensitive.*" He laughed, "Shit, I should write the copy."

"Face it, Manny, you probably do,"

injected Bernard who then turned his attention to Margo. "By the way, Margo, where are your writers? I thought they'd be here today."

Margo smiled. "Don't worry, boys, the copy's ready. It's the man that's hung us up, but I think we've found him. Go on in the dressing room, Nick, put on the jeans, then give us a look—okay?"

Nick, who had remained standing quietly by, nodded and headed for the door. He hated this part of it—marching around like some stud, being stared at, appraised—but it was all part of the game. He sauntered across the room to the private dressing room where he found three pairs of Lariat Jeans with matching sweaters, all in different sizes. He undressed, picked what appeared to be his size, then wiggled into them. Shit! They were tight. Nick sat down and pulled his high heeled cowboy boots back on, then appraised himself in the mirror. His bare chest was beautifully developed, triceps and biceps still hard and rippling from his workouts at Dukey's and the old days in the ring. He had perfect definition, and the gold chain Lucky had given him a few months ago looked terrific. He decided to forego wearing a shirt of any kind, then lit a cigarette, and sauntered casually back into the room.

Another man, slim and greying at the temples, had appeared on the scene. He stood near Margo's desk and at the sight of Nick waved his hands in the air. "Jesus, he's perfect . . . perfect! Love it without the shirt! What pecs!"

Margo laughed. "Come on, James, say hello to Nick Culletti." Nick held out his hand. "James Rice is the account executive, and he's right, you look super."

She turned to the two owners. " What do you think, gentlemen, was I right or was I right?" They fairly shouted their agreement, and Margo secretly congratulated herself, deciding that Nick Culletti had a stroke of genius for having left off the sweater. The bare chest, the cigarette, produced just the right touch of arrogance to make it all work. He was divine. She'd always known it. From the moment she's seen him in the bar, she knew Nick Culletti had that extra something that meant star quality. She'd send him in to be video taped, and her problem with Lariat Jeans would be a thing of the past.

Two days later Nick left Margo's office in a jubilant mood after signing the contract for the commercial. They were to begin shooting the following Monday, and he was ecstatic. Ernie Black, his agent, had negotiated a good deal, and he decided to stop off and pay his union dues which were way overdue.

He paused in the reception area and spotted the blonde who'd accompanied

Margo that day in the bar. Somehow, he felt she'd been good luck.

Georgia sat leafing through a magazine with Brooke Shields on the cover and glanced up as Nick came striding over and stood directly in front of her.

What a gorgeous man, was all she could think as he grinned and spoke. "Hi, aren't you Mrs. Sweet's girl friend? I mean, you were with her last week in the *Alamo Saloon*, right?"

Georgia nodded. "Of course, I remember you. You're the jeans fellow. I mean, you're the one Margo thought would be super for Lariat Jeans, and I did, too. How did it go?"

Nick continued to smile that wide beautiful grin that gave his face a curious innocent quality. When he didn't smile, he looked dark and brooding, thought Georgia, just like Heathcliff in *Wuthering Heights*.

"I got it. I mean, I'm signed. Can't believe it yet . . . still in shock, like it's a dream. Listen, come have a drink with me. Help me celebrate. Please!"

Georgia was surprised. "Oh, well, I'd love to, but I'm waiting for Margo. She wants to set up an appointment for me with Vera Best. Guess I don't actually have to see her though. I mean, I could leave a message."

She glanced at Judy, the red-haired receptionist who pretended to read but had been listening with interest to the conversation. "Judy, hon, tell Margo I'm going for a drink

132

with her new discovery, and that I'll call her later, okay?"

Judy nodded and wanted to kill. Why didn't she have such luck? "I'll tell her, Georgia. She's in a meeting now anyway."

"Thanks," said Georgia. She stood facing Nick who took her arm, and they marched out the door and into the clear, cold afternoon sunlight. Judy decided they made a glamorous couple despite the age difference.

The couple chose a small table at a little cafe called *La Cabana*. There were green plants all over the place and very few customers. It was three o'clock and the cocktail crowd had not yet begun to arrive.

Georgia looked lovely in a pale blue cashmere sweater and skirt, though she had wondered earlier if it wasn't a bit too juvenile for a woman past thirty-five. She also wore the diamond pendant Jake had returned, and as she sat there sipping wine with Nick Culletti, Georgia felt she'd gone back in time. Young again. She felt young—and free.

Nick studied her face and thought how lovely she was, how different from any female he'd ever known before. He was somewhat in awe of her, yet he felt comfortable, like she was an old friend.

"Georgia, you're the first woman I've taken out in a hell of a long time, what with my hours at the bar and all. And in my spare time I'm studying, learning scenes for class. There never seems time, and frankly, I just don't have the inclination, the urge. I liked you that first day in the saloon. You were like a good omen. I don't know what made me think that, but I did . . . I do."

Georgia smiled, "You would have gotten along great with my Grandmother Taia. She was a witch. I mean, a good witch . . . white magic. I carry a talisman, it protects me from evil, but judging by some of the things that have happened in my life, sometimes I don't think it's doing its job. For example, I had an audition for a Milk of Mango commercial last week; didn't get it. Now Margo's setting up an appointment with Vera Best—she casts the soaps and is a friend of Margo's, but I dread it." She took out a cigarette. Nick lit it for her. "You see, ten years ago I was the star of 'Mother's Children,' but I married and then, well, I drifted awhile and now it's hard to break in again, especially the soaps."

Georgia glanced at her watch. "That reminds me, I've got to check back with Margo. She'll kill me if I miss seeing Vera, even if it's for a minor role."

Nick nodded in understanding. "I wish you luck. I mean, I've had good luck, now it's your turn. I'll get the check, have to drop by and pay my union dues. May I call you sometime? Look, I won't be a pest. I just thought some evening we could go to a movie or do a scene together. Maybe you could read with me, or vice-versa."

Georgia nodded and jotted down her number. Frankly, though Nick Culletti was handsome and nice, she felt he was much too young. The last thing she needed at the moment was more man trouble!

CHAPTER SEVEN

"TROUBLE . . . TROUBLE . . . trouble! That's all I've had with you since Mama died, sneaking all over the place with the Chief of Staff. Doesn't faze you that he's married . . . doesn't bother that pretty little head one bit that he's got a wife and two kids . . . you just go your merry way, and when you're through, there'll be someone else. That's the tragedy, Trina. You don't love Max, you just love the money! I want you to pack your clothes and get out of my house . . . out! Do you hear? Out! Out!"

Georgia recited the words from the script of "Angels in White" and marveled that she'd managed to get through the first scene without a hitch. She'd been nervous a few minutes earlier, but once she'd gotten into it, she felt comfortable. The part was a small one and ran through only three episodes, but it was a new beginning. Something to get her feet wet.

The young actress who played her sister marched out the door right on cue. The director, Mickey Wren, snapped, "Cut and print," then turned to Georgia. "That's a good one, Georgia. Only two takes. You haven't lost your touch, kid. Hope you don't feel slighted—the part being so small and all."

Georgia paused for a moment before answering. "Why no, Mickey, I'm not upset. After all, I've been out of the business awhile, but I'm starting to feel comfortable again in front of the cameras."

He smiled. "God, how I used to lust after you in 'Mother's Children.' You were something—the sexiest thing on daytime television." He paused. "I mean, you still are, Georgia. I didn't mean that the way it sounded. Shit! You're not over the hill yet, kid. You've got a few good years left."

Georgia remained silent, then walked off the set and into the barnlike studio enroute to the dressing room. The building that housed the studio was enormous, with little individual sets decorated to fit whichever scene was being filmed at the moment. A large entrance into each cubicle allowed greater flexibility for cameras, makeup carts, and other equipment, while the entire ceiling area was used for a complicated array of lighting.

Georgia walked along slowly, pausing at the various sets, fascinated by the process which resulted in all this make-believe. A cameraman she recognized from the old days stopped her. "Hey, Georgia! Haven't seen you around in awhile. How's Gorgeous Georgia Bonner, or should I say Sandborne? Caught you on the Marty Saks Show. How's the off-Broadway thing? He never did give you a chance to plug it."

"Oh, hi, Charlie. I'm fine, thanks. How are you? See you're still with it. That's good." She paused, and he handed her one of his cigarettes, then lit it for her. "The off-Broadway thing sort of fizzled out. I mean, we couldn't raise the money we needed, and finally it all just seemed more trouble than it was worth. You know how these things go."

Dear God! Would she ever stop explaining herself? Questions . . . questions!

Charlie studied her carefully. "Well, kid, you still look great, but then you're not even forty yet. I mean, you started out young and all. How's about a drink sometime? Remember, I'm still the guy who can get you the close-ups." He laughed. "Oh, oh . . . I'm being paged. See you soon, I hope."

He turned before Georgia could reply and walked towards a bedroom set where two beautiful actors lay tucked neatly under heavy satin comforters. The hot lights caused them to squirm in discomfort, while the artist from the nearby makeup cart patted each damp face with a tissue then powdered them down to Barbie-doll perfection.

Georgia continued towards the dressing room and felt a knot forming inside her stomach. It would go away. It's just that things had changed. God! Everyone was so young and beautiful.

Inside the dressing area Lita Lang, the star of "Angels in White," sat in front of the long mirror and studied her reflection. She turned and smiled as Georgia walked through the door. "Hi, Georgia, you look tired. I mean, you look as if you had a row with someone. Maybe ol' Wren? The mean bird, we call him. He's a needler, but a damn good director." She faced Georgia who sat down beside her. "Beats me why in hell you ever wanted to come back in the business in the first place. Of course, we're glad to have you," she added hastily. "It's just that you were a star and all, and married to Victor Sandborne. Shit! You must have millions!"

"Stop! Please stop, Lita. I don't have millions, and even if I did, why in hell shouldn't I do what I do best? Act! Is there a law against it? What the hell is wrong with everybody?" Georgia felt the tears well up. She turned her head away. "Sorry, Lita. Sorry I blew. It's just the tension here. I'm not accustomed to it. I'll be okay."

Lita patted Georgia's arm. "You're sorry? Gee, it's my fault. I'm in a hell of a mood myself, but I shouldn't take it out on you. Some little cutie barely seventeen is being written in, and naturally she's gorgeous. I'm twenty-six but beginning to feel ninety. That's what this business does for you." Lita lit a cigarette. "I'm really sorry, Georgia. I guess I was just jealous, thinking you were rich and safely out of it all."

Georgia smiled. "Rich and out of it all? Come on, you wouldn't want out if you had a million. Look, I'm in one more scene with Roger, then I'm through till Friday. You want to come have a drink with Margo and me at The Regency?"

Lita shook her head. "Thanks, hon; but I'm on the Wiley diet. You know Dr. Wiley, don't you? Doctor Feel Good they call him, but I'm not into that vitamin therapy, just the diet part, and it's working. I've taken off six pounds in a little over a week, and I feel good. I mean, I'm not crazy the way I used to when I was on dexies."

"Dr. Wiley . . . Dr. Wiley?" mused Georgia. "Hmmm, I remember meeting him with Victor at a party at *Regine's*. Is he still around? I thought he got into trouble. Those vitamin shots—somebody told me they were speed mixed with B12," Georgia laughed. She studied her reflection in the large mirror, then touched up her pale makeup base with a special pressed powder and applied more blush.

Lita watched her curiously. "You know,

Georgia, you've got the most divine body. You're so thin, and that high butt!" She paused. "Like those black girls you see on television, your legs just go up and up, and you just ripple when you walk. It's something else! I've always admired your body. Please, don't think I'm funny or anything." She smiled mysteriously. "If I didn't know better—"

"Thanks, Lita. I work out at home, and I do a lot of walking. Also, I swim at the hotel up the street when I have the time; but speaking of diets and booze, I keep trying to cut down myself. Perrier water is really in now. Seems silly—it's just water! But somehow, you don't feel so strange when you're at a restaurant or bar ordering Perrier instead of just plain ginger ale." She appraised herself in a long full-length mirror and turned to Lita. "See you, hon. Time for my next scene."

Back on the set, Georgia rehearsed the few lines in her head, then Mickey waved her over. "Okay, Georgia, run it through with Roger here, and then we'll be ready to roll. It's short but sweet."

The scene was short but complicated. Georgia was required to slap Roger Smart soundly across the face. She hit him much too softly each time, afraid she'd hurt the burly Irishman. She hated this part.

Mickey was annoyed. "Harder! Harder for Christ's sake! You can't hurt that big bull.

141

Make it look real; hit him like you mean it! Hit him like you were hitting Victor Sandborne or Miss Kiki, that should do it!"

Georgia glared at Mickey, then smacked Roger across the face with a resounding wallop. His face contorted. She knew she'd really hurt him.

Mickey yelled, "Cut and print . . . a take," while Georgia stared at Roger dumbly. "God, I'm sorry, dear. Forgive me for hitting you so hard. That bastard egged me on. I'm really sorry. That kind of realism isn't necessary on daytime TV."

"Forget it Georgia. I really needed that," he laughed. "The scene will be great. You can bet on it. I'm strong as a bull anyway." He winked. "I'm a secret masochist." He walked away, and Georgia felt like slugging Mickey who stood calmly smoking a cigarette. Instead, she headed for the dressing room to change and meet Margo for a drink.

The Regency Bar in the plush hotel on East Sixty-First and Park was one of Georgia's favorite places. She was greeted warmly and shown to a table near the piano where Curt Meyer had just begun his first set. He waved and smiled at Georgia who looked really lovely, despite the events of the day. Sometimes she thought she must thrive on confusion.

She was all in beige; everything matched down to her alligator bag and shoes—gifts from Victor seven years ago. That alligator wore like iron. No wonder it was so expensive. Her autumn haze mink coat was also a gift, and she dreaded the day when it would go into the hock shop. In the past, it had been a great way to store furs for the summer months, and at the same time get a little extra cash. She wondered idly if Provident Loan was still providing that service, but rather doubted it.

Maybe she wouldn't have to go to those lengths, but her cash was running low. Everything cost so much more than it had even a few years ago. She was spending thirty, forty dollars a day just to exist. Her stomach knotted in fear each time she thought about money or Kiki Blake. It just wasn't fair! But what was fair, thought Georgia, glancing around the room. Nobody said life was fair.

At that moment Margo swept into the room looking glamorous as always. Georgia was proud of her friend. She had such a presence; the kind of looks that lasted, not candy box prettiness, but a dependable, well-put-together kind of beauty.

Without a word, Margo removed her beaver coat, folded it on a chair beside her, and sat down facing Georgia across the table. "Well, sweetie, how'd it go? You look drained. I thought you only had a couple of little scenes today? Looks like you just did the last act of *Camille.* You're white as a ghost!"

Georgia searched for a cigarette in her bag and glared at Margo. "Good Lord! What the hell is wrong with everyone today? Am I falling apart, or what? Christ! I'm not even thirty-seven, and everybody has me down for the count like some kind of fighter in the ring. I suppose what you really meant was that I look old. Well, those little kindergarten cuties will burn out before they're thirty!"

She paused. "I wasn't going to drink today, but to hell with good intentions!" Georgia turned to the waiter who stood silently by. "A double martini, please. And what for you, Margo dear? A nice cold glass of milk spiked with a little hemlock?"

Margo smiled. "A scotch on the rocks with a twist of lemon, please, and calm down; you must have had a really rought day, but I'm a working broad too, you know. Whatever gave you the idea it was easy? Methinks you're becoming a mite too sensitive. Look, sweetie, I'm your oldest and best friend. I've paid my dues, so that entitles me to certain rights. Invasion of privacy rights, if you know what I mean; and if you'll forgive me, Georgia, I think we're long overdue for a good talk."

She paused, studying her friend's reaction. "What I mean is, I suspect your present mood has very little to do with today's schedule or even with dwindling funds. No, methinks it's a man at the bottom of all this nervous frustration and bad humor. Probably someone you want to hide from mother. Man trouble! Come on; out with it, you'll feel better."

Georgia smiled, "God, Margo, you're so damn intuitive, and the wonderful thing about it is you mean just what you say. You only want to help, but sometimes the fact that you're so damn perfect gets to me. You know . . . perfect marriage, perfect career, perfect hostess. You are the best, and I guess I just don't want to unveil all my glaring imperfections in full view of your under-standing gaze. Oh, shit." Georgia looked straight at her friend. "Guess I'm just jealous sometimes. I mean, with you I always feel like the black sheep. Don't you dare laugh at that one."

The drinks arrived, and Georgia took a healthy sip. "As to men—or a man—well, let's just say you've got it partially right. I've gotten into a bit of a mess. Nothing earth shaking and nothing you can really do about it. I'm just not ready to discuss it as yet. I will, in time; be patient. Frankly, ol' friend, I'm a bit embarrassed and a little afraid of what you might think or say if I should reveal the darker side of my soul."

Margo answered softly, "Georgia, my dear, nothing you could ever do, short of murder, would ever change the way I feel about you. Honest. And to my dubious perfection, well, it wasn't always that way. I've had a lot of practice. You forget, I'll be fifty-three next month. You're a mere child. As to the other thing, well, that's your business of course. It's up to you." She lit a cigarette. "It's not that gorgeous child, Nick Culletti, is it? I heard you had a drink with him."

Georgia laughed, "Are you kidding? If only it were. I did have a drink with him, and he's nice. He asked me to rehearse some scenes with him, but I declined. Maybe next week. He's so young."

"Young and talented," supplied Margo. "The video tapes were fantastic, and I understand he's been signed for a supporting role in a TV movie of the week. He should be a star one day, if he plays his cards right."

Georgia's interest quickened. "Really? That's wonderful. He's got a marvelous look, that Italian macho thing that's so popular. He is awfully young though; I mean, for any practical purposes."

Margo eyed her friend and finished her drink. "I'm more than certain you'll come up with one. My money's on you, dear."

Georgia decided to walk home. It was cold, and she felt a bit light headed from the two martinis. She crossed Park Avenue and headed east. It was dark, but the windows at Bloomingdale's were illuminated, and she paused to admire the new fashions that looked so fantastic on the wooden models and so lousy when you actually put them on your own human body. Georgia paused for a moment, then crossed to Alexander's and headed towards First Avenue.

By the time she arrived at her apartment, she was exhausted. The alcohol had worn off. That was the trouble with booze; it always left you feeling like a rag unless you kept drinking. Now with grass. . . .

She unlocked her door and entered the apartment half expecting to see Jake Pierce draped across the sofa wearing a feathered war bonnet, but only the little dogs was there to greet her. Georgia picked up Powder Puff, kissed her, then went to the kitchen to put out her special food in a dish. It seemed the puppy had grown overnight into a tiny fluffy ball of heaven. Suddenly the phone rang, and Georgia went to answer, still in her coat.

It was Nick Culletti. "Well, hi! Funny you should call. Margo and I were just talking about you over drinks . . . all good . . . your ears must have been burning." She paused. "What time is it now? Oh, alright. In about half an hour. Give me a minute to jump into some slacks. No . . . no, we can read and order out for pizza, if you like. I'm not in the mood to go out again."

She hung up the receiver and wondered if she'd done the right thing. Nick was coming over with his new script. It might be fun. She'd already memorized her own lines for Friday's shooting schedule. Anyway, she was still all hyped up from her conversation with

Margo and the earlier excitement of the day. Energy coursed through her, and she decided maybe she wasn't over the hill, after all.

Georgia went to the bedroom and slowly undressed. She chose a lavender lounging set by Diane Von Furstenburg, with harem pants and a blouse with flowing bat wing sleeves. After glancing at herself in the pier glass, she took out her special mirror for far sighted people and redid her mouth with a new shade of lipstick that almost matched the ensemble. Next she touched up her eye shadow with a plum color, accented the lashes with a deeper mascara, then headed for the little gold box where she kept loose cash for emergencies. Emergencies like ordering wine from the liquor store.

Georgia opened the lid and drew in her breath. It was empty. The one hundred dollars in twenties and tens were gone . . . missing. The money had been there the last time she'd looked. She tried frantically to remember when that had been. Christmas! The time Jake Pierce had spent the entire night and following day. She felt her stomach lurch. Shit. He'd stolen from her. Well, why should she be surprised? After all, that's how they'd met in the first place.

Georgia lay across the bed and closed her eyes for a moment to calm herself. It had been some day. Of course she couldn't be certain if Jake had stolen the money or not. It was possible she could have spent it herself when she was a bit tight.

No—no point in kidding herself—he'd done it. She just knew it. Well, that was the end of Jake Pierce. Good as he was in the sack, she couldn't afford to have a thief around. She got up and walked to her dressing table where she sprayed herself lavishly with *Opium*. She'd seen the last of that crazy Indian, anyway.

At that moment the door buzzer rang from down stairs, and Georgia went to answer.

A few seconds later her own little door bell tinkled. She opened the door, and there stood Nick Culletti. He was wearing boots, a turtle-neck sweater and blue jeans. His hands were tucked in the pockets of a quilted down jacket, and he smiled that beguiling smile she'd found so attractive the first time they'd met.

"Hi, Nick. Come on in. Let me take your jacket. It looks warm," said Georgia, thinking once again how handsome he was.

The young man entered the room. "Thanks. What a nice place you've got here. It's so beautiful, like a movie set. I like all the plants and things."

"I'm glad you like it," said Georgia, wondering what movies he'd seen lately, and led him to a chair. "Would you like some wine? I had two martinis at The Regency, but I'm back to wine. Trying to cut down."

"That'll be fine," said Nick, slightly un-

"That'll be fine," said Nick, slightly uncomfortable. After giving Georgia his jacket, he sat down and placed a large canvas duffle bag at his feet. "Got the script right here. We start shooting Monday, and I only just learned the first scene. It's hard doing it alone. I mean, I needed someone to read the girl's part. Hope you don't mind. I wanted to see you again, anyway."

Georgia interrupted, "I'm delighted. Need the discipline myself. I mean, reading and memorizing lines, I'd forgotten what it was like. Let me get some wine first."

When she returned from the kitchen with two filled goblets, Nick seemed more at ease. He handed her a copy of the first page. The title was "Three Times And You're Out," and it was the story of a young fighter who became a vigilante after his father was murdered by local hoodlums. Georgia scanned the woman's part, then began to read. After half an hour she decided Nick was the next Al Pacino. He was great. They took a break, sipped their wine, now more at ease with one another.

"You're good, Georgia. Really good. I'm glad you're back working again. It's a tough racket; but man, the rewards!"

"Right you are, Nick. The rewards are great, but it takes a lot out of a person. I'm convinced some talented people should stay away from the business because of their temperament."

"What do you mean, Georgia?" Nick seemed so interested in everything she said, it made her feel important.

"Well, all I meant was that someone with thin skin, a really super sensitive nature, sometimes can't take the rejection. Like Marilyn Monroe—she was a very mixed up lady—but super talented. She took everything personally."

"Sure, I understand," said Nick. "I'm sensitive to certain things too, like I'm a sucker for animals; and those characters you see on the streets, homeless and helpless. I wish there was something I could do or say, but basically, I'm tough. I've had to be to survive." He paused. "What I mean is, since I never knew a family, never had a mother's love and all that, just grew with my own set of values, I guess that makes some strong, others weak. Me, it made strong. After the fire, my whole life was different."

Georgia's eyes opened wide. "Fire? What fire? What happened?"

Nick lit a cigarette. "I rarely talk about my past. I mean it's over, but I often wonder why I was the only one spared. I was just a little kid, and the woman up the street was keeping me for the night. My dad was sick. Well, to be more accurate, he was an alcoholic—a drunk. He used to beat the hell out of us kids, all except me. I don't remember him ever touching me, but guess I was too small for even a bastard like that. I don't remember much, to tell the truth, except always being scared. Anyway, he was apparently on one of his rampages, and they sent me away for the night." Nick looked away. "He burned down the house. Everyone was killed, even my eighty-year-old grandfather. A neighbor gave me the newspaper clippings. I still have them. Anyway, I was shipped upstate to an orphanage—the Good Hope." Nick stopped and stared at Georgia. "I shouldn't be telling you all this stuff. It sounds like I'm complaining. I hate whiners. You have your own problems."

"No, no. Please go on, I'm really interested. Don't stop now. It's like I'm just getting into it," urged Georgia.

"Well, it was nothing much really, except when I was a little older, I knew I had to get out of the place. My best friend was Lucky DiSantos. He was an older guy who knew the ropes and was really tough." Nick laughed, "The nuns were afraid of him, but I depended on him for everything. We were as tight as could be. Well, to make a long story short, we ran off and Lucky took a fall. I mean, he went to jail, and because I was a 'juvie' they sent me to Boys Town. After I got out, I was at loose ends until I met black Sam, an old guy who became my trainer. He was like a father to me."

Georgia interrupted, "Trainer? What kind of trainer? Were you an athlete?"

"Well, sort of. I became a fighter—a boxer.

But that didn't last because I got beat up bad just once, and that was enough. I decided to become an actor."

"That's quite a story," said Georgia, thinking how similar Nick's background was to Jakes—and her own. All children of misfortune; all determined to make it—make it any way they could.

She liked Nick. He was so handsome, talented, kind, and yes—vulnerable. She sensed he was afraid of women. She felt he'd had little experience with the female sex.

Her voice was soft. "Let's finish our wine; then we can get back to the script, although I think you've got it down pat. I hear the Lariat commercial is sensational. Comes out soon, right? Things happen fast in this business." She paused. "I believe, Nick, that you've got a real future; that you can become a big star. I mean it."

"Thanks, Georgia; I hope so. Look, could I maybe take you out to dinner some night? I've quit the saloon, you know, so I have more free time. I mean, then we could go to a movie or something. I haven't seen anything in such a long time."

"I'd like that, Nick. Really I would. I've got two more shooting days on 'Angels,' then I'm at liberty, as they say. Come on, let's run through that last part once more. I think you've got to show a little more fury when the lawyer plea bargains and gets the guys that shot your father back on the streets. I mean, you've really got to let the audience know you're not about to let him get away with that. Come on, let's take it from the top."

It was one o'clock in the morning when Nick finally put on his jacket and stood at the door facing Georgia. "By the way, the entire night I noticed your little dog just sat quiet as a mouse. Don't you ever take her out for a walk? She's like a little toy dog."

Georgia smiled, "Powder Puff is unusual. She's paper trained, but I do take her out on a leash sometimes. She causes quite a stir on the streets. She's so tiny. I don't walk her very often; I'm afraid someone might step on her."

Nick laughed. "Well, I'll say good night. And, Georgia, thanks for your ear and a nice evening. I can't remember when I've felt more comfortable."

"I'm glad, Nick. I enjoyed it, too. We'll do it again, soon. Good night." Georgia closed and locked the door, then undressed and headed for the shower. She was tired to the bone, but it was a nice tired—a good feeling, as if she'd accomplished something.

On Friday, Georgia worked the entire day at the studio. When she returned home, she found a notice that management planned to turn her apartment building into cooperative units. As a tenant, her own apartment could be purchased at sixty-thousand, and then would be worth about a hundred-and-fifty on the open market.

She flopped down on the sofa, the notice in her hand, and began to sob uncontrollably. Of course, it wasn't definite. A certain percentage of tenants had to agree, but it was inevitable—if not now, then sometime in the future. Apartments going cooperative had become a booming, lucrative business; in many cases badly hurting those who couldn't afford to buy. Rents were insane. Her own had risen to eight-hundred a month and was considered reasonable on today's market.

She flung down the notice, dried her eyes with a tissue, then went to pour herself a glass of wine. She had about seven-thousand in savings, three more payments due from Victor, some jewelry, furs, and that was about it. The money she made for the three day stint on the soap was minimal. What in hell was she going to do? She wondered wildly if she was too old to become a call girl. For some reason that caused her to laugh, and she felt better.

She'd really have to give this a lot of serious thought. If she had some kind of steady job, perhaps the bank would give her a loan. She could use the seven-thousand as an initial down payment, then borrow the rest. Why in God's name hadn't she learned more about business and handling money when she had the chance! Well, she'd start planning now—not be unprepared when the ax fell. Sunday she'd get the *Times* and check the want ads.

Three ads looked promising. They were for receptionists and paid two-hundred dollars a week. Monday morning she called the first one, which turned out to be an employment agency. The woman who answered informed her that the job had already been filled which struck Georgia as incredible since the paper came out on Sunday and she'd called promptly Monday morning at ten. The second was a receptionist for a massage parlor—forget about that! The third was for a real estate firm on Park Avenue. That one wanted to see her and set up an appointment for the following day.

She dressed carefully, wearing a tailored Chanel suit Victor had bought her in Paris years ago, along with shoes and bag to match. She coiled her long hair back in a knot and perched a lovely hat above her head. It looked especially fetching with the ensemble. Georgia felt a bit adventurous, as if she were preparing for a new role. Well, it would certainly be a new experience. She'd never in her entire life held a nine-to-five job; or for that matter, been interviewed for one. She donned a beige cashmere fox-trimmed coat, added a spritz of perfume, then headed for the door.

The woman who interviewed her was heavy

set and middle aged. She wore a dove grey dress, with skin to match. Her eyes were hidden behind tinted dark glasses, and she studied Georgia skeptically from across a large walnut desk.

"Miss Banner . . . Miss Georgia Banner?"

"Bonner, not Banner," Georgia corrected the woman and lit a cigarette.

"Sorry, no smoking. We don't allow smoking. Bad for the health!"

Georgia quickly mashed out the stub in a little ashtray. "I'm sorry, Miss . . . Miss . . ."

"Mrs. Quaker . . . Dolly Quaker. Sorry, I thought I introduced myself when you came into the office. I guess I was too stunned by the sight of you. I mean, we didn't advertise for a model or actress." Her voice was slightly unpleasant, as if she were irritated or needed *Preparation H*.

"Well, I simply read your ad in the *Times*, and I'm in the market for a job. It said a good appearance . . . no typing . . . good voice. I think I qualify," said Georgia calmly.

Dolly Quaker nodded. "Well, it appears you told them in Personnel that you had no previous experience, and so, all we have here on your application is your name, age, etc. I mean, we really need someone with experience. May I ask what you've done with your life up to now?"

"Well, I was an actress, a model, then I married. My husband and I were divorced before he died, and well, I need the money."

Georgia was beginning to feel foolish. "A receptionist simply answers the phones and greets people, doesn't she? I mean, every receptionist I've ever known has done that. What I mean is, you don't exactly have to have a degree from receptionist school to do the job, do you?" Georgia thought she noticed a slight smile around the woman's mouth.

"You say you were a model and an actress. What sort of actress?" Her voice contained a note of interest. "You do look familiar. I thought I recognized you the moment you walked through that door."

"I was the star of 'Mother's Children' but that was ages ago; and recently, a few scenes in 'Angels in White,' but that's it for now. I retired from the profession when I married; and really, I do need something steady."

The more Georgia talked, the more foolish she felt. Everything she said sounded insincere, as if she were lying. She hated this more than an audition. At least at an audition she knew what to expect.

"I know I've seen you before, but I never watch the soaps," exclaimed Dolly Quaker. "I know, you were on the Marty Saks Show! You're Georgia Sandborne . . . Mrs. Victor Sandborne! Why in God's name would you, of all people, need a job? Married to a millionaire and all that? Forgive me, but it just doesn't make sense. What are you really doing here, researching a part or something?"

Georgia was taken aback. "Researching a part! Why, no; I simply need a steady job." She overcame the burning desire to tell this Quaker woman she was actually with the CIA but decided to play it straight. "Frankly, my apartment is probably going co-op, and I may need a steady job in order to secure a bank loan. Look, Mrs. Quaker, what if I told you I really needed money, even this small salary?"

The woman studied Georgia for long moments before replying, "I've been in this business a long time, Miss Bonner, and I'm sorry, I'm afraid I just couldn't buy that. No; I simply couldn't buy that one, but it's been an interesting half hour—very interesting."

Georgia stood up from the uncomfortable chair, mumbled something, then stalked out of the office and headed for the elevators, tears beginning to sting her eyes. What on earth was she going to do? Trapped . . . trapped in the image of Georgia Bonner Sandborne . . . trapped . . . and without the funds to back it up!

Georgia stopped by the newsstand on Sixty-Second Street to buy the papers, then entered her apartment, flung her coat on the bed, and went to pour herself a glass of wine. She was frustrated and confused. So this was the way the real world operated. It was not unlike the theatrical profession. Above all, you had to have credentials—that was the key word: experience and creditials. Otherwise, you were out on a limb. You might just as well be invisible; and worse, if you didn't fit the mold as she had not today, you were in the same position as an actress who turned up at an audition on the wrong day for the wrong part.

Georgia sipped her wine and scanned the headlines with a sigh, then having decided to skip the usual terrifying gore of today's happenings, she turned to the society columns. Something light and gay. That's what she needed.

Suzy's column caught her eye and held it. . .

KIKI SANDBORNE, BEAUTIFUL YOUNG WIDOW OF LATE MILLIONNAIRE, VICTOR SANDBORNE, ATTENDED A GALA IN PARIS LAST NIGHT WEARING AN ORIGINAL GALANOS THAT MUST HAVE COST A FORTUNE. SHE WAS ESCORTED BY SHIPPING MAGNATE, NICO PAPPAS, THOUGH RUMORS STILL PERSIST OF HER STRANGE INVOLVEMENT WITH A SHADOWY UNDERWORLD FIGURE WHO SHALL REMAIN NAMELESS.

Georgia read and reread the article, then threw the pages to the floor. Kiki Blake Sandborne . . . everywhere she looked, there she was . . . flitting all over the globe.

Now she was in Paris! And where was she, Georgia Bonner Sandborne?

CHAPTER EIGHT

THE RITZ Hotel in Paris was Kiki Sandborne's favorite place in the entire world, and the large, magnificent suite suited her present mood. She wandered through the parlour sniffing the fresh flowers, admiring the fabric on the burnished antique gold chairs (not originals, but superb none the less), and marveling at the little crystal chandeliers that always reminded her of a tiny palace.

She made a mental note to accept the invitation of that nice maharajah who'd invited her to visit his palace in India next month, then made her way to the bathroom still in awe of the solid gold faucets—not to mention the cunning bidet. Next, she padded into the boudoir where her tiny bare feet sank inches into plush carpeting, and she peered at the canopied bed done in a batiste sheer of the palest lavender. The draperies were perfectly matched and drawn to reveal the tiny balcony overlooking the streets of Paris just yards from the Champs Elysees.

Kiki drew her peignoir more tightly around her large, firm breasts and walked onto the balcony. The sun shone brightly, and she stood there for a moment enjoying the distinct scents of the "City of Lights." No place on earth smelled like Paris. Was it *Dior, Bal de Versailles,* or just the odors wafted about from the flowers, wine, and freshly baked bread? Whatever it was, Paris possessed its own special aroma, and it was deliciously heady, making one want to love and be loved.

Kiki laughed to herself, then let the peignoir fall around her feet. She stood there in the sunlight, naked, not caring that she could most likely be observed. She was a tiny girl, only about five feet three, but with a figure that was sensational—particularly without clothes. Her legs were muscular and perfectly formed, like the legs of a doll, with dimpled knees, firm thighs, and trim ankles. Her waist was twenty inches, while her breasts were large and pear-shaped, with prominent pink nipples that invited kisses. Her face was heart-shaped with slanted green eyes and a little girl's mouth that was too small for real beauty. Her hair was brown, streaked blonde by the sun, and worn straight past her shoulders. She possessed a peculiar sexuality, at times sophisticated, almost wicked; at other times, childlike and vulnerable.

By the time Catherine Thelma Longos changed her name to Kiki Blake (she'd discovered the name in *True Confessions*), she was well versed in the art of handling men. Brought up in a pitiful two-room house on the outskirts of Detroit, she had been fondled and flattered by uncles and family friends since age five.

Men liked her breasts, her pert face, her hard little rear, even her saucy comebacks. At an early age she learned to bargain for what she wanted—there was no other way. At fifteen she was expelled from high school because one of the cheerleaders informed the Principal she was dealing a little grass. And so she was, but the little bitch who'd done the squealing was her main customer.

At sixteen she met a thirty-five year old traveling salesman, convinced him she was eighteen, and wound up in, of all places, the most famous naval town in America—Norfolk, Virginia.

The salesman moved on, and Kiki married a young sailor on shore leave. They moved into a tiny apartment near the base and within six months Kiki realized that being the wife of an enlisted man was certainly not the answer to her dreams; but she liked the redheaded sailor and when he was accidently killed on a training mission, she was genuinely sorry. However, the insurance money allowed her to dry her eyes and purchase a one way ticket to New York City.

One week after checking into the Edison Hotel on the West side of Manhattan, Kiki met a worn blonde named Steffi in an all night beauty salon. The woman dealt in introductions—introductions for a fee.

When Steffi suggested she supplement her money from the government insurance with an "entertainment service," Kiki was skeptical. "Look," said Steffi drinking her favorite Brandy Alexander, "you're a good looking kid. You got something special. Wanna give it away the rest of your life? Wanna play a sucker's game?"

Kiki had her eye on a second-hand fox coat down the street at a thrift shop and so Steffi's suggestion came at an opportune moment. Things always seemed to happen that way in her life. "Okay, tell me what to do. How do I handle it?"

That very evening, Kiki met a sixty-year-old mogul from the garment center—with a wife and four kids on Long Island—who simply wanted a beautiful dinner companion in order to cement a business deal. Simple.

Her next assignment was a Brazilian millionaire who greeted her at the door of his Sherry Netherland suite gowned in feathers and maribou, his small feet encased in three-inch high-heeled slippers.

Later that same day the garment center mogul paid her two hundred dollars to simply seduce an out of town buyer who loved pretty young women and had a difficult time doing anything about it. And so it went.

Kiki rather enjoyed her work, and pleasing men became a career—of sorts. She was very, very good at her job but soon became weary of handing so much cash over to Steffi. Her own needs had to be met; her fast growing voracious appetite for money, sex, excitement and intrigue—it was like a drug. It gave her focus and spurred her on. She adored the unexpected, wondering what tomorrow would bring.

By the age of twenty-three, she was working in a topless bar. She was the girl who made the most money, met the most important clients, and took the most chances. Temporarily, she changed her name to Valentine, and moved into a small flat near the club. She furnished the place like a dream, imagining herself as a princess in the Arabian nights. She even wore glamorous costumes to greet her guests.

But then, the unexpected happened . . . Kiki Blake fell in love!

It was a disaster. Her love life became a battlefield. The hard, brutal man she adored just used her for sex. He gave her money, jewelry . . . but never, never enough of himself. She writhed in frustration, loving and hating him simultaneously. When he was near, she was alive and aflame, as if all her senses were exposed. The man became her Achilles heel. She spent every waking hour plotting how she could possess him, but she never could, he was too like her, he knew her tricks.

And of course, Kiki was lazy; lazy in the sense that a structured life was virtually impossible for her. However, when in hot pursuit of something—or someone—she truly desired, she became a tigress. Perhaps her strongest point was her excellence as a bed partner and her uncanny ability to put aside momentary failures and forge ahead . . . upward and onward. And so, when she first met Victor Sandborne, she put aside her love obsession and concentrated on Victor.

After one year with Kiki, Victor was hooked, ready to give up his wife, Georgia, and everything else. Of course, Kiki never hesitated to apply a little needed pressure. Men! They were such children about their masculinity and of course, she prayed on that weakness. At times, she'd felt a tinge of guilt about his wife, Georgia, until she reminded herself that she, Kiki, was the most important person alive, and if you didn't feel that way about yourself, certainly no one else would.

Her marriage to Victor Sandborne could not have endured much longer. Dancing to his tune did not suit her, and so his untimely death shortly after their marriage was a stroke of luck. Well, maybe not entirely luck. She had encouraged his deepening dependence on alcohol and drugs and went to great lengths not only to keep him away from his former wife, whom he still professed to love, but to manufacture bizarre stories about the girl.

Kiki rarely gave her dead husband a thought, except when legal or money problems regarding his estate arose, and she felt not the slightest twinge of conscience where he was concerned. She had snared him by her cleverness and fascinating, almost dual, personality. But mainly it had been the sensual; his fear of impotence and his total dependence on her bizarre sexuality. If it is possible for a man to be loved to death, then Kiki Blake Sandborne was indeed a murderess!

Now she stood above on the balcony. Paris intoxicated her but finally she whirled around and walked back into the boudoir, leaving the negligee lying in a fluffy pile behind her. She drew the drapes and lay across the bed, allowing her active imagination to take over. She wondered if some man had been feasting his eyes on her nakedness. If so, was he young or old, rich or poor? Sometimes Kiki was wildly excited by really ugly men. She adored their total dedication to her body—and their gratitude.

Suddenly the phone rang. She picked up the gold instrument and purred into the receiver, "Come up, darling. It's Suite 2314."

Kiki crawled out of bed, sprayed herself lavishly with some sensuous fragrance she'd picked up in Shanghai, then slipped into a negligee that left little to the imagination. It was from the Kayto collection, made from sheer black chiffon and revealed her body to perfection. She slipped her tiny feet into high heeled Maude Frizon satin pumps and quickly ran a comb through her hair. She was tanned from the sun in San Tropez and Cannes. She smiled to herself and proceeded to answer the tinkling bell, a little shiver of anticipation running up her spine.

She opened the door silently and stood back as a tall man strode into the room, threw his coat over the satin brocaded sofa, then before she had a chance to speak, a hand reached out and struck her across the face. It was a hard blow, and she staggered back, almost falling.

"My God! What's wrong with you? Have you gone nuts or what?"

The man grabbed her by one slender arm. "I'm not nuts, my dear. It's you who are crazy. You little whore! Haven't you changed at all? I read all about you with that Greek bastard; what's his name? What's the matter, not enough money in the till, or haven't you fucked any Greeks lately? I oughta kill you, but it's not worth the trouble. You have a short memory, kid. But you born sluts always do, and that's what you are . . . a born slut!''

Kiki remained glued to the spot, then smiled a peculiar, evil, little girl's smile. With one swift movement, she slipped out of the negligee and stood naked, except for the high heeled shoes. And then she wound around the man, pressing her nakedness against the roughness of his suit, until she felt his erection through his trousers . . . felt it pressing against her bare skin . . . Then she stepped back and stood with her legs spread apart, her hands on her hips, a defiant smile on her lips. Her breasts jutted out invitingly, and her voice was a low purr. "Are you gonna hit me again, baby? Hit your little whore again? Maybe beat her up? Or shall I tell you how I've been lying here waiting for you, thinking about how it would be when you took me in your arms, made love to me. I didn't expect to be hit first." She moved nearer. "Come on, baby, hold me . . . hold me."

Without a word the tall man picked her up and carried her into the bedroom where he flung her none too gently on the bed. She lay there laughing up at him while he reached down with long slender fingers and began to fondle her breasts; pressing them, kneading them, still not speaking, but watching the expression in her eyes. He loved to watch her face when she was becoming aroused. And then he bent his head and took the nipple of one breast in his mouth; he sucked it gently at first, then harder and harder until she let out a little squeal. "Baby, careful, you're hurting me . . . hurting me . . . easy . . ."

"That's what I want to do, sweetheart. It hurts good, doesn't it?"

She didn't reply, and he abruptly undressed, dropping his clothes where he stood. When he was naked, the tall man lay down on the bed, his hands behind his head.

Immediately, with one swift movement, Kiki was on her tummy between his legs. She slipped his cock into her mouth and began a slow, steady rhythm, but only for a few moments. She knew from past experience just how long to continue. With one graceful motion she straddled him, slipping his penis inside. She sat back astride him like a horse, and using her muscular legs for balance, rode him up and down . . . up and down . . . slowly . . . slowly . . . then faster and faster until he gripped her shoulders and pulled her across his chest.

Kiki Blake had won again.

Later that day, after a bottle of Dom Perignon, the man bathed, dressed, and then stood staring at her. "I'm flying back to New York tomorrow. I've got business, and before I forget to tell you, I didn't like that little squib about the gangster boyfriend—didn't like it at all. Watch yourself, Kiki. You have a

little bit of respectability, thanks to Sandborne; try to hang on to it. I know it's hard
for a broad like you, but give it a try."

And then he was gone.

CHAPTER NINE

IN NEW YORK, Lucky sat in a large chair facing Louis Gerfinski, legendary leader of one of New York's top crime families and one of the few underworld figures without a drop of Italian blood in his veins. He was Polish and had immigrated to this country decades ago.

The man was six feet four inches tall with a head of pure white hair that was so thick it produced a leonine quality. One almost expected him to roar. His eyes were the purest blue, set in a large face so white in color that it became almost indistinguishable from his hair. The mouth was full and curved, while the eyebrows were white and thick, forming perfect arcs over the fierce blue eyes. His clothes were impeccable, and Lucky had derived his sense of style from this man who had been his idol for many years.

Mr. G. held a snifter of brandy to the light. "Good Napoleon stock. Good stuff, Lucky, good stuff. By the way, how's the world treating you, my boy . . . how's the world treating you?''

Lucky lit a cigarette. Louis knew perfectly well he was having problems. The fuckin' Colombians were giving him hell in Miami; and bootleg cigarettes from the Carolinas were becoming a pain in the ass, what with the hijacking and all. Everyone wanted to get in the act—including a few state troopers. He'd never had to pay off so many people in his life. It seemed the entire world was on the take.

He answered casually, sipping his brandy. "The world is treating me alright; that is, considering everything that's going on in Miami. I mean, those damn Colombians are like a bunch of nuts. You can't scare 'em, that's for sure; you have to work with 'em. I mean, give out more and more dough to get the stuff in. But the boys there are doin' their bit. And, we keep paying off more of the guys in blue. Still, there's always a few gung-ho undercover boys—hero stuff—you know, the kind that think they're gonna clean up the dope traffic all by themselves. Then things get a little messy, but Mario is holding the fort. He keeps things pretty much in line. I'm glad we're easing out of narcotics. Frankly, it's becoming a pain in the ass; too many amateurs.''

The white haired man smiled and sipped his brandy. "Maybe you're right. I'm too old for all that action. The massage parlours are doing well and don't cause near the trouble, providing the ladies are kept in line. By the way, Lucky, I was watching my TV, like I do each night, when who should come on a commercial but your old friend, Nick Culletti. I recognized him by the picture you showed me. I always remembered how you two started out together at the home. He's damn good, by the way. Listen, I want you should bring him to the party, you hear me? I want to meet him. You tell him he can bring a girl, but no one else, understand? He's your boyhood friend from the old days," he paused. "I'm sentimental about those things. Okay, my boy, now go. It's time for my massage."

"Fine, sir, I'll tell ol' Nick, and he'll be glad to come, I'm sure. See you soon. Thanks."

Lucky shook hands with his benefactor, then walked through the door into a large den where he was escorted out by a small compact Oriental. The little man was a black belt and could easily kill with his bare hands.

At the same moment, a sulty girl, the color of creamed coffee, clad in a white satin G-string, stood up from a sofa where she'd been reclining. She walked gracefully across the Persian rug, her bare breasts jiggling seductively as she moved. She stood for a moment, her legs apart, hands on her hips.

The white haired man glanced toward the door and motioned to the young woman.

"Come in, Francie, come in, my girl. Get yourself a brandy and put on a robe. No massage today. I want to talk."

Francie Morgan walked into the room, her head held proudly like an African princess. She filled a crystal brandy snifter, then curled at the man's feet like a sleek panther.

"I don't need a robe. I'm always more comfortable naked." She paused. "Of course, if it distracts you—"

Louis smiled. "On the contrary, my dear. It's a pleasure to feast my eyes on such beauty. Anyway, I might change my mind. But at the moment I need someone I can trust to check out a few things at one of the clubs. A woman's touch, that's what I need, a woman's touch and a woman's intuition."

He lit a cigarette and inhaled deeply.

"The Gold Cat is the establishment I have in mind. Lucky fired the last manager and hired a new one, someone by the name of Sid Levine. It appears this Levine fellow is suffering from an overdose of ambition and personal zeal where his job is concerned. Since the credit card scam, we can't afford any more trouble, especially with the help."

Louis opened a folder on the desk beside him, removed some papers, then proceeded to scan them.

"Fellows like Levine are dangerous because they are not only well educated—a degree in accounting from Columbia it says here—but basically he has nothing to lose.

He's a loser already—reformed lush, lost his family, lost a fifty thousand dollar a year job with Park Bank, and did a little time for forgery. So, you see, what we have is a smart crook. A guy who will, on the one hand, run a tight ship, be a good manager; but then the ambition starts to creep in. I know the type. I hear he's trying to change policy at The Gold Cat. That's the rumor, and while I'm certain it may be just that, I want it checked out. The bottle hustle, topless dancers, porno video tapes, a little feel . . . that is as far as the hustle goes. I'm not, after all, running a whorehouse. My places are to titillate, not satisfy."

He paused and flicked ashes in a crystal tray. "That is, of course, except for unusual circumstances—very special clients . . . very special girls. What is bothering me, Francie, is that when women get together and become dissatisfied, it then becomes a dangerous, combustible situation. I don't like that. I want harmony—peace and harmony. Remember a few years back we had that Kiki Blake girl working at the Silver Fin? I forget the name she used?"

"Valentine. She was called Valentine," supplied Francie. "Everyone called her Val. Most clever hooker I ever knew in my life. Most dedicated, I should say." She laughed a low tinkling laugh. "What about her? She fell into a pile of butter, married that millionaire, then he conveniently died."

"That's the one, Francie. Well, I'd like to think all my girls have a chance at that kind of big game. I'm sentimental about women, ever since—" He turned and faced Francie squarely. "Enough of that. You get the picture? What I want is for you to take a run over, unofficially, of course. You know the girls. They trust you. Test the waters."

The dark girl lit a cigarette from a pack tucked in the waist of her bikini and smiled. "I understand, Louis. Merry Moss is a friend of mine. She'll give me the straight scoop. You're right. If the girls are unhappy, that can be bad news. Some of them at The Gold Cat are new, a few from Europe, but the three that have been with us the longest, Merry, Bea, and Tinker Bell, are invaluable and won't put up with being pushed around —even if the guy is a college grad." She got up from the floor, kissed the older man on the forehead. "I'll take care of it; you can depend on me."

Upstairs, Francie changed into slacks, boots, and a three-quarter fox jacket; then hailed a cab in front of the building and settled back for the long ride from Brooklyn Heights into Manhattan.

It was dusk when she arrived at the small club. An enormous painting of a gold cat holding three semi-nude girls in its giant paws was exhibited at the front entrance. She sailed inside the door, ignoring the burly bouncer who at first did not recognize her.

"Sorry, Francie. Didn't see you so good in this light. How's tricks?"

"Fine, Bucky, fine. Just dropped by to have a drink with Merry. She in yet?"

The heavy-set man glanced at his watch on one hairy wrist and replied, "She's due any minute. Go have a drink. I'll tell Levine you're here."

"No, Bucky, don't! This isn't official. I'm here for purely social reasons," she lied. "What I mean is, Merry and I have some boy friend troubles to iron out. Dig?"

The large man scratched his head and smiled slyly. "Sure, sure, Francie. I gotcha."

The dark girl moved smoothly to a booth in the back and ordered a drink. She lit a cigarette and glanced around the dimly lit room. The entire place appeared to be decorated in red flocked velvet. It was everywhere—walls, carpeting, upholstery on heavy sofas in the lounge area, as well as the booth in which she sat. She leaned back and studied the bar. There were two video tapes going simultaneously, one at either end of the bar, and each exhibiting a rather tired pornographic movie without benefit of sound. That was a new addition, thought Francie, and she wrinkled her nose. The place smelled of stale perfume, alcohol, with a slight hint of disinfectant thrown in. She reached for another cigarette in her handbag and felt the cool handle of her .32 automatic revolver. She even had a permit for the gun, thanks to an ex-lover who had made Chief Inspector last year.

At that moment, two girls Francie didn't recognize undulated by and greeted a customer as he entered the dim, red-lighted room. Both women wore bikinis covering their pubic areas with straps running up between their derrieres and the smallest of leather brassieres covering their breasts. In the back of the room, a tall redhead appeared from behind a beaded curtain and presented herself on a tiny elevated stage. A pink spot picked her up and canned disco music began an insinuating beat. The girl wore a sequined bikini bottom and no top. Her large breasts were lovely, and the few customers taken in hand by the girls waiting at the door now sat watching the redhead contort her body and jiggle her breasts in time to the music. There was an all-prevading sensuality about the entire place. Tawdry, but appealing. In other words, it would not have been nearly so exotic in someone's master bedroom.

The customers seemed to be a mixture of men of various ages, some in business suits as if they'd just arrived from the stock exchange, while others lounged at the bar in dungarees and windbreakers. All, apparently, were captivated by the intangible sleaziness of their surroundings.

Francie sipped her wine in the darkness, observing everything going on around her. So far she hadn't spotted Levine. She wanted to keep it that way. She knew everyone viewed her with suspicion—and some fear—because of her close association with Louis Gerfinski, or Mr. G, as he was better known. And she liked the power. It made her feel important. Actually, she liked to think of herself as a female enforcer, at least for Louis' part of the organization. The Sicilians had their share, of course, but for the past few years Mr. G. had been in control. A Polack! Francie smiled to herself. It was just too bad Poland didn't have a few thousand Mr. G's. Moscow would be in deep trouble!

Suddenly Merry Moss appeared from out of the shadows and slipped into the booth opposite Francie.

"Hi, baby. Bucky said you were here waiting for me. Good to see you. What's up?"

Francie patted the girl's hand. "Nothing much, sweet chips. Just wanted to see how the world's treating you. You know, check in. It's been a while." She paused and studied her friend closely. "Come on, Merry, I wouldn't bullshit you. I want some info. I mean, I wanna know what's shakin' here with Levine. How's he treating the girls? Any problems? You can level with me."

Merry Moss was not a beautiful girl, but she had a certain look. Her brown hair was a mass of curls surrounding a round face with a perfect cupid's bow mouth, totally devoid of lipstick—not even gloss—just a perfect little mouth for kissing. Her eyes were a huckleberry blue with black-fringed lashes, and she sometimes wore hornrimmed glasses. She felt they gave her class. Her body was spectacular, and she was one of the girls dressed as a golden cat, tail and all. Her voice was low and appealing.

"Problems? What do you mean, Francie? There are always problems in this business, but that's to be expected. If you're referring to Levine, well he's a bit pushy. I mean he's got some ideas in his head and now the credit card scam is down the drain, the girls should add a little extra sugar to the situation, if you get the drift."

Francie took out a cigarette. "Sorry, you're losing me. What do you mean?"

"Well, he feels that for the $175 bottle, the guys should get their money's worth. You know how the hustle works—they buy the bottle, we take 'em to the back with nothing more than a quick feel, and then it's promises, promises . . . you know. 'I'll meet you later, Steve.' That shit. You'd be surprised how many guys fall for it, but the trouble is there are no repeats. Levine feels we don't have enough satisfied customers. Face it. This ain't no cat house. Shit! If I wanted to go pro, I could get my referrals from Lucy Kellogg over on Eighty-Ninth Street and make a fortune. I'm no fuckin' hooker."

"I get the picture," snapped Francie. "All

181

this come-on isn't enough. He wants you girls to put out. Is this a big push from Levine or merely a kind suggestion? How do the girls feel about it? Especially Bea and Tinker Bell?"

"Lousy," answered Merry. "Really lousy. They don't mind the hustle, but to go the whole route just for the lousy commission—it's a no-no."

"Yeah, I can dig, but keep cool. It isn't going to jell, that I can tell you. Between you and me, Levine's days are numbered if he doesn't stop. We'll let it go awhile, let him hang himself. If things get too bad, give me a call. You've got the private number. Don't worry, you know Mr. G. where the girls are concerned. Nobody leans on his ladies. That's why he's got the cream."

Merry Moss smiled and squeezed Francie's hand. "You know, I didn't want to squeal, but now that you asked . . . now that you're here . . . I'm glad. I don't like Levine. None of the girls do. He thinks he's a college professor or something. Personally, I think he hates sex; hates women. I think working here is some kind of punishment for him."

"Don't go philosophical on me, Merry. I've got to split now, we'll be in touch." Francie opened her Gucci wallet and laid a ten spot on the table. "Never let it be said I don't pay my way." She bent and kissed Merry on the forehead. "So long, sugar. See you soon." With that she was out the door and walking up Forty-Ninth Street searching for a cab. It was colder than a witch's tit!

Merry Moss slipped out of the booth and went to greet a customer she recognized but hadn't seen in a long time. He was from Texas, and she loved his drawl. "Hi, Tex. Long time no see. Want the bar or a booth?"

The man smiled and took her arm. "What I want right now is to see you, young lady. I wanna have a drink and shoot the breeze for awhile. After that, we'll see how it goes. One thing for sure, sugar, no more $175 bottles like last time . . . not this trip. Once is enough. Hell, I could of had the greatest call girl in New York for that kind of money, but I liked you, so it was worth it. Come on, let's have a drink and you tell me all about what's been happening in the Big Apple while I've been drilling in Riodosa."

Merry smiled and led the man to a booth in the back where they could be private. She liked the man from Texas. He made her feel like a lady.

In his office, Sid Levine smoked one cigarette after the other and stared at the ceiling. Lately he'd wanted to drink but had controlled the urge. He knew that would be the beginning of the end. Booze had cost him everything . . . no more wife . . . no more fifty grand a year job. Shit! He made almost as much here, but no prestige, that was the trouble, no real position. A massage parlor—topless bar—whatever you called it, it came out the same. He wanted to show the old man he had a talent for organization, new ideas. These dames should be putting out, not with everyone maybe, but the cream—like the vice boys. The dry fuck was leaving him with a lot of dissatisfied customers. The girls were lazy. They weren't doing their job. They needed discipline, just the way his wife needed it and never got it—at least not from him. She never gave him a chance. Anyway, he'd decided when he took this job that if you were going to play in mud, you'd better start trying to fight your way to the top of the heap and stay there.

It was a long, dirty slide to the bottom!

Francie returned to the large house in Brooklyn Heights located on a secluded, quiet street with trees lining the sidewalks. Almost like any middle-class neighborhood in a small town. The difference being, Louis Gerfinski owned the entire block and was, in fact, landlord to over two-hundred tenants.

He remained quiet, seldom seen in the daylight hours, traveling a great deal by night accompanied by Lucky or JuJu or sometimes his personal aide, Braskets. He appeared as a shadowy figure emerging from a large dark limousine like a giant white phantom. He was not only feared but respected. His position in the New York crime family was unique, and some said had originated with an early involvement with Lucky Luciano and Meyer Lansky. Also with a Sicilian named Nunzio Ruffito. Rumor had it that Louis and Ruffito had formed a partnership which had only dissolved with the Italian's death.

The cab stopped, and Francie paid the fare. She entered the house and went directly upstairs to her own quarters in a hurry to shower and change. Something about The Gold Cat made her feel dirty.

She bathed, then powdered her body with a delicious fragrance, and slipped into a gold lame caftan. Next she picked up a little intercom phone which was connected to all the rooms and rang Louis. The Oriental answered. She disliked speaking to Sing Jo. He was always so polite; sometimes it enraged her. His voice never rose an octave, even when he was excited or upset. She wondered when, if ever, the man showed emotion, Well, thought Francie, the boss was out. That left her free.

She went to the little bar across the room and poured herself a drink of scotch, then sat in a large lounge chair and sipped it slowly, allowing herself to unwind. She switched on the hi-fi nearby and closed her eyes. Everything was provided for her comfort in this little private suite. She possessed beautiful clothes, furs, jewels and a bank account. Louis was generous. He relied on her judgment, depended on her for sex and other creature comforts, felt comfortable with her, but still she knew he did not love her. She knew he had loved only one woman in his lifetime. There was a small room down the hall, a room kept locked at all times. But once Francie had slipped inside, and there she'd seen the shrine. Pictures, mementos, even small pieces of jewelry in little velvet boxes . . . all for a woman who was nothing more than a memory. If only she would appear. Was she dead? In an asylum? Had she taken another identity? Had she, in fact, been Louis' wife? There'd been talk . . . a wife and a child . . . kidnapped . . . murdered. Francie had never dared ask. Only Louis Gerfinski knew the true story behind the secret door, and he was keeping it to himself. Meanwhile, Francie was willing to accept the crumbs . . . anything . . . anything to be near the man she loved.

CHAPTER TEN

THE AIR had become clear and crisp with sunlight replacing long, dismal days of rain and erratic drops in the temperature. Spring chose to reveal herself in little ways. Florists along the avenue beckoned with fresh flowers and shiny green plants, and even the dogs, walked by their doting masters, appeared to have a more positive gait as if they, too, knew the worst was over.

The Lariat Jeans commercial, as well as the Television Movie of the Week, had been an unprecedented success, providing Nick Culletti with enough security for an apartment in the East Eighties. There was even an extra bedroom for Sam. The elderly black man was tortured with arthritis, and Nick still felt a certain responsibility for his friend and former trainer.

Georgia Bonner remained an enigma, a fact that was a constant source of frustration to

187

Nick. They liked one another; that was a certainty. He'd never felt so comfortable with a woman in his life, and he knew she felt the same way. Once he'd attempted to kiss her, but she'd behaved strangely—pulled away, almost crying. He hadn't understood, but he knew it had nothing to do with him personally. Something else was disturbing her. He was sensitive to Georgia and wondered at the peculiar closeness he'd felt from that first day he'd seen her in *The Alamo Saloon*. Nick believed in reincarnation and sometimes consulted a psychic named Roland Pitway who had informed him that Georgia, in a previous life, had been his sister.

He was beginning to feel a certain tension when they were together. Was it possible a sophisticated woman such as Georgia could feel the slight age difference to be a deterrent? Nick didn't think so. It must be something else, and he was determined to discover her secret.

As if an invisible force had taken over, he went to the phone and ordered a dozen roses to be sent to Georgia's apartment with a card enclosed . . . *How about dinner on Sunday? If you're free, give a call*, signed Nick.

Later that same day she telephoned. "Nick, the flowers are lovely. How kind you are! What made you do it? I mean, I haven't received flowers in such a while. I'd forgotten how good it makes you feel. As to Sunday, I'd love it. Pick me up around six, and we'll have a drink here first."

Georgia replaced the receiver and sank back on the sofa to align her thoughts. She knew she was falling in love with Nick Culletti but feared the consequences of a relationship with a younger man, especially an actor on his way to the top of the celebrity heap. Maybe she'd just be in the way. Maybe she was a mother image, for God's sake!

And, of course, there was Jake Pierce. Apparently the Indian had disappeared from her life as mysteriously as he had entered it, and for that she was grateful; but one could never be certain about a man like Jake. He was dangerous, possibly schizoid. Everything about him was excessive, especially his sexual prowess. Georgia feared him most of all because of the hypnotic spell he appeared to cast over her. When Jake was in the room, she seemed to have no will of her own, and this was terrifying. She'd never felt that kind of emotion before. On the one hand she despised the feeling, while on the other, it exerted a peculiar fascination. That ambivalence was the disturbing element.

Georgia hadn't worked since the "Angels in White" stint, and had finally dismissed the idea of securing a "straight job." Management had secured the right tenant percentage to turn the apartment building cooperative, and she had only a few months to come up with the cash or get out. But somehow things would work out—they always had in the past. Meanwhile, she looked forward to seeing Nick on Sunday night . . .

Georgia dressed carefully. For some reason she was nervous. Her hands trembled as she removed the hot rollers from her hair and placed them back neatly in their container. She chose a scarlet voile dress with a full skirt, low peasant neckline, and billowing sleeves. It was feminine and sweet but at the same time sexy. She chose a lipstick that matched perfectly and after brushing her hair until it shone, sprayed on Mitsuko and appraised herself in the pier glass. Great! She looked really lovely and felt twenty. Georgia smiled to herself and decided, as the buzzer rang from downstairs announcing Nick, to simply enjoy this new sensation.

Nick, wearing a blue blazer, white cotton shirt, and beige trousers entered the room. Georgia noticed he'd invested in a pair of Gucci loafers and appeared more at ease than he had on their last encounter. Well, why not? He was fast becoming a hot property. His confidence should be at its peak. There'd been a line in Earl's column today.

They sat and chatted for an hour, then Nick suggested a little place in the vicinity that specialized in seafood and good wines.

The couple walked hand in hand down Sixty-Eighth Street and First Avenue. People gazed at them with admiration, and Georgia noted with a certain pride that women looked at her with envy. Nick was so virile and handsome. She felt secure and protected as she held his arm, and they both laughed at the little dogs on leashes who stopped to sniff and bark at one another much to the annoyance of their owners. Powder Puff was such an angel. Sometimes Georgia forgot she was a dog. She possessed real human qualities. A responsibility, no matter how small, made a difference in Georgia's life and was important to her peace of mind. Mainly, of course, because there were no children to fill the void; no babies for her to love and care for, and, of course, there never would be. She glanced at Nick and thought what a marvelous father he would make. That was another reason she shouldn't become seriously involved with the young actor. After all, he deserved a woman who could give him children.

They reached the little cafe and proceeded to the intimate garden in the rear. It was a charming outdoor area dominated by a magnificent Japanese rock garden with stony brooks surrounded by a variety of plants and flowers. Candlelight illuminated each table, and Nick and Georgia were seated by a young man who apparently owned the place. Nick ordered a bottle of wine, smiled across the table, then took her hand.

"I know it hasn't been all that long, Georgia, but somehow I feel we've known each other for years. It's strange. I mean, I get the most peculiar feeling when I'm with you—*deja vu*, I guess." He grinned. "Is that the way you pronounce it? Anyway, it's a good feeling. I'm leaving for the Coast soon, and I'm going to miss you. Movie stars, Hollywood—somehow I dread it."

"California! I'll miss you, too. I mean, as long as you're in New York, even if we don't see each other, at least we talk on the phone. But I'm happy things are breaking for you, Nick. I knew they would. I just knew you were going to make it big, and you're already on your way. Every time I turn on the TV, there you are, doing the tango in Lariat Jeans with that gorgeous redhead. And the little dialogue is fun too. That's the first one with lines that I recall." She paused. "You're damn good. Everyone's been saying how sexy you look." Georgia smiled and suddenly realized Nick was looking at her in a peculiar way. "Nick, what is it?"

He squeezed her hand. "Georgia, the important thing is do *you* think I'm sexy?" Suddenly he felt foolish. "Sorry. That was a stupid thing to say."

Georgia interrupted. "Nick, of course I think you're sexy. Do you think I'm blind? It's just that we've been like really good friends." She sipped her glass of wine, avoiding his eyes. "Nick, I'm older than you. I'm at an odd point in my life—you know, like a crossroad. Sometimes I feel like I've been struggling forever. Sometimes I feel like I'm in an arena." She laughed. "A love arena."

"Is there someone else, Georgia? I mean, are you hooked on some guy? It's okay. You can tell me. I'll understand, really. I never want to lose your friendship, and if that's all it can ever be—"

Georgia looked deeply into Nick's brown eyes. "No, no . . . you have it all wrong. It's just that I've been hurt. My ex-husband . . . marrying again before he died, just when I thought we might get back together . . . I'm vulnerable, Nick. I just want to be careful, play it safe."

She didn't want to tell him about Jake Pierce unless it became necessary. Anyway, Jake was like a fantasy, not quite real. She wanted Nick. She knew it, and he knew it. Anything else was just an excuse. "Give me a little more time, Nick. Just a little more time."

Later in the lobby of Georgia's building they stood chatting, a bit uncertain, slightly awkward. It was two in the morning.

"Nick, come up for a nightcap?"

He shook his head. "No, Georgia. It's been a lovely evening, but I've got to get home. Lots of packing to do tomorrow." He kissed her on the cheek. "I'll call you from the Coast. Incidentally, sometime this summer there's a party for Lucky's boss. You remember my telling you about Lucky. Well, there's going to be a big bash for Louis Gerfinski, and I'd like you to go with me. Okay?" Georgia nodded, and Nick took her hands. "So long, Georgia-peach. See you soon." With that he turned and walked out of the lobby and into the darkness.

Georgia stood there for a moment staring after him, then entered the elevator and immediately noticed the strong odor of Patchouli. Hell. she was becoming paranoid. Other people wore that scent. People other than Jake Pierce.

She felt her stomach tighten as the elevator opened on the tenth floor, and she fumbled for her keys as usual. One of the hallway lights had gone out. Management was redecorating for the co op deal, and workmen had been in and out all weak. It was difficult to see the lock, and she pressed the tiny flashlight attached to her key ring. God, it was dark—darker than usual. She inserted the first key, then the second. Sounds of music from her neighbor's apartment drifted through the hall. He was an opera buff. *Carmen* at this hour!

It was then she felt the arms around her waist from behind. She opened her mouth to scream, but a hand covered her lips. Her first impulse was to bite, but the grip was too strong and she felt herself sway in terror. Then, abruptly, the arms swept her around, and she stood facing Jake Pierce. The smell of Pachouli and alcohol were stronger now.

"Jake! Jake, my God! Have you gone mad?

You scared the hell out of me!" She felt herself near collapse as his arms held her fast.

"Sorry, sweetheart. I was just waiting for you to say goodnight to your boy friend. Took you awhile."

"What the hell are you talking about?" Georgia was furious but also relieved that Jake wasn't a mugger or killer lurking there in the shadows waiting for his victim. It happened every day.

He took the keys from her hands, which were shaking badly. 'Here, let me open the door." She nodded, and the two went inside. Georgia flipped on the lights, sank down on the sofa, and began to sob uncontrollably.

Jake sat beside her. "Sorry, kid, didn't think I'd scare you that bad. Wanted to surprise you, that's all. I've been in Canada at Caughnawaga. Just got back." He stood up. "Dry your eyes. I'll get you a drink."

"No, no," muttered Georgia between sobs. "No booze. There's wine in the fridge . . . wine and some strawberries. Bring me a glass of that, please." She reached inside her bag for a hanky and proceeded to dry her eyes.

Jake returned to the sofa and handed her the glass of wine. "This will make you feel better. Sorry, I'm really sorry; but you looked so nervous there, fidgeting with the locks. I just couldn't resist teasing you a little." He shot her an evil grin.

Georgia drank the wine in silence, wanting

to hurl it in Jake's face. What the hell was wrong with this man? Was he insane or just plain mean? A little of both, she suspected.

"Look, Jake. If you ever pull a trick like that again, I don't know what I'll do. I told you last time to call me on the phone. You know what telephones are, don't you? They're all over the place."

Suddenly it occurred to her she was talking to the wall. Jake Pierce would do just what suited him and nothing else. Logic appeared to elude him entirely. He acted strictly on impulse.

"I'm sorry, Georgia. Really. I came because I wanted to see you. I hate phones. I missed you." He turned and went to the kitchen as if he owned the place, poured himself a drink of scotch, and returned to sit beside her. "I want you to go to a wedding with me tomorrow afternoon. An Indian friend of mine is getting married in Brooklyn. I want you to come."

Georgia stared at Jake in stunned silence. Incredulous! Here he came popping back into her life, scaring her half to death, then calmly inviting her to a wedding in Brooklyn. Well, she'd be damned if she'd go.

"I'm sorry; I can't. I'm busy tomorrow."

Jake simply smiled and undressed her with his eyes. "You look mighty pretty, sweetheart . . . all dressed up for the guinea actor."

How had he known about Nick, wondered

Georgia frantically. He must have followed them. She shivered.

Jake put down his glass and took Georgia in his arms, holding her tightly, looking deeply into her eyes, a peculiar smile playing around his lips. "I'll see you tomorrow at four. I'll be here to pick you up. This is a friend of mine getting married, and I want you with me. Understand?"

He stood up, and Georgia remained on the sofa still unnerved. Powder Puff, who'd been asleep in her little basket, ambled across the carpet like a little ball of fur. Georgia reached down and picked up the dog, holding her close.

Jake watched her, then walked towards the door. "I've got an appointment, angel, and it's late. Just wanted to let you know ol' Jake's back in town. See you tomorrow at four."

With that he walked out the door closing it quietly behind him.

Georgia wondered what one wore to an Indian wedding? Same as any other wedding, she supposed. She chose a beige linen dress with a matching coat, straw picture hat, matching shoes and bag, with turquoise jewelry as an added color accent.

She sprayed her hair into place, donned the hat and light-weight coat, then lit a cigaratte and sat back waiting for the buzzer to ring. How foolish, thought Georgia. Jake would never bother with such amenities. He'd slip by the doorman—as usual—and appear like some kind of apparition.

At four sharp there was a knock. She went to answer and there stood Jake dressed in western pants, short boots and a linen jacket that matched his trousers. His long black hair was combed straight back and Georgia noted the gold earring he usually wore in his ear was missing. He looked neater than usual, but still exuded that peculiar savage essence that was difficult to describe.

"You look gorgeous, baby. Come on, I've got a cab."

Georgia didn't reply but followed docilely out the door. She noticed Jake carried a package wrapped like a gift. God! she wondered wildly, was there going to be a party or reception afterwards? Brooklyn! The last time she'd been to Brooklyn was five years ago when she'd gone to Loman's to buy some clothes.

Jake opened the cab door, assisted her inside, and they were soon speeding across the bridge into never-never land. The sun was setting in a giant red ball over the river, and Georgia sat back and decided to keep quiet and enjoy the view. She hated to admit even to herself that she'd actually been coerced into coming. Coerced, because in her heart of hearts she was not only fascinated like a moth with a flame, but also deathly afraid of Jake. She sensed that he was quite capable of doing almost anything to get his way. And that anything didn't exclude killing her.

Jake said very little as the cab made twists and turns, weaving in and out of streets that appeared as remote from Manhattan as another country. Groups of men stood huddled on street corners as if plotting some mischief, and coarse looking hookers marched brazenly along the streets side by side with fat, middle-aged women carrying enormous shopping bags filled with groceries. Dogs appeared to roam free and unleashed, and Georgia noticed a skinny yellow cat scrambling about in a nearby garbage can.

At long last the taxi stopped in front of a small church located in a section of Red Hook Georgia never knew existed. She learned later that this section formed the pocket of Indians who had settled in its apartments and hotels in almost tribal fashion; however, now, with construction and iron work almost nonexistent, their very livelihoods were in jeopardy.

Jake paid the driver and assisted her out of the cab, still in his mood of silence. They walked toward the church, and Georgia had never felt so out of place in her entire life, as if she were a character in the wrong play or one of those mixed up dreams where you're either nude or wearing insane clothing while everyone else appears to be quite normal.

Even the smells were different. The unmistakable odor of marijuana filled the air. A bad substitute for orange blossoms, thought Georgia wryly.

Jake waved to a couple standing on the lawn and guided her inside the church. It was almost empty except for a scattered few occupying the pews. He took her hand and led her to a space near the altar. It was a tiny church and lacked the usual opulence of most Catholic churches. The little altar was almost bare except for candles, statues, and the usual gold crucifix.

Georgia controlled the urge to inquire if these were the only guests but noted they did look Indian in appearance. She also noticed one young couple sitting hand in hand attired in blue jeans. Certainly she felt overdressed, but it was a wedding, after all. Georgia settled back as the organ began to play and studied Jake's profile. He had been strangely silent, saying only a few words to her on the trip from Manhattan. There was a grim set look to his mouth. He seemed tightly coiled. Georgia wondered what was bothering him.

At that moment a beautiful young girl, dressed all in white, her hair braided in long dark braids to her waist, walked down the aisle toward the little altar accompanied by a middle-aged man with skin the color of dark clay. Strains of *Lohengrin* played in the background. Next, a young man appeared dressed in an ill-fitting dark suit. A small fellow stood at his elbow and clutched a tiny box, apparently containing the ring. A priest stood holding a prayer book, and the ceremony appeared to have begun. Georgia strained to hear what was being said, but it was hopeless. All she could make out was *Do you take this woman* . . . Moments later the couple embraced, and Georgia assumed it was over. Lord! This was it! An Indian wedding . . . any wedding; it was sterile and pathetic.

She sat quietly next to Jake and wanted to be any place else in the world but where she was. Jake turned to her and spoke. "It's over. They'll be going outside on the lawn. Come on, let's go and congratulate them."

Georgia nodded, and they rose and headed for the church entrance. A scattered few began to leave the pews, and as Georgia glanced around her, she realized there'd been twenty, maybe thirty people present. Suddenly she wanted to cry. Somehow she'd expected something else . . . something beautiful, maybe . . . something to make her change her opinion of Jake. At least make him appear a more romantic figure. This was sad.

And then she remembered her own wedding to Victor Sandborne years ago. How lovely it had been. Margo's living room bedecked with flowers . . . a Supreme Court judge performing the ceremony . . . a reception at "21" . . . her honeymoon in Paris,

Cannes, Spain . . . the thrill of being married to a man like Victor, someone she loved and respected, someone of wealth and power. She had thought then that everything she'd ever dreamed of was in her grasp, never once suspecting that strong, reliable Victor would, in time, turn on her, lie to her, divorce her for a girl who was no more than a prostitute. It seemed incredible, and so very long ago—almost as if it had never happened—like a dream. For a moment Georgia had indeed lost all track of time, but Jake's voice snapped her back to reality.

"God, you look like you were off on a cloud. Come on, let's say hello to the happy couple. And then we'll go over and party awhile." He patted Georgia suggestively on the behind. "I wanna show my 'yellow hair' off to all the pretty Indians. I'm certain you'll enjoy it."

Georgia remained silent but followed Jake to a little throng of people surrounding the bride and groom.

The bride was quite beautiful, and not more than twenty. She wore a white dress, matching shoes, and carried a little bouquet of violets. The groom was about thirty and not so handsome. His face was wide with a high bridged nose, prominent cheekbones, and heavy lips.

"Congratulations on your marriage. I know you both will be very happy. Vela, this is my friend, Georgia Bonner. She's an actress. You know, on TV and all." Jake's voice held a note of pride. "I'm glad you didn't wait around for me to waltz you down the aisle, Vela. Lemo here will make you a good husband."

The young bride, ignoring Jake's last remark, took Georgia's hand. "It's so nice to meet you, and I'm glad you could come. Many people I'd invited didn't. Please come over to our place for the party . . . reception . . . whatever you want to call it."

Georgia smiled and struggled for something to say. She was embarrassed. "Thank you. The wedding was lovely. I wish you all the happiness."

Jake took Georgia's arm, none too gently, and guided her toward another little group who obviously had not been inside the church. They were three men dressed in dungarees who stood whispering conspiratorily in front of an old, beat-up car.

"Hi there, Bella-Coola. Where'd you get that classy number?"

Jake smiled and once more patted Georgia on the behind. "This is 'Yellow Hair' fellows. She's an actress, society, you know; she married Victor Sandborne. You all heard of her."

Georgia felt her face flush but attempted a smile.

"Hello. I guess you all missed the wedding. Why did you call Jake Bella-Coola? Is that his Mohawk name?"

The taller man in the center of the group

answered. "Yes. He changed it to Pierce, too hard to pronounce. I'm Joe Merklin, but my tribal name is Running Rabbit. I use it for fun."

The other two young men eyed her critically but remained silent. Georgia got the distinct feeling that they looked up to Jake, probably even feared him, but didn't like or trust him.

"How interesting—the names, I mean," said Georgia, suddenly at a loss for anything better to say. She felt uncomfortable in the presence of these men and wondered why they were hanging around out here instead of being in the church for the ceremony.

"Well, Jake, the wedding's over, so I guess we'd better get started back to Manhattan. I don't see any cabs around here."

Jake shot her a quizzical look. "Are you kiddin'? The fun's just beginning. Come on, get in." He opened the door of the 1975 Ford and assisted her inside before she had a chance to ask questions. The three others climbed in as if by secret signal while the driver, an extremely handsome young fellow with sandy hair and skin the color of light chocolate, took a flask from his pocket, slugged down a shot of booze, then started the motor and gunned away from the curb, tires squealing.

"My God!" exclaimed Georgia in momentary panic. "Where are we going . . . to the moon?"

Jake patted her hand. "It's a surprise, dear. Just sit back and relax. We'll be there soon. It's only a few blocks."

The driver of the car, who everyone referred to as Coss, remained silent, his eyes fixed on the road, his foot glued to the accelerator. They made turns at such a high rate of speed that Georgia felt her mouth go dry. "What the hell? Slow down, for God's sake; I'd like to get wherever we're going in one piece!"

The men laughed and ignored her, but when the car screeched to a halt in front of a large brick apartment building, she breathed a sigh of relief. Again she wanted to vent her fury on Jake, but again she had to admit it was her own damn fault. No one had put a gun to her head.

Jake opened the car door, assisted Georgia out, and the little group headed for the front of the building. Music flooded the night from inside and again the pungent odor of marijuana.

Georgia wondered what these men did for a living. Precious little, unless she missed her guess. The one they called Coss, the one who'd driven the car, was the best looking and said the least. Running Rabbit was short and muscular like a small compact bull, and the other one she'd not been introduced to was about eighteen and wore a blue satin band across his forehead which kept his long black hair back from his eyes, eyes that were dark and slightly slanted, giving him a satanic, Oriental appearance. There was something odd about all the men, and Georgia wondered how Jake had known them.

A large heavyset Indian wearing jeans and a flowered shirt answered the door to an apartment on the first floor and ushered them all inside.

"Hi, my friends, come in. The bride and groom haven't come yet. Guess Vela had to go change, but they're in for a real bash. We got everything: food, drink, smoke, everything!"

Jake turned to introduce Georgia to the man, but he had simply walked away leaving the little group standing alone.

Georgia glanced about the large, noisy, crowded room and was struck immediately by everything Indian. A huge painting of John Smith and Pocahontas hung over the fireplace, while the battle of Little Big Horn, complete with Custer getting the tar whipped out of him, was depicted in a mural that covered half a wall. Large, beautifully woven blankets hung alongside silver jewelry and tomahawks and an enormous statue of Geronimo stood in the corner like the proverbial cigar store Indian. In one corner of the room a buffet was set up and throngs of people in various colorful ensembles were eating chicken with their fingers and drinking bourbon from large glasses. There was also wine and beer as well as little trays of marijuana cigarettes neatly rolled. Music blared from a stereo and between that and voices raised in hysterical glee, Georgia could barely hear Jake over the din.

"Come on . . . we'll get some food and booze. You hungry?"

She was, in fact, starving, though the atmosphere was not conducive to dining. Also, she felt thoroughly over-dressed and out of place, a stranger in a foreign land, the only blonde in the place. "Frankly, Jake, I'd like just a glass of wine for the moment. Then later, maybe a piece of chicken."

At that propitious moment, the happy bridal couple arrived and were descended upon by half the guests who were by now higher than kites. The place reeked of alcohol, marijuana and cheap perfume, mingled with the smells of fried chicken and sauerkraut.

Georgia, after the wild ride and all the excitement, was feeling a bit dizzy. She accepted the glass of wine, and Jake led her to an empty chair; then he proceeded to greet the bride and groom whom he appeared to know intimately. Georgia overheard one woman, garbed in a long caftan and heavy Indian jewelry, mutter, "Guess Jake got over Vela and vice-versa. Lucky for her. He'd make a lousy husband."

Georgia felt herself invisible. No one seemed to know—or care—that she was present. She sat sipping the wine and watching the passing parade for what seemed like hours, while Jake mingled about, posturing, grinning, and flirting with several pretty young Indian girls and thoroughly ignoring her. Why had he brought her here? She was confused, hurt, then furious.

At that precise moment one of the men from the wild ride, the good looking driver they called Coss, appeared at her side.

"I see Jake left you here all alone. That's stupid—a gorgeous chick like you, but Jake's crazy. You know that? Jake used to be a rodeo star, then a hard hat—you know, an iron worker—now he's just plain crazy."

Georgia started to answer, but he interrupted. "Let me get you another glass of wine, princess. I see your glass is empty, then, we'll get in a little visit." He eyed Georgia up and down and a chill ran up her spine. She sat silently and wondered how the hell she could get out of this madhouse. Red Hook, Brooklyn! She might as well have been in Tokyo. Of course there were cabs somewhere out there in the darkness.

Coss returned with the glass of wine, and she sipped it gratefully. A few minutes later she experienced a strange sensation . . . high; she felt high . . . but a different high from booze. Carefree . . . almost silly . . . she started to giggle as Jake suddenly reappeared.

"Come on, sweetheart, we're getting out of here. This place is a drag; there's another party nearby, a better one. This one stinks."

It was dark outside, and Georgia had not the slightest notion where they were headed.

A young girl in a red satin jumpsuit suddenly materialized and appeared to be joining her and Jake along with Coss and another young man whose name turned out to be Turk. They all piled in the same car, and Georgia prayed the ride would not be the roller coaster the last one had been.

At last Coss pulled up in front of a building set back several yards from the street. A silver half moon hung in the dark sky, and Georgia shivered as they climbed two flights of stairs and entered an apartment that was sparsely furnished. Music, punctuated by the sensuous beat of Indian drums, throbbed in the background, and Running Rabbit greeted them all with a tray of drinks in his hands. "Welcome to my little hideaway. I split ages ago from that stiff wedding party." He handed Georgia a drink. "You'll be more comfortable here, sweetheart."

Georgia felt a bit peculiar from the wine she'd consumed at the other party, but accepted the glass from the short muscular man with a word of thanks. He turned toward the girl in the red satin jumpsuit. "Hi, Beta. Didn't expect you, but you're a welcome sight."

The girl was Indian with straight hair worn long past her waist and dark, heavily madeup eyes. Eyes that appeared to be glazed from too much alcohol, or something else. "Thanks. I hope there's more action here." She glanced at Georgia who had settled herself on a simple brown sofa in the corner. "You seem to be the only yellow hair around. Custer's last stand." She giggled.

Georgia sensed a certain hostility and wondered if she was jealous of one of the men. "Guess you're right. You certainly have beautiful hair. I don't remember seeing you at the church or the other party. Are you a friend of the bride or the groom?"

"Well, sort of a friend. I mean, I know Vela, but I hate weddings. I just like a party. You know, have fun. How about you? You're really pretty, like a blonde goddess." Abruptly she turned away from Georgia and undulated her way across the room in the direction of Jake.

Georgia watched her in motion and decided she was probably the sexiest looking girl she'd seen in a long time. Everyone seemed so strange. And this place . . . it was so neat. Maybe it was a mess in the cold light of dawn, but the last thing Georgia had expected was the almost military orderliness that surrounded her. Candles flickered about the room casting shadows, and always in the background was the insidious throbbing of the drums. The floors were bare except for woven Indian rugs flung about in front of the fireplace and other spots, and there was very little furniture.

Georgia looked up and smiled as Jake approached her. Suddenly her head felt as if it were floating away from her body. It was a peculiar sensation. She felt feather light all over, as if she could sail about the room . . . and warm . . . her body felt so warm. Good Lord, what had been in that wine? she wondered frantically. But her thoughts were in slow motion. Why wasn't she more afraid?

Jake knelt at her feet. "Like this place? It belongs to the Rabbit. Quite a little hutch, no? He's got all kinds of things here to make you feel good. How do you feel, baby? You look good enough to eat."

Georgia's panic evaporated as if by magic, and she felt herself drifting pleasantly. She didn't reply but simply smiled and sipped more wine, then looked up to find Coss, Turk and Running Rabbit observing her closely. It seemed darker. They appeared hazy. The little candles flickered, the smell of heavy incense was almost overpowering, and the beat, beat, beat of the drums—tom-toms, a barbaric, savage rhythm that filled all time and space.

Georgia attempted to focus her eyes. It proved difficult, but she felt a certain tranquility, the panic completely erased. In its place came a peculiar peace. She felt outside herself.

Suddenly, as if from out of nowhere, came the girl called Beta. She was completely naked, and her body glistened in the candlelight. Her long hair hung to her derriere and she moved gracefully across the room. The men watched her in rapt fascination. No one spoke. She stood for a moment in the middle of the room, knowing she held center stage, then began to dance to the sensuous music. She whirled about gracefully, always moving closer and closer to the men who stood near Georgia. Her full round breasts were delicately rouged with a pink substance, and she was barefoot. Suddenly, as if choosing a partner, she smiled and took Coss' hand, pulling him to the center of the floor. She stood on tiptoes and wrapped herself in his arms, kissing him fiercely on the mouth as if she'd been waiting for just such a moment.

Georgia watched and heard his moan; then attempted to ask Jake what was happening, but her tongue felt too large and furry for her mouth. She was unable to utter a sound and felt herself becoming aroused as she stared at the two figures.

Coss' hands moved to the girl's breasts and then to her bare buttocks. She wriggled and sighed in his arms, urging him on with words. In a matter of seconds Coss was naked, while Georgia and the others remained transfixed, watching the dance of sex. The two figures continued to move together, pausing from time to time to kiss deeply. And then Coss led the girl to the Indian rug in front of the fireplace and pulled her down beside him without the slightest concern as to who was watching their erotic charade.

There was some light behind the logs, and with the candlelight flickering over their bodies, Coss began to make love to the girl. Georgia tried to tear her eyes away from the sight of the naked bodies writhing in ecstasy but found it impossible. She was burning with desire from head to toe; and when Jake took her hand, murmuring something obscene in her ear, she stood up and followed him down the hall to another room, no longer caring what had been in the drink or what was happening to the others. All she cared about at this moment was Jake's arms and mouth.

He whispered in her ear once more. "Darling, I'm here. Don't worry. I love you, baby. Get undressed. I'm going for more wine."

Georgia obeyed and undressed, then lay naked on one of the strange bunkbeds awaiting Jake's return. Her mind was a blank, her body felt as if it were on fire. She'd never experienced anything like it. And then Jake was back, naked. She wondered crazily where he'd left his clothes. He handed her the wine, and she drank it hungrily. Her mouth was so dry. She was thirsty . . . thirsty. And then Jake's mouth was on hers, kissing her deeply, hungrily. He fondled her breasts, and then his head was on her belly, lapping at her, murmuring for her to spread her legs. "Open them, baby; open them wide."

She lay there transported by the drums to another world . . . louder now. Her eyes opened wide, and there stood Turk. Where had he come from? Was it the same day? She tried to remember who the boy was, tried to connect the facts, but it was senseless. She was someone else . . . another person . . . an extension of herself floating in warmth and silkiness. Jake's mouth was feasting upon her, and Turk, also naked, was on his knees beside the bunk fondling her breasts. He sucked the nipples, moaning and muttering strange words that Georgia did not understand. And then he was kissing her lips. She felt her arms go around his neck while Jake continued to suck her. The sensation was undescribable. She climaxed, and cried out for Jake to stop, for them both to stop, but soon found herself becoming aroused again. Hot, hotter than she'd ever thought possible.

Suddenly Jake moved from between her legs and now Coss appeared like an apparition. Hazily, as if through a thin veil of smoke, she opened her eyes and saw Running Rabbit, Jake, Turk and the girl standing there watching. Next she felt other hands over her body, touching her breasts, licking her, tasting her mouth. She recognized Running Rabbit. He was smiling down at her, and his muscular naked body was wet with excitement. The others seemed occupied, taking turns with Beta on the floor. She could hear their moans of passion while she herself felt on a long sensuous voyage; one which she hoped never would end.

The drums were louder now as the dark smiling man knelt between her legs. She was so wet, but he lapped at her as if in a frenzy of desire. She reached for his head, pressing it deeper . . . deeper, and then she came once more and heard Jake's voice somewhere in the room. Or was it Jake? She wasn't certain of anything anymore . . . only the pleasure . . . only the passion.

"Enough, boys. You've had enough; it's my turn."

Now she felt him inside her, felt him moving, pounding her with his large cock as the drums grew louder . . . ever louder. Over and over she heard the girl, Beta, sighing and moaning in the background, and through a mystical haze she saw the faces of the others, watching and smiling to themselves. An audience, a participating audience, because after Jake had come, Coss straddled her and pushed himself deep inside. It felt so good. She'd never had two men that way, that close. Next Turk lingered over her breasts with his mouth for what seemed like hours, sucking the nipples and fondling her all over before he, too, slipped his hard penis deep inside her wetness. Where was Jake? He seemed to have disappeared, but when Turk moved away from her naked body, Beta appeared. Georgia climaxed again and again, despite herself, until at last oblivion . . .

When Georgia opened her eyes, she was in her own apartment in her own bed, and for one brief moment thought she'd experienced a terrible nightmare, but then she saw Jake sprawled beside her. She tried to get out of bed, but her head felt like it weighed tons. Her arms and legs were heavy. She tried to speak, but her mouth was too dry and no sound came forth. She reached for the glass of water she always kept by the bed and drank it greedily. She'd been drugged . . . drugged! No doubt about it. Drugged and used to a fare-thee-well like some sexual toy. Jake Pierce's sexual toy.

At that moment Georgia hated the man with so much passion, it terrified her. She had a strong desire to kill him, smother him with a pillow. Oh, God! The dope had made her paranoid.

She struggled to remember the night's events, but they were clouded. She got up and staggered to the bathroom in the direction of the stall shower. Soap and water . . . she craved soap and water. Georgia scrubbed herself and felt she'd never really be clean again.

After the shower her breathing became even, her panic subsiding enough for her to think more clearly. She slipped into a terry robe and made her way back to the bedroom, intent upon telling Jake that if he didn't get the hell out and never come back, she would call the police or kill him with her bare hands. But she didn't get the opportunity— Jake Pierce was gone. The side of the bed where he'd slept was rumpled and empty. Maybe he was in the living room. She padded through the apartment, but no Jake. It was a blessing because she felt murderous, soiled, and worst of all, she felt guilty. The guilt was the hardest thing to bear. That and the searing fact that she had, in fact, enjoyed it.

Georgia opened a cold beer and telephoned Teddy. Maybe he knew a good shrink. Obviously, that was what she needed. Either that or she was just a plain everyday sexual pervert. Teddy would understand. She should have discussed it with him long ago.

Teddy Morrell sat in Georgia's bedroom and smoked a cigarette. He had been patient and kind, listening to her, allowing her time to sip on her milkshake mixed with wheat germ and brewers' yeast. Since the 'episode' she had embarked on a health kick and had cut out drinking completely, at least for the moment. That was part of her penance.

She lay propped on satin pillows and observed her friend who sat opposite her reclining on a large comfortable chaise. His voice was calm and even. "Georgia, the incredible X-rated story you've related to Uncle Teddy has not shocked the pants off me as you might have imagined. On the contrary,

I knew you were up to something. You hadn't been yourself for months. Ever since that bastard robbed you and the off-Broadway thing folded, I just knew Mr. Cochise had something to do with your mood. You had been far too silent about an experience that I knew had given you a lot of pain. Now, dear girl, as your close friend and one who loves you, permit me to have my say, okay?"

Georgia nodded but remained silent.

"In the first place, you are not going nuts. You are simply a victim of your own past. I mean, we all are products of our environmnet in some way—our parents, our childhood." He lit a cigarette. "Look at the kid that tried to knock off the President. Upper middle class . . . money . . . education, but something went awry. Now, in your case, sweetie, the fact that you never knew your mother or father, that your grandmother was mulatto, that you grew like some kind of wild flower without roots, are a part of this whole problem. In other words, your attachment to Jake Pierce, regardless of his bad character, and aside from the hot sex," Teddy smiled, "went way beyond that. You somehow identified with his background on the reservation, his pain at being a displaced person. In other words, Georgia, you empathized; but in this case with a thoroughly bad individual who had no real concern for anyone but himself. Even your marriage to Victor was a mistake. You loved him but never felt worthy of him.

And then, of course, when he rejected the child after finding out about Taia, well dear, he was essentially a prick. But again you took the blame. Kiki Blake was the icing on the cake. That was a low blow I must admit. Again you were the victim. Georgia, dear, you are not crazy nor are you a bad girl. You are simply guilty of having bad judgment. And at the moment, you need to clean up your act, get out the dead wood."

He reached over and patted her hand. "And, of course, I needn't tell you never to see that crazy savage again. What you must do now is concentrate on yourself; get back your self respect; get back to work. And, dear, if you'll take this from someone who had made a few mistakes himself, get the hell over and have yourself checked out by the good doctor. Four hot Indians in one day—" He paused and grinned, "Was it fun?"

Georgia smiled, "Teddy, you're always so right about everything. I'll see the doctor tomorrow. As to its being fun—" She blushed crimson. "From what I can remember, it was pretty damn exciting, but horrible and degrading at the same time. That must have been the dope they slipped in my drink. Shit, I still feel lousy. Now, my dear, what if that crazy Jake comes back?"

"Call the cops. That's easy enough. That lunatic is dangerous, and I'll bet a nickle he's got a record. I'm certain he's done time. He's a bad number, but I don't think after what's happened he'll dare show his face. And as for right now, tonight, I'll go out and get us Chinese and we'll watch *Marco Polo*. It should keep your mind occupied."

"Thanks, Teddy. I don't feel like being alone. I'm still shaky. I'm so glad you're here. You're my dear, dear friend . . . and I love you." She paused. "Remember I told you a little about Nick Culletti?" Teddy nodded. "Well, he's on the Coast. Funny, I miss him more than I thought possible." She smiled. "Well, it figures. At least he's playing with a full deck."

CHAPTER ELEVEN

NICK CULLETTI rented two rooms in a small apartment hotel on the Sunset Strip. Originally the price had been a hundred a day, but management had graciously given the studio a rate. Highway robbery! It really wasn't that attractive, but at least it provided a little fridge where Nick kept beer, yogurt, and seven different bottles of vitamin pills.

Shooting on his scenes began tomorrow. He was nervous, but that would pass. Since the jeans commercial, and the TV movie, everything, careerwise, had been on the upswing. He could tell by the way Ira Cornfield treated him in the front office that he had something these birds thought they could make a buck on. Nick had learned long ago not to expect sentiment, or in some cases even fair play, when it came to business. Only when you brought in the bucks did the big boys give you a handshake. It was simple; if you were a hit and people bought tickets or sponsors bought TV time, a halo shone around your head, but just a drop in ratings or one wrong move, and the halo could slip and choke you to death!

Nick had met the director, an Italian in his early thirties, whose first film had been a science fiction, low budget job that had grossed a fortune. Tuto Fellito was his name, and though he spoke broken English, Nick liked and respected him. Nick's part in the series was a running one, and if the network liked the pilot and picked it up, he was in business.

The script had been written by two friends of the director who Nick considered a couple of geniuses. It was a cops-and-robbers show, with Nick playing the partner to a lady cop who was big, likeable and believable, rather than the usual TV policewoman oozing sex and vulnerability. The theme was stark realism with little glamour and a minimum of tits and ass, or T and A, just good, exciting stories that made sense with an honest look at how the system worked.

Nick walked across the room and glanced out the window at the tanned bodies frolicking in the turquoise swimming pool. Others lazed on red and blue chaises sipping from beer cans and eyeing one another, or sleeping in the sun, their eyes hidden behind large dark glasses. Palm trees were everywhere, and Nick decided that Hollywood was a world unto itself.

He went to the fridge to get a yogurt, then sat on the beige linen sofa and rehearsed lines for the tenth time that day. Oddly enough, he missed Georgia Strange, they'd never even slept together, yet he felt she was his wife.

Six o'clock the following morning the studio limo arrived. He would never grow accustomed to the early morning smog and wondered how people breathed out here. Of course, in New York you had the soot and fumes from a thousand vehicles, as well as the periodic garbage strikes that left refuse piled high on street corners. You had to be tough to survive in New York!

Hollywood, especially Beverly Hills, appeared so damn clean, but the manicured lawns of the gorgeous homes seemed always silent and empty as if no one really lived there, as if they were simply props for some play or film.

As the car sped along, Nick sipped coffee from a paper container and rehearsed lines in his head. Makeup at six-thirty, on the set by eight . . . it was going to be a rough day!

Two weeks elapsed, and Nick ached for New York. He loved the work out here, but he felt himself a visitor from another land, with people and habits unfamiliar and strange. He longed to return to the Big Apple, and if he was honest with himself, to Georgia. He'd telephoned her twice, and she seemed happy to hear from him, brimming over with questions about Hollywood and his work.

Yesterday, he'd had cocktails and dinner at The Polo Lounge of the famed Beverly Hills Hotel with a well-known journalist. The place was impressive with its intimate booths and loud speaker system paging people with names he'd only read or heard about. The entire establishment exuded a quivering excitement, an inner sanctum of those on the rise, those at the top, and sometimes those on the skids making a bid for a last chance at the brass ring. The smell of success, money, power, romance, and intrigue was everywhere. Even the waiters arrived on cue, looking as if they'd been ordered from central casting. It was here some of the biggest deals in town were made over orange juice in the morning and martinis after five.

Nick was introduced to Sam Spiegel and Joe Levine, two legendary movie moguls he'd heard about but never expected to meet in person. They both possessed that mysterious, intangible something that celebrated people seemed to inherit from the gods or built up like a treasure through the years. It was as if they held a secret key that unlocked the elusive hidden door to success. Heady stuff indeed!

Joe Levine seemed an honest, forthright character with an openness Nick liked immediately. Sam Spiegel, on the other hand, was a large, interesting man with dark eyes that didn't miss a trick. His art collection was said to be worth millions, while the jet set vied for invitations aboard his yacht and his fabulous parties on both coasts.

Each day the ride to the studio seemed less nerve-wracking, and soon Nick developed a strong sense of self confidence.

Big Sam had telephoned from their little apartment in New York, informing Nick that the rent had increased fifty dollars and a new family of wily roaches had moved in hoping to take over. Otherwise, everything was fine.

Nick smiled and looked forward to the following week when his scenes would be completed and he could return to the big town.

The plane hovered over Kennedy for what seemed like hours but in fact was only thirty minutes. Nick accepted a third drink from the smiling stewardess and lit a cigarette. It was afternoon, but the skies appeared dark and ominous through the little airplane windows. The 747 lost altitude suddenly, and the *Fasten Your Seatbelt* sign flashed on. Nick hated to admit it, but he was nervous about flying. It was one of the few things that really frightened him. They had been circling forever it seemed, stacked because of bad weather. Oh God! To be on terra-firma! Just to once more smell all the rotten, beautiful odors of the streets of New York.

They could keep L.A.; it was a cardboard community, lit up by dime store lights, thought Nick philosophically. But he'd learned a lot; the episodes in which he'd appeared in the series had been completed, and he was satisfied that he'd done well. The rushes pleased him and appeared to please everyone else. A top female agent named Doe Miller had approached him with a tempting offer, but he remained loyal to Ernie Black. After all, he'd gotten him this far and Nick had made up his mind a long time ago to remain loyal to those who had stood by him when he'd been on the drowning list—like Big Sam, Lucky, Ernie Black, and even Margo and Georgia; especially Georgia. Funny, she didn't seem to be all that ambitious for herself, but he could see how really interested and hopeful she was for his success, and that made him like her all the more. It was as if the few weeks' separation had brought them somehow closer. He couldn't wait for the plane to land so he could dial her number.

Georgia's recent experience with Jake had left her badly shaken but somehow cleansed, as if her encounters with the man had, in a way, been a purge. A peculiar way to look at it, but anything that got you through the night, thought Georgia.

She'd continued her health kick and was

exercising with Richard Simmons each morning. Her body was becoming firm and hard, and when the call came from Nick announcing he was at the airport, her spirits soared.

"Nick, you're back! I've been reading about you in the trades. I'm so proud." She paused. "What time? Great! We'll order out and catch up on everything."

Not quite everything, thought Georgia with horror. Not the Jake Pierce thing. Not if she could avoid it. "Just give me time to hop in the shower and slip into something. See you."

She hung up the receiver and felt a little thrill of anticipation. Nick was back! Good, sweet, handsome Nick! God! She could barely wait for him to arrive. He said he'd drop his bags off, then come straight over.

Georgia soaped herself, rinsed, then dried her body and stood in front of a full length mirror examining herself with a critical eye. Were there any visible signs from that disgusting orgy? If she made love with Nick, would he suspect? How ridiculous! And what made her think she was going to sleep with Nick? Maybe he'd met some gorgeous starlet of twenty in LA., maybe he just wanted to remain friends. Anyway, she'd better be certain of her own motives, no more messes; she couldn't afford it emotionally.

Georgia dressed carefully, choosing a long jade green caftan slit up both sides and pale slippers to match. She brushed her hair, then applied her makeup carefully. A fabulous new lip gloss and a bronze lipstick with blush to match added just the right touch. She misted herself with Mitsuko, and at that precise moment the buzzer rang. Lord, he'd made it in a hurry.

She appraised herself once more in the long mirror, then headed for the door, her heart beating fast. Georgia opened the door wide and came face to face with Jake Pierce.

At first she was too stunned to speak, but when she regained her voice, it was a shriek. "Get the hell out of here, you bastard! I'm expecting company. How dare you! Now, get the hell out!" She pushed the door partially closed in Jake's face, but he braced it open with his foot.

"I'm comin' in, Yellow Hair, so just relax and move away from the door before you get hurt."

Georgia moved back as Jake arrogantly pushed his way inside and stood facing her. "Now what the hell's gotten into you? You were much more friendly the last time we met." He smiled that hateful smile and touched her arm.

She recoiled and took a step backward. "I was doped the last time, Jake, but not now. Now, get the hell out of here or I'm calling the police."

"That won't be necessary," came a voice from the hall. Nick came striding through the half opened door and stood facing the tall angular Indian.

"Nick! Nick . . . I didn't hear the downstairs buzzer. This . . . this is someone I used to know." She was embarrassed, confused.

Nick's face remained set. "I believe the lady asked you to leave, friend. Kindly do so, or I'll have to help you."

"Who the hell is this kid? Where'd you pick him up from?" snarled Jake, also taken by surprise. "Oh yeah, the Guinea actor—"

"I said the lady asked you to leave, and I'm giving you another chance before I knock the shit out of you, got it?"

Jake stood for a moment staring at the muscular young man and smiled. "Oh, I see. You here for some of what the lady's puttin' out. Good stuff . . . real good stuff . . . yeah, she's a hot piece alright, but there's plenty for everybody. You shoulda seen her in action the other night after a couple of ludes—"

Nick didn't let him finish, but hit him hard with his right fist, and the Indian, taken by the surprise of a professional punch, was knocked flat on the floor. Georgia screamed, and Nick, fire in his eyes, reached down and pulled Jake to his feet. "Now get out of here, you trash. Get out of here before I kill you. I've cleaned up the streets with guys like you since I was ten, so beat it."

Jake's nose was bloody, and he reached for

a handkerchief in his pocket. His hands shook and he staggered against the wall. Nick steadied him. "You're okay. I didn't hit you that hard. Now get the hell out of here, and don't ever come back."

Jake started to speak, but blood oozed from his nose and he wiped it once more, then glared at Nick from narrowed, bloodshot eyes. "I'm leavin', I'm goin', but I'll see you again. Don't forget it." He glanced at Georgia. "Have fun, sweetheart," and then he made his way a bit unsteadily towards the elevators.

Nick closed the door and stood looking at Georgia who appeared to be frozen in one position in the corner of the room.

"Sit down, Georgia." He led her to the sofa, and she sank back still silent, her eyes wide with shock.

"Thanks. You deserve an explanation." She paused. "I didn't want you to know, but now —I owe it to you. I mean, I don't want it between us. You may hate me."

When Georgia finished the Jake scenario, pausing at times, unable to go on, embarrassed, concerned how Nick would react, but determined to clean the slate, she felt as if a great weight had been lifted from her. She glanced at Nick who had remained silent through the entire story, allowing her time to put it all in order; then he took her in his arms and held her quietly while she sobbed for what seemed like a very long time.

"Don't think about this anymore, Georgia. It's going to be all right. Things are going to be a lot better now. You'll see."

"Will they, Nick, will they? I wonder. Jake is a pecular fellow. And me, I should have put an end to it ages ago, but I kept letting him get to me. I'm beginning to think I'm the one who's sick."

Nick staightened up and looked directly into Georgia's eyes. "Look, you've had a bad time all the way around. The one thing I learned on the streets was never pass judgment until you know all the facts, and sometimes not even then. What was it someone said? You can't really know a man until you've walked in his moccasins—something like that. Don't blame yourself so much, Georgia."

He lit a cigarette. "I really care about you. I mean *really* care. I know this sounds strange, but I'm a novice with women. Just the opposite of ole Jake. I've been around some, of course, but no one's meant anything to me. That is until you—but Georgia, I've got to take it slow. I don't want you to get the wrong idea, like maybe I'm punishing you for Jake or something, it's just that right now, I just want to hold you—comfort you—understand?"

Georgia nodded. "Of course, and I appreciate that. Lord! How I need some tender loving care. Stay here with me tonight, like friends—you know, nothing more—no sex. I'd really love that." She stood up. "I'll get you a robe."

Nick smiled that beautiful grin that lit up his entire face. "I'd like that, Georgia. I'd really like that."

After milk and David's cookies, they lay down together in Georgia's enormous bed, both emotionally exhausted. Nick kissed her lightly on the cheek and covered her gently. "Goodnight, Georgia—sweet dreams."

She was soon fast asleep.

CHAPTER TWELVE

THE FOLLOWING morning dawned bleak and gray in Brooklyn Heights. Francie Morgan peered from an upstairs bedroom window watching until the long black limousine with Louis seated comfortably in the rear, was out of sight.

It was the first of the month, and for all the years she'd known him, it had been the same —Louis departing early, not to return until nightfall, returning in either a state of depression or one of agitation, but always coming directly to her quarters. It was these nights he spent with her exclusively, and it was these nights she looked forward to like a child awaiting Christmas.

They would both undress, sitting about in Chinese silk kimonos, drinking, listening to old records, talking and making love. She could thank whomever he went to see on those trips shrouded in mystery because in a way those visits somehow brought him closer to her. He never revealed where he went, and she never inquired, but it became an unspoken bond between them.

Louis relaxed in the rear of the softly upholstered car and lit a cigarette. He dreaded this trip in a way; in another, he looked forward to it. Memories of the past were both painful and sweet. He leaned back, turned down the sound of the radio, and allowed his mind to drift.

It was the beginning of the Thirties, and Louis had come to America from Poland seeking a new beginning, only to find himself in almost as much turmoil as the old country. His parents were both dead, and he had no brothers or sisters. One bad eye had left him ineligible for the army, and there had been so little in Poland to look forward to, he had simply fled.

His one friend on board ship had been a scruffy Italian lad named Nunzio Ruffito, and the two young men had stood that day like brothers as the ship docked in New York harbor. The fabled Statue of Liberty and the Manhattan skyline were shrouded in fog as they disembarked at Ellis Island, a singing in their hearts.

However, New York City was not the land of dreams he and Nunzio had envisioned. It was during the Depression and there was little or no work. The money he had saved and brought across the seas, hidden in a sock, was fast depleting itself.

A fellow he'd met on the ship suggested the steel mills. "Lots of Polacks find work there, Louie. It's a good place to make money. My brother, he works in McKeesport at the National Tube Co. You go there, Louis; ask for Mike Kevoski, he'll get you work. You'll see."

Louis thanked him, and he and Nunzio continued their lunch of keilbasa and pierogie. Today they were eating Polish; tomorrow it would be spaghetti.

"My money is almost gone, Nunzio. I'll have to give it a try. What about you? Will you come with me?"

The young Sicilian shook his head. "Sorry, *gumba*. I got other plans, my friends and cousins in Brooklyn. If things don't work out for you, then come back. I'll miss you. We been through lots together." He scribbled a number on a napkin and gave it to Louis. Sadly, the two friends parted company that day and Louis caught a bus to McKeesport.

Louis' first job at the awesome steel mills had been sweeping the floors, but after one month he graduated to firing the sweltering furnaces. He watched the men around him lose their sense of identity. Hours at the mill, then hours at the tavern, swigging down boiler-makers, eating keilbasa and blood pudding, then picking up the little girls who hung around the mills. One day melted into another and always there was the heat—the white heat of the steel furnaces like living your daytime hours in hell; and your night time hours in another sort of hell. Louis was barely twenty, yet he felt like an old man.

His first real sexual experience was with a bleached blonde of forty who afterwards demanded five dollars. He'd given it to her and gone without food until payday, but worse than the long hours, the furnaces, the money, it was the loneliness that tortured Louis. He missed Nunzio. How he missed the warm Sicilian with his broken English and strange sense of humor. At last he could stand it no longer, and after one year of torment and a hundred dollars to the good, Louis Gerfinski quit the mills and returned to New York.

Nunzio had prospered, and when Louis inquired as to how his friend had managed to acquire clothes, a little apartment in the Village, and money to spend, he smiled that secret smile of his and answered, "My friends and cousins . . . they got good businesses. Charlie Luciano, Lonzo in Harlem . . . they got things sewed up. Numbers . . . all kinds of things." He glanced down at his hands. "Louis, listen to me. We're both young, you're my best friend, we can go far. You stick with me, Louis; stick with me. No more steel mills."

At first he went to confession, pouring out

his soul to the priest, guilt assailing his every waking hour. But then it all became easier as if the repetition of dishonesty, going against the law and getting away with it, somehow diminished its importance or value until Louis one day felt almost nothing—particularly when you considered the rewards and he remembered Poland and the steel mills. His job began as a driver, then bodyguard, and at one point murder, somehow, became easier. He had struck his bargain with the devil.

He moved out of the little apartment he'd shared with Nunzio and rented a place for himself in the West Eighties. It was the first place of his very own, and he decorated it to his liking. Louis was inordinately fond of flowers and beautiful inanimate objects. He scoured the antique shops and thrift stores for furniture and in the process managed to pick up some valuable prints which he hung proudly on the walls.

He somehow divorced himself from his daily duties and spent his free time listening to records and simply enjoying the few material things and creature comforts that surrounded him. He kept his apartment as a thing sacred and apart from anyone other than Nunzio who visited rarely, having become involved with a young Italian girl he planned to marry. Louis envied Nunzio his good fortune and ached for someone he too could share his life with. Someone other than the bimbos in the bars or the prostitutes who worked for the organization. There was an emptiness inside Louis, an emptiness that had never in his entire lifetime been filled. Perhaps that was why he was so good at his work; danger meant nothing to him. He had little to lose.

After Nunzio's marriage, the feelings inside Louis became more pronounced and he found himself more and more withdrawing into a peculiar protective shell.

One Monday, he was leaving the bus terminal where he'd dropped off a parcel and was intent upon returning the locker key to his bodyguard, Vito, when he spotted the girl.

She was coming out of the station, and she walked in a peculiar way, like she was drunk or sick or something. He followed her because she appeared so young, and because she was beautiful, with all that reddish hair streaming down her back. She was wearing flat sandals, a cotton dress, and she carried a little bag made from a colorful fabric. He tailed her for blocks, and then he saw her pause, push back her hair with one slender hand, then collapse on the sidewalk. In seconds, he was kneeling beside her, her head cradled in his arms. She looked up into his face with those enormous dark eyes, eyes that reminded him of a frightened forest fawn, and then she fainted.

He had simply picked her up, explaining to those crowding around that she was his sister, that he would take care of her. Louis carried her to his apartment, and there placed her on his bed, covered her almost reverently and allowed her to sleep. Apparently she was exhausted. He sat beside the bed watching her sleep. Her face in repose was lovely, with skin a pale olive in color, high cheekbones, a perfect straight nose a bit wide at the bridge, and a full mouth completely devoid of lipstick. In sleep she resembled a glorious china doll. Her long tapered fingers were bare of rings but around her neck she wore a silver chain with something attached. Louis examined it more closely and realized it was a peculiar amulet in the shape of a bell. At last she awoke, and he spoke to her softly in muted tones.

"Don't be frightened. I'm Louis Gerfinski. I found you. You're safe now. You fainted. You must have been exhausted. When was the last time you ate?"

Her voice was weak as she answered. "I'm Scherise and I haven't eaten in two days." She appeared completely comfortable and at home with Louis, eating every spoonful he fed her and drinking a quart of milk greedily. When she was finished, she asked if she could bathe, and Louis led her to the bathroom, reveling in this beautiful, strange creature in his home. It was as if she'd been sent from another planet in answer to his prayers. He glanced at his watch and realized he'd forgotten to return the key to Vito. "Scherise, stay here. I must leave for awhile, but I'll be back. Sleep if you like, but don't be afraid. You're safe now."

Months went by and Scherise's background remained a muddled mystery. Louis gleaned bits and pieces, attempting to fit them together.

According to the girl, her father was a Norwegian fishing boat captain and her mother a mulatta from the West Indies. Sometimes while studying her skin, which was like pale beige satin with peach undertones, he found it difficult to believe she was of mixed blood—but of one thing he was certain. She was the most beautiful and affectionate woman he had ever encountered. And more than beauty, she was as bright as a dollar. She cooked and cleaned the apartment, and appeared to be not only a man's dream of heaven, but an all around treasure.

She refused to discuss her past at any length, or give a valid explanation for her appearance outside the bus station on that fateful afternoon. She said only that she had lived with her parents on a boat moored at a little seaport town off the coast of South Carolina, and was deeply unhappy in school. Unhappy in the way she'd not been accepted by the others in the community because of her mixed blood. And that she'd simply run away. Run away to find a new life.

Though the tale was a fanciful one, Louis,

now madly in love with the girl, accepted it and allowed her to remain with him. On her eighteenth birthday she became Mrs. Gerfinski in a little ceremony attended by Nunzio, his wife, and others from an "organization" that was growing by leaps and bounds.

World War II ended, and in 1946 Scherise gave birth to a beautiful blonde baby girl. Louis moved his little family to a larger apartment and had never been happier.

In Louis' rule book there was no margin for error, and this included himself. If things had been different, he might easily have headed a giant corporation. He was a perfectionist with an inherent talent for organization. His unique position as the only Polish member of the "family" served to his advantage and he moved upward, his ambition fired by his fanatical devotion to Scherise and the baby. It was as if the two had been sent to him as a priceless gift from an unknown donor, and he intended to bestow on them the best life had to offer.

Each time he carried out some order for Charles or Tony Venzetti, Louis would absolve himself of guilt by thinking, *I've got Scherise and the baby to consider now,* the beautiful little baby girl who looked like a tiny angel lying in her father's arms. Louis was calculating and shrewd, making his moves coolly, determined to build a fence of security around his beloved family.

The "organization" became divided on drugs and prostitution. Gang wars erupted. Many of Louis' friends were gunned down on street corners, in doorways. A trail of blood spread from New York to Chicago. At times, Louis watched Scherise with the baby and wondered how he'd become involved in this sordid business, but dedicated himself to surviving and moving up. He was trusted, keeping secrets as well as books. In his spare time Louis took a course in accounting, finding in himself a hidden talent. And when both he and Nunzio were given Brooklyn as their special turf, he was pleased and deeply affected by the new responsibility. His thick, once sandy blonde hair turned snow white almost overnight. and he became known among his "soldiers" as the "White Lion."

Two years elapsed and Scherise began to change. At first in little subtle ways. She became preoccupied with her appearance to an abnormal degree, shopping for clothes incessantly—clothes and cosmetics. She cut her hair and dyed it blonde. Louis hated it and made her dye it back to its natural titian. She seemed irritable, dissatisfied, vague, and Louis became concerned. He consulted a doctor who informed him it was just a delayed reaction.

"Many women experience this depression or peculiar personality change after giving birth, Mr. Gerfinski. They carry the baby nine months, then it's as if they've lost something.

Now she feels empty. It's called post-natal depression, and it will pass," assured the doctor.

"But that's ridiculous. The little girl's almost two years old," announced Louis. "And Scherise is getting worse. She's beginning to drink. Sometimes when I come home, she's drunk. She never before had anything but wine with a meal. I don't understand it."

"You'll see. She'll pull out of this. It's temporary, I assure you. Your wife is in excellent health; however, there are some new drugs on the market—tranquilizers, anti-depressants. I'll give you a perscription. Where is your wife now?"

Louis glanced at his large hands folded on his lap. "She's shopping. Yesterday she brought home five new hats."

The doctor smiled, but Louis did not. He knew in his heart that something more was wrong with Scherise. They had been too close. Also, she had been receiving mail which was unusual, and when he inquired about it, she became silent and secretive. Later he found bits and pieces of torn paper in the waste basket.

Three months later Louis consulted the doctor once more, and when he returned to the apartment that afternoon, both Scherise and the child were missing. At first he thought she'd taken the baby to the park, but when they hadn't returned by dusk, he telephoned the nurse, Angela.

"Mr. Gerfinski, your wife fired me and forbade me to tell you. I'm so sorry. She loves the little one to distraction. She'd never harm her, but your wife is not well. I can tell. She used to ramble on about her mother. How the child must go to her, how she wasn't safe here."

Louis was frantic but controlled his emotions. "What do you mean, her mother? She hasn't been in touch with her parents in years. I thought they were dead!"

The nurse's voice trembled slightly. "Mr. Gerfinski, I've been in your employ for some-time now, and I've been discreet about things I've heard, things your wife used to say. What I mean is, I think she believed the little girl was in danger of being abducted, kidnapped. She used to cut out every kidnap story from the newspapers and show them to me. And after too much champagne, sometimes she'd go on and on about how people were after her —after you—but mainly it was the child she focused on." She paused. "I don't want to alarm you unnecessarily, but I think you'd better contact the police."

The following day Louis went to Nunzio's house where his oldest and dearest friend poured wine and sat facing him in the large airy living room. "Louis, my brother. I've seen it coming. She was not a well woman. You were blind."

Louis interrupted, his voice harsh. "I don't care! I love her, and the baby. We've got

244

to do something. The police. I know how you react to that, but something has to be done. I'm going mad."

"Louis, Louis . . . calm down. We have our own methods. Our own ways. I'll make some calls. Our men will get right on it. Look, I know how much you love them both, but we must move with caution. A scandal now would be disastrous. We're becoming more organized and legitimate. I mean, the progress that's been made in only a few years is fantastic." He paused and sipped his wine. "You have the liquor stores . . . legitimate businesses; and the little clubs on Fifty-Second Street . . . also legit. Don't you see, now is not the time to drag the authorities into this. This is a family matter. Other things might surface. Charlie is having his problems and that affects us all. *Capice?*"

Louis nodded, shook hands with his friend, then went home to wait. It would prove a long wait indeed.

The searchers were unsuccessful. It was almost the way he had imagined it—that Scherise and the baby had been sent from another planet, then due to a secret summons had been whisked away leaving not a trace.

The little seaport town in South Carolina, called Edgewater, was combed by people who usually could locate needles in haystacks. However, on this assignment they came up empty handed. There had been a family of mixed blood living in the little village years earlier, but the man had become involved in a lawsuit and disappeared without a trace. Scherise had said her last name was Thorgen, but there had been no family in Edgewater by that name. Louis' people checked the census and old newspaper clippings in the local file, but came up with nothing.

Louis held himself together by simple will power and threw himself into his work. He ran ads in personal columns and at last, despite objections from Nunzio and the others, listed Scherise and the little girl with the Missing Persons Bureau.

The authorities came up with little to encourage Louis in the next few years. He was contacted on several ocassions to identify women suffering from amnesia and bearing the general description of Scherise, but it was always a false alarm, and he would return to his apartment more discouraged then ever. Louis held himself in tight rein and grieved in silence, but still continued to rise in the organization with grim determination.

One day Mario Siempres, one of his lieutenants, brought in a very young man just released from prison. The boy's name was Lucky DiSantos, and for some peculiar reason Louis was drawn to the boy who had no money nor a place to stay. He possessed a certain pride when introduced to Louis, standing straight and looking him directly in the eye without a trace of fear, but rather wth obvious respect.

"Take off your shirt, Lucky. Take off your shirt and show Mr. G. the scars," Mario ordered.

Silently and without a change in expression, Lucky had removed his shirt revealing an ugly mass on his back and upper arms.

"They did that to him in the can. The guys, they wanted him to inform on his cell mate, but he didn't break. He's a good boy, Mr. G. He needs work. He's a good driver." Mario paused. "By the way, his cell mate was my brother."

Louis hired Lucky as his chauffeur when Braskets was otherwise occupied. Besides, he had other plans for Braskets and needed someone to fill his shoes permanently.

Louis and the young man developed an immediate rapport. He liked Lucky and admitted to himself as time elapsed that he had, in fact, become a distraction from his obsession with Scherise and the daughter he had lost. He became like a son, like a healing balm to his suffering soul. They spent long nights playing chess, a game that Lucky had learned in prison and played expertly. Louis was still a driven man but he mellowed with time.

1969 . . . the U.S.A. was engaged in an unpopular war in Vietnam and Richard

Nixon was president. One afternoon on the Fourth of July, Louis would never forget that day, it was stamped in his mind like a deep tatoo, a call came through on his private line. It was long distance from Chicago, and the voice was muffled lbut distinguishable.

"Mr. Gerfinski, I got some information that might be valuable to you. I got—"

Louis interrupted. "Who is this? Tell me immediately and get to the point. I don't have time to waste. How did you get this number?"

"Look, it ain't necessary you have my name right now unless we do business. I don't want no trouble, just a little help."

"Keep talking and this better be good. Now spit it out and hurry up with it," snapped Louis. "I'm due at a dinner party for the mayor in an hour."

"Well, it's like this. I'm no pro or nothin'. I'm just a guy, well, you might term me a hustler of sorts who likes to drink. You know, I make the bars when I have the dough, from the Palmer House to . . . well . . . some of the less elegant bistros. I like women. Sometimes I pick up girls and take them home. Anyway, last night I met this dame with kinda red hair, dyed, but not bad, who liked to put away the booze better than me. But after I got to talkin' to her awhile, I see she's kinda nuts . . . you know, don't have all her marbles."

Louis' heart began to beat wildly. "What

the hell does all this have to do with me? What are you driving at? Who is the girl? Get to the point, fast; stop giving me a tap dance."

"Well," the voice continued, "this dame talks real crazy, like about how she used to live real good . . . have money . . . how she used to be your wife, in fact. I figured she was out of her gourd, but I been checkin' around the word has it you did have a wife a long time ago and that she took a walk."

Louis motioned Sing Jo for a drink and continued the conversation. "What is this woman's name and where is she now?"

The man's voice was cooler now, more in control. He had the big guy's interest. "She told me three names. First, she said her name was Ruby; another time, Irma; and the other time something like Sherry . . . Sherly . . . something like that."

"Like Scherise?"

"Yeah, maybe. But by this time she was really spaced out."

Louis' hands were wet against the receiver. "Where is she now? Where is the woman now?"

"Well, to be honest, she's sleeping it off in my pad. And, since I need the dough and all, and managed to get your number off a guy who expects me to lay a little on him, I locked her in for sake keepin'. If she's the wrong dame, no harm done. She's a coo-coo bird, though. I can tell you that, but if you want to come see for yourself—"

"I'll be there tonight, soon as I can get a flight. Name? Address? Phone number? Give it to me immediately, and don't let her go. Don't let her go, my friend . . . or you'll wish to hell you'd never been born."

Louis made a flight out almost immediately. The plane landed at O'Hare Airport, and he took a cab directly to the address the man had given him.

His heart was pounding inside his breast as he entered the rundown hotel on South Street. Lucky had begged to come along, but this was something he had to do alone. Perspiration rolled from his wide forehead and he wiped it away with a handkerchief. He located the apartment and knocked three times. Lucky had warned him it might be some kind of trap and a scam, but Louis was beyond fear. Anyway, his .38 was strapped under his coat, and he carried a knife strapped to his leg. The wait at the door seemed interminable. Why didn't the damn fool answer? He knocked again, this time harder.

At last a voice from behind the door. "Password, please."

"Warsaw Concerto," answered Louis, feeling slightly foolish. "Open up."

The door opened a crack, and a small man with a bald head peered out. "It's you. It's really you. I seen your picture in the paper and on the news. Come on in. She's asleep. I slipped her a little chloralhydrate."

Louis strode inside the shabby little room with colored lights outside that blinked on and off. He stood in the center of the worn rug and peered at the bed where a woman's figure lay sprawled.

She was fully clothed, barefoot, and her face partially hidden by her arms, crisscross, as if to shield her from some expected blow. Louis came closer.

"Turn up the lights for Christ's sake. I can't see a damn thing in this darkness."

The man complied and the figure on the bed moaned and stirred. Louis knelt beside her. He touched the woman's arms, gently removing them from her face. He felt himself sway but quickly controlled the emotions that swept over him. It was Scherise alright . . . older, heavier, her once beautiful face bloated . . . but still recognizable. He took her in his arms and she opened her eyes, eyes that still reminded Louis of a frightened forest fawn, but tonight they were bloodshot and swollen.

She smiled a sweet, almost angelic smile. "Daddy. Daddy, I knew you'd come. It's my birthday." She laughed a strange laugh that was almost a tinkle, but her voice was like that of a child. "It's my birthday and I want to celebrate, Daddy. I'm so glad you've come."

Louis wanted to weep and then his emotions changed to fury. He wanted to hit her, shake her, ask her where she'd been all these years . . . ask where his daughter was. But he realized that would be useless. This was Scherise alright, but only in body. Her mind had drifted into a never-never land, and he realized it went further than mere alcoholism. And, oh God, that meant he still might never find his daughter.

Louis, along with some of the boys in Chicago, arranged for Scherise to be transported to a sanitarium in Connecticut. After months of tests her condition was diagnosed as Alzheimers disease, degeneration of the brain cells and leaving its victim usually in a confused, helpless state of regression, all memory of the past wiped out. In today's world of medical miracles there was no known cure.

It was the most frustrating situation Louis had ever found himself in and he haunted the doctors, asking if there would ever be an improvement in his wife. It seemed incredible that his only child could be somewhere on this earth with the secret of her whereabouts locked in the mind of a mad woman.

The long dark limousine drove into the curving drive of the sanitarium and pulled to a stop, jarring Louis back to the present. It had been a longer ride than usual, it seemed. The chauffeur opened the door of the car and Louis got out, carrying the flowers and candy he always brought to Scherise. He glanced around him at the beautifully manicured grounds with the profusion of flowers in bright, brilliant colors. It was his money, and others like him, that kept this place in such splendor.

He waved at the daughter of a famous movie star whom he'd seen on many ocassions visiting her mother. They had a lot in common.

Inside the walls of the enormous building he went directly to Scherise's room. Sometimes she had not the slightest idea of who he was, but always she was glad to see him. It didn't seem to matter if she recognized him or not in her strange state. Each visit he hoped she might say something, anything that would lead him to his daughter. She would be a grown woman by now, probably with children of her own. That is, if she was alive.

Scherise smiled that vacant smile and held out her arms for the flowers and candy like any spoiled child. She was dressed in a blue satin robe he'd bought her from Bergdorfs. The nurse greeted him, her mouth set in its perpetual smile. "Mr. Gerfinski. I think she knew you were coming today. She kept asking me for the mirror. See how pretty she looks. I brushed her hair."

Louis smiled and took Scherise's hands. He stayed only an hour. It was too depressing. She had appeared to age only in the last few months. Before that, her face had remained unlined; now she looked so old it made him sad. When he bent to kiss her goodbye, she held his neck and murmured in her strange little sing-song voice, "I love you, Daddy. I love you."

Louis wanted to sob and on the ride back to Brooklyn Heights he looked forward to Francie . . . to liquor . . . to music . . . and most of all, he looked forward to holding a woman in his arms—a woman who was in the real world.

PART II
LOVE

CHAPTER THIRTEEN

GEORGIA'S REAL world had happily become filled with Nick—Nick and auditions. It was almost like beginning again, but she felt better about it, even the rejections. Even when someone informed her that professionally she'd taken a step backwards by appearing in "Angels in White." Somehow, it didn't seem to matter.

Just yesterday, Margo had telephoned to tell her there'd been some interest in her for a cameo role in a new night prime time series similar to "Dallas." She was excited, but her main interest was still Nick.

He was complicated. Far more complicated than she'd imagined. They still had not made love completely. It was there, the passion, steaming like a bubbling cauldron, but Nick wanted to take it slow, and for this she was grateful. It made her love him more because she knew that while he was adjusting to his first real emotional tie, she, in fact, needed the same kind of respite. They saw one another several times a week, but he never spent the night again after that first time. Even that intimacy seemed to frighten him.

It all had to do, she was certain, with his early insecurities, the fire, the orphanage. He was simply afraid to let go and really love her. Well, time was one thing she had. There was no one else in her life, though oddly enough sometimes her mind occasionally strayed to thoughts of Jake Pierce. Why was that kind of sex so thoroughly voluptuous? It held no emotional rewards, but the physical was almost phenomenal.

Tuesday. Nick and Georgia sat in a back booth at *Giovanni's* on Seventh Avenue and faced one another over a bottle of wine and a slow burning candle stuck inside an earthen jar. Nick was wearing Levis and a light blue turtle neck sweater. His enormous dark eyes appeared even larger by candlelight, and Georgia studied him, savoring the sight of his handsome face, and enjoying the scent of the new cologne she'd just given him. Funny how she loved perfumes, colognes, sachet, anything with a pleasurable scent. She was like a child when it came to these things. Scents and lingerie. Only last week she'd blown a hundred dollars on two perfectly outrageous negligees and gowns. One was trimmed with maribou, and the other with tiny ostrich feathers.

She'd cut way down on her drinking and excercised daily, so her body was in good shape. Forty loomed on the horizon like a death sentence, but somehow she knew it wouldn't be as bad as turning thirty—that had been the pits.

Nick was the first to speak. "You look different to me tonight, Georgia, like a living doll, all lit up inside. I mean . . . your face is so lovely and soft. You know, sometimes I try to remember the face of my mother, but it's just impossible. Sometimes if I concentrate real hard, I can almost feel her presence, or how it was when she held me, but then I think maybe it's just wishful thinking. No one can remember back that far." He poured more wine into their goblets.

"The first women I can remember clearly were the nuns. I detested them with their black and white shrouds. They always smelled so dusty. And Georgia, they hated me. I never knew why, but they hated me, even worse than Lucky. They were scared of him. Me they always called Pretty Boy and punished me if they got the chance. One day Sister Kelly called me in and said, 'If we don't cut your curls, Nicholas, you're going to turn out to be a little girl. You've already got that pretty sweet girl's face. You don't want to wake up one morning and find out you're a girl, do you, young man?'"

Georgia interrupted. "Lord! You even remember the conversation. What a cruel old witch. Go on, tell me more."

"Well, every night I used to feel between my legs to see if I'd turned into a girl." He smiled. "I remember how happy I was to find out I hadn't. I was fifteen when Lucky and I finally skipped and holed up with the Pirates, a gang in Brooklyn. You know, doing odd jobs. The leader of the bunch had connections with some numbers runners, and well, we helped out sometimes." Nick paused. "You know, Georgia, this is stuff I never talk about, but I feel I can tell you anything."

"You can," answered Georgia. "Go on."

"Well, there was this other gang—all girls. They liked me. I could never understand why, but they used to follow me around until it drove me nuts. They looked so dirty. Well, one night after a rumble, we were all back at the club house. The older guys were smoking grass, popping pills, and two of the girls came in, drank some wine, and then stripped naked and danced around on a table in front of the guys. Naturally, the guys were excited and started taking them one at a time in the back."

He finished the last of his wine and poured more in both goblets. "Each time one of the fellows would come back in, zipping up with a smile on his face, he's smirk and say the girls were asking for me. 'Go on in, lover boy. Your fans are pantin'.' Georgia, I just couldn't. I was excited, but somehow it made me feel really dirty, and I could see the guys were jealous. I didn't know what to do, and then it dawned on me. I said, 'Look, fellows, tell those bimbos I'm already taken. I'm exclusive property, and who it is is my business.' Somehow they accepted that, but still I was worried. Mamie and Jerri, the two girls that were providing the entertainment, weren't that bad. I had to prove myself some way. Lord, Georgia, I masturbated and all, had fantasies, but they sure didn't include those kind of women.''

"I understand, Nick. Go on, this is getting interesting.'' This was what she wanted to hear. At last he was opening up. She knew Nick wasn't gay. Teddy already assured her of that.

"Well, not a hell of a long time after that Lucky was picked up and I was sent to Boys Town, but before that I met a girl in the neighborhood. A nice girl. She went to high school near by and used to hang around sometimes. I remember she was pretty with long brown hair and bangs. Then one night I went to her place, her parents were out, and . . . well . . . we made it. She'd done it before, but of course I hadn't. I guess I was awkward, but at least I was a man.'' He sipped more wine.

"I liked feeling her breasts, coming, and all that, but I wanted to get away. Somehow I could feel those nuns watching me, waving

261

that fuckin' ruler in the air. Anyway, soon after that, I went to Boys Town. There wasn't any action there," he laughed. "I was surrounded by priests. And later when Sam and I started to train, I was just too exhausted to think about females, the fights left me worn out. Women just didn't seem important. There was this girl in acting class at Gladys Marlow's I kinda liked. We did a few scenes together, had a few beers, one thing led to another, and then can you beat it?—she wanted to get married! Married! Here I was working in a bar, trying to make it as an actor, and this loonie gets laid a few times and wants to get hitched! I tried to explain the situation. You would have thought she'd understand. I liked her, I really did. I didn't want to hurt her, and it was interfering with class. Well, one night she got drunk and took an overdose of pills." Nick patted Georgia's hand. "Don't worry, she recovered—but I didn't. I never felt so guilty in my life."

"God! No wonder you're woman shy," said Georgia.

Now she understood everything, and breathed a sigh of relief. "With me you feel comfortable, right? Like no pressure?"

"Right, Georgia, that was what I was about to say. With you I feel comfortable, but at the same time I want you. Don't think I don't, Georgia, because I do!"

Three days later, Nick arrived at Georgia's

apartment early. She'd been in the shower, and answered the door in her maribou negligee. It had just been handy, she hadn't planned it that way.

Nick had been to a cocktail party at his agent's, and he was high. He took off his jacket and stood staring at her.

"Georgia, come here?" She walked toward him without a word, and he took her in his arms. The negligee fell in folds at her feet, and they clung together, kissing, allowing all the pent-up passion to swell. She felt the kisses right down to her toes. And then Nick led her naked to the bedroom.

Georgia remained silent while Nick undressed slowly. She watched until he finally stood naked before her, that young, hard muscular body—a young Adonis. She drew in her breath as he slipped into the bed beside her, and took her in his arms. She felt his nakedness for the first time, the warm smooth skin, the tiny scars from the ring, the dark curls at the base of his neck. There were voluptuous kisses that warmed her very soul —tenderness combined with that marvelous positive strength. He was in command.

They drifted on a cloud of passion. So easy, so beautiful, his hands touched every part of her. His mouth found her breasts, her lips, her thighs, savoring her, drinking her up. At times they paused, content to lie in one another's arms, reveling in the new found dimension of their affection.

"Oh, Georgia—" Nick's voice was hoarse. "I never knew it could be like this!"

"Neither did I," said Georgia and covered his lips with her own mouth.

Friday morning. Georgia awakened in Nick's arms. The two had been lovers for weeks now, and Nick spent most of his time in her apartment. She lay on her side with his body fitted to hers, his arms around her as if shielding her from the world. She lay there enjoying the warmth of the moment and the delicious scent of his aftershave lotion on the satin pillows.

Now she felt him nuzzle her neck. His voice was sleepy, soft. "You awake? I could hold you like this forever."

Georgia smiled and stirred in his arms. "Oh, Nick, it's so good to wake up with you . . . so good. I used to have such nightmares, but no more." She moved out of his arms and turned on her back. Her long hair spilled over the pillow, and her face, devoid of make-up, was scrubbed clean. She smelled of Yardley soap and a delicious bath powder from Paris.

Nick raised on one elbow and looked down at her. "Good morning, baby. It's good to wake up with you, too. I'm becoming accustomed to the sight, and I've got to admit I love it." He kissed her cheek gently, then teased the satin tie of her nightgown. It opened and revealed her naked breasts. She lay there and watched him admire her, enjoying the look of desire in his soft brown eyes.

She had lovely full breasts, and she was proud of them. Her nipples stood out as if begging to be kissed. He lowered his head and gently sucked the nipple of each breast, then fondled her as if he were touching a rare treasure. "Georgia, you're so lovely all over, like a rare painting."

He continued to fondle her, then ran his hand slowly under her gauzy nightdress up her smooth thigh and between her legs. She was moist, and his fingers massaged her with a light touch. At the same time he kissed her lips until she felt her body begin to fire. In seconds she was naked, her gown on the floor in a heap. Nick was on top of her, kissing her mouth, entering her secret places, knowing she wanted to be taken. Now, at this moment . . . to enjoy the passion . . . the pleasure . . . the release. Quickly this time . . . quickly so that afterwards they could lie in one another's arms and feel the love run between them like an invisible cord, and become hungry for food, thirsty for juice, for hot coffee, secure in the safe knowledge that they had found one another. That today would be like yesterday—one of beauty, love, passion and discovery.

Saturday afternoon was the big day. Louis

Gerfinski's party was to be held at an enormous Italian restaurant in Brooklyn Heights called Venturi's.

Georgia was particularly looking forward to the event because she and Nick rarely went out socially any more. Rather, they spent quiet evenings at home or dined at little intimate bistros in the neighborhood, content just to be together savoring their newly found happiness.

An added bonus was the news that a major network had picked up the TV series, and so Nick would be returning to the Coast to resume filming almost immediately. All in all, today was a special one, and Georgia dressed carefully. She chose a pale beige linen dress by Norell that was stunning and timeless. Her shoes were by Maude Frizon and her little bag was from Gucci.

Nick wore a blue blazer, white slacks, and Gucci loafers.

The party was not informal, but it was also not black tie. Georgia imagined there would be throngs of people present, mostly Italians, Greeks, and a few of "the boys" as Nick so aptly put it. He appeared to take his best friend, Lucky's, affiliation with the underworld in stride, and so did she. After all, it was part of life and frankly she was curious, especially about Lucky and Louis Gerfinski.

Nick had regaled her with stories about the two men and all the intrigue connected with their business. She was fascinated but knew in her soul of souls that it was dead wrong; however, more than anything else on earth, Georgia Bonner admired strong, positive men, the kind who could make decisions without a backward glance and without fear of censure. She respected a man who could go out and chop down trees, fight the elements, but most of all—protect the woman he loved. A man who let nothing or no one stand in his way. She felt Louis Gerfinski was such a man, despite his tainted reputation, and she looked forward to meeting him.

Nick had hired a limousine, and at five o'clock they arrived at the large restaurant that was fortunately equipped with its own parking lot. It was filled to capacity with sleek black limousines and Cadillac sedans, some with initialled license plates. Also, there were a few FBI agents parked discreetly down the block. Nick pointed them out as they were assisted from their car.

"The Feds are here. They always are when the families, or what they think are the families, get together. They just try to take license numbers, blend in, and really accomplish very little except annoy the guests."

Georgia stood staring in fascination when a reporter touched her shoulder. She turned; a flash bulb exploded in her face.

"Georgia Bonner and Nick Culletti! What are you two doing here? Isn't this a little out of your league?"

Nick took Georgia's arm and pushed past the journalist. "It's a party! What the hell do you think we're doing here?"

The man snapped back. "Better watch it, Nick. You're not a big star yet . . . better watch your mouth . . . better watch your associates. Don't forget the Moral Majority boys." With that he turned and disappeared into the throngs of people that were just arriving. The sound of music and the delicious aroma of cooking tickled the senses.

Suddenly Lucky appeared in the doorway entrance and clasped Nick in his arms. "Nick! Nick, my man! Welcome. And this must be Georgia." He grasped her hands as Nick introduced them.

"Right you are, Lucky." Nick smiled proudly. "This is my Gorgeous Georgia. Say hello to Lucky DiSantos. You've heard me talk your ears off about him."

Georgia pressed his hands. "Lucky, I'm so glad to meet you at long last. I was beginning to think you were a figment of Nick's imagination. I'll never forget the story about the pants you made him out of a tablecloth when you two were in the home. He loves you like a brother."

Lucky smiled and snaked them all through little knots of people who were sipping champagne, or red wine, eating hors d'oeuvres and awaiting the delicious supper being prepared by some of the most celebrated chefs in New York. Music was loud, and in another room there was dancing. Georgia spotted two Congressmen and a State Senator. She found herself very warm from the crowds. This was not the intimate gathering she had anticipated. Where was Louis, or Mr. G? She could hardly wait!

Lucky led Georgia and Nick through a hallway to an adjacent room that appeared to be the inner sanctum. Juju, Sing Jo, and the two other men, along with the heavyset Braskets, milled about a small bar in the corner attempting to be inconspicuous but not succeeding. A uniformed waiter immediately asked Georgia, Nick and Lucky what they were drinking.

"White wine for me," answered Georgia, glancing around the room. The first thing she noticed was all the flowers. They were everywhere and arranged to perfection in marvelous crystal vases. Someone here was a nature lover.

Other than Georgia, there were no women present in the room except for one exquisite girl who stood hesitantly in the doorway. Lucky motioned to her, and she slithered across the room, attired in a glamorous pantsuit of pale blue with tiny insets of seed pearls. Fresh gardenias were entwined in her jet black hair giving her an exotic, yet madonna-like, appearance. She smiled and held out tiny dark hands. Georgia noticed a magnificent emerald the size of a goose egg on one finger. "Hi, I'm Francie."

"This is Georgia Bonner, and my oldest and dearest friend, Nick Culletti," announced Lucky, not bothering to give Francie's surname.

Everyone smiled, and drinks were passed. The four stood in a little cluster and seemed hesitant about approaching Louis, who sat like a reigning potentate in the far corner of the room.

He's like a star, thought Georgia, with a certain respect. He sits cloistered here while the hoi-poloi dance and make merry in the other rooms. When the timing is right, when he's good and ready, and at just the right moment, he'll make his entrance. Timing! She smiled to herself, liking the old gangster all the more.

"Come on, I want you to meet Mr. Gerfinski," said Lucky as if reading her mind. Nick and Georgia followed him across the room in the direction of the syndicate boss.

Louis looked up from a goblet containing his favorite champagne. "Well, hello there, Lucky. I see you brought your friend, Nick, like I asked, and his beautiful lady." He smiled at Georgia. "Come a bit closer. Unfortunately, my bad eye is giving me a problem today. That's always the way, just when you want to feel your best, the ravages of age—or in this case an old accident—come and spoil it for you."

Lucky introduced his two friends while

Louis took Georgia's hands and looked into her eyes. She felt a strange shiver run up her spine. "Haven't I seen you someplace before, my dear? Sounds like a line from one of those old movies, but it's true. You look so very familiar." He paused. "And your name . . . Georgia . . . how lovely!"

"I'm an actress, Mr. Gerfinski." She hesitated, suddenly intimidated. "Soap operas. I doubt you watch them."

Nick interrupted. "Mr. Gerfinski, Georgia is too modest. She's been a very successful actress as well as the former wife of the Governor of Arkansas, Victor Sandborne. Her pictures have appeared in the society columns as well as the entertainment sections."

"Well, no matter," answered Louis. "You're a lovely young woman. And you, Nick, I thought Lucky was hiding you from me. I've heard so much about when you were boys together. You were like a kid brother to him. He's proud of your success. I've always wanted to meet you, and now I have." He took Nick's hand and shook it, but his eyes never left Georgia's face for a second. He spoke to those around him, but it was obvious his interest had quickened at the sight of the blonde.

"Sorry I'm behaving like an old cripple, but I'm not coming out to greet the other guests for a while yet. You all go now. Eat, drink, have some fun. I, for one, want to forget it's my birthday." He smiled and then it was obvious that the king had dismissed his subjects by royal command. It was as if they were no longer visible in front of him.

As they turned away from the white haired man, murmuring their goodbyes, and followed Lucky out of the room, Georgia spied a State Senator along with a Councilman and a well known lawyer on their way to the throne. She smiled to herself and decided she liked Louis Gerfinski, no matter what his profession. She knew little about organized crime other than what she heard or read, but if Louis was an example, she found it hard to believe it was all as vicious as it was sometimes depicted in the movies or on television.

She took Nick's arm and smiled at him, feeling a little thrill. Sometimes she woke up in the middle of the night and hugged herself with joy just remembering they were together in that special way. Despite his youth, Georgia felt deeply secure with Nick in ways that she'd never felt before—not even with Victor. Nick was strong, virile, and tough as oak. His dreadful childhood had instilled in him a deep sensitivity and integrity she'd found in few men. Despite the specter of Jake Pierce, for the first time in years, Georgia Bonner was truly happy. How she cherished these moments.

She touched Nick's arm. "I liked him . . . the old man. He's really quite beautiful . . .

like a Norse God. Or should I say Polish. Whoever heard of a Polish Godfather?"

Nick laughed. "Right! He's a tough old buzzard. There's all sorts of stories circulated about him." He glanced at Lucky. "Didn't he have a wife and child once that were murdered or kidnapped?"

Lucky's face took on a grim look. "That's an old rumor. Mr. G. has no family that I know of. Francie has been his mistress for years. He's a very private person. How about some drinks and food? Anybody here you want to meet? Has the press been a bother?" It was obvious the subject of Louis Gerfinski's private life was a closed issue.

Suddenly Lucky glanced around the room towards the door, a peculiar look clouding his features.

Juju appeared and whispered something in his ear. He nodded to the bodyguard and lit a cigarette.

"What is it?" inquired Nick. "Anything wrong?"

"Not really. Just an uninvited guest. I'll take care of it. No problem."

Georgia looked up and grasped Nick's arm for support, for there poised in the doorway like a tiny queen stood Kiki Blake Sandborne. She paused for a moment smiling that beguiling little girl smile, then spotted Lucky, Georgia and Nick, and moved gracefully in their direction. Everyone seemed in suspended animation, and then there she was, near enough to touch, her large breasts jutting through the chiffon dress; the fragrance of some fantastic perfume tickling their nostrils.

All Georgia could think of what that she was, indeed, like a small bitch in heat. She gave out that scent. Georgia had seen Kiki only once in person at Victor's funeral, and then only for a few moments. What on earth was she doing here at Louis Gerfinski's party?

Lucky was the first to speak. "Kiki Sandborne, this is Georgia Bonner and Nick Culletti. I really didn't expect you here today, Kiki. You told me you and Nino were going to Southampton." His voice was controlled, but Georgia sensed concealed fury.

Kiki continued to smile that odd smile and answered. "Changed my mind. Paris was boring. Southampton is even more so, and you know how much I crave excitement. I figured there'd be more action here."

She glanced at Georgia. "Looks like I was right. Georgia, dear, you seemed to have replaced Victor with a much younger, better looking edition. If he's rich too, then you've really got it made."

Georgia didn't reply but turned to Lucky. "Excuse me, but I must find the ladies' room. Where is it, please."

"I'll direct you," answered Lucky, anxious to end the bizarre meeting. He led Georgia away, leaving Kiki and Nick standing together.

"My God, Lucky! How on earth do you know Kiki? There's bad blood between us; she's the last person on earth I expected to see here today."

Lucky faced her. "I'm sorry. I had no idea she would show up. I've known her a long time. I mean, we go back years. I knew all about Victor Sandborne. Now I get the connection. Nick always referred to you as Georgia Bonner. What a coincidence. Look, don't worry; I'll get her out of here as soon as possible. She can be like a coral snake—beautiful but deadly, and always where you least expect to find her."

Georgia studied Lucky's face and realized there was more to the story. "Don't concern yourself with it, Lucky. I'm certain Nick can handle her. Anyway, we can't stay much longer. Nick leaves for the Coast soon, and we want to be together as much as possible. I don't really have to go to the john. It was just a ruse to get myself together." She paused. "Now, I'm okay. I'll just sit over here and you can send Nick to me. Thanks again. I'm so glad I got to meet you and Mr. Gerfinski. I like you both."

"The feeling's mutual, Georgia. Just sorry this had to happen." He led her to a table in the corner then, grim faced, headed in the direction of Kiki who was striving to work her feminine magic on a disinterested Nick.

275

"I just couldn't believe it when she came marching in the door! I thought it was some kind of bad dream."

An hour later, Georgia and Nick were relaxing over nightcaps in the living room of her apartment. Nick shook his head. "I can't understand how ol' Lucky got mixed up with that little number. It's a small world. Did you know your arch enemy used to work in a massage parlour?"

"I knew she was a few steps above the scarlet woman when she met Victor," said Georgia. "That's why I didn't take her seriously. You know, the original Holly Harlot. But you know me, I never judge anyone; I'm in no position to and wouldn't if I were. It's just that I think she had a hand in keeping me away from Victor before he died. She was like a guard at that hospital. I resent that among other things, but let's forget it. It's old news and nothing we can do a thing about. Right now I'm concerned with your departure. God! I'm going to miss you."

Nick pulled Georgia into his arms. "Me, too. I mean, I'll miss the hell out of you, but there's no reason you can't fly out on a weekend or when I get a break, I can get on in. I won't be shooting all the time."

"I know, darling. But this is a real break for you, and I don't want you worrying about me. I mean, I don't want to interfere. Anyway, I've got to get busy, get some kind of work. Margo informed me last week that Vera Best may want me back for another few weeks of 'Angels in White.' "

Nick interrupted. "Georgia, I know you want to keep busy, but there's one thing you've got to understand." He looked into her eyes with that straightforward gaze that told you he meant what he said. "I love you. I may not be a millionaire like your first husband, but I'm gonna make it big. I know it, baby. And when I do, you'll be right there beside me, understand? After all these years I've found the one woman who really means something in my life, and I don't intend to let her go. So, just relax; this deal isn't going to take forever. Ernie called yeterday, and I'm scheduled for another commercial in Sep-temper, so, you see, money is no object."

Georgia felt her eyes mist. "Oh, Nick. You're something else. That little speech means more to me than a diamond tiara or a million in cash. I love you; I really love you so. God, I'm going to miss you."

"I'm not gone yet, darling." With that, Nick picked up Georgia and carried her into the bedroom.

CHAPTER FOURTEEN

ONE WEEK after Nick's departure, the calls began. They came at all hours of the night; three, four o'clock in the morning. Heavy breathing; sometimes music; the sound of ice against glass; then silence or a disturbing chuckle; leaving Georgia lying there alone in the dark . . . frightened and worried. Perhaps it was just a phone freak. She hated cutting off the instrument because Nick called from the Coast at peculiar hours due to the time difference. Maybe it was a wrong number . . . or some kid playing games. And then one Sunday night while she was undressing for bed, the phone jingled. She picked up the receiver, and this time a voice . . .

"Well, hello Yellow Hair. Just checking on you now that your Guinea boyfriend has taken a powder." He paused. "Just checking to see that you're all nice and safe in your bed . . . see you." And then a click.

Georgia lay awake half the night, and when Nick called the following morning, she hesitated to tell him. Anyway, if Jake should really give her trouble, there was always the police.

Saturday, Georgia was invited to Teddy's for cocktails and dinner. She walked in the door, hugged Teddy, and realized he was in a bad humor.

"God, Georgia, Billy's sat it again. Just when I thought he'd come to his senses, he ups and pulls one of his capers. He cancelled out tonight a couple of minutes ago, and I'd like to belt him one."

Georgia lit a cigarette. "I understand how you feel. It seems with you and me life never runs smoothly."

She sat down in her favorite chair and accepted the glass of wine Teddy offered her. "Did I tell you about Kiki Blake appearing like some evil genii at Mr. Gerfinski's party? Lucky seemed to know her quite well, but I was almost knocked off my pins in surprise."

Teddy stared open mouthed for a full second. "You've got to be kidding! Jesus! That dame gets around like a dirty penny. Now that you mention 'la Kiki', guess this is as good a time as any to tell you what the private investigator had to say. I would have told you before, but it sounded so crazy. I didn't want to add to your usual turmoil. It appears Billy has been spotted entering

Kiki's townhouse some nights and not leaving before the following day. Now what the hell is the lady running? First Victor, then Billy, and now Nick's friend, Lucky. I'll say this for her, she's got a lot of energy."

Georgia was astounded. "Lord, you're right. She must have a golden pussy, but Billy wouldn't be interested in that unless his sex preference has undergone a radical change. Maybe she's a transsexual."

Teddy laughed and went to fetch Georgia another drink. "Right. At least you haven't lost your sense of humor. How's everything otherwise? How's that divine Nick? There was an item in Liz Smith yesterday. I thought you probably saw it. He's really making it big on the Coast. They're comparing him to Pacino, Estrada, and Stallone . . . not bad company."

"Yes, I read it," said Georgia thoughtfully. "God, I miss him, but he'll be coming home in about two more weeks. I thought I'd like to throw a little welcome home party. What do you think? I mean, you, Margo, Ernie Black, Sam, maybe even that little prick, Marty Saks. Nick is scheduled as a guest on his show the end of next month. What do you think?"

"Sounds good to me. Maybe even invite Kiki Blake and Jake Pierce. Those two pirhanas could devour each other." He smiled. "No, seriously, I think it's a divine idea. Speaking of the devil, how's the hot Hiawatha? Any trouble?"

Georgia paused. "Well, a couple of annoying calls, but other than that, nothing. I mean, so far he's been keeping away from the apartment since Nick gave him that beating. No more unexpected visits." She glanced at her watch. "When is Margo due? I'm starving to death."

At that precise moment the buzzer rang and Teddy went to answer. "What timing. It's Margo for sure. Incidentally, I've got a few makeup samples for you both, so don't let me get drunk and forget."

"Don't worry, I won't," answered Georgia. "I'm fresh out of that golden ivory base you whipped up for me, and I can't bear anything else."

Margo sailed into the room, greeted Georgia and Teddy, then flopped into the nearest chair. "I'm exhausted, simply worn to a frazzle trying to deal with everyone's personal problems. You'd think I was Dear Abby the way things are going. I've had Lew Kaylor's wife on the phone for two hours. He's flown off to Bermuda with the new kid model, Teeny Barr. Would you believe I know the brat's father, and at the risk of dating myself, I even knew her grandfather. Quite a dynasty there."

Margo accepted a drink from Teddy, apparently in a mood of nostalgia. "Now there was a real man! Tennis pro, and the glamour stud of his day. I was just a kid, but I can remember how the females fluttered around him like a bunch of crazed butterflies. The son seems to be following in the old man's footsteps. He's been married three times since Teeny's mother, and now I hear he's in hot pursuit of an Italian princess. The kid comes by her magic appeal naturally, but that doesn't help the wronged wife. What can I say to her? 'Mrs. Kaylor, dear, your husband has fallen under the spell of an irresistible tramp who comes from a long line of heartbreakers; so there, go cry in your beer.' "

Georgia interrupted. "God, Margo, I know how it feels to be on the other end of the stick. I wish someone had given me some good advice. It's a hell of a spot to be in, I can tell you. You're one of the few people I know who has a great marriage with no sex goddesses looming on the horizon."

Margo smiled. "You're right. That is, for the moment. I don't want to feel too smug and secure; but so far my turf is sacred ground. If I ever lost John, or if he ever cheated on me and I found out . . . Lord, I'd be devastated. So far, guess I'm one of the lucky ones."

Teddy disappeared into the kitchen and then reappeared, clutching a large casserole dish in his hands. "Get ready, girls. First course coming up."

* * *

Later that night Georgia lay in her enormous bed pretending Nick was beside her. She was just drifting off to sleep with radio talk show host Dick King's voice droaning softly in her ear, when the phone rang. She answered it sleepily, thinking it might be Nick.

A silence at the other end. "Who is it, please?" Still no answer, and she was ready to hang up the receiver when she heard the chuckle. It was a low, evil sound, and then the phone went dead.

Georgia lay for long moments, her heart beating like a wild bird in her breast. She glanced at the time on her little digital clock. The red lighted numbers pointed to four o'clock. She reached over and slipped the switch that turned off the phone. She lay there staring at the dark ceiling; a cold fear around her heart. She'd think about something nice . . . something pleasant . . . like the party . . . something fabulous . . .like Nick coming home.

The welcome home party for Nick, which had begun as an intimate little gathering, was fast escalating into a full blown celebration. Georgia had invited more guests than she'd planned. Unfortunately, Lucky was out of town and unable to attend.

The apartment was bedecked with flowers. She'd spent a fortune at the florist and also hired Margo's favorite catering service to take care of the food and drink. A long bar was set up in the living room along with two efficient looking bartenders who Georgia spotted immediately as out-of-work actors. She raced around checking details and awaited Teddy's guitarist friend who had volunteered to provide a little background music. He hadn't arrived as yet, and Georgia went to the bedroom to check out her appearance once more. She wore a silver pantsuit spun from a fabric light as a feather and one that clung to her curves in just the right way. Her makeup was perfect, with cheeks naturally glowing from the excitement of the party and the anticipation of Nick's arrival. She stood in front of the mirror and smiled. Lipstick marred her two front teeth, and she quickly wiped it off with a Kleenex.

At that moment the buzzer rang, and after spritzing herself with Misuko, she dashed to answer the door. Somehow tonight nothing unpleasant could touch her. Now all that mattered was Nick.

Georgia opened the door to her neighbor, a retired four-star general, who was handsome and charming. He'd been a widower for years, and Georgia was hard put to understand why some glamour girl hadn't hooked him.

"Felix! Come in . . . come in. What are you drinking? You're the first to arrive, and I'm delighted to see you."

"Scotch on the rocks, please, Georgia. Thanks. Everything looks lovely."

Georgia motioned to the bartender, whose name was Jim, and gave him Felix' drink order along with her own.

She had no sooner settled herself across from the general when the phone rang. She went to answer. "Oh, no! You're kidding . . . well, what time do you think? Oh angel, what a bore for you. Don't worry, whatever time, even if the party is over, I'll be here. No, of course I understand. How could you have known? Are you certain the plane is safe? What? What? Oh, great . . . hurry . . . hurry."

Georgia hung up the receiver and walked toward Felix, a perplexed look on her face. "Do you believe it? That was Nick. He hasn't left L.A. yet. Something went wrong with the plane; they were delayed. Shit. He was due here in an hour from now."

She sank down in a chair and took a sip of wine. "He was phoning from the airport, and the flight was called while he was talking to me."

The general glanced at his watch. "That means he won't be here for several hours yet, and of course, there is the time difference. Well, don't worry, the party could go on till dawn."

Georgia attempted to smile, but she was disappointed. The door bell rang and Felix volunteered to answer. It was Margo, John and Teddy, their faces bright and happy. Teddy was the first to note Georgia's expression.

"What's wrong? You look like the sky just fell in on you."

"Nick just called from the Coast. The flight hasn't even taken off, so you can imagine what time he'll make it here. Oh, hell . . . the best laid plans of mice and men . . ."

"What a shame," injected Margo, putting her arms around Georgia. "But not to worry. We'll keep the party going, that's all. No one has to work tomorrow. This little shindig could go on till Sunday. Come on, sweetie, give me a nice cold drink. It's hotter than blazes outside."

Margo glanced around the apartment. "Everything looks glorious. And you, darling, I've never seen you looking better." She turned to the general. "Hello, Felix. How nice to see you. Haven't seen you since the night we ran into you at the theatre."

John, who despised parties of any sort, was delighted to see the general. They had a lot in common, as John was a retired colonel. He and Felix settled into a conversation when once more the buzzer rang its shrill, annoying blast. Everyone jumped.

Georgia went to the intercom. "Hi, Lee. Look, dear, as you know, I'm having a little party, so don't bother to announce or buzz. Just send the guests up as they arrive. You know, direct them and all, but no need to ring. It'll drive you and everyone else insane."

She went to answer the door and ushered

in Teddy's guitarist friend, Chick, as well as several other people whose names she momentarily forgot. Teddy appeared at her side, helping with the introductions. Five minutes later Marty Saks arrived, accompanied by a glorious brunette at least six feet tall and wearing a dress that looked as if it had been ordered from Frederick's of Hollywood.

The bartenders passed out drinks and a maid provided by the catering service wafted about with a tray of hors d'oeuvres. Georgia explained the Nick dilemma, and suddenly Chick strapped on his guitar and began a mournful Mexican love song. Next, he lapsed into a country and western tune, his voice raised high along with several guests who joined in the song fest. By this time the room was filling up with people, and Georgia was kept busy rushing back and forth, ushering them inside.

Her apartment suddenly seemed very small indeed, but as the evening progressed, everyone appeared to be having a great time. Georgia had instructed the maid not to set out the buffet until a bit later, meanwhile drinks were disappearing like magic and an air of joviality prevailed signaling the party was a success.

Georgia fingered the little silver amulet around her neck and smiled. God, she really was superstitious. Old habits were slow in dying. She hadn't worn the good luck charm in ages, but suddenly tonight she'd carted it out of the drawer and on impulse fastened it around her neck. Anyway, it looked nice with her silver ensemble. She noted the room was becoming uncomfortably warm, despite the air conditioning, and John propped open the front door as more guests arrived.

Lita Lang and several other actors from "Angels in White" sailed into the room, obviously high on something other than alcohol.

"Georgia, what a lovely flat. I adore it. I despise my little den in the village, but who can afford these East Side prices! Don't bother to introduce us, we'll circulate. I see Marty 'whips-and-chains' Saks is here. Mind if I make my pitch? I'd dearly love to do a guest show now that he's gone national. Nasty little pervert." And then Lita marched across the room towards the talk show host who was holding court and drinking a plain ginger ale.

Georgia was left standing in the center of the room wondering about Lita's remarks. God, she'd never forget her own guest shot on Marty's show. That was the terrible night she'd first encountered Jake Pierce—Jake Bella-Coola—or whatever his name was.

She glanced at her watch; Nick should be landing in another couple of hours, providing there was no more trouble. She peered around the room and decided with satisfaction that everyone was occupied and seemingly enjoying themselves. Voices raised in song along with loud music and frenzied conversation caused a terrible din, and Georgia hoped there would be no noise complaints. Chick sat on the floor with an adoring group at his feet, and the more drinks consumed, the better everyone imagined their voices became.

Georgia realized that though air conditioners were going full blast, the extra body heat in the room diminished their efficiency. It was becoming just plain hot. She opened her bedroom window, then flung back the enormous studio windows in the living room. The air outside seemed much cooler. At least it wasn't so stuffy, thought Georgia, spotting Billy Bright weaving through the front door. She threaded her way towards Teddy's friend and took his hand.

At that very same moment the elevator outside stopped. The door opened silently, than closed. She turned to speak to Billy who appeared to be quite drunk when suddenly a hand touched her shoulder. It was a firm touch, not rough, but positive, and even before she turned around, she smelled the Patchouli.

It was Jake Pierce, along with two other men. She recognized them immediately and for one brief instant controlled the urge to scream. Instead, she remained cool. The wine she'd consumed helped, of course.

"Hello, Jake. May I ask what you're doing

here?" She kept her voice low so the others wouldn't hear.

Why, oh why, had she instructed Lee to simply let everyone just come up? Obviously they'd slipped by in the crowds.

Jake smiled. "Hello, sweetheart. You remember the boys here. They certainly remember you."

The two men chuckled. "Hi, Georgia. Nice pad you got here. Just thought we'd drop by. You know, join the Upper East Side fancy crowd. Add a little color."

"Maybe even a little spice and excitement," laughed Jake. "I see you have a room full of celebs, but can't imagine why you'd want to leave out a few ol' pals like us. Guess you just forgot. I see Lita Lang over there, my favorite soap opera slut."

She turned to Jake. "Excuse me, but I have other guests. The buffet will be out soon. Mingle. Have some wine."

Georgia congratulated herself on her control, then went to greet her doctor and his wife.

The party was becoming noisy. Someone had turned up the stereo when Chick wasn't playing the guitar, and people were laughing, dancing, and singing in an almost hysterical frenzy. If Georgia hadn't known better, she'd have sworn Jake spiked the drinks with drugs. Five minutes later, Lee rang from downstairs to inform her that there were complaints.

Georgia stood in the center of the room and attempted to make herself heard over the din. "Let's keep it down to a howl, folks. There's been some complaints. Face it; some folks want to sleep."

Jake moved near Georgia. "Look, I've got to talk to you. Please, it's important! I knew you wouldn't answer my calls, so I took a chance. I found out about the party—"

Georgia lowered her voice to a whisper. "I've got nothing to say to you. Just finish your drink, and get yourself and your neanderthal friends out of here."

"I understand how you feel, kid, really I do, but just let me have my say. Even a condemned man gets a few last words."

He guided her near the window where it was less crowded. "What happened at the wedding was rotten. I admit it. It was all my fault." He paused, gauging Georgia's reaction. Her face remained set.

"Once I thought I was in love with Vela, and when she married Lemo, I guess I just wanted you there with me to show off. At least that's what I thought. Then the booze and stuff got to me, took over, and we all got carried away. I never meant to hurt you." His voice became taut. "And if you're honest, you'll admit you enjoyed it just a little, not having to blame yourself for all that uninhibited sex. It was a trip! Don't lay *all* the blame on me. Anyway, I'm sorry. I'll make it up somehow."

Georgia's voice was tight, controlled. "I'm not interested in your excuses, just please go! You're bad news, and it's finished. It never should have started in the first place, and it wouldn't have if I'd been in my right mind."

Jake tightened his grip on her shoulder. "Look, Miss Proud Princess. I'm not the actor, or any of the other soft, rich men you've known. I'm a hustler and a lot of other lousy things I'm not too proud of; but one thing I'm honest about—I love you. I'd go through fire for you. I've never said it before, but I mean it. I'd do anything to make you forget what happened, anything to have it like that time at Christmas . . . just you and me together . . . like real friends—"

Georgia, stunned at Jake's unexpected protestations of love, felt momentary confusion. She stood there unable to think of what to say.

And then suddenly, without a word or warning, Jake turned away from Georgia and with an incredible act of athletic prowess, with the grace of a deer bolting from its pursuer, he somehow leaped to the inside window ledge. He stood there like a giant bird and faced the room.

It all happened so fast. Conversation came to a quivering halt as all eyes focused on the strange figure that now commanded their attention. A glass fell and broke, someone coughed, then not a sound as Jake spoke, his voice clear and resonant. "See those bridges out there?" One arm swept towards the river and the open window. "Well, I help build 'em. Me and thousands like me. We didn't get our names in the society pages, but we had pride. I'm still a climber, and I'm gonna prove it. Right now I'm steppin' outside this window ten floors up." He paused. "Hell, that's nothin' to what I was used to, but I'm gonna walk that outside ledge across to the bedroom window. I'm gonna do it to prove something to a lady. A penance of sorts."

He stared straight at Georgia as an audible sigh of shock rippled through the room. "If I make it, fine. If I don't, hell, nobody lives forever." He stood immobile for a second more, then parted the drapes and stepped out onto the five-inch window ledge.

Everyone seemed hypnotized, incapable of movement, Georgia felt herself sway. "No, Jake. No! I forgive . . . I forgive—"

But he hadn't heard. He was outside now, the warm breeze playing with his hair. The moon was big and red. Someone called the cops. He was barely conscious of the crowds forming down below. A light from a police car splayed across the building. And once more Jake Pierce felt like a star. Like a performer—a tightrope walker. He smiled to himself. Faces pressed against the window. He edged along, feeling his way against the rough surface of the building. Just a few more steps and he'd be safe inside the bedroom window, there'd be cheers. Georgia

would like that. They'd be even . . . debt paid
. . . one or two more steps. It was like the old
days. Suddenly his boot heel caught on loose
gravel. He tried to shake it free, lost his
balance, his mind went blank—and down,
down his body fell, hurtling through space
towards the blue and white canopy below.
The canopy broke his fall—but it split, and he
slid through the canvas to the cold hard sidewalk.

There was instant bedlam. Everyone
talking and screaming at once. John ran to
the phone and dialed the paramedics.
Georgia, Margo and Teddy headed for the
door, but a police officer, just arriving,
herded them all back inside the apartment.
"Stay right where you are. Don't go down
there. There's already a crowd on the street.
Sit down, all of you."

His partner, a short officer with a red face,
came striding into the apartment, his face
grim. "Just relax, everyone. We've got to ask
a few questions."

Other guests headed for the bar to soothe
their nerves, and Georgia was grateful some
had left early. The two officers questioned
Georgia. "This is your apartment, Miss
Bonner?"

Before she could utter a sound, John was at
her side. "I'm Miss Bonner's attorney, and if
you'll permit me, I'll answer all questions
until she can pull herself together. This has
been a terrible experience."

Georgia's face was stark white, and she'd begun to tremble. Margo handed her a glass half-filled with cognac. "Drink this, sweetie; sit down and drink this. John will take over."

At that propitious moment Nick came striding through the door, and Georgia rushed into his arms.

Later, John and Nick accompanied Georgia to the precinct to make a statement, and as they returned to the apartment at seven in the morning, a camera crew from one of the local stations lurked near the building.

"Was there a fight? Did anyone push him? What happened, Georgia? Must have been nuts, trying to fly or something. Was he on LSD? That makes you want to walk on air," announced the little clean-faced journalist from Channel 3.

Georgia leaned against Nick and John for support. "No. No, he fell. I mean, he jumped. No . . . what I mean is he was trying to show us how he could climb—" She paused, her face tear-stained. She fingered the amulet around her throat nervously. "I don't know why. Please . . . it was an accident. Look, we don't even know if he's alive or dead."

Nick and John led Georgia into the building, the cameras still grinding.

CHAPTER FIFTEEN

LOUIS GERFINSKI watched the five o'clock news as was his habit, and sipped his first drink of the day. Suddenly he leaned forward in the chair, his interest heightened. He strained toward the screen and tuned up the sound. It was Georgia Bonner and Nick . . . Lucky's friend, Nick. The girl was crying; they were questioning her about something. He couldn't get it all; it was too fast. And then, a close up of Georgia's tear-stained face on the screen in color.

Louis watched in fascination and spotted the silver chain around her throat. Attached to it, and catching the sunlight, was a tiny silver bell.

Louis drew in his breath and felt his nerves tighten in the way he'd almost forgotten. The way it used to be in the old days when he smelled danger—or when something was about to happen that he wasn't prepared for.

He downed his drink, then telephoned Lucky.

"Get over here immediately. But before you do anything else, check the newscast and get all the dope on what happened to your friend, Nick, and his girl friend. They were just on, and I want to know precisely what happened. Also, I want to know everything about Georgia Bonner Sandborne. Everything . . . do you hear?" His voice was raised to a high pitch. "Everything from the day she was born up until now. You have the sources; use them. I don't care how much it cost, but do it. And make it fast."

Puzzled, Lucky hung up the receiver and went to work. It would take time and money. That wasn't important. Main thing—results.

The quest to discover Georgia Bonner's past was not as difficult as Lucky had imagined. A great deal was chronicled in press clippings. Lucky had friends in the newspaper morgues of thirty states, so he was easily able to locate reams of publicity on her marriage to former Governor of Arkansas, Victor Sandborne. Then there was her divorce; her soap opera days; even column items with well known men and women . . . actors, writers, even a famous lawyer who'd successfully defended an heiress suspected of being a bank robber. She really got around, thought Lucky.

The past fifteen years were no problem, but then he ran into trouble. There were walls he had to climb, and so little time.

Louis was not a patient man. He traced her childhood back to a little town called Kernsville, Arkansas—so tiny it was barely on the map. Good God, thought Lucky, no wonder she ran away at seventeen. Or was it sixteen? His source couldn't be certain . . . only that her grandmother had raised her and then died, leaving the girl alone.

She spent her early years as a waitress in Texarkana, then a model in Dallas, and after that, New York.

There ws no record of a mother or father, only of her grandmother who Lucky found out was mulatto and earned money from telling fortunes and reading Tarot cards. What a history! She must have been pretty smart to have hooked a fish like Victor Sandborne. But if Kiki's tales about the man were true, it wasn't exactly the pot of gold at the end of the rainbow.

Lucky took the information he'd gathered and went immediately to Louis who listened with interest at the long, detailed report.

"I'll have to study it further, but first I must see the girl in person. Talk to her. It's important. Do you have her number? If not, get it from Nick."

"I've got it right here, Louis. Right here."

When the phone rang for the fifth time in two hours, Georgia thought it was the hospital again. Bulletins on Jake's condition had been coming in regularly for the past few days. He was still alive, but just barely. His back was broken, multiple fractures, concussions, internal bleeding, and he was still in Intensive Care. Doctors held out little hope. Ten floors was a long fall despite the canopy.

"Hello." Georgia's voice was tired. Nick sat in the arm chair near by. "Who?" A pause. "Oh, yes, of course I remember. Well, thank you, but I have a lawyer and of course there are no charges. Everyone was a witness that he did it himself. But thanks so much for the offer. Of course, I'm very upset. He was just an acquaintance, but it was a horrible thing."

Georgia, suddenly feeling guilty, reached for a cigarette. "Tomorrow? Well, I suppose I could if it's all that important. Certainly, I'll be ready. And thanks again, Mr. Gerfinski. Thanks again."

Georgia replaced the receiver and shot Nick a puzzled look. "That was, of all people, Louis Gerfinski. He wants to see me."

"I'll bet he does," answered Nick ruefully.

"No. No, nothing like that. He says it's important we talk. He was very mysterious. My God, Nick, I could write my own soap opera the way things have been going. What on earth do Louis Gerfinksi, a gangster, and I have in common? He's sending the car to pick me up at three tomorrow, and I'm to stay for cocktails and dinner."

Georgia walked toward Nick and sat in his lap, her arms entwined around his neck. "Oh, Nick, I'm so glad you're back. You can't imagine how it feels when you hold me close.

It's the only time . . . the very only time . . . I feel really safe."

The ride from Sixty-Eighth Street to Brooklyn Heights seemed interminable, and in the rear of the air conditioned limousine, Georgia smoked one cigarette after another. The chauffeur handled the long, black car expertly, and soon they reached their destination.

Georgia was ushered into a large study by Sing Jo. The Oriental's face was mask-like as he bowed her into Louis Gerfinski's presence. The white haired giant of a man stood near the window and turned as Georgia entered the room.

"My dear! I'm so glad you could come. I've cancelled an opening in Vegas so I could spend this time with you. What do you drink? I have a marvelous Dom Perignon I've been saving for just such a special occasion. Alright?"

Georgia sat in a large hand-carved oak chair and nodded. "That sounds lovely, thank you."

Sing Jo left the room to fetch the wine as Louis walked toward Georgia's chair and stood facing her. Again she marveled at the power exuding from his large frame. He possessed an intangible strength, and underneath it all Georgia suspected an untapped sweetness.

"I know you're curious as to why I summoned you here in such haste, my dear, but it's a long complicated story and one which I hesitate to tell you at this moment. However, there are some questions I hope you will not mind answering for me." He paused, lit a cigarette, and studied Georgia's face so closely that she felt a bit uncomfortable. "Please, have patience."

Georgia attempted a smile. "Please, please, feel free to ask what you like, and if I don't wish to answer, I'll just say so."

Their eyes met and held. She felt a little chill. The room suddenly seemed cold and drafty.

"Georgia, my dear, where did you get the silver amulet you were wearing on the news yesterday? The one with the little bell attached to a chain. I couldn't help noticing it. It struck my eye, so unusual. In Poland, when I was a boy, there was an old lady who dealt in amulets—charms for those who would pay." He smiled. His eyes never left her face as he awaited an answer, and she felt the tension in the man.

"The amulet? My little silver bell? My God, that's what you're interested in? My good luck charm? Why, Taia gave it to me when I was a tiny little girl. I've always had it. She said it would ward off evil spirits." She smiled, "You see, my grandmother was somewhat of a witch—a good witch, but a witch nonetheless. And, I always obeyed her while she was alive. After she died, I rarely wore it.

First, it's not very pretty, and I try not to be superstitious, though if the truth be known, I really am . . . if I obey my inner feelings. Why do you ask?"

"You say your grandmother's name was Taia? And where did you and your grandmother live, Georgia? I mean, other than Kernsville, Arkansas? Were you always there?"

Georgia looked up in surprise. "How did you know about Kernsville? It's not even on the map, I don't believe." She smiled. "A little spot in the road. I see you've done some research. Please, tell me why?"

Louis pulled a chair near Georgia and took her hands in his.

"Please don't be alarmed. I'll explain everything in time, but now I must know about the amulet. Where did Taia get it? I mean, did she sell them? Were there any more? Or was that the only one? Think! Think! This is important."

"Well," said Georgia, feeling a most peculiar emotion beginning to take over, "there was only the one as far as I know, and she took great stock in it. She was superstitious; read the Tarot cards, palms, little roots and herbs to make people well . . . things like that. Once she sat me beside the fireplace when I was a very little girl and told me the amulet belonged to my mother. But she told such crazy stories about my parents that it was difficult to separate fact from fiction. I never knew either of them and assumed they were dead. I was never really certain if Taia was my real grandmother. She was mulatto and, as you can see, I'm very, very fair."

At that propitious moment, Sing Jo arrived with the champagne along with crystal goblets and a silver tray of crackers and caviar. He poured the wine and presented Louis and Georgia each with a glass, then passed silently out of the room.

Louis' hand trembled as he raised the goblet in a toast. "To you, Georgia, to you and to this day which may turn out to be the happiest day in my entire life."

Georgia clinked her glass to his and wondered at this mystery. All that came to mind was the line from *Alice in Wonderland* . . . "things are getting curiouser and curiouser."

"Please, Louis, tell me about the charm. Is it some museum piece of something? Is it valuable?"

Louis smiled. "Only to you and to me, Georgia. I'm going to tell you a fantastic story, and I want you to listen and try to absorb it. When I'm finished, we'll both decide togther what to do next, but I already know the outcome. I can write the ending of this scenario; I feel it in these old bones. I felt it the first time I looked into your eyes. The first time I saw you with Nick at the party. I couldn't get you out of my mind somehow, and then the newscast, the amulet. It's got to be true. It's got to be."

Georgia rode back to her own apartment hours later in a complete daze. She barely remembered leaving Louis. They had finished the entire bottle of wine while he'd related the story of Scherise and the daughter who disappeared so many years ago. He assured her he'd investigate further now that he knew the town, now that he'd met her. He seemed obsessed with the idea that she, in fact, was his long lost daughter, Gina, kidnapped by his wife so many years ago.

God! Could it be really true? Truth was stranger than fiction, people were so fond of saying. Georgia had difficulty controlling her emotions. Louis Gerfinski, her father? Her mother . . . alive but struck with Alzeimer's disease and in a sanitarium all these years! The pieces fit. Scherise was part mulatto, her father a Norwegian sea captain.

But why had Taia never told her the truth? Perhaps because she had never really known it herself. Perhaps Scherise had simply left her with Taia when she was a baby, then wafted away in her alcoholism and half madness. Perhaps she had known and realized that the safest place would be with her grandmother, away from the dangers of Louis' violent life style.

Georgia simply could not digest it all and decided to put it out of her mind for the moment. It was too much all at once, along with all the other bizarre happenings of late.

She entered her own apartment and was met by Nick, who took her in his arms and murmured, "Take it easy, kid. Take it easy. The hospital just called. Jake Pierce will live, but he may never walk again—"

The following day, Georgia went to the hospital, but they informed her Jake was still in Intensive Care and couldn't receive visitors. She left a little bouquet of flowers, feeling strangely sad.

She certainly wasn't in love with Jake, never had been, in fact, but God! The way he'd fallen, trying to win her back. Somehow it touched her. For the moment she'd put the entire thing out of her mind, and in a few days she'd go to the hospital again. She couldn't just dismiss Jake. That would be impossible.

CHAPTER SIXTEEN

"Wake up, baby. Wake up. You're having a nightmare." Nick shook Georgia gently and took her in his arms. She trembled and cried softly.

"God, it was horrible—a bad dream. I'm so glad you're here." Her voice was fuzzy. "It was Jake—he was dragging me out the window. And Powder Puff—he dropped her first. Where is she? Where is she?"

"Right at the foot of the bed," soothed Nick. "She's fast asleep like she always is at four in the morning. Come on, lie back. I'll get you some milk."

Georgia sat upright. "No, darling, no milk. Just an aspirin." She took a cigarette from the little gold box beside the bed. "You know, he looked right into my eyes before he fell, like he was trying to tell me something. I can still see him standing there."

"Come on, Georgia. He was nuts, and

mean, too, I knew guys like him when I was in the home and Boys Town. They think the world owes them a living just because they've had a few bad breaks."

"I know, Nick. It's just everything . . . the last few weeks . . . Louis Gerfinski . . . I mean, is it possible he really is my father? Sometimes I think it's just an obsession and I'm the likeliest candidate. He plans to have people check out Kernsville, try to find anyone that remembers my grandmother. You know the town is only a spot in the road. Why do you think I escaped when I was only seventeen? I never even had a birth certificate or that would settle everything. Taia said it burned up in a fire. I had to go to Little Rock for an affidavit in order to get a Social Security card."

Nick patted her arm. "Come on, Georgiapeach. If you're going to worry about everything at four o'clock in the morning, then neither of us is going to sleep, and I've a couple of important appointments in the morning. Clear your mind and pretend you're milk slowly flowing from the bottle." He smiled. "It's a silly technique, but sometimes it works."

Georgia lay back in the darkness staring at the ceiling. So much had happened. The publicity resulting from Jake's accident in her apartment ironically had given her career a bizarre boost. Vera Best, instead of cancelling her out of "Angels in White," booked her for three more episodes. Louis called incessantly, asking her for lunches, dinners, sending flowers, gifts, almost like a lover rather than a father. And tomorrow, they were lunching together at a little Italian place on First Avenue and Sixty-First street—*El Vagabondo*.

The air was chilly the following day, and Georgia wore a grey cashmere suit, matching bag and shoes, with large dark sun glasses covering her eyes, swollen from lack of sleep.

Louis sat waiting in the long black limousine outside her apartment, delighted to see her as usual. "My dear, you look lovely. Each time I see you, you get prettier and prettier." He squeezed her hand, and Georgia settled in beside him.

The car windows were shut and completely bullet proof, like the rest of the entire car which cost an estimated fifty thousand dollars to construct. The little glass partition separating the driver from the passengers was tightly closed to secure the utmost privacy. Still Louis' voice held a note of conspiracy.

"Georgia, my dear, I've been thinking. I don't want to put you through anything unpleasant," he paused and lit a cigarette, "but what I've been thinking is that if you would agree to undergo hypnotherapy, perhaps the doctor could regress you back to the time of your childhood, and you might remember your mother. That's all we really need, dear, just a faint glimmer of Scherise when you were a baby . . . when she took you . . . if she left you with Taia immediately . . . where she went. Of course, I'm certain we'll never know it all exactly, but if you could just remember her—"

Georgia looked straight at Louis, her voice even. "Then why won't you let me go to the sanitarium and see her? That could mean a lot. Anyway, I want to see her. I don't understand why you keep refusing to let me go."

Louis mashed out his cigarette after only three drags. "My dear, I've told you. I don't want you to see her in the state she's in. It's too depressing. Alzheimers is a terrible thing. There are all stages . . . all degrees. I've grown accustomed to it, but for you it would be a trauma. Why should you be put through all that?"

"Because," said Georgia with some impatience," if she is my mother, I want to know her. No matter how ill she is. Anyway," she glanced down at slim hands folded in her lap, "if she is my mother, then I should know, because I've heard that Alzheimers is hereditary."

"Oh, Georgia, they don't know that for certain. Science is coming up with more and more research. Don't put that in your head. You have enough to worry about."

The sleek black car came to an abrupt halt, and Martin, Louis' new chauffeur, assisted the couple into the clear brightness of the September afternoon. Louis insisted on traveling about without Braskets or Sing Jo when he was with Georgia, a fact that caused Lucky extreme discomfort. While the New York families were relatively calm, and Louis was, in fact, in semi-retirement, still Lucky worried about the older man's safety.

Now Louis guided Georgia inside the cave-like restaurant that was popular with not only Italians, but all New York, it seemed. The captain snapped to attention at the sight of the couple.

"Right this way, Mr. Gerfinski. We have your favorite table waiting." He marched up the stairs leading the way, delighted to have so celebrated a guest. Somehow, Louis had emerged through the years under a veil of respectability with whispers and innuendo only enhancing his charisma.

Louis ordered a bottle of wine along with scampi and spaghetti carbonara. Georgia was hungry and ate the hard Italian rolls and drank the wine almost greedily. After her third glass she was more relaxed but still totally unprepared for Louis' next statement, delivered simply and without fanfare.

"Georgia, dear, I'm making arrangements to buy your apartment. I keep forgetting to discuss it with you. The papers are on my desk. In fact, in light of what has happened, if you'd rather move out and find another place without so many memories, we can do that, too."

Georgia swallowed a bite of scampi, almost choking with suprise. "Good lord! How wonderful! I mean, I didn't really know what to do about the entire thing. I have only a month left to make up my mind. But Louis, sixty thousand dollars—"

"Sixty . . . a hundred . . . it doesn't matter if it's what you want. I want you to be happy. Now, as to the hypnotherapy—" He had dispensed with one problem and raced to the next. "As to the hypnotherapy . . . I have a doctor who will treat you exclusively—a Doctor Algin. It won't take long. A few sessions." Louis ate his spaghetti hungrily and chatted on as if he were discussing the weather.

He was so calm, so certain of himself, thought Georgia with a little spasm of irritation. Louis always got what he wanted.

Ten o'clock Friday morning a slightly nervous Georgia entered Doctor Algin's office located in a building at the corner of Fifty-Ninth Street and Fifth Avenue. The waiting room was empty. Actually the doctor was taking Georgia as a favor to Louis, having cancelled a long awaited vacation in the Swiss Alps to do so.

The fiftish, grey-haired, white-coated man smiled and ushered Georgia to a large comfortable chair. It was near a window, and she sat back glancing out from time to time at Central Park and the stately Plaza Hotel looming up in the early morning sunlight. She felt herself relax at the tone of the doctor's voice. It was even, clear, and direct but soothing. His eyes were colorless, like a rainy day; but serene, as if he knew the answers to life and found them satisfactory. Georgia honestly wanted this to work. Anyway, it appealed to her sense of the unknown.

Questions . . . questions . . . questions and answers. She barely recognized the sound of her own voice. And there were time lapses. She felt tears on her cheek. God! She was crying. Why was she sad?

The doctor's voice . . . "What's wrong, Georgia? Why are you crying? Tell me what you are feeling. Just relax and talk."

She answered, her face in her hands, her voice like that of a child. "I'm a bad girl . . . bad girl. Wet my panties. Mommy's mad." She paused. "Those boys are mean. Don't go, Mommy. Don't go."

It went on and on. Sometimes she was aware of the office, the doctor. Other times she felt a sense of spacelessness, confusion as to her whereabouts . . . but always the droning voice of the doctor. It was almost like the first time she smoked pot, a sense of not being entirely in control.

After the first session was completed,

312

Georgia felt strangely refreshed, as if she'd been on a long vacation and gotten plenty of rest.

She was required to write down all her dreams and present them to the doctor, but this part was enjoyable as her dreams had always been vivid and memorable. Each morning she treated Nick to long dissertations on her latest nightmare. He listened patiently.

Two weeks elapsed, and Georgia felt they were getting nowhere. At times, the conversations with the doctor seemed normal enough. She didn't feel out of it, or asleep, or however you were supposed to feel under hypnosis; but when she tried to remember in detail what they'd discussed, it was difficult. The most disturbing part was the time element. Always she arrived at the office early, not to leave till late afternoon. However, it seemed she'd been with the doctor only a short time, a matter of a few minutes. Later she would go home and fall into a deep sleep, ignoring Nick who was concerned and disturbed.

"Georgia, we've got to talk. I don't like what's happening to you. I don't think all this therapy stuff is going to prove a thing. Look, I think Louis Gerfinski is a sick man. His profession . . . everything he's ever done . . . has been obsessive. Now that he's getting old, he wants an heir, something or someone to give him some kind of immortality. Don't you understand, Georgia? He's taking over your entire life! Telling you he doesn't want you to be burdened with work, that he'll take care of everything. Where have you heard that before?"

Nick paused for a breath. "Listen to me, Georgia. You're headed for trouble. I can smell it. Even if you are his daughter, it's too late. I mean, you're a woman, not a little girl." Nick took Georgia's hand in his. "I know how tempting it must be to think you've found out who you truly are after all these years. I know how you feel. I understand better than anyone. But darling, you're becoming consumed. You're as bad as he is. I barely see you anymore. And now this therapy shit—"

Nick stood up and walked to the closet. "Frankly, I'm worried. I'm worried about us. Anyway, the old bastard could get a blood test."

Georgia's voice was harsh. "Honestly, Nick! I believe you're actually jealous. Jealous of a man who may very well be my father. And as to blood tests, he says they're not accurate."

Nick slipped on a canvas jacket and headed for the door. "Maybe you're right, but I just think he wants to protect his precious illusion. They could, sure as hell, prove you *weren't* his daughter if the types didn't match. Beats me how a hard guy in the rackets all these years can go so soft on one subject. See you later." And then he walked out the door.

Georgia sat and stared after Nick. Maybe

he was right. She'd go along with the therapy a bit longer and convince Louis to take her to the sanitarium. She had to see Scherise for herself.

The phone rang, interrupting her thoughts. It was, of all people, Francie, her voice cool. "Georgia, I'd like to take you to lunch, if that's possible. We need to talk. It's important."

Curious, Georgia agreed to meet Louis' black mistress Saturday at *Dart's*. Now it was Francie. Everyone wanted something.

Francie was at the bar wearing a pantsuit by Bill Blass and sipping a chilled martini. Georgia joined her and after a quick drink they were ushered to a back booth. They faced one another across the table, two women with one man between them . . . both caring in different ways.

Francie was the first to speak. "Look, Georgia, I'm going to get right to the point. I have a strong feeling you're the kind of woman who will understand and not take what I'm about to say the wrong way. If I'm mistaken, then I've made a serious error, but here it goes. First, let me tell you that I'm deeply in love with Louis and have been for many years." She looked straight into Georgia's eyes without fear of censure. "He took me out of Harlem when I was a kid on the streets and gave me a life. I adore him despite the age difference. I know what people say, but they're wrong. I love the man and would if he were a plumber or a grease monkey. We've been through a lot together. I understand his motives and in your case, I'm afraid."

Georgia was startled. "God, Francie. You sound like Nick. Why on earth should you be afraid? I mean, if I am his daughter, it won't change things for you. After all, you're his mistress."

Francie interrupted. "No . . . no, Georgia, that's not what I mean. I'm not jealous. It's just that, well . . . it's all so far fetched. I mean, he kept everything under wraps for years and when last week he leveled with me about the trips to the sanitarium, everything . . . I was stunned. Of course I knew he was visiting someone. And then suddenly he's got this notion that you're Gina, the daughter he lost over thirty years ago. I mean, Georgia, the chances are so slim. The pieces fit to a degree, but in another way they don't. Why wouldn't your grandmother have leveled with you? And Georgia," Francie smiled and sipped her drink, "while I would be flattered to have you as a sister under the skin, so to speak, you don't look to me as if you've got a drop of black blood." She paused. "Of course, I'm no expert. Face it! I've got some Puerto Rican and French in me, so who am I to make judgments. But you're so damn white."

Georgia laughed. "Francie, you are funny.

316

You know I've never really had anyone to discuss that aspect of my life with. It's nice to talk about it. Odd, it only made me unhappy a few times . . . when they teased me as a kid because of Taia and, of course, Victor. But most of the time it made me feel different in a good way. Like I was more interesting—exotic, maybe. I don't know." She paused. "Until Victor and the baby, I never truly felt I was different in the wrong way. Understand?"

Francie took Georgia's hands in her own dark ones. "Of course I do. Who would understand better? My point is, I don't want Louis hurt at this stage in his life—or you. I don't want you hurt either. You know, you could be in danger." She lit a cigarette. "Five years ago there was an attempt made on my life." She smiled. "That's when things were livelier. It's calmed down a lot, especially on Louis' end. But what I'm trying to say, I guess, is that sometimes it's better to stay clear of this type of relationship. Once you're in, for whatever reason, you're in for keeps."

Georgia answered, "I understand what you're saying, and I can appreciate your concern; but on the other hand, it's important to me to know the truth. The amulet, Louis said Scherise wore one exactly like the one Taia gave me. Could there have been two? It's so unique."

"I don't know," answered Francie. "It's just I guess I wish you and Louis could forget

317

all this father-daughter business. I'm afraid it's going to end up badly, that's all. You're all grown up. I mean, a father at this stage of the game?" She sipped her drink. "Shit! Maybe I'm just jealous. I never had an old man. Maybe I'm just a jealous bitch. I don't know anymore. Anyway, I'm taking a chance talking to you like this. If Louis found out—"

"Don't worry. He'll never know, Francie. And I'll think about everything you've said. Really I will. Nick is upset too. He feels much the way you do. Meanwhile, let's be friends, please."

Francie smiled. "I'd love that, Georgia. I like you. You know now that I think about it, you do have some of Louis' qualities. You're direct, and you don't have that bitchiness some women have. You know the type I mean?"

"Do I!" replied Georgia sipping her wine. They still hadn't ordered lunch, and she was getting queasy. "By the way, speaking of bitches, did you ever run into one by the name of Kiki Blake? Or should I say Kiki Sandborne? She married my late husband and wears the bitch crown of the world."

"Certainly I know her," answered Francie. "Her name used to be Valentine, and she worked at the Silver Fin. That's where she met Lucky. I'll tell you a little secret. She's always been nuts about him, but he only used her. I mean, he dug her, still does I guess, but never the way she wanted. Anyway, she

318

lusted after the big time—money, position, the works. They used to say she was the best little lady in the sack department because she loved her work so much," Francie laughed.

"Nothing surprises me about that one," said Georgia. "But in all fairness, she must have had something going for her to hook Victor. I mean, he did marry her, after all. Of course he was having problems and I heard she put the pressure on at some point in the game. Anyway, now he's gone and she's got everything. Don't tell me bad girls don't make good."

CHAPTER SEVENTEEN

THE ROOM was filled with mirrors on the ceiling and walls, gloriously reflecting crystal chandeliers, marvelous French antique furniture, an elevated canopied bed on a velvet dias, and lastly—a naked Kiki Blake Sandborne.

She tuned up the stereo, then stared at herself from every angle. She had taken great pains that day to clean all her jewelry after having it appraised for Lloyd's of London. Tomorrow it would go back to the vault, but tonight she would enjoy. Three diamond bracelets sparkled from her wrists while a sapphire and diamond ring, next to a ten-carat square cut diamond, covered the fingers of her tiny hand. A tiered diamond necklace hung from her throat, and diamond and emerald earrings glittered from her ears. The gems against her bare skin caused her to sigh with pleasure as she studied herself in the mirrored walls. Their reflection against her naked skin was dazzling!

She moved in time to the music towards the poudre and sprayed herself with French perfume, then continued on to the bar and made herself a stiff drink.

At that moment, the buzzer sounded downstairs. It was Lucky. She buzzed him up, excitement spreading through her entire body like a heatwave. This was perfect. She hadn't expected him so early, but she could use him. She touched herself between her legs with one diamond laden finger, then ran her palms from her naked thighs to her full round breasts. The nipples were hard with desire. Lord, how she could use him!

Lucky came striding into the bedroom having let himself in with his own key and stared at Kiki. "Good God! Aprhrodite! The goddess of diamonds . . . goddess of lust . . . etc . . . etc." He moved towards her and took her naked body in his arms. "I feel like making love to a million on the hoof, sweetheart. Don't take off a thing. I want to screw you with all your ill gotten gains dazzling my eyes out."

She smiled and slipped out of his arms. "Not so fast . . . not so fast. I want it on the white ermine coat. Today I want to lie on the white ermine coat and have you make love to me until I'm dizzy. Until I beg you to stop."

She walked to the enormous walk-in closet that housed a dozen furs and selected a long white evening coat, then flung it across the carpet and lay down on the soft white fur. It was a bizzare sight—the small voluptuous girl, her full breasts jutting forward, her small muscular legs raised and slightly parted, diamonds across her throat, on her wrists and fingers sparkling obscenely in the light. She smiled that wicked little girl's smile and crooked one jeweled finger. "Now, I'm ready, baby. Now I'm ready. Hurry up and get undressed. Hurry . . . hurry!"

After they made love, rapidly at first, then slowly, voluptuously, savoring each kiss and caress, Lucky took a quick shower, donned a robe he kept for just such occasions, and sat down opposite Kiki.

"Get me a drink, kid. I need it after that workout. You're something else."

Kiki slipped into a shortie chiffon lounger, went to the bar, and returned with a chilled bottle of wine and two crystal goblets. "Here, master, here's your drink. Now we can talk. I haven't seen you like this in awhile."

Lucky poured them both wine, then sipped his reflectively. "Look, Kiki. We've always had an understanding . . . no strings . . . no hooks . . . neither of us can function that way. I always knew it, you learned it. Now, I'd like to know what lurked inside your head the day you showed up at the boss' party?" He studied her coldly, his blue eyes devoid of their earlier desire and anticipation. "I don't like surprises, sweetheart, especially when they have to do with the boss. Don't ever do anything like that again. Our relationship is not exactly front page news, and I want to keep it that way. Understand? Nick is nuts about Georgia Bonner, and we both know what you did to her."

Kiki, now curled beside Lucky like a cuddly kitten, treated him to her special waif-caught-in-the-cookie-jar smile. Her face was devoid of makeup, and she resembled a clean cut sixteen-year old about to be punished by an irate father.

"You've lost me, dear. I mean, I came to the party strictly to see you and have some fun. Nino was out playing with the boys, and I needed a lift. As to Georgia, the injured wife, I have no regrets. I married Victor Sandborne, I didn't put a gun to his head. He was weak . . . he died . . . simple! If Georgia couldn't hold her man, it's not my fault. I feel no guilt. Sorry, darling." Kiki lit a cigarette. "It was a lousy party, anyway."

Lucky studied her for a moment. "Okay, Miss Angel of Mercy, but nothing like that ever again. Understand? You work your side of the street, and I'll work mine. Incidentally, are you and Nino still running up to Harlem to the voodoo lady? Wouldn't surprise me a bit to find out that you helped Victor on his way to the Promised Land. You would have made a great hit man, you've got the stomach for it."

Kiki stiffened. "That's a hell of a thing to

say to someone you've just laid on a white ermine coat. And to answer your question, Mr. Interrogator, I stopped seeing Kaya months ago. Almost got mugged the last time I took a run up there. Too much dope traffic. Speaking of stuff, I need some coke, okay?"

"That might be arranged when I have the time," said Lucky glancing at his watch. "Speaking of time, it's late. I've got to split. You have a way of making a guy forget business, baby. Funny, you've come a long way, but I'll never forget you that very first time—all dolled up in spiked heels and black stockings, with two sequin pasties on those gorgeous tits. You were far and away the best little hustler in the business, Miss Valentine."

Hot with fury and humiliation, Kiki wanted desperately to strike him. How dare he make love to her and leave so abruptly. How dare he remind her of her sordid past. She despised herself for her own weakness.

"Boy, talk about love on the run, next time I'll wait in the hall. Always hopping to do the master's bidding. When are you gonna wise up and ice that sentimental old Polack? he's on his way out anyway."

"Knock it off, Kiki. You know how I hate that kind of talk. After all the crap we've been through, you still manage to come across like a jealous chippie. Doesn't suit you, Sweets."

Lucky dressed rapidly, then kissed Kiki on the forehead and left the apartment.

She sat quietly for a moment, still steaming, then removed her jewelry, placing each piece lovingly in velvet boxes on the mirrored poudre, all the while contemplating her love life.

She changed the tape-deck and the room was filled with the heavy sensuous strains of *Harlem Nocturne,* flooding her soul with nostalgic memories of long, erotic nights in Lucky's arms.

Kiki had imagined that by marring Victor Sandborne and becoming respectable, Lucky would see her in a different light. However, it had done little good. If anything, he treated her more brutally than ever, and she seemed unable to break her addiction to the man. Sometimes she was consumed by vengeful fantasies involving them making love. At the crucial moment, she would plunge a dagger into Lucky's heart, and as his life blood oozed forth, he would profess his profound love for her. This bizarre image gave her momentary satisfaction.

Harlem Nocturne came to an end, and *Sweet Dreams* had just begun its hypnotic magic when the intercom rang, interrupting her dangerous trend of thought. Now who the devil was downstairs without telephoning first?

"Yes, who's there?"

"It's me. Nino! Let me up please, it's an emergency."

Kiki buzzed up Nino, wondering what her

sometime companion wanted at this hour. Lately he was behaving more strangely than usual, though he still chose most of her designer clothes and important jewelry, served as an escort when all else failed, and made an excellent errand boy. Several times a year she slipped him some dough to keep him on the leash.

In her present perverse mood, she decided to answer the door in the buff. Seeing her in the nude would send Nino round the bend, as he secretly detested most women. He'd once told her, after five martinis, that the female body turned him off, but if there was enough bucks in it—he could bear anything.

She opened the door. "Well, come in. What brings you here? Have a drink." Kiki lifted her goblet in the air and pranced across the room, allowing him a generous view of her naked rear.

Nino nervously fixed himself a drink at the long mirrored bar. He was a handsome man of around forty, half Irish-half Puerto Rican, and extremely attractive to both men and women.

"Look, Kiki. No games today. Please . . . if you've got an ounce of compassion in that heart of yours—no games. I'm in a terrible mood. Something awful has happened. I mean, try just once to think of someone other than yourself." He seated himself on the cameo brocaded sofa and took a quick swallow of his drink.

"Well, spit it out," snapped Kiki, refilling her own drink. She'd switched from wine to scotch.

"Look, I've got big problems. That last little jaunt to Atlantic City was a fiasco. I was ahead at the Blackjack tables . . . really on a hot streak, then some ugly dame peered over my shoulder and broke my luck. I lost. I borrowed some cash from the house, and then the next day they refused to give me any more so I had to get a loan from a less reputable source. If I don't pay up this time, the boys are gonna finish me for sure."

His voice broke, "I got a call, just awhile ago, Kiki, and you can fix it. You can do it just this one time. I mean, I've asked you before, but it wasn't this urgent. Just do it . . . get me out of this . . . and I promise it's the very last time. I swear. I can't take a beating. You know what they do to guys like me. They get their rocks off. Kiki, I'll do anything . . . anything!'"

"Anything?" smiled Kiki, her mind suddenly filled with memories of Victor, Lucky, and all the men in between. Nothing meant anything anymore, not even the money; the joy and challenge was in getting it! Now that she had it, she had shit, and it made her mad. Her only power was her control over others. That's how she placated herself when this frustration took over.

"How much to you owe, sweetie?" She moved gracefully across the room and sat naked in Nino's lap, her large breasts pressed near his face. He squirmed uncomfortably. "How much?" she repeated.

"Five thousand. Five grand, Kiki, and they say I only have till tomorrow morning."

Kiki rubbed the nipple of her right breast against Nino's lips and purred, "Well, sweetie, that's a break because that gives us the rest of the night. We'll start by having you get all naked and giving me a long, leisurely massage. After that, I want you to make love to me. Lucky didn't finish the job today."

She smiled at the look of shock on Nino's face. "I know you can do it if you put your mind to it. Then, if you're very good, you'll get the cash. If not—"

Nino rose slowly from the sofa and began to undress. At that moment he hated Kiki so much it excited him. Lucky for him he was slightly masocistic.

Lucky walked through the door of the Golden Cat and was greeted by Merry Moss. He'd helped her out of a scrape a few years earlier, and they were friends.

"Hi! Haven't seen you around in ages, stranger. Want a drink?"

"Sure," said Lucky. "Let's take a booth in the back." It was so dark with the dim red lights that Lucky could barely see the girl's face. The place was just as decadent as he remembered it. Christ! what kind of guys got their jollies in here, he wondered. But a hell of a lot did. It paid off big. They sat down and ordered drinks. Lucky studied Merry for a moment.

"How's Levine? Level with me, Merry. I've been getting some bad feedback. This is one of our more stable places, and since the credit card scam has been taken care of, we don't want any trouble here."

"Well," said Merry, adjusting the glasses that gave her that studious but charming look, "I hate to be a squealer, but he's back on the sauce. He disguises it pretty well, but the other night he kept the bar open till all hours. He's gettin' bad. I know all the signs. You know he wanted to change policy around here, too. Wanted the girls to lay it on the line, and Tinker and some of the others got up in arms." She laughed. "We almost organized ourselves in a union. You know, we're not hookers. And after all, the house takes a big cut. Anyway, there's something real sleazy about Sid—him with his degree. Odd, you know, I told Francie about him a long time ago."

"Thanks, Merry, I'll see you soon." Lucky stood up and walked through a door and down the hall to another door marked "Office . . . Sid Levine . . . Manager."

He knocked sharply.

"Who's there?"

"It's Lucky, Sid."

"Lucky! Oh, yeah . . . come on in."

Lucky opened the door and confronted Sid

Levine who sat behind a large desk holding a can of Schlitz beer in his hand. "Well, if it isn't Johnny Apollo. How goes it?"

Lucky ignored the remark, then pulled a chair and faced the man across the desk. "You know, Sid, I feel kinda responsible for you 'cause I hired you, even though you had a bad track record with the sauce. I thought you could handle yourself. Our deal was—no sauce."

Lucky's expression hardened. "That was our agreement, friend, and you've broken our agreement. I've given you a real fair chance. Every break. I'm not real happy, Sid. As a matter of fact, I'd like to beat the shit out of you." Lucky's voice became a soft snarl. "I hate making mistakes; Mr. G. doesn't like me making mistakes. It reflects on all of us, understand?"

"Come on, Lucky, you're makin' a mountain out of a little ant hill," responded Sid, a whine in his voice. "This is nothin'. This is just a little brew . . . nothin' hard." He held the can up to the light.

Lucky knocked it out of his hand with one swift movement. His expression didn't change.

"Look, Sid, we both know you're an alkie, and alkies can't take beer, wine or nothin'. I'm real disappointed, and to add to my mood, rumor has it you were trying to do a little policy changing around here. I told you when I put you in how the deal worked. After we canned that Nickles bum with the credit card scam that almost got us all busted, I told you the score here, and you simply chose to ignore my orders. I don't take kindly to that. I want you off the premises tonight. You're gettin' off real easy."

Lucky reached inside his pocket. "Here. Here's a grand. That should take you to the nearest bar. Now get your shit and get out."

Sid sat and stared at Lucky, his eyes red with fury. "What the hell do you mean? You can't just come in here and fire me. I've straightened this fuckin' place out. Got those dames in line. They're a bunch of lazy pigs, by the way. You got nerve marchin' in here tellin' me I'm through." Sid jutted his chin with the usual false bravado of the drunk. "Keep your grand. I'm stayin' right here."

Lucky slowly advanced forward, his blue eyes cold and without expression. He reached across the desk and pulled Sid to his feet, then shook him like a cat shakes a captured mouse.

"Now hear this, you lush, you're fired. Pure and simple. I put you in, and I'm putting you out. Your interference with the girls, the sauce, just on general principals. Be out of here in an hour, and if you know what's healthy for you, don't come back!"

With that Lucky turned and walked out the door.

Sid sat for a full minute, his mind in a whirl. He hated Lucky with such fury at that moment, it was all consuming. And that bastard, Louis Gerfinski! Who did this bunch of ignorant, uneducated fools think they were anyway? He'd finished third in his class at Columbia. Those fuckin' idiots had the audacity to fire him, Sid Levine, with two degrees. He'd leave this filthy den of female pigs all right . . . this den of cheap twists pickpocketing the dumbos that sneaked through the doors to get their rocks off. This bunch of bimbos. He'd take the cash and leave. He'd be glad to get the hell out of this slime, and one day soon, he'd be back where he belonged at the top of the heap. He drained the last of the six pack, then glanced at his watch. Still time to hoist a few before the bars closed.

At three in the morning, Nino crawled out of Kiki's bed exhausted and humiliated.

She sat bolt upright. "Where the hell do you think you're going, my friend? I'm just getting my second wind. Get back in this bed."

"Kiki, please . . . please . . . enough . . . enough!"

Kiki stretched herself languidly and ran one hand up her naked thigh. "What's the matter, sweetie, don't you dig girls?"

"Kiki, please . . . just give me the money. I've only got a few hours." Nino's voice trembled, he felt near tears, but fear and panic kept his eyes dry.

Kiki lit a cigarette. "Look, I didn't say for

332

sure I'd give you the cash. I said maybe. Yes, I seem to recall that there were some conditions attached, and I said just maybe, if you were a real good boy. Anyway, I've changed my mind."

She watched Nino's reaction with a secret pleasure, then continued. "What the hell, Nino, maybe this little episode will teach you a lesson. Maybe you'll learn once and for all that you are not a gentleman gambler. You can't afford it, sweetie, really you can't. Now get dressed and get out. I want to get my beauty sleep."

Nino lunged across the bed like an enraged lion whose trainer has for one split second lost control. His mind was blank except for the urge to kill . . . maim. He grabbed a startled Kiki by the neck like a rag doll and felt the warm pulse of her throat, watched her terrified eyes as she struggled to escape. His strong hands continued to choke her, continued to press, until all the life was squeezed from her beautiful naked body.

Then silently, and with an amazingly clear head, Nino helped himself to the jewelry on the poudre, left the apartment, and disappeared into the night.

CHAPTER EIGHTEEN

Louis and Georgia relaxed in the rear of the limousine as Martin guided the car over the East River Drive out of Manhattan and toward Connecticut. At last Georgia had won her battle to see Scherise. Louis, against his better judgment, had agreed to take her to the sanitarium in order for her to meet face to face with the woman who might be her mother.

"I hope this is the right thing to do, Georgia. I have been hesitant because I felt it would depress you. At times she's not coherent; other times she simply sits and stares into space. It varies, but mainly she's like a lost child. Once she was the most beautiful woman I'd ever seen, but now—"

Louis' voice was sad. "Alzheimers is a mysterious illness. If only they had a cure. How the poor thing managed to survive before I found her is a mystery."

"Look, Louis, I don't care about all that," said Georgia. "What I mean is, if she's my mother, then I just want to know . . . just want to see her . . . love her in my heart. Don't you understand?"

She smiled at Louis. "Like now I have you in my heart; you're my father no matter if it's blood or not. You've been so kind to me—the apartment, the gifts. You know, Louis, I guess I married Victor as a father substitute because I'd never known the love or security of an older man. After Taia died, I was so all alone." She paused. "It wasn't easy."

Louis lit a cigarette. "I don't want to hear. I can't bear to think you were deprived. I can't stand it. But never again. That I can promise you."

He peered out the car window. "We're almost there. It's so beautiful this time of year. Everything's green."

A half-hour later the car pulled into the curved driveway of the sanitarium, came to a halt, and Georgia and Louis were assisted out by Martin. Louis took Georgia's arm and guided her through the entrance of the large building. Suddenly she was flooded with a peculiar sense of forboding that made her feel temporarily weak.

A doctor in a white coat greeted Louis as they entered the large reception area, then paused at a desk, waved on by a nurse who obviously recognized Louis. They continued to walk toward a room at the end of the hallway. Suddenly Georgia stopped short. Louis looked at her.

"What's wrong, dear? Cold feet?"

At the same moment, a piercing scream reverberated through the corridors, and Louis took Georgia's arm. "It's nothing. Just someone whose medication isn't working right or someone who's had an upset. I'm used to it. I told you, it wasn't any picnic."

He paused and turned away from Georgia. "Here comes Dr. Sawyer. He's Scherise's main doctor, but by the size of the bills, you'd think she had a dozen."

A thin, beige man with salt and pepper hair and hornrimmed glasses too large for his face greeted Louis. "Good afternoon, Mr. Gerfinski. How are you today?" He glanced at Georgia with undisguised curiosity.

Louis shook his hand. "Dr. Sawyer, this is Georgia Bonner, a friend of the family." No need to involve the doctor in the unfinished scenario.

"Hello, Miss Bonner," answered the doctor. "Nice to meet you." He turned his attention to Louis.

"Mrs. Gerfinski is doing about the same. We've changed her medication and also she has a new nurse. Lucy had to return to the Islands. She's just had her lunch, and I'm certain she'll be happy to see you. You'll both exuse me now, I'm making my rounds. Nice to have met you, Miss Bonner." And then he turned and walked away.

Louis and Georgia proceeded down the hallway, and Georgia noted the absence of hospital smells. The odors of urine, antiseptic, and harsh soaps were missing. As the two approached the door of Scherise's room, Georgia paused.

"Just want to be certain I look okay."

Her hand trembled as she took out her compact, and Louis pretended not to notice. "You look fine, dear, just lovely. Come on, let's go and meet her. She may be sleeping. They keep her sedated. I guess she's less trouble to them."

Louis tapped at the door, and a small, pretty Irish nurse greeted them with a smile.

"Hello there. I'm Mary, the new nurse. You must be Mr. Gerfinski. Come in."

Louis and Georgia entered the large, airy room and Louis approached the bed, motioning Georgia to remain in the background near the door. He stood for a moment, then handed the box of *Godiva* chocolates to Scherise.

His voice was soft as if he were speaking to a child. "You look lovely today, my dear. And I'm glad because I've brought someone to see you. She's a friend." He motioned to Georgia who walked toward the bed slowly, hesitantly, a small bouquet of violets in her hand.

Scherise was propped up on large pillows; her long red hair, now streaked with grey, was caught back with a lavender ribbon. Her once lovely olive skin was sallow and high prominent cheekbones sunk in at the side of her face where two teeth were missing. She wore no lipstick and held a small white Bible on her lap. Her enormous fawn-like eyes studied Louis for a moment. They were vacant eyes, like large, dark pools that had no bottom. Her mouth was set in what had begun as a smile, but changed abruptly to a frown at the sight of Georgia now standing near the bed. She did not utter a word but stared at the girl with a look of such fury and hatred that Georgia drew in her breath.

Georgia offered the flowers and started to speak, but suddenly without warning Scherise sprang from the bed and lunged at the young woman like a savage beast. Her long nails ripped at Georgia's exposed white throat and the girl rushed screaming towards the door, blood staining her cashmere sweater a brilliant red.

Louis and the nurse grappled with Scherise as a shrill, heart rendering shriek filled the air, followed by a flow of obscenities that were so startling even Louis was stunned.

Scherise writhed in his grasp with the strength of ten demons and managed to free one hand, pointing it wildly towards Georgia who stood cowering in the hallway.

"Whore! Whore of Babylon!" Her voice rose so loud that other ambulatory patients filled the corridors. Louis attempted to cover her mouth with his hands, but it was useless.

She bit him. Mercifully, two security guards and a doctor rushed into the room and took over.

Louis stepped back, perspiration dripping from his brow. The guards wrestled Scherise to the bed where a nurse produced a long hypodermic needle. In a matter of seconds she was quiet, saliva running from her lips.

One of the doctors took Louis' arm. "Come with me. Dr. Sawyer will want to see you."

Georgia stood quietly in the far corner of the room wincing with pain as a nurse cleaned and applied antiseptic to her scratches. They were not severe, but she trembled visibly as Louis walked towards her.

"My God! Are you okay? I've never known her to react so violently. If anything, she's been passive." He studied the scratches on Georgia's throat and arms with horror. "Come on, we'll go to the doctor's office. It's just down the hall."

Georgia was ashen. She fumbled in her purse for a cigarette. "It was all so sudden . . . the way she jumped at me like a wild cat. I'm sorry, Louis, I've got to sit down."

Louis nodded and led her to the office. The doctor stood waiting at the door and motioned them both inside. "Sit over there. Make yourselves comfortable. Fix Miss Bonner a drink, there's a bar in the corner. I'll be back as soon as I've checked on Mrs. Gerfinski."

Georgia sank down on a leather upholstered sofa, and Louis went to the bar and poured them both drinks of brandy. He handed a glass to Georgia. "Something crazy happened to Scherise. I don't understand it."

Georgia took a long sip of the liquid and faced Louis. "Indeed, something happened! She was jealous! Don't you get it? She saw me and was jealous, like any normal woman. She may be sick, but some emotions are left intact. She thought I was your girlfriend. That I was a threat. Don't you see!" She started to cry. "The poor thing, you're the only one she's got, and here I come all neat and painted. What the hell did I expect? That she'd recognize me with some hidden maternal instinct and say Gina . . . Gina . . . my baby?"

Georgia dried her eyes with a hanky from her purse. "I've been stupid and selfish, Louis. You were right. This part of your life I should never have invaded."

"It's not your fault." Louis patted her shoulder kindly. "I know that her emotions are unpredictable, but I've never before had anyone with me. Funny . . . I never gave it a thought . . . I mean about the jealousy. Of course you're right, you're right."

At that moment Doctor Sawyer returned and sat down behind his oak desk facing Georgia and Louis.

"She's resting nicely. They've given her heavy medication. She should sleep through

340

tomorrow. This entire thing poses many questions. Mrs. Gerfinski has never before exhibited violent tendencies. Sometimes she's fussy with the nurses when they bathe her or insist she eat all her food, but mainly she's docile and childlike. I'm afraid, Mr. Gerfinski, that in the future it would be ill advised to bring a visitor. It appears to have triggered something we are not prepared for." He shook his head. "Alzheimers is a mysterious illness. We're learning about it every day."

Louis finished his brandy and stood up. "Of course, doctor. It will never happen again. Now, I think we shall be leaving. The drive back to the city is a long one and this incident has upset my daughter very much."

A look of shock registered on the doctor's face. Louis ignored it and guided Georgia out the door, down the hallway, and towards the long sleek limousine in the driveway. Martin stood waiting beside the car, happy they were ready to leave. He hated this place.

Georgia and Louis were silent on the drive back, exchanging only a few words, both deep in their separate thoughts. Louis took Georgia's hand. "I'm so sorry, dear. Really I am. Will you continue with Dr. Algin or do you want to stop the sessions altogether? Whatever you want, Georgia. Whatever you want."

Georgia remained silent, staring out the car window as Louis continued. "I understand. You're afraid of the outcome. You don't want to know if that wild tainted creature back there is, in fact, your true flesh and blood. That's it, isn't it?"

Georgia turned away from the window and faced Louis. "You may be right, I'm not certain. The sessions are making me aware of things that are upsetting. I mean, Dr. Algin is pricking little things in my psyche that are sensitive. But maybe that's good. Let me think about it, after a good night's sleep." She paused. "Is it really that important we know for certain?"

Louis faced Georgia. "Legally, it doesn't matter all that much. I've arranged my affairs so that everyone is taken care of after my death, including you and Scherise. I feel you are my daughter, I just have that gut feeling. Always did, right from the start. Of course it would be wonderful to know for certain, and there is one outside chance that I haven't investigated. It's a long shot, but a chance."

Louis took Georgia's slim hands in his own large ones. "I don't want to discuss that at the moment, because there's something else I should have mentioned to you before now."

"What's that?" asked Georgia, her senses still reeling from the hospital episode, and Louis' declaration about his will. "Any more surprises today and I might just pass out. I hope this is a good one."

"It's a good one all right, and I'm sorry I

didn't tell you before, but I sometimes do things on the spur of the moment and expect everyone to go along." He smiled. "I forget you're not a part of the 'organization.' Pack a bikini and a toothbrush, because day after tomorrow, we leave on a Caribbean cruise. The Villa Rosa sails at ten o'clock in the morning."

Georgia was stunned. "A what? Oh, Louis, I'm not prepared. I've got appointments . . . Nick—"

"Break them. It's important that you get away for awhile." He lit a cigarette. "I'm selfish, Georgia. I need it, too. I need to be alone with you."

Georgia remained silent and recalled Francie's words. It's dangerous. Once you're in, it's hard to get out.

Later that evening Georgia arrived home to find Nick in the bedroom deeply engrossed in his script. He wore briefs and nothing else. She dreaded telling him about the cruise. It would only confirm his fears about Louis' possessiveness.

She remained standing in the shadows, studying the man she loved. He looked so young, handsome, and for all his time on the streets and in Boys Town—vulnerable. Love and passion, tenderness and desire, were new to him. She was far more experienced in these matters, and she so wanted to preserve Nick's illusions. She sometimes hated herself for the twinges of maternal love that Nick inspired in her, but she'd grown to accept it.

At last he glanced in her direction. "Georgia, you were so quiet, I didn't hear you come in. How was the hospital? I mean, how was the sanitarium? And speaking of hospitals, I checked on Jake Pierce today. He's doing okay, although why you'd care is beyond me. Your milk of human kindness runs thicker than mine."

Nick patted Powder Puff curled by his side. "I almost went home tonight. Sam's feeling lousy, and I knew you were out with Papa. Come around here where I can see you."

Georgia slipped out of her lynx jacket and sat on the edge of the bed. "The meeting with Scherise was a horror, and I'm not up to discussing it at the moment. Matter of fact, I just want to be with you and forget the day. But there is something I have to tell you."

She paused and lit a cigarette. Better get it over with. Better tell him and be done with it. "Well, here goes. Nick, Louis has arranged for the two of us to go on a cruise leaving day after tomorrow. Lucky my passport is in order." She paused. "Please don't be upset, Nick. Please try and understand."

Nick dropped the script in his lap and sat straight up facing Georgia. "You're what? A cruise? Just like that—a cruise. Lord, I knew something was brewing. Georgia, we've got to talk. I've tried to stay out of your business, but things are getting out of hand. You and

Daddy Warbucks are becoming a real item. You're not the same girl I know and love. You're someone else. You seem to be under a spell, or in a trance, or like a puppet with Louis pulling the strings. Maybe that doctor neglected to snap you back. Maybe you're walking around hypnotized. I don't know if you're Georgia Bonner . . . or Gina Gerfinski . . . or Mrs. Victor Sandborne. Talk about your multiple personalities. I'm really concerned, Georgia. I don't think even you are aware of how your personality has altered since Louis came on the scene. I love you, Georgia. I don't want our relationship to end."

Georgia moved slowly to the bed. She sat next to Nick and ran her fingers playfully through his thick, black hair.

"Stop it, Nicky. I love you. Nothing is going to change that. I'll be back to myself again. Really I will." She smiled. "Three different women could be interesting. Right now this particular one wants to get all naked and lie beside you. This woman wants to kiss you, make love to you, and lie in your arms forever."

As she spoke, Georgia began slowly to undress, flinging a sweater here, a brassiere there. At last she was completely nude and Nick eyed her with undisguised pleasure.

"Boy, you've got a hell of a way of changing the subject. Come here . . . come here."

He took her by the shoulders and pulled

her down on the bed across his lap. He lowered his head and kissed her breasts, her long white throat, working his way to her mouth. The deep, sensuous kisses intoxicated Georgia whose emotions were slightly askew. Nick's tongue was in her mouth and she kissed him back with an all consuming passion, seeking the temporary oblivion of his arms. Over and over they kissed until the waves of desire were almost unbearable.

They moved together in the rhythm of love until both were satiated. Georgia lay in the warmth of Nick's embrace and whispered in his ear, "I love you. I really and truly love you. Try to be patient. Give me time. I need some time."

Nick whispered back, "I love you, too, babe, but cancel the cruise."

CHAPTER NINETEEN

Hot white heat . . . suntan oil sweet and sticky . . . tall tropical drinks served by smiling waiters . . . nights filled with music and a moon so big and white it turned the sea to a shimmering silver. The cruise ship Villa Rosa cut through turbulent Caribbean waters, her passengers filled with rum and the desire to escape. Curacao in the West Indies, then Caracas, Venezuela, with a short stop in Puerta Cabella was the chartered course.

Grinning natives bartering their wares greeted passengers arriving from the ship by motor launch to the island of Curacao, and Georgia and Louis filled baskets with colorful beads and strange wood carvings. They spent a lazy afternoon dining on fresh lobster, shrimp, and even squid, shaded from the blazing sun by a straw thatched roof. Georgia vetoed the idea of a refreshing swim having noted the wires set up to keep out the sharks. Their evil fins could be spotted in the distance cutting the waters like a surgeon's knife.

Hours later they returned to a ship alive with romantic couples, a few singles searching for adventure, and one young man traveling with his dowager mother who changed jewels as frequently as she changed clothes.

Georgia was introduced as Louis' daughter, but she sensed that story was accepted with a grain of salt. She began to enjoy the stir she and Louis created as they made their nightly entrance for cocktails and dinner.

"You're as white as a ghost," observed Louis on their fourth night at sea. "What's wrong?"

Georgia smiled through her tan but sipped her wine slowly, hoping to relieve the queasiness she'd been fighting all day. "I'm okay. It's a little rough out tonight."

The following day, however, she remained in her stateroom, drinking champagne and popping Dramamines. By the time the ship reached Caracas, Venezuela, she was feeling much better. A motor launch took them ashore, and the awe-inspring sunset viewed from the palatial terrace of the world famous Tamanaka Hotel filled Georgia with a sense of wonder. If only Nick were here to share this beauty, it would all be perfect. She sat with Louis in a reclining chair near an aquamarine pool sipping a tall pink drink, and felt a sudden pang of loneliness. Georgia was wary of life when it became too placid. It seemed always then that fate stepped in creating mischief, upsetting the balance, blocking sunshine from the days and adding blackness to the nights.

Louis patted her tan wrist. "What are you dreaming about? You seem off on one of those fluffy white clouds. By the way, do you want to stay here tonight and meet the ship tomorrow in Puerta Cabella, or shall we finish our drinks and go back now? It's a hell of a trip by car through the mountains, and the roads aren't that great."

Georgia accepted a second drink from a red coated waiter with a tan face and answered, "Whatever you say, but I think I'd prefer to go back now. I hate long drives in the heat."

An hour later they returned to the ship and sat on deck sipping gin and tonics, watching the sharks slice through the blue waters of the Caribbean. Georgia looked at Louis and felt a strange contentment.

When they entered the dining room that evening, Georgia was wearing a pale pink cotton sundress threaded with gold and displaying three new gold bracelets purchased by Louis in Caracas. Heads turned. Both she and Louis enjoyed the stir they created and later on deck laughed together in blissful camaraderie.

That night, lying in her stateroom, an

enormous tropical moon flooding the port-hole with light, Georgia thought of Nick. God, she missed him. He'd been furious when she left, but the trip had been worth the aggravation, though she still felt slightly seasick. She'd thrown up earlier, but the champagne had helped. She'd gotten a good rest, a good tan, and time to become even more dependent on Louis Gerfinski. Not once had she even so much as glanced at a newspaper.

Lucky and Juju greeted the couple as they disembarked from the cruise ship.

Georgia, anxious to cut the red tape of customs and return to her apartment, turned to Lucky. "How's Nick? Have you heard from him? Seems we've been gone forever. God, I've missed him."

Lucky answered quietly, sensing the urgency in her voice. "Spoke to him only once since you've been gone. He's been on a roll. Commercials . . . cover of *People* . . . columns . . . you know. And another thing, Georgia—" He paused, his voice strained. "Kiki Blake has been murdered. It was days before they found her body. They're looking for a guy named Nino."

"Murdered! Oh my God! Thank the Lord I was in the middle of the ocean. I would have been high on the suspect list. She wasn't my favorite person, but I'm sorry she had to go that way."

Louis appeared at that moment informing everyone there would be no wait in customs. As usual, he was in command. On the walk to the limo, Georgia paused at the newsstand and bought a copy of *People Magazine*, her mind still in turmoil. Kiki murdered! She deserved it, but what avenging angel had done the deed?

Inside the rear of the car, Georgia settled in beside Louis and studied Nick's handsome face smiling at her from the magazine cover, thoughts of Kiki's untimely demise wiped from her mind. As she read the detailed article on Nick accompanied by several candid pictures, her stomach tightened. The little printed black words describing Nick's frequent visits to *Limelight* with his glamorous co-star were like blows. She couldn't believe what she was reading. It was like she didn't exist, like she was invisible in Nick's life. The article went on to describe Nick's other romantic interest, another actress, who if her picture did her justice, put Bo Derek to shame. Georgia felt a sudden dizziness, like she might faint, but she fought it off. She quickly closed the magazine, lit a cigarette, and attempted to avoid Louis' curious gaze.

"What's wrong? Feeling sick again? I thought once we were off the ship—"

"It's nothing, Louis. Maybe Kiki's murder. Murders always upset me, no matter who they happen to . . . and I have a slight cramp, a spasm. I'll be fine once I get home."

The car came to a halt in front of the building in the East Sixties, and Lucky separated the luggage, then assisted Georgia out of the long, black vehicle. She thanked him and turned to Louis, whose eyes followed her every move.

"I'll speak to you later after I've unpacked." Her voice was surprisingly calm. She simply had not digested the article. Nick with another woman. God! She never should have left him. Maybe it was all just publicity, lies. Maybe he'd have an explanation.

Inside the apartment, Georgia stared at the luggage in the center of the living room and decided to forget about unpacking until later in the day. She opened the blinds to the sunlight and went directly down the hall to retrieve Powder Puff from her neighbor. Back in her own apartment, she kissed the little dog's cold nose and sat her on the bed like a tiny toy just as the phone began to ring. It was Nick.

"Thought you'd be back by now. I'm sure you've heard the news about the murder, so I'll skip over that. It's depressing as hell, even though she was a bitch." His voice was tight, not filled with its usual boyish enthusiasm.

Georgia felt warning signals go off. She decided to avoid the subject of *People Magazine*.

"Yes, I've heard about the killing of Kiki, and you're right, it is depressing. Just got in a few minutes ago. I thought you might have been at the dock to greet me, or maybe surprised me here at the apartment, but no such luck. I guess you were too busy. Anyway, the docks are hell to get to with all that stupid traffic." She was talking too fast, prattling on, and she couldn't seem to stop. "It doesn't matter. I'm back safe and sound, and I missed you. God, Nick, if you could have seen that moon over the Caribbean . . . it was glorious . . . just like in the movies. And we almost ran into a hurricane, but it passed us by. I wish you could have been with me."

There was silence, then Nick answered, "Georgia, I've been very busy working, and well . . . I need to talk to you. Are you in the mood for me tonight?"

"Of course," she answered, sensing disaster. "Come around at six, if that's okay."

They hung up and Georgia decided to unpack after all in order to keep herself busy . . . keep herself from thinking too much about the discussion she and Nick would be having later. Somehow she knew it wouldn't be a happy one.

Georgia answered the door barefoot and wearing a shortie robe. Nick walked inside the apartment and they stood looking at one another for a moment without speaking.

At last Georgia broke the silence. "Well, hi. Come on in and sit down. Want a drink?"

Nick followed her inside the living room and sat down on the sofa. "A glass of wine,

Georgia. That's all. Just a glass of wine. I'm bushed and if I drink too much, it'll only make me more tired. Did you enjoy the trip? You look well." His voice was strained.

"Oh, fine . . . fine. Glad to be back. Louis had business as usual, and I needed to get back." She'd be damned if she'd mention the *People* article, and the other blurbs in the *Star* and *Enquirer.* "Here's your wine." She handed him a glass and sat opposite him.

"Well, tell me everything." Her voice was hollow and lacked its usual luster. She felt a fraud, like she was playing a scene. She wanted to fling herself in Nick's arms, tell him how much she loved him, how much she missed him, beg him not to leave her, not to desert her for some shimmering little teenaged starlet, but she just sat and felt all empty and queasy inside. She already knew.

"Look, Georgia. This isn't easy. First let me say that I love you. I really do. That's not the problem." He paused. "The problem is your confusion about your identity, this thing with Louis. The two of you are like two desperate people feeding off one another's weaknesses."

Georgia started to interrupt, but Nick stopped her. "And it's not just that either. It's my career; I've got to make it, Georgia. It's all I've got. I mean, you're important, but now you're confusing me. Am I supposed to feel guilty when there's a column item or something about me?"

354

Oh, here it comes, thought Georgia sipping her wine. Here it comes. She remained silent and let him continue.

"I don't know if you saw the *Star* and *People Magazine.*" He paused, studying Georgia closely. "You know the thing about my dating Lee Vance, my co-star in 'Precinct,' and Marcie Ridge—"

"Nick, please stop this, will you?" Georgia felt herself become stronger. "Of course I've read it. I'm not your keeper. If you want to date your co-star, or anyone else for that matter, who the hell am I to tell you not to." She lit a cigarette. "I'm also not your mother —I'm your lover. I want respect and consideration, but I don't own you. Let's for God's sake be honest with each other. We've had a wonderful relationship. Let's not spoil it now by lying. I've got the distinct feeling that you want out. I mean, that you want a breather. Maybe you've got a thing for Lee, or someone else. After all, dear, I'm the only full fledged affair you've ever had, so maybe you want to sample the wares out there now that you're becoming a great big movie star."

Georgia felt tears welling up, and it infuriated her. She so wanted to carry this off with a little dignity . . . no such luck. She felt her face dampen. "Please. Don't drag this out, Nick. Just go. Please. We'll be in touch."

She stood up and Nick remained seated on the sofa, a tortured look on his face. "God, Georgia. I don't want to lose you, but maybe you're right. A breather . . . that's what we need. I've got to go to the hospital now. Sam is sick." He stood up and walked towards Georgia. "I'll be in touch."

Georgia turned and faced him. "Go on, Nick. Go now. And do what you have to do. I hate people making other people feel guilty. It's been too good." Her face was wet with tears. "Please go. We've said everything there is to say." She ran into the bedroom and listened as Nick let himself quietly out the door.

Later that night, Georgia lay staring into the darkness. All alone again. No Nick to shield her from the demons of the night. The impact of his desertion had not fully taken hold yet. The reality of it would be bitter, and, of course, she would feel some guilt. If she hadn't taken that cruise with Louis . . .

Suddenly she felt old. Undesirable. God, she was mixed up. Sometimes she wondered why her life appeared to have all the suspenseful elements of the soap operas. It was almost as if she'd taken the scripts and applied them to her own existence, or that somehow they had seeped into her subconscious.

Grandmother Taia would have known what to do. She, and the cards, would have put her on the right track. How silly. Maybe she was cracking up, becoming crazy—like her mother; but if, in fact, Scherise was her mother, wouldn't she have felt something positive that day at the sanitarium instead of that terrible repulsion? There were no answers.

Georgia slipped out of bed, located the bottle of valium in the medicine chest, and popped two fivers. That should knock her out for the rest of the night. She crawled back into bed, closed her eyes and was soon fast asleep, her last thought before drifting off that Kiki Blake Sandborne was dead, and she, Georgia, felt absolutely nothing.

Billy Bright on the other hand, felt a great deal and he had no intentions of sleeping. Banner headlines and follow up stories about the strangled beauty had diminished somewhat, but he'd kept close track of every word, and studied each day's report with more than passing interest.

At first, the cops appeared hot to ferret out everyone in Kiki's little black book; but abruptly, like bird dogs on a brand new scent, their interest now centered entirely on her little known companion, Nino Comprez. He had become the prime suspect in the Glamour Girl Murder, as it had become known, and was being sought everywhere. A dark young man had been picked up by mistake just yesterday, and released with much fanfare. He looked remarkably like Nino, and oddly enough turned out to be his second cousin, Pablo.

Billy nervously fixed a drink, spilling half a jigger of scotch all over his favorite robe. He cursed out loud, then telephoned Teddy. "Look, friend. I've got to see you. It can't wait another minute. I can't sleep, and I can't think, and I'm about to lose what's left of my mind. And what's more, I've screwed up on three orders of wallpaper. Teddy, I need you. Please get your butt over here—pronto!"

Billy replaced the receiver and sat down to enjoy his drink. He was relieved that Teddy was on the way. Butterflies filled his stomach. Suddenly the telephone rang. He waited three rings before answering, somehow knowing, with a twinge of panic, who was on the other end of the line.

Teddy Morrell slipped into jeans and a cashmere sweater, wondering what the hell Billy's call for help was all about. Maybe, at last, there'd be a showdown of sorts. Maybe he'd get some answers to some unanswered questions.

The fact that Kiki Blake had been murdered only added to his confusion about Billy. Christ! Could he have done it? Not likely, but the plot thickened. Teddy slipped into a topcoat, checked the bills in his Gucci wallet (a gift from Billy), and then proceeded outside to hail a cab. It was late and there weren't many, but finally a cruising taxi pulled up to the curb and Teddy crawled in with a feeling of relief. He hated being on the streets alone at this hour. New York had become a violent, unpredictable jungle— even on the posh East Side.

Billy opened his apartment door barefoot and wearing his favorite silk robe. He held a drink in his right hand and appeared to be slightly drunk. "Thank God you're here! Come on in and have a drink. You'll need it."

Teddy entered Billy's superbly decorated apartment and marveled, as he always did, at the beauty of the place. The living room was done in black and white with bright touches of scarlet at propitious spots. It was masculine, but done with simplicity and elegance, a room both male and female would find attractive and comfortable. Bookcases, TV unit and bar were built cleverly into the wall in order to conserve space and give the impression of roominess. A faint odor of incense wafted from a Chinese urn, while soft music played in the background.

Teddy built himself a tall drink and sat in an overstuffed chair opposite Billy. A hurricane lamp burned brightly nearby casting a soft glow over the room. Teddy leaned forward, his curiosity piqued. "Let's get on with it, BIlly. What's the problem? Before you begin, however, I've a confession to make and it might make matters a little easier." He paused. "I've had a P.I. on your tail, my friend, and it appears you either have a taste for the ladies I was unaware of, or Kiki Blake was running a male brothel. So get on with it, and don't spare the horses."

Billy's face registered momentary surprise. "Sorry you wasted your dough, but I have to admit I'm a bit flattered. And now for the moment of truth." Billy took a quick swallow of his drink. "Here goes, Father Morrell."

"Cut the funny stuff and get on with it," snapped Teddy impatiently.

"Okay, okay . . . but I'm nervous. You see, I know a little bit more about Kiki and the Glamour Girl Murder than you think."

"Let's hope you didn't do it," responded Teddy. "Just continue. Sounds like a mystery."

"Well, it is, sort of. You see, Kiki had this fellow who did things for her. You know, got her grass, picked out her clothes, and when she'd flit off to Europe, he'd house sit for her. She'd let him stay in her fancy town house in order to keep things safe from the rip-off artists. Anyway, Teddy, this is the part I'm frightfully ashamed about. I met this person at *Bogarts* one night and we had dinner. After that, I saw him for drinks a few times, and when Kiki left the last time, I don't know what possessed me, but I did while away a few nights with him at her place."

360

He paused, noting Teddy's expression. "Look, I know this sounds like a copout, but it meant nothing and I was trying to break it off. Matter of fact, I was having a little problem breaking it off. You see, Nino, that's the guy's name, had this gambling addiction. I mean he fancied himself Jimmy the Greek, and he never had any dough. He was always after me for a buck." Billy lit a cigarette. "Now here comes the bad stuff."

Teddy sipped his drink. "Hurry up. I just love suspense stories."

"Well, this is suspenseful all right," said Billy, his mouth in a grim line. "Nino just disappeared. I mean, he used to call all the time, usually for a handout, and then suddenly I never heard another word. Odd, right? Then the shit hit the fan and every time I picked up the *Post* or turned on TV, there was a picture of Nino on the most wanted list. I felt as guilty as sin for just having known him. You know what a good Catholic I am, Teddy. I almost went to the priest, but I was too embarrassed. Anyway, day before yesterday, my fears were realized, Nino called sounding terrible. His voice was shaking, and he said how frightened he was because of all that had gone down. Of course he said he didn't do it, but wanted to skip town for obvious reasons. He even offered to lay some jewelry on me if I'd give him some cash. Can you imagine the nerve of that number? Of course I refused, and I never heard another word until tonight. There was Nino on the phone again with that nervous voice." Billy's voice began to rise. "What the hell should I do? I don't know where he is, but he might call back. Teddy, I'm so upset I could scream."

Teddy studied Billy for a moment before replying. "First let me say, my friend, that I really care a great deal for you. I believed we had something special. I fancied that though I've had women in my life, our kind of feeling was unique, something that no one else could shatter. Like brothers in a way—loving brothers. Don't panic, I'm not going to deliver a long moral lecture, but I will say I'm disappointed!

"Now to get to your problem. I think your best bet is to call the police and tell them exactly what you know. That way, if Nino calls again, you're off the hook. If they want to put a tracer on the phone, that's their business, but you're in the clear."

Billy interrupted. "I know you're right, but we really don't know if Nino killed Kiki. He said she gave him the jewelry."

"Come on, Billy, stop being so naive. Of course he did it. You'll simply tell the cops that you've heard from him, and that if he calls back you'll try to find out where he is. Chances are he won't call back."

Teddy finished his drink and stood up facing his friend. "Christ, Billy, if this doesn't

362

teach you a lesson, then nothing will, and I'm running out of patience. Nino is undoubtedly at the airport this very minute bound for Rio, and if what I've heard about Kiki Blake is true, then I can only wish him bon voyage!"

CHAPTER TWENTY

LOUIS SAT quietly on the plane bound for Little Rock, Arkansas, and rationalized over and over to himself that he was doing the right thing. He was aware that Lucky and Francie were disturbed by his obsession regarding Georgia, but he had simply lost all perspective where she was concerned. At his advanced age, and having escaped death and imprisonment during the many years of his involvement with life in organized crime, he had not only few illusions left, but regarded his quest for the identity of his daughter as something of a last act . . . a kind of epitaph . . . something that would, in a way, give meaning to his bizarre lifestyle.

His affection for Georgia confirmed that what he felt was a true miracle. That she was, in fact, Gina Gerfinski, the little girl spirited away by his sick wife so many years ago. He was determined to make certain.

He had been told that an old black woman named Aunt Necie, a witch of sorts, lived in a wooded section outside Kernsville and possessed knowledge of the history of that area since the early nineteen hundreds. Aunt Necie was reported to be ninety-one years old.

The plane lost altitude and prepared to swoop in for a landing. Louis fastened his safety belt and hoped he'd have no trouble finding the little town. A Hertz car had been reserved in the name of Mr. Smith, and Louis, despite Lucky's desire to accompany him on this trip, had refused, feeling that it was of such a personal nature he had to go it alone.

The car was waiting, and after filling out the aggravating forms and paying the pretty Hertz attendant, Louis drove away just as the sun was setting over the fabled Ozarks. The drive was approximately one and a half hour from the Little Rock terminal, and Louis felt certain he'd make it by dark.

He drove through mountainous terrain surrounded on both sides of the highway by dense forests and heavy foliage. A deer scampered across the road, and Louis felt, as the sun sank deeper into the lush foliage, that he was in another land. It was so quiet. He passed very few cars on the highway and soon found himself on a rough, red dirt road. It was getting dark, and he overheard the sound of an owl and watched a squirrel scamper up a tree nearby.

He stopped the car, turned on the dash-
board light, and consulted a map. Kernsville
was five miles from the next fork in the road.
What a desolate place, a perfect place to hide.
No wonder his men were never able to get a
lead on Scherise's whereabouts. He con-
structed a scenario in his mind, how Scherise
must have felt when she abducted the little
girl. She had become terrified that Gina
would be kidnapped. Her mind was so
umbalanced that she, no doubt, lost sight of
reality. Confusing fact with fantasy. But, of
course, she had kept track of her own
mother, and that would be the logical spot to
take the baby. Louis pictured Scherise
frantically hiding during the day, traveling
by night.

At that moment his train of thought was
interrupted and he came upon a crude sign
that read "Kernsville, Arkansas . . . Population 1,500 . . . 1 mile." Louis lit a cigarette and
continued to drive.

He drove into the tiny town and assumed
he was on the main thoroughfare which was
dotted with a post office and what appeared
to be a movie house; and at the end of the
second block a diner that advertised catfish
for supper. The place was called the Blue Cat
Cafe.

Three cars were parked in front, and Louis
continued to drive slowly, assuming the
motel was on the outskirts of town. He was

correct, and almost immediately drove into the driveway of the Red Hollow Inn. A single sign, illuminated by three or four not so dazzling lights, blinked off and on giving the place an eerie quality.

Louis drove to the office, registered, parked his car in the little stall, and was shown to a clean room furnished with a single bed, wash basin, shower, and a TV which ate quarters.

Louis thanked the old man in coveralls and asked for some ice. The man allowed as to how he'd not only bring him ice, but some freshly baked corn bread straight from his wife's table. Louis smiled and thanked him, wondering what he would think if he knew he was entertaining one of the country's most notorious crime figures.

Louis fixed himself a scotch—he always carried his own brand when traveling—and decided tomorrow would be time enough to visit Aunt Necie. He was tired from the drive, and the scotch relaxed him enough to sleep. The bed was lumpy and hard, but he slept well and awakened the following morning to the sound of a rooster crowing loudly in the distance. He climbed out of bed, shaved, and dressed quickly, wondering where he'd be able to get a cup of coffee. At that moment, the old man knocked on the door.

"Mr. Smith, good morning Mr. Smith. Got you some good hot coffee and some of my wife's good biscuits."

Louis opened the door wondering why he was getting such service, but decided there were few customers this time of year.

"Thank you. That's very nice of you."

He invited the old man into the room, and while he sipped the coffee, decided to ask some questions.

"Umm, delicious. I needed that. I'm going on a fishing trip later in the week, not too far from here on the White River. Have to meet some other folks." He paused. "I had a friend lived here a long time ago. Guess she's dead by now."

The old man cocked his head and scratched it. "Who would that be? I been round these parts a long time. I'd be knowin' just 'bout everybody. What's her name?"

"Well, her name was Taia. She had a little girl . . . raised her . . . her granddaughter, I believe."

The man studied Louis for a moment before answering. "That would be ol' Taia all right. Strange old lady. Kept to herself most of the time. All kinds of stories about her and that white girl livin' there with her. Guess it was her granddaughter. That's what they said, all right. That girl was the most beautiful thing I ever did see. She kept to herself, too, like some kind of forest creature —always in the woods with the animals, that one. After the old lady died, she took off. I hear she made it big up North. Wouldn't be surprised. Pretty enough to be a movin' picture star. But they kept to themselves . . . a real mystery there. Seems like they was always there, she and the old lady. Seems like there was an old man there, too, sometimes. He had real funny white-grey hair and drank a lot of moonshine. Then he went off. That the one you mean? That your friend?"

The old man looked at Louis slyly. "You ain't foolin' me. You're some kinda writer. A few years back we had people askin questions, poking around in other folks' business. We don't like that kinda thing here with outsiders. Everybody 'round these parts minds their own business." He smiled a toothless smile. "You one of them writer fellows? I won't let on if you tell me."

"No. No, really, I'm not," answered Louis, pleased at the information he'd been able to ferret out of the man. "I'm just curious about a few things. I knew Taia before she moved here to Kernsville. Not well, but I was just curious about what happened to her and the girl. She was just a tot when I saw her last. I hear there's an old woman still lives around here who knows about everyone and everything in these parts." He paused. "Aunt Necie —ring any bells?"

The man stared at Louis, his eyes narrowed. "Aunt Necie, huh? Now I get it. You're one of them ghost fellows . . . psychics, whatever. We had them all over the place a few years back trying to find out about Aunt Necie and her magic. She's another one keeps to herself. Has a cabin about two miles back in the black bottoms. You'll never find it alone. I can get you a mule, and my boy can lead you there. He won't stay though. Don't cotton to Aunt Necie and her lizards. He'll take you, though. Give him a few dollars, and he'll take you. But why anybody'd want to see that old crazy black biddy, I'll never know."

"Fine. Fine. When can your son leave? I'd like to make the trip as soon as possible," smiled Louis.

"I'll go get him now, but figure you better start early tomorrow. These things take a little time. How much you plan on givin' him?" The man studied Louis slyly. "Better give me a little to hold 'cause he'll just run up to Little Rock and spend it on some no-good."

Louis reached inside his wallet and handed the man a fifty dollar bill. "I'll give your son more after I meet with Aunt Necie."

The old man studied the crisp bill, thanked Louis, then ambled back towards the motel office.

Louis sat down on the one chair and finished the coffee which was surprisingly good. He felt a peculiar mood of expectation which had been lacking in his life for some time. It was almost the way he used to feel when he first started with the organization, years and years ago. Bizarre twists and turns of fate . . . danger . . . a sense of the unknown. He felt almost boyish, the way he'd felt when he'd decided to run away from Poland and come to America. He felt good. Good and just a little bit scared.

The trip through the woods to Aunt Necie's was not a pleasurable one, and Louis was glad the boy, Ray, had insisted on the old, sure-footed mule. Louis rode while the boy led the animal through the undergrowth and woods of the Ozarks. The two said little to one another, concentrating on their journey. Small brown rabbits peeped out from behind the brush, and Louis spotted squirrels and raccoons chasing about over tree stumps left by a woodsman's ax.

It was ten o'clock in the morning and quite chilly. Louis wore a warm lumberjacket while the young man was dressed in a fur lined sheepskin coat. Sunlight shimmered over the trees and cast shadows both dark and light. Where the trees and foliage became thick and heavy, it was dim and mysterious.

"This here's the black bottoms," announced Ray suddenly. "We're gettin' near old Necie's place. It's not far from here. Reckon you can make it back by yourself, Mr. Smith?"

"Yes, of course. I'm certain I can find my way back. If I can't, I think this old mule will remember the way," answered Louis, with some humor creeping into his voice.

Suddenly it occurred to him how utterly

foolish and ridiculous this entire thing had become. He had to laugh. Louis Gerfinski . . . syndicate boss . . . famous . . . powerful . . . rich . . . here he sat astride a mule in the middle of nowhere enroute to the lair of a ninety-one year old witch. He chuckled, and the boy stared at him. "It's nothing," said Louis. "I just find all this very amusing."

Louis noticed smoke curling in the air and then his eyes rested on a tiny log cabin nestled in a clump of trees. A brook trickled along one side of the house while tall pines and weeping willows stood like guardians of the land. A purple mist seemed to hang over the area and a peculiar aroma filled Louis' nostrils. He tried unsuccessfully to place it.

Ray halted the mule a few paces from the cabin and Louis dismounted, feeling he'd never stand straight again. His thighs ached.

"We're here," said the boy, his eyes wide with both fear and curiosity. "This here's far as I go."

Louis handed him a bill from his wallet and smiled. "Thanks, Ray. I'll return the mule later tonight. Is Aunt Necie home? Looks like there's a fire in the chimney. That's a good sign."

"Yeah. The old lady's home, all right. If she'll see you, that's the trick. They used to tell real bad stories about this place when I was a kid. People gettin' lost and never comin' back. Strange creatures hiding all around, and that old lady conjuring up spirits

372

and things." He glanced at the bill hungrily and folded in into his pocket. "I gotta get back now. Thanks."

He turned and made his way rapidly over a hill, leaving Louis and the mule standing side by side.

Louis walked slowly towards the house, leading the mule who had suddenly became stubborn. He tied the animal to a nearby tree and continued toward the cabin. A large old fashioned black washing pot sat outside and fire wood was stacked in neat little piles at the side of the house.

Abruptly, Louis turned and spotted the shadow of wings as a large eagle came swooping overhead, circling ominously as if to attack. For one split second he experienced real fear, then realized the bird was simply appraising him in much the same way one of his own men would appraise a potential enemy, then, finding him harmless, retreat. The large bird circled once more, then flew back to its perch beside the house. Apparently he was trained by an expert.

Now Louis was at the door and again smelled the strong pungent odor of cooking. He stood patiently for a moment wondering if he should knock or call out, when suddenly the door opened revealing a small dark woman, a bandana covering her head and men's shoes on her feet.

She was very tiny and wrinkled, but when she smiled, Louis was astounded. Her smile was that of a much younger woman, and she appeared to have all her teeth. Her neck was covered with multi colored beads along with a small snake that curled cozily about her throat like a necklace. And when she spoke, her voice had a peculiar lilt. "Come in. Come in. You had a long trip. Come sit by the fire."

Louis had not anticipated this warm welcome and entered the little cabin door. It was dark and cozy inside. A fire burned in an open hearth and light from candles and oil lamps illuminated walls papered with old newspapers and magazine covers.

Louis took the old lady's hand. Her tiny black eyes appraised him from head to foot. No need to lie to this creature. She'd find him out in a second. She appeared as supple as a jungle vine. "Hello there, I'm Louis Gerfinski. May I sit down?"

She motioned toward a wooden bench by the fire. "Sit there. I'll brew you some herb tea. I knew you'd be comin'. I just didn't know when."

Pondering this, Louis sat down and awaited the tea. At last the old woman handed him a steaming cup of pale liquid and dark, hot bread, served on surprisingly good, hand painted china.

"You are Aunt Necie, are you not?" questioned Louis while sipping the tea slowly. "This is excellent. Such an odd taste."

"Thank you. I'm glad you like it. It's a special brew. And to answer your question, yes, I'm the one they call Necie. I've been called a few other things, too."

She smiled that odd smile once more and continued. "What can I do to help you? I'm willing to help now. Once I wasn't, but now I'm willing. It's the girl. You've come about Taia and the girl."

Louis had ceased to be surprised at anything the old witch said or did. He nodded, and Necie sat down opposite him in an old oak rocking chair. She closed her eyes and began to rock to and fro, almost as if she were lulling herself into some kind of trance. Her voice was soft.

"It all started a long time ago back in the days when couples of mixed blood had it real hard—almost impossible, I'd say. One cold day along comes this pretty mulatto gal with a white man, and they move into a little house on the outskirts of town. It was cheap, and off the beaten track. Taia—that was the woman's name—was good as gold, and we became friends. I took her under my wing, taught her the cards, how to heal with herbs, everything I knew. She was like a sister. But the man, that was another story. He was no dang good, plain and simple. Went and lost his fishin' boat shootin' craps one night, drunk on moonshine."

Necie stood up and poked the coals in the open hearth, then added paper causing the flames to shoot forward, orange and bright. "No, he was no dang good, that one; and when he gets himself killed in Texarkana, me and Taia didn't shed no tears. And there was a daughter. She'd run off years earlier and the old guy wouldn't let Taia look for her. Said it was just one less mouth to feed. How she wanted that girl . . . prayed every night. And me . . . I made spells just to help things along. Years ago I'd been burned at the stake. I'm a real witch, you know.''

Louis had no doubts on the subject and wished he was privy to some of her dark secrets, but remained silent allowing her to continue, barely able to conceal his mounting excitement.

Necie wiped her face with a red bandana, an exact duplicate of the one on her head, and went on. "Well, one day out of the blue, the daughter shows up . . . seems she'd kept in touch with the mother all along, and clever ol' Taia just never let on to the old man. Anyway, now, here she comes all dolled up like some movin' picture star and draggin' a kid with her. I saw right away the kid was fine, but the woman, well, she had a sickness. I spotted it right fast.''

Louis could bear it no longer. "She brought a little girl with her, didn't she? A little girl named Gina? That's it for God's sake, isn't it? Tell me. Tell me!"

The old woman studied Louis for a moment. "What if I told you no. No, that she brought a boy with her—a son. What would you say then? How would you feel? Like all white folks, you're impatient."

Suddenly Louis became agitated. Was there something in the damn tea? Christ! Maybe this was a set up. Could his enemies have gone to this extreme?

He stared at Necie and started to speak, but she interrupted, at the same moment lighting a foul smelling little cigarette. "Join me in a smoke? I grow my own. It's special."

Louis shook his head no. "Please go on; tell me more."

"Well," said Necie puffing on the cigarette, "Taia's daughter stayed only a short while. The child—" she paused and stared at Louis for a full moment before continuing. "The child, a beautiful little girl, was left here with the grandmother. The mother came back only once, then went away again. No one ever knew what happened to her. It was a mystery. Taia was left with the little blonde one to raise, and she loved her like her own. The girl grew like a wild flower . . . beautiful and free. She turned out fine. I kept track after Taia died, and the girl left these parts. My spirits told me some. My smoke told me more. I knew Taia could rest in peace. Just like I knew someday you'd come." She paused. "You are the girl's father."

It was a statement of fact, and Louis was momentarily stunned.

"How did you know?"

"Do not ask. Remember, I am a witch. We have many secrets."

Louis thanked the old lady and attempted to give her cash, which she refused. He turned and walked out the door of the cabin feeling suddenly as if he had the energy to race over the hills to the motel, sprout wings like the old lady's eagle, and fly himself back to New York.

CHAPTER TWENTY-ONE

GEORGIA SAT in front of her TV screen watching Nick accept an Emmy for his role in "Precinct." He looked so handsome, so self-assured, as he made his short acceptance speech, and then sat down to thunderous applause.

Georgia sipped a glass of wine and felt like throwing things at the set. There he was, her Nick—a big, fat success—and here she was watching him on TV from her living room. She wondered who his date was and suspected it was that little starlet he'd been linked with of late. However, according to the columns, he seemed to be playing the field, a fact that was little comfort to Georgia.

The second Lariat Jean commercial, due to his popularity on the new series, had been an even greater success than the first. Georgia wondered if he was as miserable without her as she was without him. She doubted it. At least one positive thing had developed. According to Margo, Georgia's audition on tape as the vixen, Marilee, in the new night time series, "Millionaire's Row," had turned out mildly sensational. If she signed, it would be a big upward step in her career. But at the moment that was the last thing on her mind.

Suddenly the camera panned the audience and focused on Nick and the girl by his side. She was brunette and beautiful, but Georgia didn't recognize her. She sat there smiling at the camera, her full, lip-glossed mouth forming little silent words, as she gazed at Nick with adoring eyes. Georgia wanted to scream, but instead snapped off the set and went to bed.

That night her sleep was filled with garbled scenes. Large ominous shapes pursued her through dark, eerie caverns and muddy waters. Nothing made sense, nothing but the terror that possessed her, and that seemed real enough. She was running . . . running . . . pursued by giant waves from an angry sea. And there were sharks swimming about . . . prowling about in murky waters seeking their prey . . . sharks with human, smiling faces.

Suddenly Georgia was wide awake, trembling, lying there staring at the ceiling, attempting to shake the clinging nightmare. She lay still a moment more, then sat upright and reached for a cigarette.

She felt so alone. Nick's defection was the hardest to take. Not even a call, a note, as if their intimate, loving alliance had meant

nothing. Merely an interlude. She tortured herself, picturing him with other women—the
brunette from the Emmys, the female lead on
the series—all beautiful, talented, clever, and
young. She envisioned him making love with
them, having fun, sharing secrets. God, did he
tell them about her? Had Louis been simply an
excuse for him to move on?

And what about Louis, with his obsession
and life of intrigue, strangely untouched by it
all, like a man encased in glass. If he was in fact
her father, what then? How would it all end?
Right now all she really cared about was Nick,
and he was out of her life.

Georgia ground out the cigarette and lay flat
once more, struggling to find a comfortable
position. Her fingers strayed to her smooth
tummy. It felt so distended. Odd. Of course
she'd skipped two periods, but that had
happened before. Somehow this felt different.
All the frantic excercising had not diminished
the annoying little bulge. Lord, maybe she had
a tumor!

The following day, Doctor Manze fit Georgia
into his busy schedule because of the urgency
in her voice. The humiliating examination was
routine, feet in stirrups, doctor's hands soft
and painless. "Does that hurt, Georgia?
Breathe in and out, dear. Don't tense up." At
last. "You can get dressed now, dear. Wait in
the outer office and I'll see you in private when
I'm free. Due for a delivery at the hospital in

381

two hours." He glanced at his watch, dismissing Georgia with a wan smile.

In the waiting room, Georgia nervously flipped pages of *Vogue* but actually saw nothing except the plump, expectant mothers sitting patiently, and waiting for the good doctor's approval. There were several other young women, who smoked and stared out the window towards the park. Georgia felt separate and apart from everyone, like she was from another planet. She, after all, could never bear children, and sometimes being in the presence of pregnant women made her uncomfortable.

At last the nurse smiled in her direction, "He'll see you now, Miss Bonner. You know the way."

Georgia marched down the hall towards the doctor's private sanctum, and prayed there was nothing seriously wrong. She stood in the doorway for a moment and observed the white coated man seated behind an enormous oak desk, his expression revealing nothing of what he might be thinking. He would have made a good executioner, thought Georgia wryly, as she entered the room.

"Come in and sit down, Georgia. We have to talk, and as usual I'm running late."

Georgia sat in a small, uncomfortable chair with a leather back and lit a cigarette.

"Georgia, will you kindly put out that cigarette. You know how I feel about smoking."

She obeyed, wanted to strike him. "Okay it's out, now what's the story on the tummy bulge? Am I gonna live? And please, no fairy tales."

The doctor faced her squarely. "Georgia, I really don't quite know how to tell you this, considering your past history, except to simply say that we are not infallible. I mean, science makes mistakes, and in your case there's been a big one." He cleared his throat. "As far as I can determine at this time, without further tests, you are about three months pregnant."

Georgia felt herself sway, then everything went dark. She awakened on the doctor's couch with a nurse wafting ammonia under her nose. "Feel better now, dear? Doctor had to rush to the hospital, but he said to tell you not to worry about a thing, and I should schedule another appointment for you in two weeks."

"I'm all right, I guess," said Georgia sitting up and adjusting her blouse. "I'm fine now, and I'll just grab a cab and go home."

Back in her apartment, Georgia lay on her bed and contemplated the shocking news. This changed everything. Pregnant . . . almost thirty-eight . . . a series in the offing . . . Nick. Lord! On the one hand she was thrilled, on the other terrified and confused.

Frantically she began to count. Jake Pierce. That horrible orgy. No, thank God that had been months earlier. She was safe. It was Nick's child. She breathed a sigh of relief. It *was* Nick's and despite everything she was going to have it.

Should she tell him? Maybe he'd come back just for the sake of the baby . . . just because it would be the right thing to do. She couldn't bear that.

The phone rang interrupting her thoughts. It was Louis, back from his mystery trip.

"Georgia, I've got to see you. Lunch tomorrow okay?" His voice sounded excited—different.

Georgia smiled into the phone. She felt euphoric, safe—Louis was back. Her security blanket.

"Tomorrow will be fine. I've missed you, I wish it was today."

She returned the receiver to its cradle and smiled happily. Everything would be all right now.

The following noon, Georgia stood in the hallway enroute to the waiting car, and admired herself in the large mirror near the elevator. She was delighted at the secret she carried inside herself. That very morning she was positive the child had kicked; but wasn't it too soon? She'd had little or no experience with babies. No brothers or sisters, just that time spent working at the Foundling Home several years ago. How she'd loved to diaper the cuddly little creatures. How she'd longed to take them home. Now she'd have her very own. She hugged herself happily and wondered if she should tell Louis her secret or keep it just that—a secret. She'd wait and decide later.

The chauffeur skillfully guided the car through midday traffic toward Louis' town house in Brooklyn Heights. They were dining at a special restaurant in his neighborhood.

As Georgia watched him proceed majestically down the steps toward the car like a white haired Norse warlord, Abe Lincoln's old quote came to her mind. *By the time a man is forty, he has the face he deserves.* Judging by that, Louis Gerfinski had lived a virtuous life. His broad face remained unlined, the eyes hard, but with a hint of concealed merriment, the mouth wide and generous.

Today his cashmere coat, shoes, gloves, and scarf were a gun-metal grey and all matched perfectly. He wore no hat, and the wind ruffled his snow white hair. He walked with a jaunty gait, like a man with a purpose, a man with a mission.

He slipped into the back seat alongside Georgia, adjusting the heavy mink throw over his lap and gave her a quick peck on the cheek. "How are you? You look well. I missed you and wanted to see you as soon as possible."

Georgia squeezed his hand. "I missed you, too. Tell me all the news. So much has happened in only a few days." She snuggled under the mink throw, feeling luxurious and safe for the first time in a while. Gone were thoughts of Nick and her pregnancy. She was here with someone who really cared about her and she decided to savor the moment. There were all too few of them.

"Sorry dear, you'll have to wait." He took her hand and seemed different somehow, as if he were concealing some secret. "We're going to do this right. Lunch at Mama Da's . . . champagne . . . the works." His eyes sparkled. "First, I've got a little something for you. A present." He reached into his pocket and presented Georgia with a velvet oblong box.

"Oh, Louis, you've done too much already. Lord, you know how much I love presents."

She sat for a moment holding the box, then opened it with a squeal of delight. It was an exact replica of her amulet, but copied in gold and studded with diamonds. The stones caught the sunlight and sparkled in Georgia's hand like something alive.

"Put it around my neck this very moment. I knew I didn't wear any other jewelry for a reason. Put it on! Quick . . . quick."

Louis fastened the chain around Georgia's throat.

"Oh, Louis, it's gorgeous. Why on earth did you do it? You've already given me the world with a ribbon tied around it."

He smiled. "After all, the amulet is what first brought us together."

At that moment the limousine came to a halt, in front of the small restaurant called Mama Da's, a place that catered to a few discerning neighborhood people and others with dedicated palates.

The cuisine was varied, but the house specialty was a baked bass with almonds and a sauce that made one forget diets.

A young man in a plain business suit ushered Georgia and Louis to a secluded table in the rear of one of the three small, intimate rooms that made up the restaurant. A fire burned in an old fashioned fireplace, and fresh flowers peeped from small crystal vases at each and every table. Plants hung in profusion and the aroma of some delicacy wafted from the kitchen nearby.

Once seated, they were greeted warmly by Mama Da herself. After presenting the menu, she retreated quickly to fetch the special wine Louis had ordered earlier.

Minutes later, the wine poured, goblets raised, Louis smiled at Georgia, his eyes shining brightly, almost as if he had a fever. Georgia wondered at his mood, but found it contagious. She glanced around a room that appeared to be empty of patrons other than one lone man sitting at the small bar in the rear. This was their own private party. She suspected Louis had arranged it that way.

"To you, my dear. To you, Georgia." He paused dramatically. "I mean to you, Gina. To you my darling child, my darling daughter, all grown up . . . to you!" Tears appeared on the man's cheeks.

Georgia held her glass tightly, allowing the words to sink in. "Louis! Louis, you mean it? You mean you found out for sure? How? How?"

Her voice rose; her hands trembled. She felt

herself tingle with excitement and delight. To know for certain . . . to be sure who she really was at last!

That moment would be frozen in her mind forever. The little restaurant with sunlight filtering through the one window bathing the room in a shadowy glow. The crackle of the fire on the hearth. Louis' eyes filled with pleasure and satisfaction.

It all happened so quickly that when she was asked to reconstruct the scene later, her mind was a blank. Only the look of surprise on Louis' face remained etched in her brain. The shadow of the man at the bar moving quickly—suddenly—like an animal given a whip command by his trainer, a few steps to their table. At first she thought it was a friend; he stood for one split second, then a blast . . . once . . . twice . . . glass splintered . . a flash of light. Louis fell backwards, champagne flowing over the clean white tablecloth.

Georgia remained in a sitting position . . . frozen . . . blood everywhere . . . people running, screaming . . . shrieks from the chef who stood in the doorway . . . Louis on the floor . . . complete disarray . . . Georgia on her knees, cradling Louis' head in her arms . . . his mouth forming words . . . blood oozing from his lips . . . gurgling sounds . . . his voice so low.

"Gina, Gina—say it, say it please! Call me Father just once—just once."

Tears streamed down Georgia's face. Her dress was red with blood. She didn't stop to consider it was her own. "Father, my darling father. Daddy, Daddy, don't leave me. Please don't leave me."

Louis tried vainly to speak once more, but the effort proved too much. His eyes opened wide for one brief instant, then he was dead. Georgia sat on the hard floor paralyzed, clutching his body to her breast, rocking to and fro.

The entire place was in chaos. No one seemed to know what had happened. Police and the paramedics arrived simultaneously. Georgia, still covered with blood, accompanied the officers to the precinct, making a valiant effort to avoid falling to pieces. Somehow her old habit of "grace under pressure" came to the fore, and she managed to call Lucky and John, answering questions as best she could.

An hour later, she was hustled out of the station house and through a barrage of eager reporters who screamed questions and snapped pictures. She was assisted into a police car by John, Lucky, and a sergeant who observed her with open admiration as he lit and handed her a cigarette. "You're some cool lady. A lucky one, too. Damn lucky to be alive!"

The following morning a fifty-year old neighborhood man turned himself in filled with drunken remorse. The horrendous story he spewed forth to the detectives was an all too familiar one. His beautiful teenage daughter had become hooked on drugs, turned to prostitution to support her habit, then just three weeks earlier she'd hung herself in the bathroom. Insane with grief, the man vowed to kill anyone involved in drugs. In his madness, Louis Gerfinski had become a symbol to be obliterated.

The girl's mother, tears streaming from her eyes, followed her husband into the precinct. "Joe didn't mean it. He's a good man. He's been nuts since Joanie died, even went after me with a knife. Blamed everyone. I tried to get help, but the officer said he had to do something first. Now he's done something," she sobbed. "Oh, God! I can't believe he's gone and killed Mr. Gerfinski." The woman was led away by a large, rawboned matron with a bored expression on her face.

POLISH GODFATHER MOWED DOWN WITH ACTRESS DAUGHTER.

There was a picture of Georgia and a long detailed account of her life as a soap star, as well as her celebrated marriage to former Arkansas Governor Victor Sandborne. The article went to inform the readers of the *Post* that Georgia was Louis' long lost daughter, and told of the events that had led to that discovery.

She cut off her phones, still in a state of shock, and went to Margo's where she remained in seclusion until the day of the funeral.

At Campbell's, Georgia, Francie, and Lucky sat together in the first pew reserved for family, and near the closed coffin covered with the most beautiful arrangement of flowers Georgia was able to order. There were many people present at the simple ceremony. People that surprised even Georgia—Congressmen, a State Senator, lawyers, Sing Jo, Braskets, and an assortment of men who could have stepped out of an old Humphrey Bogart movie along with well-dressed matrons, accompanied by their husbands, a stage star who Georgia recognized, and of course—the press.

Later, Georgia, Francie, and Lucky shared a limousine for the long ride to the cemetery. They all remained silent, suffering in their own private ways. It was a cold, wet day. Throngs of strangers, as well as friends, followed the casket to its final resting place. Some stood, umbrellas open, while others milled about, paying their last respects to a man some loved, other feared and hated.

Georgia, dressed entirely in black, wiped her eyes with a small handkerchief. It had taken three valium to get her through the day. She felt sick and numb inside, like a robot, standing there watching them lowering the casket into the earth. Somehow none of it seemed real. Once again she experienced the peculiar sensation that she was performing in one of the soaps, that this was all make believe and soon the director would yell, "That's a take . . . wrap it up!"

Lucky and Francie stood near by while Margo, John, and Teddy waited several feet away to be available if she should need them. She'd stay the night with Margo. She couldn't bear the thought of being alone, facing the curious, the thrill seekers. A mobster's daughter—a *rich* mobster's daughter. Louis' lawyer had already contacted her regarding the provisions of the will. She was well taken care of. How ironic, thought Georgia, that a man like Louis, with so many known enemies, should be cut down by a simple father out to avenge his daughter's death. Ironic, indeed.

Of course, now there was someone else to consider—the baby. So far she'd told no one, not even Margo. Strange. She'd lost her father just as she'd found him, but a new life was on the way. Somehow that gave Georgia some small comfort.

Lucky touched her arm. Francie was not bearing up well. She could hear her muffled sobs. She really did love Louis, just as she'd said. It wasn't just the money and power. Georgia felt real sympathy for the girl.

The brief ceremony was ending now, and she found herself trying to concentrate on what the priest was saying, but the words held no meaning. Inside, she experienced a deep, throbbing sense of loss, as if a real part of herself had been left back there under the rich black earth. The dismal, gray day did little to lighter her mood and she moved slowly away from the others in order to gain control of her faltering emotions. A cool breeze ruffled her hair, and she thought how stupid she'd been for not having worn a hat, or at least a scarf. Her swollen eyes were hidden behind dark glasses. She had a strong desire for a good stiff drink.

Margo, Teddy and the others were moving toward the waiting limousines, allowing her time alone. Suddenly, someone touched her elbow and she turned, finding herself temporarily without words. Was she dreaming? It couldn't be!

Nick stood there in the mist, wearing a beige trench coat and looking drawn and weary in the dim light. They stood staring at each other for several endless moments before Nick finally spoke.

"Georgia, don't look so stricken. It's really me. I didn't mean to startle you. I've been standing here in the crowd through the whole thing. I haven't called because I've been going through hell—and I know you have, too."

All the remaining color had drained from Georgia's face. "God, I never saw you at all!" She was suddenly flooded with insecurity. It occurred to her that perhaps Nick had come out of a sense of duty merely to pay his respects. Maybe his girlfriend was waiting for him in the car. Lord, she was much too fragile right now to bear up under that kind of jolt!

"Why did you come, Nick? It's been weeks . . ." Her voice held just the slightest tremor, though she tried to control it. "Weeks!"

"I had a lot of thinking and sorting out to do, Georgia," he said quietly. "Maybe this isn't the time or the place to tell you what a fool I've been, but when I read about the shooting, all I could think of was how much I love you." He took her arm gently. "And then I thought, Christ, what if it had been my girl dead! My beautiful, darling Georgia shot down. And I couldn't stand it. I'm back for good, if you'll have me. I want you on any terms. Life is shit without you. I mean, a successful career doesn't mean anything if you have no one to share it with."

Georgia managed a smile through the tears that started to roll down her cheeks. "Your timing always was perfect, and I'm not about to question a miracle. I have so much to tell you—but right now I'm just going to hold onto your arm and feel safe for the first time in ages!"

Nick nodded, smiling too, and handed her a clean handkerchief from his pocket. "Here— blow your nose. And your mascara is running from behind those shades. Let's get out of here so I can hold you in my arms and tell you how we're going to spend the rest of our lives. I want to marry you, Georgia, as soon as possible. We'll start all over again, and this time there'll be no Jakes or Kikis or anyone else to come between us."

Obediently Georgia blew her nose. In an instant, her misery had been changed to exultation. Just then she felt movement inside her belly.

She turned and smiled radiantly in the direction of her father's grave. She was sure that he, too, knew she'd won the final round in the love arena . . .